Murder
Takes
Time

GIACOMO GIAMMATTEO

FRIENDSHIP AND HONOR SERIES BOOK 1

Murder Takes Time

GIACOMO GIAMMATTEO

INFERNO PUBLISHING COMPANY

MURDER TAKES TIME
by Giacomo Giammatteo

INFERNO PUBLISHING COMPANY

For more information about this book, visit
www.giacomogiammatteo.com

Print ISBN 978-0-9850302-0-9
Electronic ISBN 978-0-9850302-1-6

It is not the oath that makes us believe the man,
but the man the oath.

– Aeschylus

CHAPTER 1

RULE NUMBER ONE:
MURDER TAKES TIME

Brooklyn, New York—Current Day

He sipped the last of a shitty cup of coffee and stared across the street at Nino Tortella, the guy he was going to kill. Killing was an art, requiring finesse, planning, skill—and above all—patience. Patience had been the most difficult to learn. The killing came naturally. He cursed himself for that. Prayed to God every night for the strength to stop. But so far God hadn't answered him, and there were still a few more people that needed killing.

The waitress leaned forward to refill his cup, her cleavage a hint that more than coffee was being offered. "You want more?"

He waved a hand—Nino was heading towards his car. "Just the check, please."

From behind her ear she pulled a yellow pencil, tucked into a tight bun of red hair, then opened the receipt book clipped to the pocket of her apron. Cigarette smoke lingered on her breath, almost hidden by the gum she chewed.

Spearmint, he thought, and smiled. It was his favorite, too.

He waited for her to leave, scanned the table and booth, plucked a few strands of hair from the torn cushion and a fingernail clipping from the windowsill. After putting them into a small plastic bag, he wiped everything with a napkin. The check was $4.28. He pulled a five and a one from his money clip and left them on the table. As he moved to the door he glanced out the window. Nino already left the lot, but it was Thursday, and on Thursdays Nino stopped for pizza.

He parked three blocks from Nino's house, finding a spot where the snow wasn't piled high at the curb. After pulling a black wool cap over his forehead, he put leather gloves on, raised the collar on his coat then grabbed his black sports bag. Favoring his left leg, he walked down the street, dropping his eyes if he passed someone. The last thing he wanted was a witness remembering his face.

He counted the joints in the concrete as he walked. Numbers forced him to think logically, kept his mind off what he had to do. He didn't *want* to kill Nino. He *had* to. It seemed as if all of his life he was doing things he didn't want to do. He shook his head, focused on the numbers again.

When he drew near the house, he cast a quick glance to ensure the neighbors' cars weren't there. The door took less than thirty seconds to open. He kept his hat and gloves on, walked into the kitchen, and set his bag on the counter. He removed a pair of tongs and a shot glass, and set them on the coffee table. A glance around the room had him straightening pictures and moving dirty dishes to the sink. A picture of an older woman stared at him from a shelf above an end table. *Might be his mother,* he thought, and gently set it face down. Back to the kitchen. He opened the top of the black bag and removed two smaller bags. He set one in the fridge and took the other with him.

The contents of the second bag—hair and other items—he spread throughout the living room. The crime scene unit would get a kick out of that. He did one final check, removed a baseball bat from the bag, then sat on the couch behind the door. The bat lay on the cushion beside him. While he stretched his legs and leaned back, he thought about Nino. It would be easy to just shoot him, but that wouldn't be fair. Renzo suffered for what he did; Nino should too. He remembered Mamma

Rosa's warnings, that the things people did would come back to haunt them. Nino would pay the price now.

A car pulled into the driveway. He sat up straight and gripped the bat.

NINO HAD A SMILE on his face and a bounce in his step. It was only Thursday and already he'd sold more cars than he needed for the month. *Maybe I'll buy Anna that coat she's been wanting.* Nino's stomach rumbled, but he had a pepperoni pizza in his hand and a bottle of Chianti tucked into his coat pocket. He opened the door, slipped the keys into his pocket, and kicked the door shut with his foot.

There was a black sports bag on the kitchen table. *Wasn't there before,* Nino thought. A shiver ran down his spine. He felt a presence in the house. Before he could turn, something slammed into his back. His right kidney exploded with pain.

"Goddamn." Nino dropped the pizza, stumbled, and fell to the floor. His right side felt on fire. As his left shoulder collided with the hardwood floor, a bat hit him just above the wrist. The snap of bones sounded just before the surge of pain.

"Fuck." He rolled to the side and reached for his gun.

The bat swung again.

Nino's ribs cracked like kindling. Something sharp jabbed deep inside him. His mouth filled with a warm coppery taste. Nino recognized the man who stood above him. "Anything you want," he said. "Just kill me quick."

THE BAT STRUCK NINO's knee, the crunch of bones drowned by his screams. The man stared at Nino. Let him cry. "I got Renzo last month. You hear about that?"

Nino nodded.

He tapped Nino's pocket with his foot, felt a gun. "If you reach for the gun, I'll hit you again."

Another nod.

He knelt next to Nino, took the shot glass from the coffee table. "Open your mouth."

Nino opened his eyes wide and shook his head.

The man grabbed the tongs, shoved one end into the side of Nino's mouth, and squeezed the handles, opening the tongs wide. When he had Nino's mouth pried open enough, he shoved the shot glass in. It was a small shot glass, but to Nino it must have seemed big enough to hold a gallon. Nino tried screaming, but couldn't. Couldn't talk either, with the glass in there. Nino's head bobbed, and he squirmed. Nothing but grunts came out—fear-tinged mumbles coated with blood.

The man stood, glared at Nino. Gripped the bat with both hands. "You shouldn't have done it."

A dark stain spread on the front of Nino's pants. The stench of excrement filled the room. He stared at Nino, raised the bat over his head, and swung. Nino's lips burst open, splitting apart from both sides. Teeth shattered, some flying out, others embedding into the flesh of his cheeks. The shot glass exploded. Glass dug deep gouges into his tongue, severing the front of it. Shards of glass pierced his lips and tunneled into his throat.

He stared at Nino's face, the strips of torn flesh covered in blood. He gulped. Almost stopped. But then he thought about what Nino had done, and swung the bat one more time. After that, Nino Tortella lay still.

He returned to the kitchen and took a small box from the bag on the counter then went back to the living room. Inside the box were more hairs, blood, skin, and other evidence. He spread the items over and around the body then made a final trip to the kitchen to clean up. He undressed and placed his clothes into a large plastic bag, tied it, and set it inside the black bag. He took out a change of clothes, including shoes and plastic covers for them. Careful not to step in any blood, he went back to stand over the body.

Nino lay in his own piss, shit, and blood, eyes wide-open, mouth agape. *You should never have done it, Nino.*

He blessed himself with the sign of the cross while he repeated the Trinitarian formula. "*In nomine Patris, et Filii, et Spiritus Sancti.*" Then he shot Nino. Once in the head. Once in the heart. *An eye for an eye. And then some.*

Before stepping out the door, he removed the plastic covers for his shoes, placed them into the bag, then closed and locked the door behind him. The wind had picked up since he arrived, bringing a cold bite with it. He turned his collar up and tucked his head into his chest.

Forgive me, Father, for what I have done.

He walked two more blocks, almost to the car, when an image of Donnie Amato appeared in his head.

And for what I still have to do.

CHAPTER 2

A BIG MISTAKE

Four of Tony Sannullo's men waited outside of Cataldi's restaurant, alert for signs of trouble. A gold Lexus pulled up, and a big man dressed in a Brioni suit stepped out. Paulie "The Suit" Perlano straightened his blue silk tie, ran a comb through a full head of dark hair, then walked up to the guys gathered by the door.

"Hey, Suit," one of them called.

"Hey, Paulie," another said.

"Anyone tell Tony yet?"

Four heads shook at once. "You fuckin' tell him," one of them said.

Paulie stood on his toes and peeked in the window. Tony "The Brain" Sannullo sat alone at a round table that seated six, his back against the wall. An espresso sat to the right of his crossword puzzle, and he chewed on the end of a ballpoint pen. Despite the advice he'd received all of his life, Tony was a creature of habit. On Friday mornings he took his espresso, along with breakfast, at Cataldi's.

Paulie shook his head then walked up three steps to go inside. "He's not gonna like it."

Anna Cataldi greeted him. "*Buongiorno*, Paulie. Beautiful day, huh?"

"That depends," Paulie said, but then he laughed. He had an easy laugh, the kind that came from frequent use. "How you doin', Anna? How's that new baby?"

"Good, Paulie. And your kids?"

"Hey, Anna, kids are kids. They're always good. Pains in the ass, but good." As they walked toward the back, Paulie asked, "He in a good mood?"

Anna raised her eyebrows and shrugged. "It's February."

"Ah, shit."

"Yeah," she said, and waved Paulie on.

He headed toward Tony's table, the rumbling in his gut a combination of hunger and nerves.

Tony scratched in one of the final answers of his crossword as Paulie came to the table. "When are you gonna dress like the rest of us, Paulie? Nobody wears suits anymore."

Paulie fidgeted with his silverware while he stared at Tony's crossword. "Still got a few to do, huh?" Nobody liked to interrupt Tony's crosswords.

"You got a seven-letter word for radiant or dazzlingly bright?"

"Sure, Tony. It's right on the tip of my tongue."

"Starts with an 'f.'"

"Yeah, I got one—fucking—as in *fucking brilliant.*"

"That's my buddy Paulie. I knew I could count on you." Tony chewed on the end of his pen while the waiter brought another espresso for him and a new one for Paulie. "*Fulgent.* That's the word I was looking for."

Paulie fidgeted more. *Might as well spit it out.* "Okay, Mr. Fulgent, if you can take your nose out of that puzzle for a minute, I got something to tell you."

"What?"

"Nino Tortella got clipped last night."

"Shit." Tony slapped the table. "How?"

"Same as Renzo."

"You know what this means."

"Yeah, I know. There's no way Nino didn't talk. Might be a couple of guys smart enough not to talk, but not Nino."

"Anybody seen Donnie Amato?"

Paulie sipped his espresso. "I called. Got no answer."

"Send a couple of guys to warn him."

"You know how hardheaded Donnie is. He thinks he can handle himself."

Tony slugged the last of his espresso. "Fat chance of that." He tossed two twenties on the table. "I've got to call Tito. Catch up with me later."

Paulie narrowed his eyes. "You didn't have anything to do with this, did you?"

"You know who's doing this."

"We shouldn't have done it, Tony. It was wrong from the get go."

"Tell me about it," Tony said, and headed for the door. *Lot more people are gonna die now.*

CHAPTER 3

TIES TO THE PAST

Detective Lou Mazzetti pulled to the curb and got out of the car, his creased Oxford loafers splashing slush onto frayed pant cuffs. He buttoned his coat, positioned his hat to cover a bald spot, then went up the walk toward the old brick house. The house was still in nice shape—most were in this neighborhood, a community of predominantly Italian and Irish, but with a good mix of Poles and a smattering of Jews. Lou nodded to a patrolman stationed at the door as he climbed the steps. Today he felt as tired as he was old.

"How is it?" Lou asked.

"Neighbors didn't hear anything, but they didn't get home till late." The patrolman shook his head. "Looks the same as the first one."

Same as the first one. A disturbing thought, but as Lou examined the scene it proved to be true: dead male shot once in the head, once in the heart. *And damn near every bone in his body broken.* No shell casings, and he felt certain the crime scene unit would find hairs, blood, skin, and DNA from a wide assortment of people. Lou looked at the medical examiner, Kate Burns, a pretty girl with skin as pale and freckled as her Irish name suggested. "Anything?"

Kate shook her head, wrapped up her kit and tucked it into a bag. "I'm sure we got his DNA, but it's mixed in with the rest."

"Process it all."

"I'll process it, but unless you get something more, it won't do you a damn bit of good."

DETECTIVE FRANKIE DONOVAN STEPPED through the door and wiped slush from his Moreschi shoes using a monogrammed handkerchief. He unbuttoned his cashmere coat, hung it on a rack behind the door, then surveyed the crime scene with the hazel eyes he inherited from his father. Rumor was he got the Irish luck from his father, too, but that's where the gifts stopped. The dark skin, bold nose, and brown hair came from his Sicilian mother, along with a birthmark on his neck, which his grandfather swore resembled a map of Sicily. It was a dark pigment, almost black, and it sat just below and left of a solid, square jaw that looked as if it might shatter. He'd had it hit enough times to know it wouldn't.

"I just ran into Kate. She said we got nothing."

"Hey, Frankie." Lou walked over and gave him a slap on the back. "They told me you were coming. Anybody fill you in?"

"The lieutenant gave me the basics. He said you've had three now."

Mazzetti nodded. "Three, yeah, but this might be the worst."

Frankie motioned for Lou to join him in the kitchen. "Lou, listen, I—"

"Donovan, don't worry. I knew the captain was gonna give the lead to someone. I'm glad it's you."

"Thanks, Lou."

"Let me fill you in. First one was bad, like this. The guy makes them suffer. Kate says they're dead before he shoots them."

Frankie listened as Lou went over the details, then he spent time walking around. He checked the body, looked at the mess on the floor, picked a few things off the dresser then headed toward the kitchen. "What's this?" he asked, looking at an evidence bag on the counter.

"Rat shit."

"You said there were no clues."

"I bagged it, didn't I? But it's no clue; it's rat shit." Mazzetti laughed.

"You want more? We got cat hairs in the sink, but he doesn't have a cat. There's probably dog shit in the bedroom, or who knows, maybe in the fuckin' freezer. But no dog. And we got enough DNA to represent half the criminals at Riker's." Mazzetti waved his hand in the air, as if to surrender. "It's the same old shit. That's why I got no leads after three killings."

"Guess we got too many clues," Frankie said, and picked up a brown paper bag at the end of the counter. "What's in here?"

"Dead rat. Found it in the fridge. How's that for a psycho? You think this guy ate them?"

Rat shit and a dead rat. "Mazzetti, I want everything you've got on these murders. Every scrap of information. Every photo."

"I just told you. We got nothing."

"Get it ready for me."

"You know something?"

Frankie remembered the time Nicky and Tony broke into Billy Flannagan's house and stuck a rat in his fridge. "Maybe I do."

"Don't you think you ought to share?"

Frankie considered his answer carefully. Some things even partners didn't share. "I'll think on it."

"What the hell are you talking about? Is this how you work with a partner? I'd have been better off with Jumbo."

Frankie opened the door, turning to Lou before leaving. "I think somebody sent me a message. If I'm right, you don't want to know."

FRANKIE PULLED INTO A parking space and walked toward his apartment. Alex and Keisha, two of the kids from the building, were sitting on the stoop. He was in a hurry to get upstairs, but he always made time for these two. Alex was ten years old and, like a lot of young street kids, he was nothing but ribs and skin. Keisha was twelve and going through one of those slightly chunky phases that young girls hated. "What are my two favorite brats doing out in this cold?"

Alex didn't bother to look up. "Not everybody hates cold like you, FD."

"You know why we're here," Keisha said.

Frankie sat next to them, shivering when his ass hit the concrete. He reached over and rubbed Alex's head. "Your mom got company?"

Alex's chin rested on his hands. "Yeah."

"Besides that, how's it going?"

That drew a smile. "Not bad, FD, how 'bout you? Still catching bad guys?"

"Not so much catching as looking for, but it keeps me busy." Frankie put as much enthusiasm as he could muster in his voice. "I've got to get out of this cold. Why don't you two come up? I'll make dinner."

"I've tasted your cooking," Alex said.

"Guess it's just me and my girlfriend."

Keisha straightened her skirt, grabbed hold of Frankie's hand and walked inside.

Alex followed. "I didn't say I wasn't coming. Your cooking's bad, but it's better than what I've got."

Frankie kept his smile as they walked up the stairs. What he wanted to do was bust Alex's mother and haul her ass to jail. He *would* if he could figure a way to keep Alex out of child services.

When they hit the second floor landing, Keisha's mother poked her head out the door. "Keisha, time to eat, baby."

"We're eating with FD."

She stepped into the hallway, hands on her hips and a stern look on her cocked head. "Girl, how many times have I got to tell you—Detective Donovan doesn't need you and Alex keeping him from work. Lord knows we need some people arrested in this city. We could *use* some arrested right here in this building." She gave Frankie a raised-eyebrow stare when she said that.

Keisha protested, but her mother put a stop to it. "No arguing." As she walked back into her apartment she turned. "Bring Alex if you want."

Alex sniffed the air then looked at Frankie. "FD, I'm taking a pass on your invite. You smell that pot roast? Gonna be *way* better than what you make."

"Don't be surprised if I come down to eat with you guys," Frankie said, and started up the steps toward his apartment. He was relieved to have the night free, but sad the kids weren't joining him. Some people had soft spots for dogs or cats. For Frankie, it was kids. He couldn't refuse a kid in trouble. Maybe because of his own troubled youth, or maybe he just thought he could make a difference.

By the time he reached the top of the stairs, he had his tie off and his shirt unbuttoned, despite the chill of the stairway. He turned the key and pushed open the door, greeted by a vast emptiness. *An empty house for an empty person.* That's what Mamma Rosa used to say. He shrugged, as if accepting the inevitable, made his way to the kitchen, opened a bottle of Chianti, then took a shower.

When he came out, clad in shorts and a T-shirt, he poured a glass of wine and sat at his desk. Writing opened his mind and let him think differently. He thought about the day and the crime scene. *Rat shit and a dead rat.* The rat held special significance. To any other detective it would have been nothing, but to Frankie it said a lot. If someone from the old neighborhood was involved it reduced his suspect list from millions to a handful. At the top of that handful were two people—Tony Sannullo, crew boss for the Martelli crime family; and Niccolo Fusco, otherwise known as "Nicky the Rat."

He clicked the top of his rollerball pen, took a narrow-lined notebook from the drawer and started. Frankie used computers for almost everything, but he preferred to write the old-fashioned way, with a pen on paper. The pen felt comfortable in his hand. Even the nuns back in grade school told him he'd be a writer someday.

Anyone with penmanship like yours will learn to write. That's what Sister Mary Thomas told him. Maybe her inspiration kept him going when he wanted to quit. Frankie sipped the wine, put ink to paper and wrote:

'This story started about thirty years ago, down by Philly. But that's a long way off and a lot of years past. Even so, my memory is clear on this—how you ask—it's easy for me. Tony, Nicky, and I were best friends.

So how did Frankie Donovan, a Brooklyn Detective, and Tony Sannullo, a mob boss, and Nicky "The Rat" Fusco, come to be best friends?'

Frankie set the pen down and leaned back in his chair. He didn't feel right telling this story. Maybe that's why he couldn't get started. People say that the past holds the key to the future. Frankie didn't know how much of that was true, but he knew someone from the old neighborhood was involved with these crimes. If he hoped to solve them he'd have to figure out where things went wrong. Frankie put his hands behind his head and kicked his feet up. *If this is about the old neighborhood, then it's really Nicky's story. Maybe he should tell it.*

CHAPTER 4

WITH LIFE COMES DEATH

Wilmington, Delaware. Summer—32 Years Ago

My mother's name was Maria Fusco. They say she struggled with her pregnancy, and that the first eight months felt more like eighteen. Morning sickness lasted four months, then headaches, back pain, stomach cramps—all the things she didn't want, especially with her first child. Rosa Sannullo, her neighbor and best friend, said it was a sign, and not a good one. Trouble in the first few months meant the baby might get toothaches or gas pains. The second few months meant a troubled youth. But problems throughout the pregnancy usually meant a bad child, the sign of the devil at work. Rosa always blessed herself when she said this, and she always carried a *cornicello*—an amulet to ward off evil—to clamp onto the child the moment it was born.

Rosa stayed with my mother the whole day, dabbing her head with a cool cloth when the fever came, spooning *pastine* in her mouth when it waned. "Eat, Maria."

"Not hungry," she mumbled. "Where's Dante?"

"Dante's still working. But listen to me. I've had four babies, tended to eight or ten more, and I'm about to have another. You need to eat for the baby. He needs strength."

Maria's laugh was weak and forced. "You keep saying *he*. How do you know it's not a girl?"

Rosa scoffed. "A girl would never cause so much trouble. Girls wait until they are grown—*then* they cause trouble." She raised her head toward heaven and sighed. "*Dio santo.* You don't want to know the trouble they cause then."

Rosa scrubbed the pot she cooked the *pastine* soup in, then set it aside to dry while she finished the dishes. "Besides, you need to have a boy so he can play with my Antonio." She rubbed her swollen belly and laughed.

Maria shifted to her side, holding her stomach. "Maybe I should go in."

Rosa bent down, put her hand to Maria's stomach. "Water hasn't broken, but he *is* kicking hard. That's a good sign." She stood, thinking. "But if you have pain, maybe we should go in. I'll get Dominic."

ROSA TALKED ALL THE way to the hospital, and all the time holding Maria's hand. "Betty McNulty asked about you. And that Snyder woman down on Chestnut Street."

Maria nodded. "She's nice. How is her little girl doing? Didn't she have trouble at birth?" Maria's hands flew to her stomach. Her knees raised. "Rosa." Her teeth ground together, forehead wrinkled. "Oh, God. It hurts."

Rosa patted Maria's head while she squeezed her hand. "It will be all right. Hold on." She leaned toward Dominic and whispered. "*Sbrigati.*"

"I *am* hurrying, Rosa." Dominic stepped on the gas, but every block Rosa yelled more. Half a mile later his tires screeched as he pulled into the hospital entrance. He jumped out, flung open the back door and pulled Maria out, carrying her in his arms.

Rosa held the door open and shouted. "Get a doctor. This woman is having a baby. And she's bleeding."

An attendant met them in the hall with a wheelchair. He helped Maria out of Dominic's arms, then rushed her toward the operating room. Rosa grabbed hold of a doctor talking to a nurse. "*Dottore*, get in there with Maria. That woman is having a baby. *Sanguina.* She's bleeding."

They waited five or ten minutes before Rosa remembered no one had told Dante, Maria's husband of ten years. It was difficult to tell at times which one loved the other more. He doted on her and she waited on him as if it were her only job in life. "God help me, Dominic, we didn't tell Dante."

"Calm down, Rosa. Do you know where he is working?"

"Some job…" She scratched her head. "By the waterfront. Down on Front Street."

Dominic nodded. "I know the one."

Within half an hour, Dominic returned with Dante, his face etched with worry. He rushed over and hugged Rosa.

"How is she?"

"She was in a lot of pain."

For more than an hour they sat, and paced, and worried. As Rosa prayed on her rosary beads, Dante got up for the third time. Paced more. Wrung dry hands. "What could be wrong?" His brow was a wrinkled mess.

"Please sit," Rosa said. "Worry wears the heart raw."

Dante came back to the sofa and sat. "We cannot lose that baby. It's all Maria has lived for."

Rosa looked into his eyes and held his face. Dante Fusco was a stone-mason, a strong man. But even more, he was a respected man. She hugged him again then waved to her husband to leave them alone. "It will be all right, Dante. Try not to worry."

Minutes later a doctor came through the double doors of the waiting room. He looked around as he took the green mask off his face. "Mr. Fusco?"

Dante jumped up and ran to him. "I am Dante Fusco. How is Maria?"

The silence seemed to last a year. As the doctor reached for Dante's hands, Rosa was up and running to him.

"I'm sorry, Mr. Fusco," the doctor said. "We couldn't save her."

Dante heard the words and knew their meaning, but he could not accept them. Something twisted inside of him. Snapped. Broke. He stared at the doctor. No tears. "And the baby?"

"You have a healthy boy."

Dante nodded, then turned and walked away. Walked past Rosa, waiting to console him. Then past Dominic, returning with coffee. He walked out the door and all the way home, never stopping for anything, thinking about nothing but Maria. About the life they would never have together.

THREE DAYS LATER ROSA went with Dante to get the baby. Dominic drove.

"Dante, a baby cannot go unnamed for so long. If it does it will lose its soul."

"Once I get him home I will find a name."

"I always liked Gianni," Rosa said. "Or Vittorio."

"I will think on it, Rosa."

Rosa blessed herself. "Think all you need to—just give him a name before Satan does."

As they neared home, Rosa reached over and blessed the baby. She had already put the *cornicello* around his neck. "He should be breastfed. Two blocks over, the Snyder woman's neighbor just had a baby. She could feed him. And that Irish girl on Maryland Avenue—Camille, I think her name is—her baby is only three months old. She should have plenty of milk. Those Irish always have good milk."

Rosa leaned back, rubbing her own enlarged stomach. "This little one is kicking. I think he wants to come out and play."

"How do you know it is a boy?"

"Because she's a witch," Dominic said, from the driver's seat.

Rosa brushed her hands in the air. "Because I already have four boys, and I have the same feeling I had with them. I must have done something very wrong for God to punish me like this." She blessed herself when she said it. "*Dio Santo.* He kicked again. We might not need that Irish girl. It looks as if Antonio will here before the doctor thinks."

Dante patted her arm. "You're a good woman, Rosa. Thank you for your help." He leaned forward then said, "And thank you, Dominic. I appreciate all that you and Rosa have done."

"Don't forget what I said about breastfeeding. He already looks skinny."

Dante sighed. "Rosa, I know how you feel, but babies do fine with formula." He kept a firm, yet soft, grip on the baby, wrapped in a blanket Rosa knitted. He looked at its twisted features, pinkish face, curled feet. *Not a good trade for Maria. Not a good trade at all.*

My father didn't give me a name until I was five days old. Rosa warned him not to wait, said Satan might claim me.

Niccolo Conte Fusco—that's the name he gave me. I guess it's questionable whether he did it in time. Some, like Rosa, swear he did; others… well, others might say he waited too long. Far too long.

CHAPTER 5

COPPERS

Wilmington—26 Years Ago

I woke up happy on my sixth birthday. August first was the day I was born, but Mamma Rosa made me celebrate two birthdays—the day I was born, and the day Pops named me, just in case the saints mixed them up.

School was more than a month away so we had plenty of time to do things. Plenty of time to get into trouble, my father said. He was mostly right. Tony, Frankie, and I ran that neighborhood, at least in our minds. We were six, going on eight, and wishing we were ten.

Smoking cigarettes was old hat by now. It was one of the things we lived for. Anytime we were far enough away from home or the prying eyes of a neighbor, there were smokes dangling from the left side of our mouths. Had to be the left side too. I don't know where that came from, but somebody we saw and admired must have done it that way.

I was still lying lazily in bed when the front door opened. I heard feet pounding up the stairs.

"Get your butt up, Nicky." Tony came in, followed by Frankie.

Frankie's real name was Mario, named after his mother's father, but he didn't like the way *Mario* sounded with *Donovan* so he went by his middle name. If we wanted to piss him off, we called him *Francis*. Worked every time.

"Christ's sake, half the day's gone," Tony said. "Let's go."

I jumped out of bed, started dressing. "What's the rush?"

"You guys are gonna help with cleaning."

"You prick." Frankie said, and wrestled him to the bed.

We all laughed, then ran up the hill toward Tony's house. The hill we lived on was steep, not San Francisco steep, but the kind of hill that was great for stick-boat races in the gutters after a summer rain, or for catching rides on the bumpers of cars when it snowed. Anyway, we were kids and running up hills was fun.

"This better not take too long," Frankie said.

"We'll be done in no time." When Tony opened the front door, the sweet smell of garlic hit me. I was hungry before the storm door banged shut.

"Good morning, Mamma Rosa."

"What are you boys up to?" She shut off the upright vacuum and pulled a dust cloth from a pocket on her old plaid dress to wipe the end table.

"We're helping Tony clean," I said. A few steps later we were across the living room and into the dining room.

"Coffee is in the pot, Nicky. And taste my sauce. Tell me what you think."

Mamma Rosa called it "sauce" like the Americans did. Many of the immigrants called it "gravy" or "ragu" and got insulted if you said sauce. It was one of the few American customs Mamma Rosa adopted early on, and *nothing* was more important to her than her sauce.

"I'll taste it in a minute, Mamma." Coffee was always brewing at Mamma Rosa's house, and something was usually cooking. I thought it was the way *all* houses smelled—that wonderful aroma of coffee, and garlic, and red sauce. I poured a half cup of coffee and dipped my finger in the sauce. "*Perfetto*, Mamma."

Mamma Rosa stopped cleaning to tend her spaghetti sauce. Every now and then, she wandered over to taste it, frowned, then added a pinch of garlic or a sprinkle of cheese. No matter how many times the recipe was tweaked, it seemed to need a pinch of something to make it *perfetto*.

"Nicky, taste this again."

She hummed one of her favorite old Italian songs as she cooked. I never knew the names of them, doubted she did either, but they sounded good. I dipped my finger in and tasted the sauce. "*Perfetto*," I said, and gave her a big hug.

Mamma Rosa treated me the same as her own kids. I remember her saying that raising me and Tony together was a blessing. To her, everything was either a blessing or a curse, and she embraced both with appropriate passion.

"It's for your birthday. Not today, the other one." She leaned against the stove and laughed. The way her belly shook made me smile. "Aren't you glad I gave you two birthdays?"

"Sure am, Mamma Rosa. That's one extra time I get your meatballs."

Tony raced down the steps into the kitchen. "Ciao, Mamma. We're done."

"Where are you boys off to?"

"Try to find some work. Maybe stack boxes at the grocery store," Tony called over his shoulder.

"Don't spend all you earn."

"We won't," Tony said.

We headed out the front door, down three worn concrete steps and across the yard, the smell of fresh-cut grass tickling my nose. Six more steps took us to the sidewalk.

Frankie acted nervous before we hit the next street. "I'm almost out of cigs."

"Need to get some money," Tony said.

I checked my pack. "I got two."

"One," said Frankie.

I gave both of them a hard glare. "I'm not stealing any."

"Let's go to Johnny's and carry bags," Tony said.

Frankie took a long drag on his last cigarette. "Nobody's gonna pay us to carry bags."

"Up those hills they will. Find us a couple of sweet old ladies, and *bam*—we got some bucks."

We walked ten blocks to Johnny's Meat Market, inconveniently situated halfway down one steep hill and at the bottom of another, ensuring that most everyone had to carry their groceries up a hill. For two hours we asked people if we could carry their grocery bags, hoping to earn tips. By mid-morning we earned enough for a pack of cigs, but only one.

"Screw this," Frankie said. "Go get some, Nicky."

The cigarettes were in racks above the checkout counters, too high for any of us to reach. "I'm not doing it."

"I'll do it," Frankie said. "Get in position and make it something good."

Tony and I went in and moved to the right while Frankie pretended to look at comic books. Tony bumped into a metal rack of canned beans. When the cashier came to help, Frankie jumped onto the counter and grabbed packs as fast as he could.

All of a sudden a customer yelled, "Hey, kid, get the hell off there."

Frankie leapt off the counter and dodged a stack of magazines, but ran into the arms of Johnny, owner of the meat market. Frankie scrambled to get away, but Johnny had "butcher hands," as we called them; there was no way Frankie was breaking his grip.

Frankie's old man would kill him if he got caught, so instead of running, I rammed into Johnny's side, breaking his hold on Frankie. We ran for the door but Johnny caught me, holding me like a vise.

I SAT IN THE chair at the cop station, scared shitless. Two cops had been grilling me for an hour. It was a hot, sticky day, and they had the windows closed, probably on purpose.

The tall cop, Moynihan, handed me a bottle of Coke. "Remember your name yet, kid?"

"I gotta pee."

"Not until you tell us your name."

"And who you were with," the other cop said.

"Already told you. Wasn't with anyone."

The second cop, a young black guy, leaned down to look me in the eye. "Johnny said two other boys were with you, and one of them stole cigarettes. A customer said the same thing." He smiled. "Nobody will get in trouble if you tell us what happened."

"Two other dagos," Moynihan said.

I looked up at his Irish-whiskey face and nose. "I know the kids you mean. I don't know their names, but I think they were dirty micks."

Moynihan reared back to smack me but his partner shook his head. He stepped in close and whispered, "Johnny said they were dark-haired and looked Italian. The one who stole the cigarettes had a birthmark on his neck."

I stared at the black cop. "No offense to you, sir, but they must've been black Irish." I turned to Moynihan after I said it. "I really gotta pee, bad."

Moynihan sneered at me. "As soon as you tell us who you were with." He laughed as he left the room.

I waited, then waited some more. I had to piss so bad it hurt. I stuck my hand down my pants and held my dick, squeezing it to stop from peeing. It helped at first, but soon got worse. I thought about telling them my name, but knew it would hurt Rosa. Besides, I couldn't get Tony and Frankie in trouble.

Twenty minutes later they returned. Moynihan wore an are-you-ready-to-talk-kid smile. I gave him a screw-you smile in return. "Bring me any Coke?"

Moynihan looked around the room, checked under the table, then looked in the trash can where I'd pissed. "You little fuck." He stretched across the table and slapped me, knocking me from the chair.

His partner grabbed him, but he shook it off. "Tommy, leave it alone."

Moynihan yanked me up with one hand and slapped me again. "Little bastard." He slammed me into the chair and shoved it into the table, squishing my gut. "You'll tell us who you were with before you leave here, or I swear—"

By then I was crying, nose bleeding.

"That's enough. I'm through with it," the partner said.

The door to the interrogation room opened.

"Pops." I pushed the chair back and ran, jumping into his arms.

My pops was a short, muscular man with a hooked nose and dark complexion. When he was angry he got a terrible, scary look in his eyes. He hugged me then set me down. He cleaned the trickle of blood from my lip, wiped my nose with a handkerchief from his back pocket then folded it and put it away. Moynihan turned his head when Pops glared at him. It was that day I realized how frightening Pops' eyes were.

"Who are *you?*" the partner asked Pops.

Pops picked me up and headed for the door. As we were leaving I heard Moynihan whisper, "You know who that was?"

"No idea."

"Dante Fusco."

"Oh, shit."

"Yeah."

I didn't know why that scared them, and I didn't care. I was glad to be going home.

CHAPTER 6

CONFESSION

Wilmington—25 Years Ago

It was the summer before second grade, and we were worried about something that wouldn't happen until springtime—confession. It loomed larger than the shadows and noises that followed us when we took shortcuts through the woods at night. None of us said we'd tell the truth, but nobody was brave enough to say they'd lie to a priest either. In the absence of a solution, we didn't talk about it.

During the last week of August, we made lots of trips to the smoke shop. This was where the important people in the neighborhood went. The guys who dressed nice, drove Caddies, and laughed as if the world were a great ball of fun. The smoke shop was full of colorful characters: Mikey the Face, Patsy the Whale, Tommy Tucks, Charlie Knuckles, Nicky the Nose, Paulie Shoes, and a host of others. It was run by Doggs Caputo, a tough little bastard who never smiled and always sported a five-o'clock beard. Doggs also had a thing about nicknames—everybody had to have one. If he gave you one, it normally stuck.

On Thursday, the week before school started, Tony and I went to buy cigarettes. While we waited, Doggs came out. He shoved the frames of

Coke-bottle glasses through wiry hair that should have been cut a month ago. Should have been combed, too. "What are you kids doing here?"

"Just hanging out," Tony said.

"What's your name?"

"Tony—"

I kicked him before he got out the rest.

He finished the sentence with, "Nothin."

I stared at Doggs. "What difference does it make?"

Doggs swaggered over, flipped his cigarette at my head. I ducked, glared at him.

"So, we got Tony fuckin' Nothin' and Mr. fuckin' Nobody, huh?"

At times it seemed as if every word out of Doggs' mouth was an "f." And he was clever in how he used the word; he used it as a verb, a noun, an adjective, even tacked on some letters and managed to use it as an adverb. When he got really pissed, he strung them together in the same sentence. He stared at Tony and me, lit another cigarette, then laughed. It was such an unusual occurrence that the Whale rushed outside.

"What's goin' on?" Patsy's voice rolled down the street, rumbling like a bowling ball down a lane. Whenever he talked I expected to hear pins shatter at the end of the sentence.

"Go back inside," Doggs said. "I'm having a conversation with my new friends." He tousled the hair on both our heads and started to walk away, then turned back, staring at me, then Tony. "What the fuck, you two brothers?"

"Just friends, why?"

"You look like brothers."

"Yeah, we hear that all the time," Tony said.

Doggs squinted as he looked at me. "You the kid Moynihan couldn't bust at the station?" He bent down, looked closer. "Look at me, kid." When he stood again, his head was bobbing. "Yeah, I thought so. You're Dante's boy all right. Got those same fuckin' eyes." He opened the door to the shop. "Patsy, get a couple packs of Winstons. One for Tony Nothin' and one for Nicky the Rat." He turned back to look at me. "It is Nicky, isn't it?"

"I ain't no rat."

"That's right, boy. And that's why you're getting the name. Not many kids your age keep their mouth shut. Got good blood, though. Guess I'm not surprised." He grabbed the cigarettes from Patsy, tossed a pack to each of us. "See me next summer. Maybe I'll put you to work."

"We can do it now," I said.

"You'll do it when I say, Rat. Now get out of here before I take back those cigarettes."

"Thanks, Doggs," Tony said.

"Yeah, thanks," I said.

As we walked home, I wondered what Doggs meant by "good blood," but Tony distracted me.

"The Rat," Tony said.

"Sounds like a goddamn squealer."

"Bullshit. Everybody's gonna know. Christ's sake, you got the name from *Doggs*." We walked about half a block before Tony spoke again. "Besides, it's like Johnny Viola, you know how they call him Johnny Handsome."

"Yeah, guess so," I said, and whistled. "He sure is an ugly fucker."

"Ugly as a goddamn peach seed."

We both laughed as we walked the rest of the way home. "Johnny Handsome," I said, and smiled.

SEPTEMBER CAME FAR TOO fast, and with it the first day of school at St. Elizabeth's. We walked the corridors along with hundreds of other kids, looking for our classes and wondering who our teacher would be. There were only two options: Sister Mary Leona or Sister Mary Thomas.

Sister Leona was ancient—jowls like a bloodhound and eyes so squinty it was hard to tell if they were open or closed. Frankie said she taught his grandfather. Judging by what we saw, I didn't doubt it. Of course, an old teacher had its benefits: worse hearing, worse eyesight, couldn't hit you as hard.

On the other hand, Sister Mary Thomas was the meanest, nastiest, most horrible person God ever put on this earth. She was also the nicest, kindest, sweetest, and most caring person God ever put on this earth. Which side you got depended on who you talked to and on what day, or even what time of day. She stood a few inches above five feet, but when she walked the corridors with her fiberglass yardstick or her pointer, she was a giant. Some kids said the yardstick twitched as she walked, looking for someone to hit. And she was as quick as a cobra when she struck. If you found her singling you out, you'd better hope your ass was padded because there was a good chance you were getting whacked. One kid, Jimmy Borelli, got hit so often he brought a pillow to school so he had something soft to sit on.

I walked down the hall, careful not to attract attention. When I saw Sister Mary Thomas I turned my head.

"Niccolo Fusco."

The words echoed off the walls. Her voice demanded a response. Ignoring a call from Sister Thomas was like ignoring a call from God.

"Yes, Sister?" I said, framing a smile.

She waved her pointer. "I was fortunate enough to get you in my class this year. Room 118. Class starts at 7:50."

"Yes, Sister." I gave her my I'm-so-lucky smile, but inside, I cried.

"Shit," I whispered. "I got the witch."

Before Frankie or Tony could answer, another command came from behind us. "Oh, and you, Mr. Sannullo, and Mr. Donovan. You were fortunate enough to get the witch too."

Tony gulped. Frankie's eyes almost bugged out of his head. And I damn near fell down.

"Yes, Sister," Tony said. "We'll be there at 7:50 sharp."

Sister Thomas wore a smile, but her voice carried a threat. "You do that."

As she walked away, we looked at each other with raised eyebrows. We'd heard about nuns having eyes in the back of their heads, but did they have some kind of God-enhanced hearing, too?

THE YEAR FLEW BY, and before spring arrived, Tony earned his nickname. "The Brain" he became known as, and for good reason. There wasn't a math problem or question asked in any class that he didn't get right.

The First Communion celebration was near the end of second grade. Prior to that, all kids did their first confession—it was the day we'd dreaded since last summer. The nuns taught us how the priest was God's representative on earth, and how he couldn't tell anyone what was said in the confessional.

"So it's all right to tell your sins to him," the nuns told us. "No one will know."

On Saturday afternoon we met at the church. I got put in Father Dimitri's line, tenth from the front. I felt sorry for the first one to go. Must have been scary. My stomach churned as I stepped inside, closed the curtains and knelt. It was dark in there, and the infamous "divider" separated me from Father Dimitri, but I recognized him. That made me think he could recognize me too. I didn't like that, but it was too late to ditch out, so I took a deep breath and repeated the ritual. "Bless me, Father, for I have sinned. This is my first confession."

Father Dimitri mumbled some nonsense in Latin, made the sign of the cross, then told me to confess my sins. Twice I almost started, but then I said, "Father, I've done a lot, but I don't think I can tell you."

"It is all right to be afraid, my son. This is just between you and me. No one else will know but God."

"See, now you're already bringing somebody else in on it," I said, getting ready to stand. "I think I'll just keep it to myself."

"If you do not confess, I cannot absolve you of your sins. You will not be able to receive First Communion."

I was in a jam. If I didn't get First Communion, everyone would know something terrible was wrong. *What would Pops say? What would Mamma Rosa say?*

"Listen, Father, I'll make a deal with you. I'll tell God what I've done, and He can absorb me, or absolve me, or whatever it is He does. That way, it'll be between me and God. I *know* He ain't telling nobody."

A long sigh followed. "But you have to do penance, and I have to administer that based on your sins."

Shit. Another problem.

"How much for someone who's been really bad? I mean, I didn't kill anybody or anything."

"I cannot—"

"How about I do a rosary? That should cover it. Jimmy Borelli was in here before me, and I saw how fast he finished his prayers. You couldn't have given him much." I laughed, but in a low voice, then whispered, "I *know* what Jimmy Borelli has done, Father. If he finished with a few Hail Mary's, a rosary from me is plenty. Trust me."

A pause followed. I thought I heard Father Dimitri laugh. Finally, he said, "All right, my son. Say a complete rosary, and may the Lord go with you."

As I walked out, I realized he hadn't actually said my sins were forgiven. Now what could I do? I couldn't go back in there. Sister Mary Thomas stood at the front of the church, making sure all the kids were in line and well-behaved. I walked up and got her attention.

"Sister, suppose for some reason a kid has sins and can't get to a priest. Suppose he says his sins to God instead. Will that work? Does it have to go through a priest?"

Sister Mary Thomas rubbed my head and put on her friendly smile. "If this…child was sorry for his sins and told God, I'm sure it would be all right."

"So if another kid maybe forgets a few sins while he's in the confessional, but remembers them later and tells God about them, he can maybe just say a few extra prayers to make up for it?"

She stopped rubbing my head and looked down. Her face had that almost-mean look to it. "This…kid…better be really sorry. And he better remember all of his sins the next time. But I'm sure God would forgive this kid." She whacked me lightly on the butt with her ever-present pointer. "Go say your penance."

I smiled as I sat in the pew, saying the rosary. Sister Mary Thomas had just made my day brighter. It was almost summer, and now I had a clean soul. That left a lot of room for fun. I got to thinking about religion and how it worked. Decided the Catholics had it right. The Jewish kid on Third Street didn't get his sins forgiven like this. If he did something wrong he had to live with it, or go talk to the person, or settle it all up when he died. I wasn't sure how it worked for him, but it wasn't like this.

Nah, the Catholics have it down pat. Do something bad, tell God about it, then start all over. I liked that.

CHAPTER 7

INVESTIGATION

Brooklyn—Current Day

Frankie finished his wine, sat back in the chair and relaxed. He thought about what Nicky used to say about confession. *Do something bad, tell God about it, then start all over.* That defined Nicky's whole life. He was the one who bought into that confession bullshit, but he would do it himself, with God. And it was always on a Saturday, as if it were a magical day for confessing.

Frankie wanted to sleep but couldn't get that dead rat off his mind. He headed to his desk, spread the files, and sorted them by date. Renzo was killed nearly two months ago. The second murder, Devin, followed three weeks later and had as many differences as it did similarities. Devin was Irish, not Italian. Lived in an apartment, not a house. And most puzzling of all, he wasn't tortured, just shot—once in the head, once in the heart. But the preponderance of evidence at the scene was the same. Frankie felt certain both murders were mob-related. It was a shame that people thought that way, but if two guys named Tortella and Ciccarelli got shot in Brooklyn, people assumed they were connected even if they were wearing priests' collars and carrying chalices.

Whoever did this had powerful motivation. Frankie just had to figure out why. *Why kill a person like this? Why make them suffer? Why shoot them after they are already dead? Why shoot them in the head and heart?*

A new thought occurred. Based on Mazzetti's statement, Frankie had assumed they were already dead, but he needed confirmation. Frankie scrolled through his contact file until he found the listing for Kate Burns. He dialed her number, recalling the days when she was on his speed-dial list, back when he thought he might finally have a relationship that would last. At least they still got along.

The phone rang a few times before she picked up.

"Hello."

"Kate, it's Frankie."

"And I mistook you for the shy type."

"I need to know if these guys were already dead when he shot them."

A pause followed. "You mean Mazzetti's murders?"

"Yeah, there were three."

"I know how many there were, but the first two weren't the same. The second guy was just shot. But the first one..."

"Renzo," Frankie said.

"Thanks, the names are always a blur to me. I remember wounds."

"That's what makes you so attractive, Doctor."

"Screw you," Kate said. "Anyway, the first guy, Renzo, he got it bad. He was definitely dead before he was shot."

"And Nino?"

"I haven't confirmed it, but I'd bet on it."

"Thanks. Sorry I bothered you at night."

"Before you go, I thought you'd like to know that the actual murder weapon was a Louisville Slugger. I'm guessing we'll find the same with Nino."

"Yeah, me too. Thanks again."

"Goodnight, *Detective* Donovan." She cooed the title.

"I love you, too," he said, and hung up. He regretted saying that to her—didn't want to make her think... *Nah, she won't.*

As he went through Tommy Devin's file, he saw something in the inventory that stopped him cold—thirty-two packs of Winstons.

Thirty-two packs. Another link to the past.

If he assumed the murderer was Nicky or Tony, that still left a big question—how did they know the victims? To figure that out, Frankie had to know the victims. After picking up his favorite fine-point marker, he started making a chart. "Who are you, Nino? And what did you do to piss someone off so bad?"

There was no doubt that someone was sending Frankie a message, but were they warning him off, or giving him clues? Was this *really* tied to the old neighborhood, or was he reading too much into it? Maybe the guy bought four cartons and happened to have thirty-two packs left.

Frankie pulled a cigarette from a pack on the table. He lit it and sucked hard on that first drag. A memory brought laughter along with the smoke, damn near choking him. Nicky hated it when Frankie strained the cigarette. But that was back when cigs were important. Hell, back then they were *everything.*

CHAPTER 8

THE OATH

Wilmington—21 Years Ago

My eleventh birthday was the best of my life. Pops took off from work and invited Tony and Frankie to see the Phillies play. We smoked a whole pack of cigarettes before noon, knowing we'd be dry the rest of the day. An hour later we piled into the car with Pops. It was August-hot, but despite that, and the fact that our team didn't win, we had a great time. Not only did we get to go to the ball game, but we celebrated my birthday dinner the next night at Tony's house. Mamma Rosa made my favorite meal of meatballs and spaghetti. Nothing fancy, just the most delicious damn meatballs in the world and homemade pasta. When I thought I'd died from pleasure, Rosa brought out a plate of sfogliatelle—shell-shaped pastries stuffed with ricotta cheese. The sfogliatelle took this from the best meal to one made in heaven. I stuffed until my stomach hurt. It was a great way to kick off August.

I was no longer just Nicky; I was "Nicky the Rat." The name Doggs gave me stuck, much to my dismay. Names were like that; they either stuck, or they didn't. Frankie was hanging out more at Tony's house, swearing he couldn't stand to be in the same block with his father. He never told us about the beatings, but we saw the marks on his back when we went swimming. We spent most nights in Tony's basement playing pool. The table was nice, but the basement floor wasn't level, front and back sloping toward a drain in the middle. And the steps were always in the way, forcing the use of a short cue that made us feel like dwarfs.

Tony was kicking Frankie's ass at nine-ball, winning all his cigarettes. While he did that, I played with a spider that lived in the rafter supports just above the old oil tank, a 250-gallon metal behemoth that sat in the corner, covered in soot and stinking like a factory. The other guys teased me about the spider, but they knew better than to kill it. She was mine.

By early March we'd saved enough money to make a deal with old-man Burczinski to rent his garage down off Broom Street. There was a line of row-houses with a hill behind them and a string of detached garages below. Must have been thirty garages, all covered by a flat roof. We sealed the deal with Burczinski then collected junk furniture to put in our hangout.

A few weeks later, a kid named Tommy McDermott joined our group. He was what we called "Black Irish." He looked more Italian than Irish, but that's where it stopped. Tommy thought beef stew was the best meal in the world. If it was, he was the luckiest guy in the world, because that's what the McDermotts served five days a week. The other two days were pot luck, but no matter what, potatoes accompanied the meal.

The McDermotts had nine kids: six boys and three girls, and the half that weren't rail-thin were just plain skinny. Tommy's dad was a fireman, probably because he couldn't make it as a cop. There was an old joke in the neighborhood that held more truth than not—Mick kids grew up to be either priests or cops, and dagos grew up to be priests or gangsters. With a few exceptions, they weren't far off.

Tommy came into the group almost by accident. I was stealing cigarettes from Johnny's store and, as I ran out, Johnny hot on my heels, I passed Tommy. I shot him a glare, as if to say, "Don't you dare rat us out."

It took me ten blocks to ditch old Johnny. Probably because he got winded going up the steep part of the hill on Maryland Avenue. That son-of-a-bitch could run for an old fuck. After that, I took a roundabout way back to the hangout, careful when I entered in case the cops had gotten wind.

Frankie let me in, a cigarette dangling from his mouth. "Where you been, Nicky?"

"Nobody came?"

"No, why?"

"That McDermott kid saw me get the cigs. Johnny chased me for half a mile. Maybe more." I looked around, peeked outside. "Thought the mick might have ratted us."

Frankie took a long drag. "If he didn't give you up, maybe he's all right."

"Yeah, we'll see. If we go another week without a cop coming for us, I'll be impressed."

A week went by, then another. Finally I admitted that McDermott didn't rat us out. I waited for him one day after school. "Hey, mick. Come here."

Tommy McDermott looked at me with hard blue eyes, deep-water blue, like the color of the ocean. "You thought I'd rat you out?"

"You know better."

"Fuck you, dago. I'm not scared of you. I just don't rat."

I looked him over, stared him up and down. He was poised to fight. "All right. I'll buy that." I held out my hand. "You can hang with us if you want. But we got rules."

"If any of those rules involve fuckin' my sister, stand in line. Everybody wants her, and she ain't giving it out."

I laughed, then laughed harder. "Okay, you'll fit right in. C'mon, I'll introduce you to the other guys."

We walked to the garages, trading stories. I lit a smoke, handed one to Tommy, who bummed a light from me, then we slowly made our way down St. Elizabeth's Street, across Broom Street and around to the garage. By the time we got there, the cigs were gone. I called in as we approached. "Yo, Frankie, comin' in."

The door opened, and we ducked in. "This is Tommy McDermott. Tommy, this is Frankie Donovan. We'll find him a nickname soon."

Tony flicked a cigarette butt at us from his perch on a worn old sofa.

"Oh, yeah," I said, "And the one with the shit-eating grin is Tony "The Brain" Sannullo. Hate to say it, but he's the smartest guy I've ever seen."

Frankie passed cigs around. "Guess we need to give you a name, unless you're okay with Mick."

"Name's gotta fit, right. I *am* a mick."

I roared. "Told you you'd like this guy."

Frankie crashed on the sofa and pulled out the latest *Playboy,* compliments of Tony's older brother. We drooled over it, discussed which girl had the biggest tits and the best ass, then smoked some more.

"I gotta go eat dinner," Frankie said. "See you back here later."

"What's going on later?" Tommy asked. All eyes went to him.

"Before we tell you, you better know this. Once you're in, you're in. Any ratting after that, and you're dead. No excuses."

"What am I in for?"

"Cigarettes—a whole shitload of them."

"I'm in."

"Be back here at 8:00."

BY 8:05, NERVES WERE getting the better of us. "He ain't showing," Tony said. "I told you we shouldn't trust him."

"You didn't say shit, Tony, so shut the fuck up."

"Probably scared shitless."

"Not everybody gets scared," I said.

Tony spat. "Yeah, and not everybody's a freak like you, Nicky. Some people *do* get scared."

I patted him on the back. "Don't worry. I'll take care of you, little brother."

Tony swung at me just as Frankie came through the door, out of breath and sweating. "He's coming up the hill."

"Alone?"

"Yeah, he's alone."

When Mick arrived, I got everybody in a huddle. "All right, listen. Before we do this, Mick needs to swear the oath."

"What oath?"

"The rules we got," Frankie said.

Tommy looked at each one of us. "Spit it out."

"Friendship and honor," I said. "That's it. Two rules."

"Who thought this shit up?"

Frankie pushed him. "Tony did."

Here we were, eleven years old and nothing was more important than our friendship. Not family, not girls, not even cigarettes. Back then, we'd have died for each other. Or so I thought.

"Tony will explain it all," I said.

Tony crushed his butt on the floor and stared at Tommy. "*Friendship* means we look out for each other. Nobody ever rats or betrays anyone else." Tony waited for Mick to nod. "*Honor* means nobody fucks with one of us and not the others. We stick up for each other. And it means we don't run, unless we all run. So, if there's a fight and we're gonna get our asses kicked, either we all run, or none of us run."

"Good by me," Mick said. "How do we do this oath? We cut ourselves or something?"

"We're not dumb micks," I said. "We swear to it, that's all."

"Swear on our mothers' eyes," Frankie said.

"So you're not dumb micks, just dumb dagos." Mick's laughter got us all going. But after that, we swore on our mothers' eyes, and everyone took it seriously. Since I didn't have a mother, I swore on Mamma Rosa's eyes. That was as serious as any oath got.

CHAPTER 9

MIKEY "THE FACE" FAGULLO

We did the job that night for the Borelli's, and several more over the next few months. During the next year we picked up odd jobs, and occasionally got a cigarette heist to supplement the habit. Through it all, we managed to earn enough to pay Burczinski rent for the garage, which became the perfect hangout. We also started hanging out more at Mick's house, mostly to stare at his sister Patti. Now we had a perfect triangle: Tony's house to eat, the hangout to smoke or look at dirty magazines, and Mick's house.

One hot Saturday morning, the three of us were sitting in the garage with no breeze. It was humid as hell. Frankie paced, straining every cigarette he smoked. The rest of us sat there sweating. "Let's go to Mick's," Frankie said.

"Why, so you can drool over Patti?"

"Fuck you, Tony. It's too damn hot here."

"It's no cooler at his house."

"At least he's got fans," Frankie said. "I'm going. If you want to come, okay."

Tony and I followed Frankie. It was only eight blocks, but Frankie must have fucked Patti a dozen times in his mind. Patti had grown into a beautiful girl with a great body, and she was, as Frankie described her, "fuckably sweet." Half the boys in the neighborhood came to the McDermott house under the pretense of visiting one of the brothers, but they were really there to see Patti, hoping to get a glimpse of her in underwear, or, God forbid, to cop a feel as they squeezed past her in the hallway.

As we turned the corner to Tommy's block, I tapped Frankie on the shoulder. "Get that glazed look off your face. Tommy's dad is gonna know what you're after."

"I'd eat her pussy right in the middle of church."

I roared. "You said that with such conviction I believe you."

"You don't know what pussy tastes like and you never will," Tony said.

Frankie glared, as if to challenge him, but he was right. Twelve years old, and none of us had eaten pussy. Had done about everything else, but no one had sampled the forbidden fruit. "I'll let you know as soon as I do, Tony."

Well, there it was. The dare was out there. It wouldn't be long before somebody got a taste.

THE NEXT DAY TOMMY came to the garage with a possible big job. He overheard his older brother, Jack, talking about a freight train loaded with cigarettes. It was unlocked and wouldn't be unloaded for two days. His brother planned on hitting it the next night.

"It has to be tonight," Tommy said. "Gonna have to be late too. The store doesn't close till nine, then they take time locking up and shit."

"Jack will be pissed."

"He'll be out for blood," Tony said.

"Screw him," Mick said.

"Easy to say that now, Mick, but if he finds out he'll kick all of our asses."

I thought for a long while. "I say we go for it." The other guys agreed. "All right. We tell our parents we're spending the night at each other's houses, like we always do. We'll hang around till eight, then leave. Meet here at nine."

BY 10:20 THE MARKET was dark except for two lights inside and one each at the front and back on the outside. Tony found the open boxcar within five minutes; it was full of cigarettes. "This is perfect."

"Perfect my ass," Frankie said. "How are we gonna get them to the garage without anybody seeing?"

"We got shopping carts," Tony said. "They hold a lot of cigs, but we can't risk more than one trip."

"No, Frankie's right," I said, then thought it through. "Tony's right too. We might make it to the hangout one time, but these carts are noisy. We can't risk it twice."

"Who you selling these to?" Mick asked.

I almost didn't say, but hell, he was one of us now. "Couple of spics on Harrison Street."

"I got an idea," Mick said. "Mary Sitarski lives just around the corner. She's got a shed out back they never use. Her dad used to butcher chickens or something, but he's sick now, so nobody uses it. We can stash them there until the Puerto Ricans come get them."

I smiled. "Just might work."

"Best part is," Tommy said, "there's a path through the woods at the end of the lot. We don't even need to go on the road."

"Let's do it," I said. "Once we sell these to the spics, we'll have a pile of cash."

"How much for Mikey?" Mick asked.

"Nothing."

Tony grabbed my arm. "Nicky, you telling me that Mikey doesn't know about this?"

"Nobody knows but us."

Frankie was shaking his head. "We gotta pay The Face his due."

"Let me worry about The Face." I stared each of them down. "We gonna get this done, or what?"

We loaded seventeen shopping carts full of cigarettes into Sitarski's shed that night. Tommy told Mary the next day what we'd done, swearing her to secrecy and promising her a small cut if she kept quiet. Three days later, the Puerto Ricans picked up the cigs, and I collected the money— four hundred and seventy bucks each.

FOR TWO WEEKS WE were on cloud nine, then, while walking up Union Street, we saw Mikey "The Face" Fagullo.

"Nicky, there's The Face," Tony said.

"Take it easy. He might not know."

"He knows," Frankie said. "You don't steal in Mikey's territory without him finding out. We should've settled with him."

Mikey started across the street. "*Ciao, ragazzi.* What are you doing up here?"

They called him The Face because the guy couldn't leave his face alone. He was always rubbing it, or scratching it, or looking at it. If he passed by anything resembling a mirror, he stopped to look at himself. He'd lean in close and pinch his cheeks, try out a few smiles, then move on until he hit another reflection.

I tapped Tony's arm. "We need to get out of here."

"Let's go," Tony said, and we took off.

The next day, while we were sitting in the garage, the door opened and in walked Mikey, followed by Tommy Tucks and Pockets.

"Don't know why you ran away," Mikey said. "I just wanted what was due. You guys stole from my neighborhood. When you do that, you gotta pay the dues."

Mick darted for the door. Tommy Tucks grabbed him and tossed him back inside.

Tommy Tucks got his name from the extreme habit of tucking in his shirt. There was no doubt that if you were with Tommy for more than five minutes he'd be tucking in his shirt, or straightening it, or doing something with it at least once. He hung out with a guy named Pockets, who always had his hands in his pockets. When the two of them were together it was a sight. The whispers around the neighborhood were that Pockets had his hand on a knife. Other people said his hand was always on his dick. Either way, you didn't want to shake hands with Pockets.

Tony stepped up to Mikey, looked him right in the eyes. "Sorry, Mikey. Didn't mean to cut you out."

Mikey slapped him playfully on the side of the head. "I didn't think so. You fuckin' boys make me laugh. But don't worry. Pay what you owe and we'll be square."

"Our cut was four seventy each," Tony said.

Mikey smiled. "Since it's your first time, let's see…how about fifty percent?"

"That's two hundred thirty-five bucks."

"Yeah, how about that. No wonder they call you The Brain." Mikey's smile disappeared so quickly, it had to have been a fake one. "Now, pay up you little fucks."

"We don't have it with us," I said.

"Get me the money or Pockets tears this place up."

I looked to Tony, then to the others. They all nodded. "All right." I went to the sofa in the corner, lifted the cushion, reached inside a hole and pulled out a brown grocery bag.

"Nine hundred forty," Tony said with a sigh.

"Fuck, that kid's good," Mikey said.

I counted it out, then handed Mikey the money and put the bag away, already thinking of where we could hide it after this.

"Good job, boys," Mikey said, then turned to Pockets and Tucks. "Don't leave marks where they can be seen."

It didn't register at first, but it didn't take long. Tommie Tucks and Pockets pulled out two short clubs and started beating our legs and upper body. "Don't hit the face," Mikey said.

They only hit us a few times, probably less than a minute, but it seemed like forever. I could barely stand, and Mick was spitting blood. Tony and Frankie were holding their legs and trying to stand.

"Go get the bag," Mikey said to Tucks.

He walked out, returning in a minute with a grocery bag. Mikey tossed it to me. "Just to show you there are no hard feelings," he said, then they walked out.

"Cock-sucker." Tony yelled.

"That whore will get his," Mick said.

"What's in the bag?" Frankie asked.

I dumped it out on the ground. "Smokes," I said. "A lot of them."

When we were done counting, there were thirty-two packs of Winstons. Not worth the beating we took, but something. I sat on the sofa shaking my head. "This was my fault. I should've paid Mikey his due."

"We were in this together," Tony said. "Nobody argued."

Soon they were all nodding. "Guess so," Frankie said.

I smiled. "The important thing is we stood together. We stood by the oath."

"I don't care if we have to die," Tony said. "We'll keep the oath."

I stared at each of them one by one. "Somebody breaks this oath, and they *will* die."

We put our fists together and raised our hands in the air. "Friendship and honor!" everybody hollered at once.

CHAPTER 10

MORE EVIDENCE

Brooklyn—Current Day

"Oaths." Frankie got out of bed and thought back to his youth. Friends were all that mattered back then. Frankie hated life with his parents, and Mick's didn't have time for him. Tony had the best mom and dad anyone could want; he just didn't get it. And Nicky—no mother, and a father who doted on his dead wife. The four of them were good for each other.

"Where are you, Nicky?" Frankie asked while he brushed his hair. "Are you still in Cleveland, or are you here?"

He set the brush on the vanity and went to the closet. He grabbed a pair of olive pants, matching socks, and a beige knit shirt, putting them on in that order. Next he took the shoe trees from a pair of black Moreschi lace-ups, smiling as he slipped them on. The one thing he wouldn't compromise on was shoes. As he made his way to the kitchen, he thought again about the oath. Friendship and honor were part of the oath, but the unspoken part was betrayal.

That made him think of Nino—he did *something* to piss someone off.

Frankie drank his coffee then headed out. When he got to the station, he parked, grabbed his folder of notes, then walked inside and up the steps to the second floor. "Where's Lou?" he asked Carol, the all-knowing receptionist perched at her desk and guarding the detectives' room like Cerberus did Hades.

"He's checking on leads. And he said to tell you that he won't tolerate a partner who's late. But Vinnie's here."

Frankie was already moving away when Carol's voice caught him. "The lieutenant wants you in the office."

Frankie knocked before entering. "Hey, Lieu. You wanted to see me?"

Morreau didn't look up. "Where are we, Donovan?"

"Same place we were yesterday. We got nothing."

He stopped writing and stared. "Three bodies and not a single lead."

"Lieu, I—"

Morreau stood. Stretched seemed more like it. When he was sitting he seemed normal, but once he stood his body parts elongated, like those trick mirrors at the boardwalk. "I don't want excuses. Find this prick and get the pressure off me."

"Yes, sir. Is that all?"

"That's all."

As Frankie passed Carol, he forced a smile. "Tell Vinnie I'm looking for him. Suggest he bring coffee."

She saluted and clicked her heels, then rounded up Vinnie.

Vinnie was a young detective who managed to get a badge through connections.

"What's up, Donovan?"

"How were the bodies found?"

"You got all the pictures. Nobody moved them."

He also had an attitude, Frankie now remembered. *A real smart-ass attitude.* Maybe he didn't like that Frankie took over the case. "I meant how were they *discovered*?" Frankie leaned close to Vinnie. "If you fuck with me, I'll make sure you get assigned to the Island."

Vinnie must have thought Frankie really could do that. "Sorry, sir." He shuffled through papers, searching. "Let's see, Tommy Devin, the second vic…neighbor called it in. Said she smelled something rotten coming from the apartment."

Frankie nodded.

"First…okay, here we go. First one is Renzo…"

"Ciccarelli."

"Right, so Renzo was called in to 9-1-1."

Frankie sat up straight. "What?"

Vinnie read more. "Yeah. A neighbor said they were walking by and heard a cat, or maybe a baby, crying."

"Give me that." Frankie reached for the report and read it through. "Why didn't I have these files before?"

"I don't know, sir. But—"

"But nothing, look at this." He tapped the folder with his finger. "Cat found in the bathroom with door locked. Food and litter box inside. Toilet bowl open."

"Guess he kept the cat in the bathroom. So what?"

"You remember that house? Do you think someone could hear a cat crying if they were passing by on the sidewalk? With the cat in the bathroom?"

Vinnie took the report back and frantically went through it.

"Forget about that for now," Frankie said. "How about Nino?"

"When he didn't show up for work and they couldn't reach him at home, somebody called the cops."

"Somebody?"

"Guy he worked with." Vinnie scrambled for the name. "John Hixon."

"And that's all? You sure there are no other calls?"

"No, sir." He sat rigid after he said it.

Frankie thought about the cat, lit a cigarette, then laughed like hell. In fifth grade, Nicky found a cat at lunch and kept him in the coat closet all afternoon. He gave it a bowl of water and some food. Every time it meowed, the nun threw a fit trying to figure out where the noise was coming from. Several kids got beaten that day because she thought they were making the noise.

Judging by the look on Vinnie's face, the laughter must have taken him by surprise. "Something funny, sir?"

"Nothing," Frankie said, but chuckled to himself. Nicky always liked cats. Frankie's smile disappeared as those nagging thoughts returned. *Rat shit. Dead rats. Winstons. Now this.*

More proof as far as he was concerned. No way Nicky the Rat was going to let that cat suffer, or be left alone with its dead master. Still, all this was circumstantial.

But *someone* called this in, and that someone was probably the killer. Time to see if it was anyone he knew. He poked his head out the door. "Carol, can you get me the 9-1-1 call from the Ciccarelli case? Not the transcript. I need the voice."

"Might take a while, but I'll get it."

"Thanks," Frankie said, and returned to his files. He called Mazzetti, got another cup of coffee, finished that, then grabbed his coat. "Carol, I'm going to meet Lou. If you get that tape let me know."

As Frankie drove to meet Mazzetti, another thought hit him. He had been leaning toward Nicky because no one had seen him in months, or even heard from him. *Not since he called and said he was in trouble. But what if Nicky's dead and someone is trying to make me think it's him?* He said a silent prayer, and, as he did, another question arose. When Nicky called he mentioned a girl. *Where does she fit in?*

CHAPTER 11

ANGELA

Wilmington—21 Years Ago

Several months passed with little of importance. During late November, Angela Catrino started coming by Tony's house to learn how to cook from Rosa. Angela's mother died the month before and the responsibility fell on her to take care of her father. He asked Rosa to teach her.

Rosa had been blessed—or, as some said, cursed—with five boys, when all her life she dreamed of having a girl. When this opportunity came along, she welcomed Angela into her home.

Angela came by almost every day. She was a quick learner and a diligent worker. If Rosa said go to the store and get something, Angela ran. And when Rosa gave instructions, Angela memorized them as if they were a history lesson. She had the uncanny ability to watch Rosa do something once and, like a machine, copy it. That wasn't as easy as it might seem. In Italian families, recipes were an ever-changing process; what was written down was seldom adhered to. During the cooking process, pinches of garlic, or cheese, or drops of olive oil...anything, were added. And all dependent upon the continual tasting that went on.

Angela was more than sharp; she was respectful. And because of that, Rosa taught her everything. Didn't hold back like some of the old Italians.

Angela even wore the same kind of apron Mamma did, with a pocket to hold the wooden spoon on the right. The only difference was Angela wore a white-and-green checkered apron; Rosa's was white-and-red.

She soon became one of the guys. She was around so much we gave her a name—Angela "No Tits" Catrino—though no one would dare say it in front of Mamma Rosa. Angela had become "off limits" with Mamma. She was as protected as Paulie Shoes was from Doggs.

Everyone called her "No Tits" for the obvious reasons. Aside from missing the two lumps on her chest most teenage boys found a necessity before striking up a conversation with a girl, and besides the fact that her father would have killed anyone who touched her, she was a nice kid. Cute, too. As the months rolled by, I grew accustomed to seeing Angela at Tony's house. Pretty soon her name went from No Tits to Angela, then to Angie. Before long, I was getting pissed at the other guys for teasing her.

On the first hot Saturday in late spring, we went swimming then headed to Tony's house. Being wet, we had to use the back door, so we rounded the corner and headed up the alley, a two-and-a-half foot wide strip of concrete between Mr. Ciotti's ever-present stone wall and the back side of chain-link fences. The wall was five feet high but loomed above us like the Iron Curtain. On the left, the fences ran back-to-back, clotheslines strung from the houses to steel poles buried in a lump of concrete at the end. Occasionally there was a young kid tied to the pole to keep them from running away while their mother draped laundry over the line, giving it that fresher-than-heaven smell. The houses were only seventeen feet wide, so it didn't take long to get to Tony's house. His was the fifth on the block.

We popped open the gate and raced up the sidewalk, the whole backyard filled with the wonderful aroma of Mamma Rosa's sauce and meatballs. A smile covered my face long before we burst through the back door, still in our swimsuits.

"Hey, Angie, you cooking meatballs?" I reached into the pot and grabbed one. It was hot as hell, so I had to bounce it from hand to hand to keep from burning.

"Get out of there, Nicky." Angela swung the spoon at me. She must have missed on purpose, because the kitchen was so small I could barely squeeze by without bumping into her, which wasn't bad.

I bit the outside of the meatball. "Pretty good."

"*Pretty* good?" Angela stared, her hands planted on an apron covered with sauce. She looked like a young Mamma Rosa.

"Could use some more cheese in the sauce."

She splashed water on me from the sink, then went after me with the spoon again. I ducked into the basement, laughing. I went down a few steps then crept back up and watched through the door. Angie dipped her spoon into the pot and tasted one. "He's right. It needs cheese." She whispered it, almost to herself, but I heard.

Rosa sat at the table, silent. She watched as Angela added Parmigiano to the sauce. "Pay no attention to that boy."

"I think he's right. It needs cheese."

Rosa smiled ear to ear. "Whatever you think, dear."

After that, I found more reasons to be at Tony's house, particularly when Angela was there. I was thirteen and in love, and my dick ached every time I saw her. I couldn't help it. She wasn't gorgeous like Sandy Miller, but there was something special about Angie. The way she smiled. The way she laughed. I particularly liked the way she twirled her hair around her index finger whenever she was thinking or nervous. And the way she gave me shit right back when I teased her. Come to think of it, I liked everything about her. Soon, I worked up the nerve to ask her out, which meant hanging out at the park or on the corner with the guys. It was nothing formal, but to Angie that was fine. She said a trip to Delmonico's in New York couldn't have been better.

After that day the word was out. Angie was under my protection.

CHAPTER 12

A STACKED DECK

Wilmington—19 Years Ago

We were thirteen, and Doggs hired us to work a big game at the smoke shop. I put on my black pants, black socks, and pointed black shoes. I grabbed a pale green shirt from the closet and tucked it in, then tightened the belt till my gut damn near burst. I wore green more since meeting Angie. The guys teased me about it, but I defended my choice. I checked the mirror a few times more than necessary, combed my hair for the third time, then ran downstairs.

"Where you going, Nicky?" Pops was in his chair reading.

"Doggs is having a game. Wants us to work it."

"Who's 'us'?"

"All of us—me, Tony, Frankie. Paulie Perlano, too."

"Who?"

"You know Paulie. We call him The Suit."

Pops never looked up from his book. "You boys stay together. And remember your manners. It will earn you more."

I was halfway up the hill to Tony's house when Suit called. Paulie's parents were poor, so poor he only had one white shirt to wear with his school uniform. No matter what time of day you went to Paulie's house his mom was washing or ironing clothes. She had five boys and six girls, and their uniforms had to be washed every night. They might have been poor but there was no way Mrs. Perlano was going to send her boys to school in a dirty shirt. Paulie swore that when he got older he'd have a closet full of suits. That's how the name got started.

"Hey, Nicky. Check this out."

I looked at him and whistled. Suit had a new shirt. "Where'd you steal that?"

"My brother got a raise. Bought three of us new shirts."

I ran my hand over the material, gave a soft whistle. "Nice shit."

Suit smacked my hand away. "Let's get Tony."

We picked Tony up then walked to the corner to get Frankie.

"What's up, Frankie? Why so glum?"

"Same old shit. Always one parent that's a prick."

"At least you got two parents."

Frankie looked at me with a sad face, one I'd always remember. "Sometimes two parents aren't so good."

"Hey guys, let's forget the depressing shit. We got a game to work." Tony tried lighting a match while he walked but it wasn't working. "Gonna be a big game."

"Lot of tips," Suit chimed in. "*Lot* of tips."

I scoffed. "*If* you're lucky enough to get a winner. Get a loser, and they'll be borrowing from *you*."

"You're just pissed 'cause you always get losers," Frankie said.

The other guys laughed and I was forced to agree. "Can't catch a break on that."

"Who's playing?" Frankie asked. His mood seemed to be brightening.

"Everybody. Charlie Knuckles, Mikey the Face, The Whale, Jimmy the Gem, Paulie Shoes. Probably more."

"Who *ain't* playing?" Suit asked.

We set a fast pace to the smoke shop, where Nicky the Nose was standing duty for Patsy. He let us into the back room, checking the street first to make sure no one was watching. As soon as we entered, we heard Patsy "The Whale" Moresco's laughter rolling through the room. If you judged happiness by laughter, Patsy was the happiest man alive. Tony used to say that if you wanted to find Patsy, follow the laughter, and he'd be at the end of it, his big fat palm banging on a bar or a table—something.

"Frankie, get your ass over here." Patsy sat at the bar, on a stool that looked too frail to support him, his meaty hand clasped around a drink.

Frankie ran over, eager to get an early start on the night. Serving drinks earned good tips, but it was usually a bad omen. The guys who drank typically lost in the game, and that's where the big tips came in.

Pretty soon, everyone had shown up, and Doggs assigned the players. Tony got Paulie Shoes and Charlie Knuckles, and he couldn't have been happier. Knuckles almost always won, and he was the best tipper. People would think with a name like "Knuckles" it was because he had big knuckles. It was the opposite. Charlie blamed it on the nuns beating him with rulers, and though it didn't make sense, it earned the nickname. Paulie Shoes was another story—he loved shoes. When he was a kid, he spent all his money on them. He had ripped pants and shirts with frayed collars, but his shoes were always new. Paulie Shoes was a 50/50 shot, but if he won big Tony would be in business.

Suit got Tommy Tucks and Patsy. Frankie got The Nose and Pockets. And I ended up with The Face and Doggs. I was hoping for Jimmy the Gem, but he didn't show; still, I wasn't unhappy with the pick. Face could do good if he caught cards, but Doggs was too tight. Only way he'd win big was if the other guys got drunk or went on tilt.

Before we started, Doggs brought out a coffee can with a lid. "I just caught eight goddamn cockroaches in the back room," he said. "I'm gonna let the fuckers go. The one who kills the most bugs wins ten bucks." Doggs knelt on the floor, turned the can upside down then opened the lid. Eight roaches ran like hell as soon as they hit the floor.

Frankie's eyes lit up. "That ten bucks is mine."

Tony and Suit laughed like hell. This job was tailor-made for Frankie.

The Donovans had the misfortune of living next to the DiNardos, who reigned over an empire of cockroaches, water bugs, flies, and an assortment of other pests. That would've been okay if the bugs had respected property lines. But those German roaches must have inherited more than an ancestral name, because they always tried grabbing new territory. No matter how much concrete sealant or stucco Mr. Donovan put on his basement walls, those bugs found a way to breach the barrier. During hot summer nights, when everyone had their windows open, the screams of the Donovan girls echoed for blocks whenever a roach ran across the floor or, God forbid, across the bed.

Frankie was invisible to his father. The only praise he earned was for killing bugs, so he got good at it. Got to be so he could out-think a roach, knowing which way it would turn before it moved. He could stomp a roach and catch a fly at the same time. Doggs didn't know it, but he had entered a fixed race.

Frankie went into action, stomping, whacking and even using the broom handle to kill the bugs. Within a few seconds, Frankie killed every roach before anyone else got one.

Mikey the Face laughed so hard he choked. "What the hell was that? Did you see that shit? Frankie killed them fuckin' roaches like he had a machine gun."

"Frankie, hell," Doggs said as he peeled two fives off his wad of bills. "Gentlemen, meet Bugs Donovan."

While Doggs congratulated him for a good show, Face peeled a five from his stack and tossed it to Frankie. "Here you go, Bugs. One helluva job." Everyone laughed, but this time the laughter held a note of respect. Killing was killing. It didn't matter if it was roaches or people; killing took finesse, and these guys respected it.

Frankie finally had a name. We tried forcing names on him before, but they didn't take. Names weren't like that. You couldn't force them. Had to come on their own. 'You gotta earn a name' Paulie Shoes always said.

Doggs checked to make sure the doors were locked then took his usual seat, back to the wall so he faced the main entrance. "You hear about Moynihan getting whacked?"

I plopped a drink on the table in front of Knuckles. "Not sorry to hear that. He always busted my balls."

"Guess that'll teach him to pick on Little Nicky," Doggs said. Everyone laughed, as if they knew a joke we didn't.

I looked over at Tony and Frankie, but they shrugged. Guess they didn't know either.

The game kicked off at eight. Before long they were heavy into play. By ten, Knuckles was up a grand. He tossed Tony a ten-spot and a leash. "Take Pisser for a walk. And make sure he does it all."

Tony stuffed the ten in his pocket. "What kind of fuckin' name is Pisser?"

"Watch your mouth, you piece of shit."

"Where you want him walked?"

Knuckles grunted. "That's more like it. Take him to the park. And be patient. That dog will piss on everything he sees."

"Jesus Christ, Knuckles I don't have all night."

Knuckles laid his cards on the table and turned to stare at Tony. "You got ten dollars, you shit. If I tell you to walk that fuckin' dog to Philly and get him a cheesesteak, that's what you'll do."

Tony headed toward the door, his hand waving in the air. "Okay. Okay. Fuck."

"Watch your *fuckin'* mouth. I already told you." Knuckles turned to Doggs. "I don't want that kid no more. Next time give me The Rat or Bugs." He shook his head as he picked up his cards, mumbling. "Can't stand ungratefulness in a boy."

Shoes crushed his cigar out in the ashtray. "Hope he doesn't run into Chinski's dog. That son-of-a-bitch is nasty, and it can run."

"Should be in a race," Face said, then looked around the room. "You know, that ain't a bad idea. We should get all the dogs in the neighborhood and have a race. Bet on them."

I smiled, but I wanted to laugh at him. *How the hell is he gonna have a dog race in the neighborhood?* I'm stuck with two losers, and now Face was thinking about dog races instead of cards. *Just win a pot,* I wanted to tell him.

Suddenly an idea hit me. When Face said we should have a race, it reminded me of the way those roaches ran when Doggs dumped them on the floor. Face was right; the neighborhood needed races, but not with dogs—with roaches.

CHAPTER 13

WHAT'S IN A NAME?

Brooklyn—Current Day

Frankie drove home with the heater cranked up to 75. He circled the block looking for a parking spot, then saw Keisha and Alex playing step ball. He picked up energy drinks and beef jerky, which Keisha loved, then came around again. On this pass, Alex flagged him down. Frankie lowered the window. "What's up?"

Alex pointed to construction cones blocking part of the street next to the curb. "Saved you one, FD. Figured that might be worth something on a day like this, knowing how you hate the cold and all."

Frankie laughed as Alex cleared his spot. The kids called him *FD*. He didn't know if it stood for his initials or "fuckin' dick" but he didn't care; they said it with respect.

"Who's got five for old FD?" Frankie said as he got out of the car.

"Sure as shit ain't me," Alex said, and held his hand out to bump fists. "You know we don't do that slap-five shit no more. How old are you?"

"Too damn old, I guess." Frankie tossed a pack of jerky and handed them the drinks. "How's my best girl?" Keisha was an adorable kid, twelve years old, with smooth chocolate skin and long hair she wore in pigtails.

"Waiting for you to make my day. You're the only one who laughs, besides me and Alex."

"You're both full of shit." Frankie started to walk away but Alex called him back.

"Hey, FD. How 'bout you stay and share a smoke with your little buddy?"

"You're too damn young to share a smoke," Frankie said, but he stopped at the stoop and handed one to Alex, then stood around to talk.

"FD, why you always jiggling change in your pocket?"

"To remind myself that I need real money. Cheese. Green. Whatever you want to call it."

"If you don't think that change is real, hand it over to Alex."

Frankie laughed, but he gave Alex his change and went inside. The steps to his apartment were worn from years of tired feet scraping them. He was tired, too, and wanted nothing more than to go to sleep. But he knew he'd end up working; he couldn't get his mind off the girl. If Nicky had anything to do with this, the girl was a key. When Nicky called, he said she was in trouble, and not the kind of trouble that got solved in a back room of a dark alley. This was mob trouble, and these killings had mob written all over them. Of course that brought Tony Sannullo into play too. Tony knew about the girl. And he knew a lot more than what he was saying.

Three cold beers later Frankie quit work, thought about popping in an old movie, but decided to open his mail instead. He had the normal assortment of bills, and a large padded envelope addressed to Mr. Mario Francis Donovan.

Who the hell sent this?

He pulled the tag on the envelope, opened it, then reached inside, drawing his hand out immediately. "What the fuck?" Several roaches lay next to the package. Frankie grabbed the envelope by the bottom and shook it. More roaches came out. "Eleven," he said, and remembered the significance. There was no question now that this was someone from the old neighborhood. Only a few people knew about that—Tony, Paulie, and

Nicky. Maybe a couple of others. Frankie thought about it until his brain felt fried, then went to bed, falling asleep in minutes.

WHEN IMAGES OF THE roaches woke Frankie for the third time, he decided to get up and take notes. Years ago, he started keeping notepads by the bed, a little thing called the NiteNote. Greatest thing his ex ever bought him. He pulled the pen from the NiteNote, which kicked on a battery-powered light, then wrote on the 3x5 cards it held.

Bugs and roaches. Not coincidence.

Frankie decided to make a few charts.

Nicky:	Tony:
Friends	Friends
Honor	Honor
Girls	Girls
Nuns	Nuns
Prison	Mob
Fearless	Conniving
Smart	Smart
Rosa	Rosa
Tito	Tito
Cleveland	Brooklyn

Frankie learned early on that this line of thinking proved successful. As he went through the case, he would write down anything that coincided with these words, adding more as he went along, and perhaps scratching some off. Already he could fill something in, and he wrote next to the "Smart" column—killer is definitely smart. Has us confused. Knows police procedure. As more thoughts came to mind, he filled in the chart. When he hit a lull, he stepped back to look at it from afar. Sometimes it made a difference.

Right now Frankie wished he could distance himself from the case. But this was his first big homicide, and he needed to trust that his legendary Irish luck would pull him through. It had done a good job so far: it had helped him survive gang fights, a broken marriage, seven years on the force—street duty, robbery, drugs, back in robbery—all without compromising his morals.

He lit a smoke, vowed to quit once again, then laughed at his predicament. At least he could still laugh. Nicky could laugh too, but not Tony. A laugh from him was as rare as a curse word from Mamma Rosa.

Frankie got up to make coffee. Might as well take advantage of all the vices. He needed to be sharp for this analysis. He owed both of them that much, especially Nicky. And if this was Nicky, then Frankie had to help him. Nicky would do the same. He *had* done the same, many times. Frankie laughed at the memory of when Nicky backed down four guys just by staring at them. Never said a word. Of course he *did* have his father's eyes. *That* was a scary man. Frankie often wondered about him, ever since that day in Schmidt's back yard, when Nicky thought Mikey the Face was going to kill his father. It was the day of the roach races.

CHAPTER 14

ROACH RACES

Wilmington—19 Years Ago

It was an early morning meeting and everyone was there: Tony, Frankie, Mick, Paulie and me. Tony recruited Paulie because we needed extra help. I wouldn't go so far as to call Paulie stupid, but Tony manipulated him like Gepetto did Pinocchio.

I got everyone's attention then laid out the plan. "We do it just like the track. We'll make odds and take bets."

"People in this neighborhood will bet on anything," Tony said.

Bugs lit a cigarette and handed one to Mick. "Yeah, Shoes and Patsy bet on what color gum balls come out of the machine—twenty bucks a pop."

"Who's gonna catch the roaches?" Mick asked.

"Bugs is—who do you think?" I said.

Five minutes later, Bugs headed down to DiNardo's basement with a jar. He was supposed to get eleven roaches, ten for the race and one extra. He came back within twenty minutes, holding a jar full of frantic, nasty roaches.

"Twelve," he said. "Got an extra one in honor of Suit."

We laughed our asses off. Suit didn't like the number eleven. There were eleven kids in his family and he lived on the eleventh house on the street, number 1111. "Too many fuckin' elevens" Suit's father always said, and Suit took it to heart. If he was eleventh in line at school, he'd push somebody out of the way so he could be tenth. He wouldn't even play football because there were eleven guys on the team. Suit avoided elevens like Paulie Shoes did thirteens.

We all got a good laugh, but then got to work. Tony's job was to write the numbers on small pieces of paper, which Paulie glued onto the roaches' backs. Bugs painted a small circle on the concrete, about the size of a coffee can, then another one about eight feet in diameter, making it almost four feet from the coffee can to any part of the circle. This was no scientific calculation, it was dictated by the space we had on the German kid's concrete pad. The concept was simple: Suit would put the roaches in the coffee can, then we'd turn it upside down in the little circle. When he lifted it, the roaches would scatter, heading in all directions. The first one to cross the line won.

"How do we do the odds?" Suit asked.

Never being too good at math, things like odds boggled Suit's mind.

"We should ask Doggs," Tony said.

I nixed that idea. "He'll be betting. Can't trust him if he stands to make money."

"Who we gonna trust?" Tony asked.

"Sister Thomas." Bugs said, and acted like it was a good idea.

I smacked him in the head. "You're gonna ask Sister Thomas to calculate odds for our races? What the hell is in your head?"

"Doesn't she always say to put what we learn to practical use?"

Tony was all smiles. "He's right, Nicky. Nothing more practical than this."

"You ask her. I've had my beatings for the month."

Tony and Bugs braved Sister Thomas' wrath and discovered not only was she willing to help, she was well-versed in race-track odds and how to calculate them based on previous performance. This made us wonder about the life of nuns in general, and of Sister Mary Thomas in particular.

"When are we gonna have it?" Mick asked.

We decided on Saturday and tacked signs to telephone poles throughout the neighborhood. By 12:30 on the day of the races, we only had four people in the backyard, not counting us. We were damn disappointed. But by five to one, we had thirty, maybe forty, paying customers. I tapped Mick on the leg. "This is gonna be big."

At one o'clock, Suit gave a loud, shrill whistle, signaling the start of the first race. The crowd gathered around. Must have been fifty people crammed into Schmidt's yard. Bugs stood on the concrete stoop and announced that bets were closed for this race, then Suit grabbed the coffee can and set it down on the little circle. He tapped the bottom of the can, making sure all the roaches were on the concrete, then slid the lid out from under it and lifted the can.

Roaches scattered everywhere. Frankie's sisters screamed. Everyone except the DiNardo kid stepped back a few feet. Calls from the experienced track people drowned out the others.

"Come on, number two!" Mr. Schmidt yelled, his roach being in the front, but at the last minute the roach turned and ran the other way. He laughed and tore up his ticket. "That's why I don't go to the track."

Number five raced across the finish line a second later, followed by numbers seven and ten. I tapped Tony on the shoulder. Nervous as shit. "How'd we do?"

"Two fifty-cent bets on number five." He looked at the books, then said "Got a few show bets on the ten, but won't cost us much."

For the second race we dropped the odds on numbers five and seven and raised them on two and nine. Then we prayed and got ready for the next race. It turned out to be almost a repeat of the first, with number five winning. This time number ten came in second, and number two rushed to a third-place finish. Number nine again finished last.

Mr. McDermott and several of his firemen buddies came in just before the third race. It was a surprise he showed, but when he bet five bucks on number nine he shocked everyone. He had nine kids so we figured that was why. Tony nudged me and Bugs, then whispered. "Nine's a dog. Got no shot at winning."

We were still laughing when the sound of car doors slamming echoed up the alleyway. Mikey the Face stepped out of a Caddy, with his normal contingent of hangers-on. He pranced down the alley like he owned it, comb already out and messing with his hair. Paulie Shoes was with him, as were Tommie Tucks, Pockets, and Patsy Moresco, though how Patsy fit into that Caddy with four other guys was a mystery. The gate squeaked open, and Face came in, still brushing his hair as he walked across the yard. When he got to the odds board, he stared at it while he scratched his cheeks and picked at an imaginary beard.

"Number five's won two in a row, huh?"

"Both of them," Tony said. "Odds are going down on him, though."

"Those odds ain't going nowhere." Mikey pulled a wad of bills out of his pocket, peeled off two C-notes, and plunked them down on the table. "Two C's on number five."

Tony almost shit. Even though the odds were even money on number five, we couldn't cover the bet. Tony hesitated, looked up at me.

I shrugged, looked behind me. Pops stood against our fence, two houses away, just watching. I had hoped for support, but Pops turned and walked back into the house. My heart sank. Not that I blamed him. Who was going to stand up to Mikey, except maybe Doggs. Still, I felt a little ashamed. Pops hadn't even come down to see the races. I turned back to Tony.

"Do whatever we got to."

Face picked up the bills and waved them in front of Tony. "What the hell, kid? You takin' the bet or not?"

"We don't have that kind of money, Mikey."

"What are you doin' holding a race if you can't take a bet?"

"Why don't you bet less, Mikey? There's ninety-six bucks in the till." Tony stood up, faced Mikey. "We'll cover you for ninety-five. Come on, we're kids."

Mikey the Face was usually all smiles. Today he looked mean. Word on the street was he lost big a few nights back at Doggs' game. Maybe he was trying to make some of it back. Whatever it was, he was showing no mercy. He leaned in close to Tony, snapped the bills—crisp hundreds—then backed Tony right into his seat. "You either take the bet or you close down this piss-ant operation."

The gate creaked open and Pops walked in carrying a cigar box. When he got to the table, he handed me the box.

"Cover the bet," he said.

I opened the lid to a box filled with money.

"Holy shit. How much?" Suit asked, not thinking about the cursing.

It was an assortment of ones and fives and tens. I pulled out a wad and handed it to Tony. "Count it," I said, while I started on the other stack of bills.

Tony finished first. "Two hundred seventy-eight."

Suit and Bugs stared at me, waiting. As I rolled past the last few bills, my eyes lit up. "Two hundred forty-nine," I said, and almost instantly Tony totaled it.

"Five hundred twenty-seven." He turned to Face, grabbed the two C-notes from his hand and stuffed them into the betting box. "That's two C's on number five," Tony said, and wrote it in the book.

I stared at Pops, proud as anyone could be. I didn't know where he'd gotten the money, but it was the proudest I'd ever been of him, except maybe that day at the cop station.

Face snatched the bills back. "Decided not to bet."

He turned and walked straight into Pops, who stood as stiff as Ciotti's stone wall. Those hawk eyes he was known for burned into Mikey the Face. "You laid the money down. It was a bet."

My pride turned instantly to fear. Face would kill him for this. "Pops, it's all right. I—"

"Stay out of this," he said. His eyes never left The Face.

I shook, not knowing what to expect, certain only that Pops would be killed. *I'll go get Doggs.*

Bugs tugged on my arm, whispering like we did in church. "Nicky, you see what I'm seeing? Face is scared shitless of your old man."

I nodded but said nothing. No one made a move to help Face or back his play. Not Tucks, or Pockets, not even The Whale.

Face yanked the bills out of his pocket and threw them at Tony. "Put it on number five." He moved to the other side of the yard, mumbling. "What the fuck's two bills anyway?"

When people saw Mikey bet so much on number five, many of them followed. Soon we had almost four hundred bet on that one roach. Just as Tony was about to close the book and get Suit to announce the third race, a voice rang out from the back. "Don't close the betting."

I turned to see Sister Mary Thomas, her smile as bright as the sunshine. Tony looked up at me, as if to ask, "what the hell" and I shrugged. The crowd parted like the Red Sea for Moses, then she handed a one-dollar bill to Tony.

"Anthony, I would like to bet on number one, please. To win."

Tony smiled, wrote it down and took her money. "You got it, Sister."

She leaned toward him and whispered, "You should close the betting on number five."

He nodded, then looked at her as if he forgot something. She leaned close, and he whispered, "Sister, if you've got any juice upstairs, ask God to hold back on number five."

"Anthony Sannullo," she said, as if indignant, then winked at him and walked over to stand beside Mrs. Donovan.

"Fix is in," Tony whispered to Bugs.

Suit whistled, alerting them of the third race, then he put the coffee can on the ground. I made the "sign of the cross," whispering in Latin while I waited for the lid to come off. "Go." Tony shouted, and the roaches scattered. Like every other race, number five broke for the front, heading straight toward Sister Thomas. Numbers two and six were close behind. I heard a shout from the crowd and looked in the other direction to see good old number nine crossing the finish line. I could have kissed that roach.

In ten seconds, it was over. Number nine won, with number five coming in second, ensuring us of a *very* successful day. Face tore up his handwritten ticket and stormed out of the yard. Once he was gone, Pops headed for home. I ran to him, threw my arms around his waist. "Thanks, Pops. I can't believe what you did."

He tousled my hair. "Sometimes you have to stand up for what is right. Mikey was wrong. I reminded him, that's all."

We had three more races then closed down because one of the Donovan girls stepped on two of the roaches before Bugs could collect them. Two more got hurt legs when he scooped them up. That didn't leave enough for good betting. After everyone left, and after we cleaned up the Schmidts' yard, we went to my house and counted the winnings.

"Six hundred ten bucks." Suit said.

"That's…"

"One twenty-two each," Tony said. "I'm saving mine."

"I'm buying clothes," Bugs said.

"Clothes? You got enough for three people now."

"Hey, screw you. I like nice clothes, okay?"

"I'm buying my brothers a shirt so Mom don't have to iron so much."

"That's *doesn't* have to iron. You let Sister Thomas hear that grammar and she'll kick your ass."

"You let her hear that mouth and she'll do worse," Pops hollered from the other room.

"Sorry, Pops."

"What about you, Nicky? What are you buying?" Tony asked.

"I don't know."

Tony laughed. "Yes, you do. I can tell by that look in your eyes." He punched me in the arm.

"Haven't decided."

Tony stared at me, then laughed. "It's a gift for Angie isn't it? I *knew* it." He looked at the other guys, trying to stir them up. "What a pussy Nicky is. Buying a gift for little Angie."

The laughing pissed me off at first, but I soon joined in the fun. It was far too good a day to get pissed off. Besides, I didn't mind them making fun of Angie. But if anyone ever hurt her I'd kill them.

CHAPTER 15

FORBIDDEN FRUIT

Wilmington—19 Years Ago

I had been falling for Angela for a long time; it just took me a while to realize it. The truth probably didn't hit me until I decided to spend my share from the races on a present for her. Not a ring—that would have been too obvious, so I opted for a bracelet. Doggs had a hot one that was worth four or five times the price, but I told him I wanted it "clean" for her, so he hooked me up with a jeweler who owed him money and got me a good discount. I had to borrow money from Doggs, but he said I could pay it back over time. I was about to leave, but stopped.

"Hey, Doggs, how come The Face was afraid of Pops?"

"What are you talking about?"

"At the races. I know you heard."

Doggs got that mean look on his face, and his eyes scrunched up. "You ever looked at your old man? He's a fuckin' beast. Strong as a fuckin' ox. He could rip Mikey a new ass and shove it down his throat if he got pissed off." Doggs poked my chest with his finger and stared at me. "Let me tell you something, Rat. Nothing pisses off Dante like someone fuckin' with his kid."

I couldn't help smiling; in fact, I couldn't stop. "Thanks, Doggs."

"Yeah, get outta here."

For almost three weeks, I had that bracelet in my drawer at home, waiting for the right opportunity. It arrived a few days later when a friend of Tony's invited us to a party at his house Friday night. His name was Eddy Chinski and his parents were gone for two days, leaving him to watch the house. I asked Angie to come.

When we got to his house it was already crowded and most people were walking around with beers. I grabbed two bottles, opened them, then motioned for Angie to follow me to the living room. When we got there, I started up the steps.

"Where are you going?" she asked.

"Come on up."

"I'm not following you to the bathroom."

Chinski's house, like all of the ones in the neighborhood, had one bathroom, and it was upstairs with the three bedrooms. The downstairs had a small living room, a smaller dining room, and an even smaller kitchen. "I'm not going to the bathroom," I whispered. "Come on. I want to show you something."

She eyed me suspiciously, almost like Mamma Rosa did, but then she started up the steps.

I looked around when I got to the top, then went into Chinski's parents' room, closing the door after Angie got in.

"Nicky, I—"

"Don't worry. I want to give you something, and I don't want everybody to see." I pulled the small box out of my pocket and handed it to her. "It's nothing much, but I thought you'd like it." I shrugged, turned my head to the side. Looked for a reaction. *She probably thinks I'm an ass already. Shit, shouldn't have done it.*

The box was black and looked classy, the kind girls like to keep. Angela opened it real slow then stared at the bracelet. It was gold with six small diamonds spaced around it. For a few seconds she didn't say anything.

I shoved my hands into my pockets, fidgeted. "If you don't like it, I can take it back. I just…"

She grabbed hold of me, pulled me to her, and kissed me. "Nicky." Tears were in her eyes. "I can't believe…I mean, *really* can't believe it." She kissed me again. "I *love* it. It's beautiful. I can't believe you did this. Where did you get the money?"

I shuffled my feet, embarrassed. I felt sure my face was red. "Remember when we had those stupid races? I saved since then. Just…I don't know, just waiting for the right time."

"This is the best gift I've ever gotten." She kissed me one more time, softly, deeply. "Why don't you lock the door."

The way she kissed me, and the way she said that, made my whole body throb. "Listen, Angie, I didn't give you the bracelet for that…I mean, I don't expect you to do anything…"

"Lock the door," she said. It was a command.

Under the right circumstances I knew how to be obedient, and this was one of those times. I locked the door, shut the curtains, and climbed into the double bed, then took off my shoes and socks. Angie climbed in next to me, pulled a blanket over us and got close, bare feet tickling mine.

"I can't believe we're alone," Angie said.

"I know. Great, isn't it?"

She kissed me softly. Slid closer.

I returned the kiss, tongue tasting hers. I felt her tense. Wrapped my arms around her, squeezing gently.

She giggled. Relaxed. "I can't believe we're doing this."

I kissed her neck. Nibbled on her earlobe, dropped down to her neck again, started to bite her.

"Don't make any marks. My father will kill me." She pushed me back then reached down and pulled her top off. "Take yours off."

I stripped off the shirt, snuggled in next to her. Her skin was on fire. "Take your bra off."

She kissed my neck, biting lightly. "Undo the straps."

I reached behind her, breathing growing more excited. Soon the strap was undone and she slipped her arms out. I pressed against her again, let her warmth excite me. The kissing grew more passionate. I went to her neck and down to her breasts. I let my fingertips trace up and down her side, lightly tickling her.

"Not much there for you to kiss."

I thought she sounded embarrassed. "I don't really care about tits."

"If you don't, you're the only boy who doesn't."

I stopped, came back to face her, kissed her. "I'm serious. You're the smartest and funniest person I know besides Tony, and I sure as shit ain't kissing him."

She gave me a little love smack. "So you're just kissing me because I'm smart?"

"Your nice ass might have something to do with it."

Angie laughed, then dug her heels into the bed and lifted. "Take off my pants."

I slid her pants off, underwear too, and tossed them on the floor. After taking mine off, I moved beside her. We were on fire. As we kissed, my hand ran down her back, down between her cheeks, softly. Angie's leg wrapped around me, her foot sliding up and down my leg. I felt like I would burst into flames. I moved down to her breasts, kissing, then lower, to her stomach, letting my tongue and lips work on her. God, but her skin was smooth. And she smelled so nice. I licked her navel while my hands tickled her sides. Felt the goose bumps on her as I did.

"Come back up, Nicky."

When she said that, I hesitated. Part of me was relieved, wanting her to stop me. This was new territory, and despite my show of bravado I felt...inexperienced. I kept kissing her stomach, moving to the side. She never said anything else, so I went lower, below the navel. Let my hand slip lower too. Ran the tips of my fingernails down her thighs, just barely touching her, enough to feel me. No more.

"Nicky..."

I slowed down again, remembering what all the older guys said about girls, how they always said no but meant yes. I wanted more than anything to keep going, but I didn't want to push her. My fingers gently caressed her as my lips moved lower.

"Do you want me to stop?" I almost hoped she said yes, but she said nothing. The silence gave me courage.

I kissed some more just below her stomach, slow, deliberate...then slid down her leg, inside her thigh. At that point instinct took over. I kissed her all the way down, all the way to her foot. Nibbled on a toe, then let my hands run up and down her legs, softly caressing. Intermittent kissing. Then I went back to her thighs, kissed all the way up, gently pushed her legs apart. Very gently. Kissing all the time.

Angela grabbed my head, started to pull me up toward her, but stopped. I let my tongue flick across her. She moaned, lightly. I licked softly all around her. Up and down, then across. Traced a circle around her, then focused on the clitoris. Paying special attention to it.

"No," she said, but pressed me closer. Spread her legs wider.

I touched her gently with my fingers, spread her wide, then used my tongue to explore her. I licked her silky smooth skin, tasted her wetness. "God, you taste good."

Angela pushed herself into my face and held me there.

We made love then. When we finished she rolled over on top of me. We kissed and laughed, and then she lay her head on my shoulder, arm draped across my neck. "I love you, Niccolo Fusco."

I kissed her forehead then her nose. "And I love you, Angela Catrino."

I knew the moment I said it that my life was changing. I vowed again that if anyone ever hurt Angela, I would kill them.

CHAPTER 16

MORE CHARTS

Brooklyn—Current Day

Frankie got to the station before Mazzetti did, before any of the morning shift except Carol. It was tough to beat her in. "Morning, Carol. You're looking sharp."

"Compliments are not necessary, Donovan, but yes, I did get your tape. It's on your desk."

He leaned over and kissed her cheek. "You really *are* the best."

Frankie pretended not to see the blush on Carol's face; instead, he got coffee then hurried to his desk. He was listening to the tape when Mazzetti came trudging in. "What are you listening to?"

"The tape of Renzo's 9-1-1 call."

Lou waited while Frankie played it twice more, his ear in close. "Anything?"

Frankie sat on the edge of the desk. "I didn't tell you this before, because I wasn't sure."

"Yeah, I remember. Crazy thought and all."

"That's right. And I'm still not sure. I thought this might be a guy I knew leaving me clues. I wanted to see if I recognized the voice."

"And?"

"I want to say no, but one time I thought I detected a Philly accent."

"There are plenty of guys from Philly up here. You can't pry that accent loose with a crow bar."

"Don't I know it," Frankie said. "Been trying to lose mine for years."

"So we're back to the grind."

Frankie tossed his cup into the trash. "Guess we are, partner."

They worked the rest of the day, catching up with the few people they hadn't interviewed yet from the neighborhood and on pestering Kate Burns about DNA evidence. She had turned up some stuff, but there was an inordinate amount of it at the scenes and the system was already bogged down. By late afternoon, Frankie called it quits. Lou had already left for a dentist appointment. "Going home early, Carol. See you tomorrow."

THE CHART WAS WHERE Frankie had left it, hanging on the wall to the right of a poster featuring Bogart and Mary Astor that he picked up at a garage sale. Looked good keeping company with *Casablanca*. He grabbed a marker and started writing. It was time to find answers.

Nicky:	
Friends	—*Who are friends? Me, Tony, Suit. Anyone else?*
Honor	—*Don't ever run. If this is Nicky, he definitely isn't running.*
Girls	—*There is a girl, but who is she? And what does she have on Tito?*
Nuns	—*Sister Thomas—does she know anything? Would Nicky tell her?*
Prison	—*Have no idea what he did in there.*
Fearless	—*No shit.*
Smart	—*Has us confused. Knows procedure.*
Rosa	—*Her teachings would have affected him.*
Tito	—*What's the connection with him?*
Cleveland	—*What the hell were you doing in Cleveland?*

Then he stared at Tony's chart:

Tony:

Friends	*—Me, Nicky, Suit, Tito, Manny.*
Honor	*—Not sure if it still means anything to him.*
Girls	*—Has wife, Celia. Others.*
Nuns	*—Never had the respect for them that Nicky did.*
Mob	*—Seems to be in tight.*
Conniving	*—Can no longer trust Tony.*
Smart	*—Smartest guy I know.*
Rosa	*—His mother—but did he learn from her?*
Tito	*—Does he obey? Or just work for him?*
Brooklyn	*—Knows what's going on.*

Okay, enough of that, he thought, happy with what he accomplished.

Time to look at the files again. Files usually held the key to a case. They just had to be reviewed over and over again. Just like the nuns taught them in school. *Never give up. If you are stuck, go to the beginning and start over.*

First file: Renzo Ciccarelli. No occupation. Three arrests for gambling. No convictions. Killed in a house. No one heard or saw anything. Tons of evidence. Tortured before shot.

Second file: Tommy Devin. A plumber in the union. No convictions. No arrests. Killed in a house. No one heard or saw anything. Tons of evidence.

Third file: Nino Tortella. Car Salesman. Twelve arrests, all minor. Three convictions. No jail. Killed in a house. No one heard or saw anything. Tons of evidence. Tortured before shot.

Donovan stared at the data. Not much to go on. At least he hadn't found it yet. It was there, he felt sure, but he had to sift through it. He drew three columns on a new sheet of paper: Renzo. Tommy, Nino. Underneath them, he penciled in the things they had in common and what was unique.

Several things caught his eye: Rat shit. Shot in head and heart. Killed at home. Preponderance of evidence. All of these went under each name as common to all.

A few items stuck out. Torture—only Renzo and Nino got penciled in. Dead rat—only Nino.

Unless they just didn't find one at the other scenes.

Frankie made a note to ask about that. He stared, flipped through the papers, then read again.

Cigarettes at Tommy's house. Picture of mother turned down at Nino's. Nicky would never dare let anyone's mother see them be hurt so bad. Not even as bad as he must have hated poor Nino. Frankie wrote two more notes.

If this is Nicky, why *did he hate Nino?*

'Check and see if pictures turned down in other two houses. See if there were pictures.'

That was one more clue on the bad side for Nicky. After working two more hours, Frankie quit. His eyes were tired and things were not making sense. He jotted down one final note:

'Find everything these three had in common. Need the link.'

He thought about what he had learned. On one side it pointed to Nicky: rat shit, rat in the fridge, the 9-1-1 call, cigarettes, roaches, picture of Nino's mother turned down.

But Tony also knew about the rat, the cigs, and the roaches. He wouldn't have bothered calling about the cat or turning the picture down, but…he *was* smart enough to have thought about it if he was framing Nicky. And of the two of them, Tony was the one Frankie pictured doing this. Either way, the killer was sending Frankie a message—but what? Was he telling Frankie who would be next? And if it was Nicky, *why* was he killing these people? *Why* had he disappeared to begin with? Why had he never called back?

Frankie wrote another column on the paper. *Who else?* Under it he scribbled more thoughts. If someone else was doing this, they would have to know Nicky's habits. Have to be from the neighborhood.

He settled onto the cushion, deciding to sleep on the sofa tonight as he thought about what to do. He knew what he *should* do. He should go in tomorrow and tell the lieutenant that he wants off the case, that he suspects one of his old friends is the killer. Frankie scratched his head, closed his eyes and imagined the scenario. None of it good. How does he tell them that his absolute best friend is an ex-con and might be the one killing these people? And what if they ask about the rest of his friends...the ones who were mobsters. Either way he was fucked, but then again he'd been fucked from the moment he was born into that hellhole of a house.

He remembered times growing up when he wished his father would just go away, not come home one day from work. After some of the beatings he wished that he would die. When he was little and still believed in shit, he got scared that God would do something to him for thinking such thoughts. Later, when his hate had turned to his mother, he didn't care. At that point the only friends he had were Nicky and Tony. Now Nicky was missing and Tony...well, Tony was still Tony. He always had a way of being a prick and he knew just how to get under Nicky's skin.

CHAPTER 17

A NEW DIRECTION

Wilmington—19 Years Ago

After the night we made love, Angela and I were inseparable. I had sampled the forbidden fruit, but there was no way I was telling the guys about it. They would spread the news, then I would have to kick their asses. It was better to keep it quiet. Let someone else have the glory of being "first."

Soon afterwards, I stopped hanging out with the guys and did everything with Angie. I left Tony, Bugs, Suit, and the rest of them to fend for themselves, though I saw Tony every day at his house and we got together when we worked Doggs' games. Things were different with Tony, though. He had been messing with drugs, and it showed.

One day when I came into Tony's house, Rosa and Angie were in the kitchen. Mamma Rosa had the wooden spoon in her hand, waving it like a conductor's baton as she talked to Angie. She held that spoon so much that sometimes she reminded me of Sister Thomas, who was never without her pointer or yardstick.

"Taste that again," Mamma Rosa said to Angie. "Is it right?"

"Tastes good. Not as good as last time, but—"

Rosa administered a loving pat to the back of Angie's butt with her spoon. "That's what's wrong with young girls. Not as good as last time means not good at all." She rinsed the spoon, stirred the sauce, put the spoon to her lips and tasted. Her eyes squinted as she sampled it. "Nicky, come taste this."

I smiled at Angie, then took the spoon and tasted the sauce. "I think it's perfect."

Rosa threw her hands up in the air. "*Perfetto.* Of course it's perfect. You are young and in love." She shook her head as she stirred. "How am I going to teach Angie if you don't help me?" She wagged the spoon in my direction. "Just remember, you might be tasting this sauce for a long time. Don't be telling her little love lies."

Angie and I were still laughing when Tony came into the kitchen. "Nicky. How did I know I'd find you here? I was hoping to get a minute with my own mother, but I guess that's out of the question when you and Angie are around."

I laughed, but it was fake. There was something in his voice, and more importantly in his eyes, when he said that. "Guess you'll have to get a new mom," I said, trying for levity.

Before anything serious happened, Mamma Rosa whacked both of us with the spoon. "There's plenty of me to go around, boys." She pulled us to her and hugged us, like she did when we were little. I thought right then that no matter how old I got, or how much trouble I was in, a hug from Mamma Rosa would make things okay.

Tony laughed—a real one this time—and threw a punch.

I kicked at him. He dodged, threw a spoon at me. "Hey, Rat, it's Saturday night. Come out with us. We're working a game."

I wanted to say no, but Angie signaled for me to go. "Sounds good. I'll get dressed."

"Better hurry, Nicky," Rosa said, then smacked Tony with her spoon. "If you don't want another one, get ready to go," Mamma Rosa said. She stared at him over her glasses with that look of hers that brooked no argument.

We got to the smoke shop in half an hour. While waiting for the game to start, Tony and I swept the floor.

Doggs came up to us. "You boys are getting a little old to be working the games, aren't you?"

Tony shrugged. "We doing something wrong?"

"Nothing wrong, but there's a new crop of brats waiting to take your place." Doggs looked around the room. "Besides, I got things you can do to make more money."

Tony stopped sweeping and leaned on the broom. "Like what?"

Doggs stared at both of us through narrowed eyes. "One fuckin' word..."

"Doggs, holy shit, man, we've been working for you for eight, nine years now. You can trust us."

He shrugged. "All you gotta do is pick up a few things. Deliver a few things. Like I said, nothing much."

"You talking numbers and payoffs, or are you talking drugs?" Tony looked at Doggs and raised his eyes. "If it's drugs it'll cost you a lot more."

Doggs smacked him across the head, hard. "What the fuck's the matter with you, asking me a question like that?" He smacked me, too, but not as hard. "I'm a legitimate fuckin' business man. No fuckin' drugs."

"All right," Tony said. "Don't get so worked up. I had to ask, right?"

It was obvious that Doggs' patience went out with his last utterance of *fuck*. "So what is it, you in or out?"

"I'm in," Tony said.

"Count me out."

"Nicky, what the hell? Why not?"

"Just count me out, that's all." I wanted nothing to do with Tony's schemes anymore. He was getting way too involved with shit that could put us away.

"It's Angie, isn't it? You shit. You're probably not even getting any of that, and you're letting her control your life. Go fuck Sally Jenkins if you need to get it off, or let me have a shot at Angie. I guarantee she'll put out for me."

I shoved Tony against the bar, then punched his face, drawing blood. He came after me, but Doggs smacked a cue across my back and whacked Tony in the head with the broom. "Cut the shit or I'll kick both your asses."

I pointed a finger at Tony. "Shut up about Angie, or I swear I'll beat your fuckin' brains out." It was the first time in my life I was ever really pissed at Tony. We had gotten in fights before, even fist fights, but I had never been pissed like this.

Tony stared at me, but I stared him right back. "Fuck you," he said, then turned to Doggs. "I'm in, and you can count on Bugs. Suit, too, if you got enough work for three."

Doggs nodded. "I got enough," he said, then stared at me. "You keep your fuckin' mouth shut, Fusco. Hear me. I don't give a shit who your father is."

"You know I will, Doggs, but I don't want your work anymore. Not if Tony's involved." I put the broom up then headed for the door. As I walked home I kept hearing what Doggs said in my mind. *'I don't give a shit who your father is.'* What the hell did he mean by that?

THAT MARKED THE START of the real split from the group. I was out, and Suit was in, which was fine by me. For a long time, Tony had acted different. I think it started because of Angie, but it soon snowballed into everything else. He was jealous of my relationship with Mamma Rosa, with the other guys, but mostly Angie.

Several years went by, and though I ate dinner at Tony's house, it was only because Mamma Rosa insisted on it. She knew something was wrong between us, but she never asked, and we never said anything. Angie still came over on Tuesdays and Fridays to cook with Rosa. She'd long since gotten to be an excellent cook; now she came just to perfect her skills, and, of course, to see me.

One day, when Angie and I were out walking, Tony caught up to us at the park. "Hey, Nicky, what's going on?"

I was surprised to see him. "Just hanging out with Angie."

"Let's go to my house. Got some stuff to show you."

He grabbed my arm, but I shook it off. "I'm gonna hang out here."

"Come on. Bring Angie with you."

I stared at Tony. I didn't know what was going on, but he was acting strange. "I'll see it later."

Tony turned his head. Shook it. Seemed to be losing control. "You *need* to come with me. Really."

"Why? What the hell is going on?" I was getting pissed.

He turned to Angela. "Tell him to come."

She looked worried. "Nicky, maybe you better."

"Tony, tell me. Goddamnit."

Tony looked like he didn't know what to do. He grabbed hold of me, and I could tell something big was wrong. "It's your Pops, man. He's dead." He started bawling, hugging me as he did. "I'm sorry I had to tell you like this."

I couldn't believe what I was hearing. I ran down the street, tears already forming. "No." I ran all the way down Clayton Street until I hit our block. Rosa was waiting to intercept me. I should have known she'd never let me see Pops by myself.

I took the concrete steps from the street two at a time then raced up the walk. She grabbed me before I hit the door, wrapped her arms around me. "Nicky. Oh, Nicky. I'm so sorry."

"Let me go, Mamma. I gotta see Pops."

She opened the door, letting me inside. He lay there on the floor. Blank. Dead.

I ran to him, but it wasn't Pops. It was just a lifeless body. I hugged him, but felt nothing. Kissed his forehead, but felt no warmth. After that, I cried. And cried.

I felt a presence. A hand on my back. When I turned, Rosa was there with tears in her eyes. I hugged her. "Mamma Rosa, what happened?"

"I was out back, and Dante called to me, but by the time I got in here, he was almost gone. He had a heart attack, Nicky."

I couldn't say anything. All I could do was cry.

The ambulance came and took him away. I kissed him goodbye as they loaded him on the stretcher. I wanted to ride with them, but they wouldn't let me.

"It is time, Little Nicky. Come with me. We'll call Jimmy."

"Jimmy" was Jimmy Maldonaddo, the last of four boys who had inherited their father's funeral business. They buried damn near everyone in the neighborhood, no matter what the nationality. I couldn't let go, but Rosa insisted. Finally, I stood and walked out the door with her help.

By the time we got to her house, Tony and Angela were there. I hugged and cried with both of them. My two best friends. As I struggled with emotions, I heard Rosa in the background.

"Grief is the pain the heart needs to heal." She was praying on a rosary as she said it.

I hugged her again. "What am I gonna do? Pops is gone."

CHAPTER 18

A GATHERING OF FRIENDS

Wilmington—15 Years Ago

I stayed at Rosa's house the first night, not wanting to be by myself. The next day, though, I went home. The furniture was still there, nothing had moved, but the house felt...empty. I shivered as I walked across the living room.

This was more than empty. Or maybe it was less than empty. It was lonely.

I noticed new things for the first time: the echoes of my shoes on the hardwood floor, how dark the rooms were when the lights went out, how deathly silent it was with the television off. I wondered what Pops must have felt like all those nights I spent at Tony's. Pops here by himself, without mom. Loneliness must be the worst thing there was.

By two in the morning I still wasn't sleeping, so I got dressed and went out. As I walked the hill a window opened in Bugs' house. "Yo. Nicky. Hang on."

A few minutes later, Bugs crept out the front door, lighting a smoke by the time he hit the street. He dragged hard on it, like he always did, then handed me one. "Sorry about your Pops, Nicky. Shit, that's bad."

Bugs wasn't the best at offering condolences, but I knew he meant it, and he was a good friend. "Feel like walking?" I asked.

"I don't care. I hate that house."

We walked for a half a block in silence, then Bugs said, "Let's see if Mick's up."

"You interested in Mick, or Patti?"

Bugs hit me. "Maybe the three of us could do something. You know, take your mind off things."

"It's two in the morning." It was so ridiculous I almost laughed. Regardless, we went to Mick's, tossed a few rocks at his window and eventually got him out.

The three of us roamed the streets for hours. Didn't do shit. Just talked. Reminisced. Smoked. When we saw the Connor brothers delivering the morning papers, we knew it was time to go home. Damn near daylight anyway. As I walked in the house I realized that this was what having friends was about.

Friendship and honor, I thought. *Just like Tony says.*

I GOT UP AT eight. Showered and dressed, then went to Tony's house. Arrangements had to be made for Pops. It wasn't something I wanted to do, but I knew I'd have help. The smell of Rosa's meatballs hit me as I climbed the steps to her house. I hated to think of something nice on a day like this, but Rosa's spaghetti and meatballs seemed to help any situation. As I opened the screen door, I thought about Mamma Rosa. She had simple solutions for everything, and most of them had a root in food.

Rosa blamed air conditioners for half of the woes of the world. Said they kept people inside, made them stop socializing. "Once you stop talking with your neighbors you find things wrong with them," she said. "And if you keep the windows closed at night, people holler more at each other, or worse—at their kids. If half the neighborhood is listening, people will be more careful with their words."

Worst of all though, she blamed those vile air conditioners for blocking the sweet smell of food being prepared. There was something magical about the smell of sauce and garlic from a whole neighborhood, Rosa always said. Tony and I used to laugh about it all the time, but Mick disagreed. "That's okay for you dagos; tomato sauce smells good. But over by my house all that's getting cooked is potatoes. And let me tell you, potatoes smell like shit when they're cooking." We used to laugh our asses off about that.

I stopped, took a final whiff of the sweet-smelling sauce, then walked in. "Morning, Mamma Rosa. Sure smells good in here." Angie stood behind her, white-and-green apron covered in sauce. I didn't think she would have been here this early.

Rosa's face lit up. She set the big wooden spoon down, the same versatile spoon that both stirred the sauce and beat our asses, and then she ran for me, arms open wide. She squeezed me a few more times than necessary, then shoved me toward the table and into a chair. "Sit, Nicky. You need breakfast."

As she stirred the sauce, she yelled upstairs. "Tony. Carlo. Get down here and have breakfast with Nicky." She turned to Angie. "Make some espresso for the boys."

I jumped up from the table. "I can get that, Mamma—"

The spoon wagged at me, and her eyes slapped me back into the chair. "Sit down. Angie will get it." She brought a meatball over, skewered on a fork. "Taste this. See what you think."

As I nibbled on it, she kept talking. "I called Jimmy Maldonaddo." She looked my way, made sure I saw her face. "He said to tell you how sorry he was. Said to tell you your father was a good man."

I nodded. Nobody had much to say about Pops when he was alive, but now people were coming out of the woodwork to sing his praises.

"Jimmy will take care of everything," Rosa said. The wake will be tomorrow night, and the funeral the next day. Father Dimitri will do the ceremony." She looked at me again, but this time with business eyes. "He'll be put next to your mother."

"Of course," I said, but then the embarrassment hit. "Mamma Rosa, I..."

"What?"

"I don't…how am I gonna bury Pops? I can't pay for any of it."

She let her spoon fall into the sauce—a cardinal sin—and then she reached for me. "Nicky. *Mio bambino.* Don't worry about things like that."

I pushed away. Looked into her eyes. "I can't ignore it. Pops needs to be buried, and I've got nothing."

She smothered me in her arms. I felt her crying. "Don't you worry, Little Nicky. I'll take care of your Pops. A lot of people owe your Mamma Rosa favors. And it's time they paid."

ROSA TOOK OFF HER apron, told Angie to finish the sauce, then went upstairs to dress. She put on her finest checkerboard dress, her best pair of nylons, and her black walking shoes. She grabbed her purse from the dining room table and walked up the street toward the funeral home. Dominic, her husband, had been sick for a long time and could no longer drive. It didn't matter much; Rosa loved to walk. Before long she was knocking on Jimmy Maldonaddo's side door.

He greeted her warmly, but before he could say anything else she started in on him. "I won't have Dante Fusco buried in shame. Nicky's a good boy, and he needs to see his father buried right." She wagged her finger at him as if it were her wooden spoon. "You owe me, Jimmy Maldonaddo."

He held up his hands in mock surrender. "Rosa, please. Dante took care of everything before he went. Everything is paid for."

Rosa looked at him, then mumbled, "Where the hell did he get the money?" It puzzled her, but Rosa was not one to look a gift horse in the mouth. She moved on to the cemetery. She found the same situation every place she went. Dante had paid for the cemetery, the wake, the flowers, had even paid the priest.

She walked home from the church, shaking her head as she came in the back door. She walked straight to Nicky. "Everything is taken care of."

"I don't know how you did it, Mamma, but you know I appreciate it."

She grabbed a pot for coffee. "I didn't do anything. Your father had it all taken care of." She shook her head. "I don't know how, Nicky, but he has everything paid for. You have no need to worry. He'll have a nice funeral."

Rosa got me to Jimmy's place early. I wanted to wait until the last minute, but she insisted. Tony and Bugs were with me. Suit, Mick and Chinski would be there any minute. I was glad to have them up front near me. I was going to sit with Rosa and Tony, but the rest of the guys would be in the row behind me. Rosa said it would be okay since they were going to be the pall bearers. I didn't have any family so I asked them. I think they were honored. Tony's brother Carlo was the sixth one.

Jimmy Maldonaddo's wakes were held in an old house on Union Street. It was actually two row houses that he had converted into a funeral home. The building sat at the middle of the block, right where the breezeway came in, allowing access to the back of the building. Five short steps led up to a small brick porch, then in another door to a waiting area. This is where the sign-in book would be, and where people gathered before going in to pay their respects.

Bugs and Tony and I were standing near the back of the room, away from the casket. I stared down the hall and saw that a few people had formed a line in the waiting room. When I looked the other way, I saw Mamma Rosa pacing and praying on her rosary. "What's the matter?" I asked Tony.

"It's a wake, Rat. You know how bad she is at anyone's wake, but this is your pops." Tony tugged on my sleeve. "You get everything? You know how damn superstitious Mamma is."

I checked the pocket inside my jacket. "Got 'em."

After a few more people gathered, Rosa came down the hall to get me. She waved Bugs and Tony away as if they were pests. "Go on. Take your seats." She patted my back. "Are you ready?"

I nodded. "Guess so, Mamma."

She squeezed my hand. "I'll stand with you if you want."

"That would be good. I'd like that. Maybe Tony, too."

Her smile told me she approved. "He would be honored," she said, but then her smile disappeared, and her brow furrowed as if a great burden had come upon her. "Did you remember the items for the coffin?"

I patted my jacket pocket. "I've got them right here."

She held out trembling hands. "Let me see what you have."

I pulled out the picture of me when I was little, maybe five years old.

Mamma Rosa closed her eyes, and shook her head slowly. I thought she was going to cry. "You were such a beautiful baby."

I waited, then handed her a more recent picture of me, then the picture of my mother. She held them as if they were treasures, nodding the whole time.

"And the lighter?" she asked.

I pulled out Pops' favorite lighter. It was so old that the metal was worn at the edges, but it still worked. Pops was never one to give up on something just because it was old.

Rosa seemed to be getting more nervous. "The cigarettes?"

I took them out of my jacket and gave them to Rosa. She felt the pack, looked inside. "There's not more than a half a pack, is there?"

"Only nine." I almost laughed despite the occasion. Rosa was so superstitious. I still remember her words the first time I went to a wake with her. I asked why people were putting things in the coffin, and she looked around the room, then whispered to me.

"When someone dies, even though we miss them, we don't want their spirit coming back. So we put the things that they will need to be happy in the next life—pictures of their loved ones; their favorite lighter, half a pack of cigarettes—"

I asked her why half a pack. Why not a whole one?

Rosa said some people put whole packs in, but she felt if you did that, the spirit might think there was an endless supply and come back for more. If they saw only half a pack, they would know they got all there was. She then added that she had never seen a spirit come back when only half a pack was put in.

I reached over and hugged her. She *was* a saint. "We better get in line."

She motioned for Tony to join us. "And don't forget to save your items until last," she said as we formed the line at the casket. I tried not to look at Pops as we passed. I had some time alone with him earlier, and there would be a chance afterward.

Just as they were about to let people in, Rosa left me and hurried to the front room, grabbing Angela on her way. Rosa ushered her past the waiting line and brought her to the front.

Angie paid her respects, taking time to say her prayers, then she placed a picture of us at a school dance in his pocket. Tears were already building inside me. I didn't know how I was going to last the night. She hugged me, then Rosa and Tony, then took a seat with Bugs. There weren't many people, not compared to a lot of the wakes in our area. Most of the ones that showed up were the parents and brothers and sisters of my friends. Mick's whole family came, so that was eleven right there. Tony whispered that the only reason they came was to have Rosa's food at the gathering afterwards. He might have been right, but that was a small price to pay. Having a lot of people at the wake was a symbol of pride. It meant the person was respected. After about half an hour, the line was down to nothing. I thought we were going to wrap it up. It was a little embarrassing not having many people there.

Just as I was thinking that, the front door opened and in walked The Face with Tommie Tucks and Pockets. They came in, knelt in front of the casket and said their prayers, then offered condolences. They each put something in his casket, but I didn't see what. While they were in line talking to Rosa, Doggs and Paulie Shoes came in.

I thought the floor might have groaned when Patsy the Whale showed up, and Nicky the Nose was there, hanging on to his coattails as if he were a lapdog. Charlie Knuckles came in with a guy named Monk, and Jimmy the Gem grabbed the door behind them before it closed. And they kept coming: Johnny Handsome, Ralph the Angel, Sammy Smiles, Lefty, Bobby Glasses, Four Fingers Joey, and more. My tears dried and my heart swelled. *This* was respect. The whole neighborhood showed up. Everybody who was anybody had come to see my Pops.

We waited about ten minutes after everyone had passed. Rosa said it was time for me to visit with Pops. As I moved toward him I heard footsteps coming across the hardwood floor. I turned to see Sister Mary Thomas, rosary in hand, walking toward me. She grabbed hold of me and hugged. Wouldn't let go.

"I'm so sorry, Nicky."

I thought I heard tears in her voice. Maybe I did, but I couldn't be sure. She went to the casket right away, knelt and started praying. She must have said as many prayers as everyone else combined, the way she flipped through those rosary beads. Guess with all of that practice it gets easier. When she finally stood, she bent over Pops and laid something in the coffin, just inside his coat.

I thanked her, then Rosa did. After that it was time for me. I was tempted to see what she had put in there, but that wouldn't have been right. I said some prayers. Laid the pictures in there with him. Put the lighter by his right hand, then the smokes by his left. He always smoked with his left hand. After that, I looked around to make sure nobody was close, then I leaned in and sang him the lullaby he used to sing to me when I was little.

CHAPTER 19

THOUGHTS OF DEATH

Brooklyn—Current Day

Frankie pulled down the street to his apartment, finding a parking spot half a block down. He noticed Alex on the steps when he went by, so he stopped at the store and got him a Heath bar, Alex's favorite. He was a great kid, with a personality that went into high gear the moment anyone talked to him.

"Hey, Ace, how's it going?" Frankie had given him the name from their time spent playing cards in Frankie's apartment while his mother was "busy."

Alex raised a weak hand to wave. Frankie tossed him the candy from about ten feet away, like he always did. Alex missed it.

"Whoa, what the hell's going on?"

"Nothing."

"All right, well, let me know if I can do anything."

"Yeah."

Frankie started up the steps then stopped. He knew *exactly* what was wrong. Alex's mother was all but a whore and she chased that poor boy outside every time a new boyfriend came by. He pictured Alex's face, his runny nose, and realized his own life was not that goddamn important. He went back outside, sat next to Alex and watched the cars go by.

After about a minute, Alex looked at him for the third time. "What's up, FD? Why you sittin' here?"

"I felt like shit too. Thought I'd join you."

Alex shrugged. "Suit yourself."

"Cold?"

He shrugged again.

Frankie took off his coat and wrapped it around Alex, then lit a smoke.

"You got one of them smokes for me?"

Frankie almost snapped at him, but caught himself. Alex didn't need to hear more shit today. Frankie handed him a smoke and offered him a light from his own cigarette.

"Thanks, FD."

They sat in silence while they smoked, then Frankie started talking, almost to himself. "I knew a guy growing up who had a mom like yours. When he was little he thought she was the best damn person in the world..." The silence lingered as he stared across the street at nothing.

Alex looked at him. "Then what?"

"Then he found out she had a lot of boyfriends."

"Like my mom?"

"Yeah, I guess sort of like that, except his mom was married."

Alex straightened up, pulled the coat tighter around him. "Did the dad know?"

A gust of winter air rushed down the street; Frankie shivered. He put his arm around Alex. "Yeah, he knew."

"That's shit," Alex said. "What'd he do to her?"

Frankie crushed out his smoke, didn't answer. After a few seconds, Alex asked again. "Hey, FD, what'd he do?"

"He took it out on us," Frankie said.

Alex handed him the last of his cigarette, almost to the filter now. Frankie took a long drag then handed it back. "How about I cook dinner for us?"

Alex took off the coat and handed it to Frankie. "You got a deal. I'm hungry."

Frankie cooked dinner then they watched an old movie. Alex had gotten to like the old black-and-whites from watching so many with Frankie. When he laughed it reminded Frankie of the old days, when he and Nicky and Tony used to laugh so much.

After a while, Alex's mother came looking for him. She always knew where to find him if he wasn't on the stoop. She was polite, and she showed the proper amount of concern. And she was embarrassed, unable to meet Frankie's glare, but Frankie knew she would do the same thing next week and the week after that. He almost said something to her; instead, he said good night to Alex and said he'd see him tomorrow.

It was too late to work, so Frankie listened to music then went to bed, hoping to get a good night's rest.

Nino Tortella's mutilated face kept popping into Frankie's head, waking him from what could have been a good sleep. He sat up, drank water from a bottle he kept on the nightstand, actually a folding table he got at the garage sale along with the Bogart picture, then turned the lights on. There was no reason to turn the lights on other than to try to wash the image of Nino from his mind. *This can't be Nicky. He wouldn't do that to someone.*

He told himself that but he didn't believe it. Didn't want to face the tough decisions that would follow if it was true. After all, Nicky had saved his ass a lot of times—saved his *life* at Woodside. As Frankie thought about it, he remembered how scared he was that night. It was never easy going to a gang fight. As kids they pumped themselves up as they walked toward the scene, but that was all for show, to keep each other from turning and running. Once you were there, pride kept you, but the fear only got worse.

Frankie remembered his stomach roiling, the sick feeling he got like he would throw up, and how, in the end, he was able to channel it all into hatred for the Woodside guys. All of that fear focused inside a raging youth wielding a chain and a club.

He took another sip from the bottle, wiped the sleep from his eyes and looked at the clock. It was almost five. Not a good time to be trying to go back to sleep, but sure as shit not a good time to get up, either. He thought about death a lot since Woodside. After that he no longer wanted his father to die. Not even his mother. When Frankie faced death that first time it changed his perspective on things. A lot.

Frankie leaned back, sucked hard on a smoke. He could still hear that gunshot as if he were right there. He remembered turning, seeing somebody go down, then seeing the guy turn the gun toward him, all in slow motion. He thought he was going to die that night, and he didn't like it one bit. *I would have died if not for Nicky.*

CHAPTER 20

DEATH IS FOREVER

Wilmington—13 Years Ago

We had the funeral the next morning. The guys from the smoke shop really made me proud, driving their Caddies and Lincolns in the procession to the cemetery. Rosa insisted we take a different route home from the gravesite—to confuse the spirits. That was fine. It gave me time to think before everyone gathered at her house.

Rosa had been cooking for two days. The rest of the neighborhood chipped in too, bringing foods of all types for the celebration. It seemed odd to celebrate someone's death, but that's what we did. At Italian funerals there was an unspoken hierarchy regarding the burden of entertainment. The primary job fell to those furthest from the deceased and moved forward in a downward scale. Friends were charged with telling humorous stories to keep the family laughing. After friends, the burden shifted to distant relatives, then to closer ones until it got all the way to the siblings. It was a magnificent, protective circle designed to keep the parents or the children of the deceased from feeling too much grief at once.

Since I had no family, this burden fell onto my friends and Rosa. The problem was, there weren't many funny stories about Pops. No one knew him well enough to have much to say; instead, they told tales of things I had done and talked about Pops' reactions to them when I got caught. The stories made me laugh, and definitely helped. Mamma Rosa always said a pound of laughter cures ten pounds of grief. In hindsight, I think she might have understated it.

AFTER THE FUNERAL I thought I'd have to move out of the house, but Rosa said Pops had an insurance policy. It turned out to be enough to pay off the house and give Rosa money to help take care of me. So I stayed at home, but pretty much lived with Tony. I wasn't about to turn down Mamma Rosa's cooking. Besides, Angie still came there twice a week, which made it convenient.

For the next two years, I spent all my time with Angie. Tony still hung out with Bugs, Suit, Mick and Chinski, but for me there was only Angie. We were more than in love—we loved each other's company. We went to the beach together, to dances, to the park. And when I wasn't working, we went out on Saturday nights, sometimes just walking.

One of my fondest memories was when we borrowed a car, hooked school and drove to Wildwood during a snowstorm. It was crazy, because the roads were bad, but Angie and I never had such fun. We walked the beach in the snow, waves crashing on the shore and us freezing our asses off. When we got too cold we'd go back to the car, turn on the heat and keep each other warm. Angie wanted to walk the boardwalk, so we did, letting the wind-blown snow sting our faces as we laughed and huddled together. Nothing was open; no one was there. It felt as if we were in one of those end-of-the-world movies, and we were the only two left.

As we walked, I told Angie to close her eyes and pretend we could see the lights of the boardwalk. Soon we heard the pitchmen hawking their games and the screams of the people on the roller coaster. We even smelled the popcorn and pizza. We walked until we got too cold, then headed back. We made love in the car, then walked the beach one final time before leaving. It was a memory we would never forget.

Two weeks later, as I was dressing to go to work, I heard a pounding on the door. It was Frankie's sister. "Hey, Donna. What's up?"

She pushed in, nervous. "You've got to help them."

"Help who?"

"Frankie. Tony. All of them."

I took her by the hand. "What's going on?"

"They're fighting the Woodside gang. One of them was bothering me. I…" She started bawling.

"Calm down. Tell me what you know."

"Frankie said he'd kill them all." Donna held her hands to her face. "Oh, God, Nicky. He could get killed."

I laughed. "Donna, we've been in a lot of fights. He might get hurt, but he won't get killed. Trust me."

"I'm not *stupid*, Nicky. These guys have guns!"

My gut tightened. "How do you know that?"

She shrank before me. Cried harder.

I grabbed her by the shoulders and shook her. "How do you *know*, Donna?"

"I was with one of them. When Frankie caught me, I lied." She grabbed my collar. "I *saw* the guns."

"Goddamnit." *Fuck me. Fuck me twice.* "Where are they meeting?"

"The clearing in the woods. Just past the ball field over the hill."

"Go home. I'll take care of it."

"What are you going to do?"

"Go *home*, Donna."

I ran to the smoke shop. Patsy Moresco was guarding the store as usual. "Hey, Patsy. Need to see Doggs."

"He's gone for the night."

I pounded my fist on the counter. "Fuck."

Patsy waddled over, put his big thick arm around me. "What's wrong, Rat?"

"Bugs and them are in trouble. They're fighting Woodside, and I heard they've got guns."

Patsy squeezed my shoulder with his meaty hands. He looked about the shop, then leaned in close and whispered. "Tell you what, Little Nicky. I'll take care of you, but know this—your mouth's a fuckin' trap, you hear?" His look bored through me. I nodded, not knowing what to expect.

He reached behind his pants, pulled out a .22, cleaned it off and handed it to me like it was poison. "I don't give a fuck if this gun kills the president. Far as I'm concerned, I never seen this fuckin' gun. Never heard of this fuckin' gun. Don't ever *want* to hear of, or see, this fuckin' gun." He grabbed my cheeks and made me stare straight at him. "You got me?"

I nodded. "Thanks, Patsy. I won't forget this." As I started for the door, he hollered.

"That's wrong already. I *want* you to forget this."

Patsy's warning hit home. I got that sick feeling in my gut that Sister Thomas always told us about. I wanted to toss that gun and go find Angie...but my friends were in trouble. "You got it, Patsy. Gotta go."

As I RAN, I played the scene over in my mind. Bugs was going to be filled with rage and ready to kill someone. Bugs was a lethal combination— the fight of the Irish and the vengeance of the Sicilians. To top it off, I think he took the bottled-up frustration from his home life and took it out on whoever he fought. Once he got to that point, nothing could stop him short of knocking him out. And he'd probably be the one to start things off.

Chinski I hadn't known as long, but I knew him enough to know he would be scared shitless. I'd be surprised if he didn't piss his pants by the time they got within ten feet of Woodside. But when it came down to it, he'd fight. We could always count on Chinski for that, and, like a lot of the polacks, he could take more than a few punches.

An image of Mick crossed my mind. That crazy Irishman would be right there with Bugs, itching for the fight no matter who might get hurt.

He had gotten so used to fighting his older brothers at home that fighting kids his own age seemed like a cakewalk. Mick was a wild one, and he didn't care what the weapons were. He fought with his mouth, his hands, or anything he happened to pick up.

I was halfway across the ball field, cutting through a game in progress, when I thought of Paulie. He was a brute. Like a lot of big guys, his nature was to be nice, but push him over the line—and no one could tell what that was—and he was unstoppable. Tony was the only one he listened to when he got like that. Paulie would pick the guy who looked to be the most dangerous and go after them. And once Paulie got started there was going to be big damage.

That left only Tony. But saying "only Tony" did him an injustice. He was the most dangerous guy in a ten-block radius. It didn't matter if it was a gang fight or a one-on-one; absolutely *nobody* wanted to fight him. He'd be the first one into battle, even before Bugs. That thought spurred me to run faster. Mamma Rosa would never forgive me if something happened to Tony.

As I crested the hill the scene came into focus. Ten of the Woodside gang stood against five of us. *Six now,* I thought, and pushed harder. By the time I arrived, things had become disturbingly clear—Bugs was fighting two guys, one of whom had a chain. Bugs' head was bleeding badly.

Mick, armed with a half a cue stick in each hand, was fending off two of them. As I moved into earshot I heard the crack of bone when he struck one of them on the head—a small wiry boy about our age. I couldn't tell for sure, but it looked like Bobby Lewis, a kid we went to school with. Blood ran down his face. He went down, wailing.

Chinski and Suit were fighting back-to-back, holding their own against three guys, but both showing wounds—Chinksi on his left arm and Suit on his side, blood staining his shirt. I wouldn't have wanted to be the guy who ruined his shirt; Suit would probably kill him.

"About time you got here!" Tony yelled.

The sound of his voice brought me back into it, as if I'd never left.

"Hang on." I wrapped my left arm with my shirt to protect against knives, then jumped in with Tony, who was fighting three guys. He held a chain in his right hand and the butt end of a cue stick in his left. Good combination, even against knives—especially against knives. With a knife, a person had to get in close, and somebody good with a cue or a chain wouldn't let that happen. Tony was good. He whacked a guy in the head just as I joined him, but a Woodside kid darted in and cut him on the right side. Tony yelled, stepping back. The other guy dropped his blade. I picked it up, poised to fight, blade in hand.

It was easy to join the fight. My friends were in trouble and I had to help. Our code demanded it. But that didn't mean I wasn't scared. I thought about what Mick and some of the others always said about me not being scared of anything. It wasn't true. I *did* get scared; I just didn't show it.

When I joined the fight, it distracted the guys Tony was fighting. Two of them turned toward me, so Tony moved against the one on the far right, hitting him with the cue, then wrapping the chain around his hand and pummeling his face. Blood poured from the guy's nose. He backed up quickly, letting Tony move against one of the two I faced. I positioned myself on Tony's weak side and faced two Woodside guys, staring into their eyes. The first one Tony hit with the cue stayed out, crawling away to safety. Now the second guy was out too. The odds were getting close to even. We liked that. As I moved in to strike the guy in front of me, I heard Bugs yell.

"Gun!"

The sound of a shot slammed my ears. The fear I had controlled until now raced through my veins. I gripped my blade tight to keep from losing it, and looked to Bugs, praying he was okay. I ran toward Bugs and Mick, ignoring the Woodside guys. Nobody seemed hurt. I thanked God for that. Just then a second shot went off. Mick went down, the side of his face exploding with blood and flesh. Some of it hit me. I wanted to run, hide, get it off me. Instead, I screamed. "Mick!"

I ran toward him. The Woodside guy turned, aiming his gun at Bugs. I saw fear on Bugs' face. "Run, Bugs!"

I reached in my pocket and pulled out Patsy's .22. The hard steel felt cold in my hand. It felt...different. Not like a knife or a cue. The gun had a dangerous, powerful feel.

I took quick aim and fired. Once. Twice. Then again. The second shot hit him in the face, dropping him. And before I knew what was going on, I turned and fired three more times, hitting one more of them in the arm. They ran.

Tony grabbed my arm, tugging me away. "Let's go, Nicky. We can't stay here."

Chinski ran.

Mick lay bleeding at my feet. "Mick!" I screamed, and knelt next to him.

Bugs, Paulie, and Tony joined me. Mick had a hole in his face, and blood poured from his mouth. We checked his pulse and heartbeat. He was real bad. I used my shirt to wipe his face, closed my eyes, and started giving him mouth-to-mouth. The taste of his blood made me want to throw up, but I focused on helping Mick, praying I was doing it right.

Help me save him, God. Please?

"Gotta get him to a hospital," Bugs said.

Paulie was crying. "I'm going to call an ambulance. Keep Mick alive."

Sirens wailed in the background.

"Cops," Tony said. "We gotta go."

I turned my head to the side, spit blood. "We can't leave him."

"He's dead," Tony said. "You'll get caught."

I looked up at Tony, certain that my eyes reflected what I felt. If I hadn't been so concerned about Mick, I'd have gotten up and beaten his ass. "He's one of *us*."

"Don't you fuckin' rat," Tony said, then grabbed Bugs. "Let's go."

Bugs was caught in a half-step, one foot ready to follow Tony, the other planted, intent on waiting it out with me. I never hated Tony more than that moment. As far as I was concerned Tony and I were done. "Go on, Bugs. I got it."

I tried reviving Mick, and I put pressure on his face to stop the bleeding, but it wasn't working. The more I tried, the more I prayed. Guilt overwhelmed me. Maybe God would have listened if I'd lived a better life.

The sirens drew closer, only about a block away. I wanted to run, get the hell out of there before the cops came. Then I felt Mick grab my hand. "You're gonna make it," I said, holding back tears.

Mick moved his head to the side. "Tell my mom."

My throat closed up, but I kept breathing air into Mick. When the ambulance came down the street, I almost ran, telling myself there was nothing more I could do. But I looked at Mick—blood covering his face, his deep blue eyes crying, and pleading with me. As long as I live I will *never* forget that look in his eyes; it was sorry, and sad, but mostly it was empty. Earlier I had wished I was a doctor so I could save him. Right now I would have traded that for being a priest. I think Mick wanted to confess. I felt for him, thinking how scared he must be.

The sirens got closer. I glanced over my shoulder and saw them coming over the hill. I got up on one knee, ready to run. Mick squeezed my hand, and his eyes…his eyes… I got down beside him again. No way I was leaving him to die alone. Even with only a snowball's chance in hell of saving him, I had to try. I took a deep breath and started in again. *Hold on, Mick. Please?*

I heard the footsteps approaching, then felt the hands on my shoulders, lifting me from him.

"Stand aside," somebody said. They checked him out, then scooped Mick onto a stretcher. Before they got to the ambulance, the one checking him was shaking his head.

When I turned to look behind me, two cops were there. One had his gun drawn. "Hands behind your back," he said. The other one cuffed me before I said a word.

On my way to the station, I cried. *The Mick is dead. Who's gonna tell his mom?*

CHAPTER 21

CONFINEMENT

It was Sunday, the day after the fight, and they still had me locked up. I told the cops I wasn't talking until I got a lawyer, then I used my one call. By the time Mamma Rosa showed up, they had all but convicted me. Three of the Woodside guys had been hauled in, but they weren't talking. I shot one dead and the other guy took a shot to the arm. I told them what happened. It would have gone better if I had just shot the guy who got Mick, because the other guy had no gun.

Rosa cried. Angie did, too, when she got there. I told her not to worry, and before she left, I gave her a pack of matches. "Put these in Mick's casket." She looked at me funny. "He'll understand."

Mick had stolen enough lighters to open up a store, but he was always asking people for a light. Now he'd have one if he needed it.

WITHIN A FEW WEEKS, they processed me and sent me to trial, and then the judge for sentencing. When the gavel slammed down, seven years came with it. I almost shit.

Seven years.

My public defender mouthpiece grabbed my arm, but I shook him off. "Seven years? Jesus Christ. They started it."

The gavel hit again. The judge added thirty days for contempt.

"Shut up or you'll get more," the lawyer whispered to me.

I struggled, but I managed to keep my mouth shut. Angie ran to me, crying, but the bailiff held her back. Mamma Rosa, too. I was allowed a quick hug before they took me away.

"See you soon," I said, with more than a little pleading hanging on each word.

At first, the worst thing about prison was missing Mick's funeral. After a while, that was a distant worry. I found out quickly that the cops sent word ahead of me that my nickname was "The Rat." First thing I learned in prison was that the guys didn't stop to ask how you got the name; they just kicked your ass. I could have killed Doggs for giving me that name. It cost me three days in the prison hospital.

Fortunately I never got back-doored. They were going to do it once, but I was saved by Teddy 'The Tank' Moresco. He was Whale's brother, and he was as big as Patsy. With Tank's protection, the beatings stopped. I ended up with a nasty scar above my right eye, but that was a small price to pay.

After the next few weeks, I reflected on what were the worst things. I didn't mind the clothes or the shoes. Didn't even mind the isolation. Hell, I'd lived with Pops all my life and he wasn't much of a conversationalist. What I did miss, though, was the food. This was the worst food I'd ever eaten in my life, even worse than Mick's house. I winced as I thought it.

Mick. Dead now. The thought made me more serious than ever to do my time and get out. It made me look at things differently, too, and once I'd done that, I soon grew used to my new surroundings. I even came close to forgiving Tony for what he'd done that night at Woodside, leaving the Mick like he did.

The prison was about fifty miles from home. Not so far when driving, but Rosa had never bothered to get a license, forcing her to rely on Tony, who always seemed to be too busy with one thing or another to bring her to visit me. Despite that, she managed to get there twice in the first two months, using a combination of buses and favors called in from friends. I begged her to stay home. Her legs were getting older than she was, so even walking to the bus stop was too much.

"Just write," I told her, but she wouldn't hear of it.

"As long as I can put one foot in front of the other, I'll be here." She said it with such conviction that it made me realize Rosa could do anything she wanted. It pissed me off even more that Tony didn't bring her.

Angie managed to catch a ride with some friends a few times. Her problem was more with her dad. If he found out she'd been to see me, it would have meant serious punishment. He didn't like me before I went to jail, and now I was a pariah. Tony and Suit came twice, both times bringing Bugs and Chinski, but they didn't like coming; I could tell. And they only stayed long enough to make it official. After the visits stopped, they said they'd write. At first, I didn't open the letters.

I was pissed that my friends didn't come personally, but after a month of no visitors, each of those letters became little treasures, each word a hidden gem. Soon, even the letters stopped.

Everything was changing. Seemed like what happened to Mick and me affected all of them. Tony planned on moving to New York. Doggs hooked him up with some people, and he was taking Suit with him. Bugs got a girl pregnant and asked her to marry him. Said he was going to move, maybe go to college. I said a silent prayer for Bugs, knowing how he dreaded the thought of marriage.

My biggest surprise came near the end of the third month. It was a particularly tough day, and they told me I had a visitor. I was surprised because it was late, and when I walked into the visitor room, my heart jumped.

"Angie." I couldn't run, but I walked as fast as the guards allowed. "God, it's good to see you."

She hugged me. We kissed, then I just stared. "I can't believe you're here. Who brought you?"

"Tony. He's waiting for me, but he said I can't stay long."

"He didn't come in?"

She shook her head. "He's running some important errand for Doggs and said he has to hurry. He's picking me up in twenty minutes."

"I can't believe he didn't come in. Isn't he going to New York soon?"

Angie got that look on her face, the one that told me not to worry about little things. "You know what an ass he's been."

"Still doing drugs?"

She nodded. "Dealing them too."

I couldn't believe it—Tony dealing. But Angie was right. I had no time to worry about it. "Twenty minutes is fine. Even two minutes is okay." We talked about everything. She caught me up on all the news I didn't know, then we just stared at each other. I could see the pain on her face and in her eyes. I thought about the years that were left. What kind of life it would be for her to wait for me. Suddenly her pain became real.

Angie started twirling her hair around one finger, and I felt her pain growing. It was that, more than anything, that made my decision. "You should stop coming."

She started to object, but I stopped her. "This isn't right. I got five, six more years, even if they let me out early. You can't wait." I stared into those huge brown eyes. "I won't *let* you wait."

She stood, kissed me on the lips. "You go to hell, Nicky Fusco. I'll do what I want." With that, she walked out.

ANGIE LEFT THE PRISON more depressed than when she went in. It was bad enough to come all this way, but to see Nicky like that... She wished there was something she could do to make his time easier. As she paced the sidewalk, waiting for Tony to pick her up, she thought about what he said. She looked at her watch, checking. It was already dark and, not surprisingly, Tony was late. Ten minutes later, the sound of screeching tires alerted her. She jumped back just as Tony came to an abrupt halt at the curb. Two guys Angie didn't know were in the car with Tony, one in the front and one in the back. Angie took one look at Tony and knew he was messed up. "You don't need to be driving, Tony."

She didn't intend to, but she probably put too much of Mamma Rosa in her admonishment.

"Just get in."

"If *you're* driving, I'll find another way home."

"This is bullshit," he said, but he got out, told the guy in the back to drive, then opened the back door and climbed in beside Angie.

She looked at him through squinted eyes. "Have you been doing drugs?"

"Shut up, Angie. For once, just shut the fuck up. You sound like my mother."

Angie smacked him. "Don't talk to me that way. Your mother—"

He grabbed her wrist and glared. "Yeah, well, my mother isn't here to protect you. Neither is Nicky."

Tony continued drinking and snorting cocaine as they drove. Angie had never seen him this bad. "Let me off at the next light. I'll get a ride home."

"And tell my mother how bad I treated you? No thanks."

Angie crossed her arms, riding in silence but keeping a keen eye on the road. Something didn't feel right. She didn't know the other two guys, and Tony was completely out of it. When they stopped at a traffic light, she tried to get out.

Tony yanked her back in. She struggled, smacking him, but he hit her and pulled hard on her arm.

"Stop it. You're hurting me."

He pulled her close and pressed his lips to her mouth. "Why don't you give me some of what Nicky's been getting?"

Angie punched him in the side of the head, repeatedly. She used her legs to shove against him and kick. Tony hit her hard, three times in the side of the head, pressing her down onto the seat. She fought, but couldn't stop him from spreading her arms out. Then he punched her twice in the side.

While she fought for breath, gasping, he ripped her pants off, spreading her legs at the same time. She screamed for help from the two in the front seat, but they ignored her.

"Tony, don't you dare!" she cried. "Don't you goddamn dare." He was too far gone to listen. He kept it up until he was done, then moved to the other side of the car, straightening his clothes. "You say anything about this, and I'll kill you. Got that?"

Angie pulled her pants up, slid all the way against the door and hugged herself. She didn't cry. She wouldn't give him that pleasure. She didn't say a word until they got to her house.

As she got out of the car, Tony pointed a finger at her. "Remember what I said."

She leaned forward, narrowed her eyes. "You remember this night, Tony Sannullo. One day you'll pay for it."

Angie cried most of the night. She cried during each of the four baths she took; cried while she scrubbed the sins of Tony Sannullo from her body; and then cried more while she lay in bed wishing she were dead. When that failed to make her feel better, she decided to write to Nicky and tell him what happened.

> *Dear Nicky:*
>
> *I hate to bring you news like this, but something terrible happened. When I came to see you last...*

Angie wrote for an hour, crumpled up three letters, and pressed so hard with the pen on two more that she had to throw them away. After two more attempts, she got up, paced, imagined what Nicky would do when he read it. She wanted him to kill Tony. But she knew that wouldn't happen. So what *would* happen? What could he do?

She tiptoed to the bathroom so she didn't wake her father, then locked the door. Avoiding the mirror had been difficult when she took her four baths. Now, she purposefully stared into it. She was bruised by her ear, but she could cover that up by doing her hair differently. The last thing she wanted was her father seeing it. Her lower lip had been cut, and her side hurt bad from where Tony punched her. But that was nothing. The cuts, bruises, the aches—they would all disappear in days. What Tony did to her would not. She thought about his threat to kill her and scoffed; what he had done was far worse.

But the question remained—if she told Nicky, what could *he* do?

He could get angry, go crazy, hate the world, maybe take it out on a prisoner who looked at him the wrong way. He could do a lot of things, but nothing would help her, and worse, it would hurt him. She decided not to make Nicky suffer with her. Telling him would be giving him a death sentence.

She looked at the mirror again. An angry, bitter person stared back at her. She tried telling herself to be strong, but it didn't do any good. She wondered how she would get through the night, let alone the next day, and the endless ones that followed.

Angie brushed her teeth, combed her hair, unlocked the door, went to her room, and tore up the last version of the letter. She would not tell Nicky, or Mamma Rosa, or anyone else about this. She would have to trust in God to help her get through it. With the decision made, she folded her hands and prayed.

CHAPTER 22

BAD NEWS NEVER STOPS

During the next three months, Angie didn't make it to see me, but she wrote often. Her letters were more than treasures.

When I got a visitor one Saturday, I got excited, thinking it might be her. It turned out to be Mamma Rosa, and she had Sister Thomas with her. I never expected to see her again.

"What a surprise."

Rosa held my hands, rubbing across my fingers as if they were rosary beads. Her face looked sallow, her eyes full of worry. "Dominic is getting worse. I don't know if I can get here for a while, Nicky."

I reversed the position of our hands, patting hers while I spoke. "Don't worry about me. Stay home and take care of him." For the first time she looked old. "How about Tony? Is he okay?"

Rosa nodded. "He wanted to come help with Dominic, but his new job is keeping him busy. He said to say hi, though, and that he'd come see you soon."

I nodded, knowing it was a lie but not wanting to upset her. "You know how sorry I am, Mamma Rosa."

"I know."

Sadness had overtaken this woman I loved. I asked about Bugs and Paulie. She cheered up at that. Then I worked up the nerve and asked about Angie. I hadn't seen her in so long.

Mamma Rosa was silent.

My stomach twisted. "What about Angie?"

She reached into her purse and handed me a letter. I knew what it was. Wouldn't touch it. Couldn't.

"Take it with you," I said, and walked away.

Sister Thomas called me back. "Niccolo Fusco."

I went back. Commands from nuns die hard.

She stood with her hands on her hips. "Rosa came all this way to see you."

Rosa stood, shaking her head. "No, Sister, don't—"

"Sister Thomas is right. That was rude."

Rosa reached for me. "I have to go anyway, Nicky. You take care, and I'll see you soon."

"Mamma, have you seen Angie? Is she okay?"

She looked as if she would cry. "I don't know what's wrong. I haven't seen her for weeks. She had a friend drop this letter off at the house."

Mamma put the letter on the table. I held back tears. "Thanks for bringing it, Mamma. I appreciate it."

I hugged Rosa, then she walked away. Sister Thomas stayed behind. "I'll bring her by when I can."

"Thanks, Sister." I turned my head. I still had a hard time looking her in the eyes.

There was a long, awkward silence then, "Would you like me to bring Father Tom?"

"No."

"You might feel better if—"

"No."

"Fine, Niccolo." She pressed the letter into my hand. "Only cowards walk away from things."

I took the letter, but I didn't read it. Not that night.

Not ever, I thought. *Not ever.*

But by the end of that first week, my courage disappeared. Late one night I opened it, using contraband candles to read.

Dear Nicky:

By now you're probably upset because I didn't come see you, especially after my promise to visit you often. I'm sorry I upset you. Now, though, you're going to be really upset, because what I have to tell you isn't good.

I won't be coming to see you anymore. Not this week. Not ever again. There are a lot of reasons why. My father forbids it; I have no ride; people will talk. None of those matter, though. If it were only my father, I'd fight him. I would run away. I'd change my name. I'd do anything to be with you. But we both know I can't be with you. Not now. Not for years.

And if it were just you telling me to forget you, I could deal with that. But the problem, Nicky, is I know you. And I know me. If I waited for you, it would break your heart. Maybe make you more bitter. And if you grew bitter, it definitely would break my heart to see you that way. I don't mind sacrificing. I'd sacrifice anything for you, but I won't be a martyr and let myself be destroyed. We'd both lose.

Now for the tough part. I know you already thought this was tough. It wasn't. I'm going to have to go on with my life. I don't know what each day will bring, let alone each month, or the seven long years you'll be gone. I'll be thinking of you every day. When I cook, I'll pretend it's for you. When I do the dishes, I'll turn suddenly and splash suds at an imaginary person standing behind me. And when I go to sleep at night, I'll dream of you lying with me, feeling your touch, and hearing your heartbeat. I'll do this every day until you get out and come rescue me from whatever boring life I'm living, for it will surely be empty without you.

You might never forgive me for this. I hope you do. And I hope that no matter what happens, you are happy in your life. Truly happy, the way Mamma Rosa is. But you have to promise me one thing.

When you get out, and when your life is straightened out. When things are good in your life and you feel good about yourself, find me. Please? No matter where I am, Nicky, find me.

Do you remember the first night you touched me? We both shivered with excitement. Can you ever forget the feeling of lying in each other's arms afterwards? Can you ever forget the feeling? I want to feel that way again. And not just one day, or one time, but for the rest of my life. So, you find me, Niccolo Fusco. Damnit, you better.

Ti amo con tutto il mio cuore,

Angie

Ti amo con tutto il mio cuore. I love you with all of my heart.

The saying Mamma Rosa had taught us. Nothing pleased me more. It made her words more special.

I went through periods of being pissed at her for her stance, and then proud of her. That was the Angie I knew and loved. What would I have done in her shoes? I tried telling myself that it didn't matter, that I couldn't put myself there, but I ran the options through my head anyway. On days when I felt good, I applauded her decision and used her words for inspiration; other days…were not so inspiring.

TWO MORE WEEKS PASSED with no visitors. The only letters were from Rosa. Dominic had passed away. He had been sick so long that his death must have been a blessing and a curse for her. As all things were, it seemed. I hadn't heard anything from Angie, but I hadn't expected to.

Another month passed. It was Friday, and they told me I had a visitor. My heart jumped. I damn near raced to the room. I hoped to see Angie, prayed I would, but I expected to see Mamma Rosa. As I turned the corner to the room, the familiar habit of the Benedictine nuns waited for me.

Sister Thomas. What's she doing here? I felt for sure I had pissed her off the last time. It didn't matter; I was glad to see her. "Sister, what brings God's best representative on earth to the prison today?"

I expected the wonderful smile that only Sister Thomas could manage, the one that somehow lit up her entire face, even though it was mostly covered. Instead, I saw a grim expression that was foreign to me, at least from her—but it was too familiar on so many others. My gut wrenched. I started shaking my head before she said it.

"Rosa Sannullo is dead, Nicky." She grabbed me before I fell. Helped me to a chair.

The guards had to rush over, because I was screaming. And crying. And crying.

CHAPTER 23

ANOTHER FUNERAL

Rosa's arrangements were handled by Jimmy Maldonaddo, same place Pops went. The prison guards got me there late, but they let me go in without cuffs. The only stipulation was that I couldn't associate with anybody but Tony or his brothers.

Bugs and Suit were in the next room. When I waved to them, Bugs stepped toward the front of the room. My heart stopped. Angie stood behind him, looking as if she were the angel sent by God to get Mamma Rosa. She smiled and waved at me, mouthing something I couldn't make out. She tried to come see me, but the guards stopped her. Suit said something to her, and she turned toward him. When she did, I noticed her stomach seemed swollen.

Goddamn. She's pregnant. It had been six months since I was in prison…She didn't look *that* pregnant.

I asked Tony but he didn't know anything or, if he did, he wasn't saying. I knew some women didn't show much until near the end, but still…I buried the emotion and focused on Tony. Had to help him.

It was a huge wake. I knew by the time the night was over there would be hundreds attending. Tony was proud. I was too. When it was my turn, I went to the casket, knelt and blessed myself. I said my prayers, then closed my eyes and prayed some more. This was a woman who deserved a path straight to heaven, and I wanted to make sure God knew that. Afterwards, I stood, leaned in and kissed her forehead. I took a picture of me and Angie from my pocket and placed it next to her. Then I laid her wooden spoon next to her left hand, half expecting her to reach out and grab it. With a final sign of the cross, I left, delivering myself to the guards, patiently waiting by the door.

As I was leaving, Tony handed me an envelope. "This is from Mamma."

I tucked it into my pocket, then went out with the guards. They asked to check the envelope, but they didn't open it, just felt for weapons before handing it back. As I left the funeral home, I wondered again about Angie. Was I nuts, or was she pregnant? I had to find out. And if she was pregnant, was the baby mine?

It has to be. She wouldn't be with anyone else.

ONCE BACK IN MY cell, I pulled the letter out and started to read.

Dear Nicky:

My sweet 'Little Nicky.' How I will miss you now that I am gone. You were my sixth child. My baby. I know you are suffering where you are. And I know what you sacrificed for Tony and the other boys. I will never forget you for that. What hurts me the most is what happened with Angela. I loved Angela. If you were my sixth child, she was my seventh. I loved her like the daughter I never had.

Someday you two will be back together. You were made for each other. Even an old woman like me could tell that.

It will be tough for you, Nicky. Prison does more than confine a man. It strips him of his freedom, pride and self-confidence. You must overcome all that. Don't allow them to do to you what they do to the others. I know you, Niccolo Fusco. I held you when you were coughing blood as a baby. I bathed you in alcohol when the fever almost took you. And I watched over you and prayed when every other sickness came through and—with God's blessing—spared you.

You have the strength to do whatever you want to do. But you must remember, Nicky: Your life is what you want it to be. Always remember—God and Satan both have room for one more soul.

Ti voglio bene,

Mamma Rosa

I folded the letter neatly. Perfectly. Then I tucked it into the envelope and slid it under my pillow.

I swear, Mamma Rosa. I will never do you wrong again. Ever.

CHAPTER 24

THINGS IN COMMON

Brooklyn—Current Day

Five in the morning is a terrible time to get up, but when you've been thinking of death all night, the morning is more welcome. Frankie managed to plant a smile on his face as he walked to the kitchen for coffee. He often wondered how people survived before coffee, but knowing at the same time there must have been a substitute. Even Mamma Rosa needed coffee to be fully alert and civil.

As he waited for it to brew, thoughts popped into his head. He jotted them down then headed to the station. Carol met him at the top of the steps with more coffee.

"How the hell did you know I was here?"

"Ted saw you pull into the lot. And if the coffee's not hot, don't bitch at me."

"I'd never do that. Not to your face, anyway." He ducked her punch, then asked, "Lou here?"

She nodded to the "war room," as Lou called it, the place they'd set up to work on this case.

"About time you got here, Donovan."

"You sleep much, Mazzetti?"

He lifted his feet from the chair where they rested and plopped them on the floor, shoving the chair toward Frankie so he could sit. "If you ever get married—which is doubtful, but if you do, and after it's been thirty years—you'll know why I'm here early."

"You're right. I'll never know."

Lou nodded toward the files in Frankie's hand. "What have you got?"

"Some stuff I got thinking about this morning." He set the notebook on the table, grabbed the files on the case, and spread them from left to right in the order the victims were killed. Frankie stuck his head out the door. "Hey, Carol, if you're not too busy, we could use your magnificent handwriting in here."

Mazzetti stared at Frankie as he stretched his neck. "Anybody ever tell you that birthmark on your neck looks like Sicily?"

"Only about a million times."

"No shit, though. It really does. Goddamn amazing."

He continued staring until Carol came in a moment later, with the slight swagger that was both sexy and don't-you-dare-try untouchable. At slightly over five feet, and a hundred pounds tops, she wasn't physically threatening, but she carried herself as if she were an Amazon. And if someone pissed her off, the look in her eyes was usually enough to deter any repetition of whatever set her off to begin with.

"What do you need?"

Frankie pointed to the posters. "We need you to fill in the details."

She sighed, but Frankie knew she loved doing this; she liked anything that took her away from the grind at her desk. "Okay, call them out to me," she said. "But go slow. I don't have a damned keyboard."

Frankie picked up the file. "Renzo Ciccarelli. Groceries spread all over the floor. A lot of them crushed. Brought them home in a grocery bag."

Lou had Devin's file. "Tommy Devin—"

"Whoa," Carol said. "Spell Ciccarelli."

Lou spelled the name then continued. "Items at the Devin scene include a bottle of Jack Daniels, found on floor next to body, unbroken. No receipt, and it hadn't been opened yet."

Frankie moved to the next file. "Nino Tortella. Pizza box on the floor."

Lou got up. "We've been through this already, remember? The pizza place said Nino stopped once a week, religiously. Devin was in that liquor store every day, and Renzo went to the grocery store at least twice a week." He looked at Carol. "You want more coffee?" When she shook her head, he continued. "And another thing. They weren't killed on the same days of the week. They were about three weeks apart, but not exactly."

"I just thought of this last night," Frankie said. "If we look at the case like we have been, it doesn't seem like anything—liquor, pizza, and groceries—nothing in common. Different days of the week. Different parts of town." Frankie walked to the charts. "Look at where everything was found. Liquor bottle next to body, groceries spread all over floor—next to body, pizza box on floor—next to body. If we look at that from the killer's perspective, every one of them had something in their hands when they came home. He *wanted* them to have their hands full, to make it easier to take them."

Lou moved by the charts. "And that means he was watching them. Probably for a long time, so he could tell exactly *when* they'd have their hands full."

"Which explains the three weeks or so between killings. This isn't some nut bag killing random people; this is a serious-as-shit killer taking his time to do it right."

Lou scratched his chin as he stared at the charts. "So this guy sits in the house waiting for them to come home, knowing their hands will be full."

"Exactly." Frankie said, and slapped Lou's extended hand.

"Good work, Donovan. Let's find out where this guy watched from. We might get a lead to break this case."

As they left the building, heading toward Lou's car, Frankie's adrenaline was pumping. At the same time, though, he was scared. A lead might point to the wrong people.

CHAPTER 25

REFORMATION

Delaware Department of Correction, Smyrna, Delaware—13 Years Ago

When Mamma Rosa died, it devastated me. Each day pushed me beyond limits I thought were impassable. There were days when I felt great, dreamt of a getting out and starting a new life with Angie. But they tended to be overshadowed by the concerns that she wouldn't be waiting for me, or—even worse—that the baby wasn't mine. On the good days I clung to the words she wrote in her letter. 'Find me, Niccolo Fusco. Damnit, you better.' But on other days, I hated her, cursed her for leaving me here, so lonely.

I fought it every day, but I was losing the battle. Two weeks after the funeral, I got into a fight in the yard and almost killed a guy. After that, I *did* begin a new life. Trained every day. Boxed. Ran. Practiced martial arts. Lifted weights. Ran some more. I met a Chinese guy who taught me mental training—Qigong, it was called—a set of breathing exercises that he swore had powers to heal. My goal was to learn, so I followed him, focusing on the exercises at night when I was alone in my cell. After a lot of practice, I got to the point where I could feel the essence of the *qi* flow through me, or at least, he said that's what it was. I didn't know what it was, and I didn't care. It helped me relax and sleep. I had nothing better to do with my time.

By the end of year two, I could run ten miles at a good clip. Smokes were long gone from my daily routine; they went with my first month of serious running. Funny thing was I still missed them, every day, all day.

Just as I was getting to accept my new life, Tank Moresco got released, taking my protection with him. I had settled into a habit of taking a shower after my evening run. One day three white guys tried to backdoor me. It was probably a good thing it happened in the shower; the soap prevented them from getting a good grip. Once I slipped away, it gave me all the time I needed. I ran, letting them build momentum, and then I stopped, did a quick spin, and charged them. I hit the first one in the throat. When he went down, face first, I jammed my heel into the back of his head, slamming him into the tile floor. At the same time, I threw a bar of soap at the one nearest me. He tried to protect his face. I used the opportunity to punch him in the balls. Then I grabbed hold of them and yanked him off his feet. The back of his head hit with a thud, blood mixing with the water running toward the drain. The last guy ran, but I caught him and took him down. I grabbed a fresh bar of soap from the ledge and jammed it up his ass. He screamed when it went in. Guess it was bigger than it looked. I kicked him in the face as I stepped over him, then turned to them as I left the shower.

"Try anything again, and I'll kill every one of you."

The guards put me in solitary for a week. That was all right; it allowed me time for meditations. I became more aware when I meditated, things suddenly coming to me as realities. One of them was how fighting worked. You didn't have to be the best boxer or the best martial artist or the best shot with a gun to win. Fact is, during the heat of the moment—and I'm not talking competitions here, but when life is on the line, or more importantly when death is on the line—that's when it shows who has what. I realized that any one of the guys in the shower should have taken me, same as that night against the Woodside guys. I just wanted it more. Willing to risk more to get it. That night of meditation changed my life yet again. Gave me new insight.

A few days later the guards let me out. I saw the fear in their eyes when they looked at me. After that day I saw it in everybody's eyes.

For the next few years, I trained in everything. Not just the physical, and not meditation, but books. I learned history, math, science, law, English. Even geography. Sister Thomas sent me books, and I absorbed everything I could. I'll have to say that, of everyone I came in contact with, she was the only one who could stare me down. Must have been a psychological thing from childhood, but regardless, she managed it. I guess Sigmund Freud would have something to say about that. Probably say I wanted to fuck Sister Thomas—Freud's answer to everything.

By year six, my physical presence and appearance had changed, and my knowledge base had grown tenfold, so I focused on developing social skills. "Connections" we called it in the streets. I decided if I was going to make any headway, I had to make a deal with the blacks. They were the second biggest group in the prison, but they stuck together better than the whites.

I waited for a sunny day then walked up to the blacks. The circle of beefy bodyguards parted to let me through then closed around me like hyenas circling a lion. The leader was a guy named Monroe. He wasn't big, but word was that he was as tough as anyone. As tough as me, some people whispered.

Monroe was sucking the last bit of life from a cigarette when I approached. "You got balls coming in here like this."

"Yeah, well I figured you'd want to know why I came before you barked orders to your dogs."

I thought that pissed him off, but he laughed. I was counting on that. "You're the Rat?"

"That's what they call me."

"I hear your protection left. That what you coming to me for?"

I shook my head. "Cigarettes," I said, and stared. Looked right through him. "I can get all the cigarettes you—or anyone else in here—needs."

Monroe had been sitting on a bench. He stood now, face to face with me. "Why you bringing this to me? White boys want your pretty ass? Who knows, maybe I like white-boy ass too. Been in here a long time."

I smiled, got closer, our faces almost touching. "You've got ears, Monroe. I know you heard what happened to the last ones who tried that."

He seemed to want to back up, but he held his ground. "Yeah, I heard." He laughed again, and when he did, several of his men joined him. "So tell me about this deal," Monroe said, and motioned for me to sit next to him on the bench.

It only took half an hour to hammer out a deal. I would arrange delivery of cigarettes, smuggling them in through visitations and guards. He would handle distribution. I got twenty percent and didn't have to touch anything.

After we completed negotiations, we shook hands. He called to me as I walked away.

"I thought you would have asked for protection."

I turned, letting my eyes hold him. "Don't need it."

Monroe laughed louder than I have ever heard him. "You're one crazy fuck, Rat. I like you."

"You, too, Monroe. Nice doing business with you."

I walked across the yard with a huge smile on my face. Not only had I made a deal that would bring me money, but it would be invaluable for connections. And as far as protection...I didn't have to ask. That would have weakened my position. Besides, they knew if something happened to me, the cigarettes dried up. That was far more important than a piece of white ass.

News traveled fast about my status. After that I made contacts with everyone—Hispanic, Italian, Jew, Irish—didn't matter. I figured that when I got out, all of my contacts would be valuable. Early on these deals caused me trouble. Prisons are gang—and territory—oriented. Freud would have probably said it was because we all wanted to fuck each other. The way I figured it, some of the guys in there must have read his books and taken the message to heart.

After a particularly troublesome negotiation with another group, two guys attacked me. I killed one, blinded the other. I *had* to send a message. The attacks stopped, but the fight earned me three more years on my sentence. I did the time easy enough, counting the days until I could see Angela and start a new life.

During the final years of my sentence, Nicky the Rat—the guy they beat up when I first came in here—ruled this little kingdom. Even the guards chipped in to throw me a party for my release. I didn't hold any delusions that it was out of love—from the guards or the inmates. They just wanted me out of there.

As for me, all I dreamed of was getting back with Angie. Maybe get married. Live together forever.

CHAPTER 26

MARRIAGE LASTS FOREVER

Brooklyn—Current Day

Frankie "Bugs" Donovan stared at the blank walls of his apartment, cracking his knuckles while a cigarette dangled from the left side of his mouth. He kept his eye closed so the smoke curling around it didn't sting.

Marriage lasts forever. That's what his mother always told him. And he figured she should know, having put up with his father all of those years. When he was little, he used to ask why she stayed, but the only thing she said was "marriage lasts forever." He could still hear the way her voice trembled, as if "forever" was penance for her sins.

Penance, my ass. No priest would have been so lenient. Even Mary Magdalene was a repentant sinner. Bugs slugged the last of his wine. If he could muster the energy, he intended to pour himself more.

The refrigerator hummed a steady beat from the kitchen, and the fan in the living room dragged a breeze he was grateful for, even if it did carry the stink of the city streets. He looked around at what his wife had left him: a picture of Humphrey Bogart from a *Casablanca* poster; his wine rack and a few bottles of Chianti; the fridge—thank God for small favors—and the chair he sat in.

Fuckin' whore.

Even as he said it, he knew he was wrong. She was no more to blame than he was. She was pregnant at nineteen, and he asked her to marry him, promising to take care of her and what would be his offspring—another new Donovan. Not that the world needed any more Donovans, but...duty was duty. They got married, but in the eighth month, misfortune took the baby, leaving them together, alone. Some kids made it marrying young, but usually they were kept together by the babies. When that was taken away there wasn't much left. Not at nineteen. After all, what did an Irish/Italian kid from the streets have in common with an upper-crust girl whose family could trace their English roots back a few centuries? Nothing. Less than nothing. Might have been different if she had been Irish, Polish—hell, even Jewish. Kids of immigrants understood each other. The old, established ones didn't. Even worse, their families didn't.

This line of thinking provided enough energy to get his lazy ass up and into the kitchen, where he poured more wine. As he came back into the room, he lifted the glass to Ingrid Bergman, staring at Bogie with those sorrowful eyes. "Here's looking at you, kid." And once more he slugged it down. He didn't like his job right now; in fact, sometimes he hated his job. Bunch of idiots in suits trying to act like God. He didn't mind putting away the bad guys, but they could stuff that pretentious bullshit up their asses. Half of the cops he worked with acted like they were in the manger with Joseph and Mary. Sister Mary Thomas would have beaten their asses for implied blasphemy.

When he succumbed to moods like this, he felt like quitting, screw being a cop with the rules and bullshit. It would be nice to be back on the streets with Tony and Paulie...and Nicky. Damn, they had fun together. He couldn't remember the last time he laughed like he had when Nicky came back. Frankie sucked hard on his cigarette, recalling the excitement—and the danger—of the old days. He hadn't felt whole since then, and it all worked because of Nicky. He was the glue who held it together.

Goddamn, I miss him.

He meandered back to the kitchen—it was easy to meander in an empty apartment—and poured another glass of vino. He laughed. Knowledge was king, and he knew when he started referring to the wine as *vino* that he'd had too much. He punched the cork in tight, realizing too late that the bottle was empty, then went to recapture his throne.

As he plopped down in the seat, he looked at the plaque on the wall—a forgotten treasure when he took inventory moments ago—and said his name aloud. "Detective First Class, Mario F. Donovan."

Frankie was as screwed up as his name, but he'd known that all his life. He'd been screwed since birth. Italian first name with Irish last name. Olive skin with eyes that only sometimes matched. Loved to eat, but couldn't cook. Worst of all though, on the outside he was a cop, but inside he was still a gangster trying to get out. That's what bothered him the most.

It made him wonder about Nicky's time in prison and what it felt like for him when *he* got out.

CHAPTER 27

RELEASE

Wilmington—3 Years Ago

August twenty-first was a beautiful day, unseasonably cool, clear skies—and it was the day I was getting out. I packed my things—a lighter I didn't use anymore, pictures of Angela and Rosa Sannullo, and a letter from each of them.

It took an hour to process my papers, ridiculous paperwork that should have taken ten minutes, but I had learned patience in prison, if nothing else. When the outside gates finally opened and I stepped outside, I almost didn't believe it.

I stopped, stared. Breathed deeply. Somehow *this* air was cleaner.

A horn beep alerted me, and I jumped, turning toward the sound. An older model station wagon sat across the street. When the door opened, out stepped the most beautiful sight I had seen in years—Sister Mary Thomas.

I'll be damned.

It was August, and even though a decent day, it was still warm to be wearing a long black habit. It covered her head, most of the face, and the rest of her body. Despite that, her smile stretched from ear to ear. I raced across the street, embracing her. "Sister Thomas, what are you doing here?"

She patted me on the head, like she did when I was in first grade, then gave me one of her famous smiles. "Someone had to greet you, Niccolo. Now, get in and tell me all about your plans."

We made small talk as she drove toward Wilmington. I thanked her for the books she had sent me, and I told her how much I'd learned. We both avoided the subject of Angie, and it hung like a curtain between us.

"You must be eager for some good food," she said, and stopped at a small diner where a lot of the locals went. She slid into the last booth on the right, tucking in her habit as she did. I sat opposite her. "Tell me about yourself, Nicky. How is your life now?"

I smiled. Couldn't do anything but smile today. "Sister, I just got out. I don't know what the hell…heck, I'm going to do, but right now life is great."

She laid her two magnificent hands on top of mine. Stared at me with her two magnificent eyes. "I have prayed for you all of these years."

The waitress came, and I ordered coffee.

"Coffee for me as well," Sister Thomas said, "and perhaps some pie." She glanced at the menu again. "Apple pie."

I declined the pie. Had never been a big fan of apple pie.

As soon as the waitress left, Sister Thomas peppered me with questions. "What will you do, Nicky? Where will you go?"

"I don't know. I've only had ten years to think about it."

We laughed, then talked more until the coffee came. When I saw her pie, I changed my mind and ordered some. Sister Thomas shook her head. "Share mine. I forgot how big it was."

"You sure?" I asked. When she nodded, I turned to the waitress. "Just another fork then."

"So really, what are your plans?"

"I'm going to get a job, then I'm going to see Angie."

"Nicky…"

I stared. Braced myself. The way she said "Nicky" told me something was wrong.

"I don't know if you know this, but Angela is married." She squeezed my hand. "She has a child."

Sister Thomas could have hit me with a hammer and it wouldn't have hurt as much. I remembered the letter Angie sent, the one I treasured. Her words had been my mantra through the toughest times in prison; they kept me going when I wanted to quit. 'Find me Nicky. No matter what happens…' *What a crock of shit that was. Now she's married. Jesus Christ, is that somebody else's baby? Did she…*

I sipped coffee while fighting the urge to cry and curse at the same time. I didn't trust my voice to speak her name, so I changed the subject. "I heard Tony's in New York. I'll probably go see him."

"No reason to leave Wilmington. The economy is booming. We have…"

I downed the last sip of coffee, grounds and all. "I always wanted to see New York anyway; besides, I haven't seen Tony or Suit in a long time. Be good to see what they're up to."

A frown crossed her face. "Up to no good is what Tony Sannullo is. You would do better looking up Frankie."

I stared, probably blank-faced. I know I spoke with more than a little anger in my voice. "Forgive me, Sister, but I haven't heard from anyone but you since Mamma Rosa died. I don't know what anybody's doing."

Silence fell between us, then tears welled in her eyes. She squeezed my hand again. "I'm *so* sorry. I didn't know, or I would have…" She stared straight at me, shook her head as if chastising herself. "I should have come more often. I thought you knew about Angela."

Knew about Angela? I know *now.* "Just tell me what's going on with Tony."

She raised herself up with a big sigh, the kind of sigh only nuns and moms can accomplish, and then she composed herself. "Tony Sannullo is a mobster. There's no nicer way to say it. And Paulie is hanging onto Tony's coattails like he always has." She smiled now. "But Frankie is a detective in Brooklyn."

"A what?"

The smile remained, one of those impossible-to-wipe-off smiles. "He's a detective, and I hear he's doing quite well for himself."

The waitress refilled my cup. I picked it up and gulped some down. Shitty coffee, but better than what I'd had for ten years. "Son-of-a-bitch."

"Niccolo."

Embarrassment flushed my face. "Sorry, Sister. Prison will do that to you."

We chatted about a lot of things for the next hour. I tried getting Sister Thomas out of there several times, but she kept drilling me with questions. The only thing on my mind was Angie, and the only thing I wanted to do was get the hell out of Wilmington. I was lucky that Delaware had abandoned its parole laws. If you served your time, you were free when you got out.

"I can't talk any longer, Sister. I've got to get going." I stood, reaching for money, but she insisted on paying. I let her, since I had almost nothing with me and didn't know how much it was going to cost to get to New York. Most of the money I earned from the cigarettes was squirreled away in a bank account, compliments of one of the financial guys in prison. The rest of the money—what I got when Rosa sold my father's house—Tony had with him in New York. One more reason I had to get there.

Sister Thomas paid the bill and, as we approached the car, she turned to me. "Where can I drop you?"

It only took a second to think. I had decided in prison that I wasn't going to be like Tony or go with him, but where else did I have to go? I sure as shit wasn't staying here in Wilmington with Angie and her husband. "The train station."

"So, it's New York."

I nodded.

"May God go with you."

We rode to the station in silence—almost silence; she hummed one of her silly tunes.

Her and Mamma Rosa, I thought. When we got within a few blocks of the station, her humming got louder. She was always humming, and it was always a happy song, though back in school she seemed to hum the loudest just before she whacked me with the pointer or whatever she had in her hand. I half expected to be beaten right now, but I didn't see a pointer or yardstick, so I felt safe. She turned the corner onto Front Street, and, as we pulled to the curb, I grabbed my things. Just before closing the door, I hesitated, turned back toward her.

"Sister, I—"

She shook her head. "If you are going to ask me to take a message to Angela, the answer is no. I taught you better than that. Do your own dirty work."

Now I was embarrassed. My head drooped.

"I'll drive you to her house if you want."

"No thanks, Sister."

She beeped as she drove off. I waved, but didn't bother to turn around. There was a train waiting for me, and it was going to New York. I had mixed feelings about going there. On one hand, it would be great to see the old gang again, but on the other, I didn't know if I even wanted to see Tony after what he'd done the night Mick died. I learned to forgive a lot in prison, but I had a rotten feeling about it all.

CHAPTER 28

A CLEANSING OF THE SOUL

Wilmington—3 Years Ago

Angela Catrino-Ferris dragged her tired body up the hill toward the three-story brick building that housed St. Elizabeth's. Kids of all ages rushed past her on their way home. School had started a week ago, and most of the kids were still in summer mode with a boundless supply of energy waiting to be expended. She had long ago learned the joy of walking, one of many things Rosa Sannullo taught her. A smile that accompanied any thought of Rosa lit Angie's face.

The smile broadened as she crossed Banning Street. Sister Mary Thomas stood at the door, waving to the children as they left, the ever-present pointer in her hand in case it was needed on some of the more rambunctious ones. Angie waved to her and climbed the six steps to the landing.

"Angela, how nice to see you. How is little Rosa doing?"

Angie blushed. "She's fine, Sister, but I'm sure you know that. You're the only one she talks about."

A vague smile appeared, one only nuns can produce—the kind that told nothing. It could make a person feel warm or frighten them, depending on their state of mind. Sister Mary Thomas ushered the last few kids out the door, nodding and waving to their chants of "goodbye, Sister Thomas" or "see you tomorrow, Sister Thomas." When the last of them had gone, she turned to face Angie. "Come up to the classroom, Angela."

Angie followed her up the stairs, amazed at how fit Sister Thomas was for her age. When they got to the second floor, they entered the first door on the right, same as it had been many years ago. The door closed behind them, and Angie broke silence. "Why did you want to see me, Sister?"

"It's nice that you still get to the point right away." Sister Mary Thomas set her pointer on the desk, erased the chalkboard, and pulled a desk next to the one Angie sat in. "I pass Rosa in the hall quite often. I've seen bruises on her too many times to blame it on accidents."

Angie lowered her head.

Sister Thomas wrapped her hands around one of Angie's. "Would you like to talk about it?"

She kept her head lowered. "Sister, I have wanted to talk to you for a long time, but…"

Sister Thomas waited five, perhaps ten seconds. "But?"

Tears welled in Angie's eyes. "There are things I can't tell anybody. Not even you."

Sister Thomas stood, walked a bit across the room and back, mostly in small circles. "I'm not going to tell you that you can trust me. You know that. I'm not going to tell you what you need to do. You know that as well. What I will remind you of is what I taught you in my class: Embarrassment and guilt are the two most powerful deterrents to truth. They are also two of the worst reasons to avoid the truth." Sister Thomas reversed her course and stopped in front of Angie's desk. "Talk to me if you like, or go talk to Father Tom. Do whatever you have to…but if I see bruises on that child one more time…" Somehow the pointer had gotten back in her hand. It wagged as if it were a cobra ready to strike.

"Sister, it started just a short while ago. I think Marty realized Rosa wasn't his daughter."

Sister Thomas looked at her. "She *does* bear a resemblance to her father."

Angie lowered her head, embarrassed. "Yes, Sister, I know." She buried her head in her hands and sobbed.

Sister Thomas rubbed her shoulder, then moved the long hair from Angie's face. "I think Father Tom is in church now. I'm sure he would be glad to hear confession or just talk."

Angie lowered her head, nodded a few times, then hurried for the door. As she placed her hand on the knob, she turned. "Thank you."

Nuns could do many things others couldn't. Along with their smiles, they had perfected the art of nodding. The one she gave Angie had forty years of comfort in it. "Go on, child. Go see Father Tom."

ANGIE FELT LIKE RUNNING, but she didn't know which direction to go—see Father Tom…or run home and hide. Sister Thomas' words pounded in her head.

Embarrassment and guilt are the two most powerful deterrents to truth.

After all, isn't that what she'd been doing, hiding from the truth? When she exited the school, she turned right.

Church it is.

The one block that separated the back of the school from the front of the church seemed like a mile, and the barely measurable incline seemed like a mountain. Angie wiped a bead of sweat from her forehead, blaming it on September heat, but suspecting nerves. Despite the obstacles, she made it. A blast of cool air hit her as she opened the door into the vestibule, stepping onto the floor that she had always found so beautiful. She hadn't noticed the floor in so long, perhaps it was because her head was lowered today.

Seems like even shame can open up new worlds. She crossed into the church with a few steps, treading carefully so she made no noise, and dipped her hand into the holy water to bless herself.

Father Tom was speaking with a nun at the front of the church. Angie grew anxious as she waited, but made her way down the center aisle, then she genuflected and slid into a pew about six rows back. She blessed herself, lowered her head, and prayed. Her prayers continued for a moment, until she heard the almost imperceptible sound of footsteps leaving the altar. Angie added that to the list of nuns' special powers—perhaps they had taught ninjas long ago, or maybe even *been* ninjas; they *did* wear black robes.

She risked a look to the front. Father Tom was heading in her direction.

"Angela." He whispered it, the way everyone does in church, but her name seemed to echo.

She did her best to lower her voice. "Father Tom, I…"

Priests didn't have all the powers nuns did, but they had some of them, and he recognized a troubled person when he saw one. "Would you like to talk?"

"I don't know, Father. I came—"

"For confession, then? There's no need to wait for Saturday."

Angie's face lit up. She stood. "I think I would like that, Father. If you don't mind."

He gestured with his right arm, indicating the confessional he would use. Angie followed, spread the curtains, and knelt on the pad. She blessed herself as she said, "Bless me, Father, for I have sinned. It has been eleven years since my last confession."

A hesitation followed that made Angie nervous. She half expected him to come out of the box and chide her.

"Eleven years is a long time, my child. God is overjoyed to have you back."

She couldn't speak; the words stuck in her throat.

"Go on, my child. There is nothing to be afraid of."

"Father, I…I have sinned."

He waited. "Everyone sins. Even priests."

"I married a man I did not love…because of a child."

"You were pregnant?"

"Yes, Father."

"While that is not…condoned by the church, it is not the most grievous sin."

"My husband sometimes beats our daughter. I have thrown him out, Father, but still…when he sees her…"

She sat through silence. For the first time she realized that a priest didn't have a handbook of answers back there, that for more serious things, a priest might have to think before they spoke. She prayed he thought this through right.

"There are several ways to deal with that. He needs counseling, and she should get some as well. But, regardless tell him if he does it again you are going to the police. And make certain that you do, Angela."

She gulped. She had never had a priest call her by name in the confessional. Angie felt like finding a place to hide—forever.

"Does he hit *you*?"

"Never." The shame struck her. Maybe he should be hitting *her*, instead of Rosa.

"Why does he hit her?"

"I don't know. I…" She shook her head, the tears that had dried resurfacing. "Yes I do know, Father. She's not his child. He knows it, and he takes it out on her." Angie paused. "He's a good man, Father, it's just…"

"Just what?"

"He never hit her until I told him the child wasn't his. It's my fault." More silence. Angie felt like running through those curtains, out the door, down the block, and all the way home. She wondered if Father Tom had ever experienced a person as foul as she was.

"I'm proud of you for coming here. Go home to your family. Convince him to see someone, and make sure you protect your daughter."

"I will, Father. Thank you." She wasn't smiling, but she already felt better, and there was no shame this time when he called her by name.

"Oh, and Angela, say a rosary before you leave."

"Yes, Father. Thank you." She blessed herself as she stood, barely able to contain her relief. Why hadn't she done this years ago?

She opened her purse, took a rosary from a small pocket on the side, then knelt in the pew closest to the altar; somehow it made her feel closer to God. She mouthed the prayers as she counted the beads, each one relieving another burden from her heart. After finishing, she hurried from the church to get home. Tonight she would cook Rosa's favorite meal. She had to hurry, though, because right now she had the courage to tell her. If it waited too long, she might not. The truth was sometimes a horrible thing.

CHAPTER 29

WHERE IS THE EVIDENCE?

Brooklyn—Current Day

Lou Mazzetti climbed the stairs one at a time, each one a struggle. His right hand gripped the rail and each time he lifted his foot, he tugged himself forward and up.

Frankie stood at the top of the steps, laughing. "Slow going, Lou?"

"Screw you, Donovan. They ought to put detectives on the first floor."

"The higher the floor, the greater the power."

"Fuck power. I just want to get to work without having a heart attack." He stopped at the top, panting.

"Quit smoking, and you won't have to worry."

"You won't laugh so much when you have to carry me up these steps."

"When that time comes, I'm getting a new partner. Won't even think twice about it."

"I thought you were aiming for one anyway."

"What are you talking about?"

"You know damn well what I'm talking about. You're handing out descriptions of people to the waitresses at the diner as if we had a suspect." He pointed an accusing finger at Frankie. "You're still not sharing what you know, and it's pissing me off."

"I'm going to get coffee," Frankie said. "You coming?"

Mazzetti made his way into the door where Carol sat guard. "Hold Donovan's calls, Carol. He'll be busy all day, getting his ass kicked by me."

After getting coffee, and making his morning rounds to say hi to everyone, Lou Mazzetti walked to the war room. The table, once covered with files, pictures, and notes, was cleared. Everything had been transferred to a large wall-to-wall poster board. Lou stared. A new chart showed the three people they talked to yesterday who "thought" they remembered a man in his thirties, medium height, dark hair, dark complexion.

"All that legwork and we didn't get shit."

Frankie closed the door behind Mazzetti. "About yesterday, I—"

Lou waved his hand at him. "Forget about it. Just tell me what we've got here."

Donovan smiled. "We're catching shit. For some reason, Nino's murder got the chief's attention."

"Anybody tell the chief this was just another guinea hoodlum?"

"Need I remind you that you're a guinea?"

"Don't exclude yourself; you're just a dago hiding behind an Irish name. The difference is, we're not hoodlums."

We're not hoodlums. Lou's statement hit Frankie hard. If he wasn't a hoodlum, he'd better start acting like a cop and go after whoever the hell was doing these killings.

"No matter. The chief's putting pressure on us."

"Let's get to work then," Lou said, and as they reviewed the evidence, a call came in. Lou picked up the phone. "Mazzetti."

"Where's Donovan?"

He handed the phone to Frankie. "Kate."

"Hey, Kate."

"Got a new lead for you, Detective. A good one."

"Don't keep me in suspense."

"It's you."

There was silence while he waited for the rest. When it didn't come, he continued. "Me what?"

"A positive match on your DNA at the crime scenes for Renzo and Nino."

"Funny, Kate. Now what did you want?"

"This is no shit. It's taking a while to process this much DNA, but we got your evidence, and it's not from innocent contamination. We have hairs found *under* the blood. Hairs that could *not* have come off you during the investigation."

Frankie turned his head away from Lou and lowered his voice. "I'm sure there is a way to explain it. Figure it out."

"I'll do what I can, but I'm not covering up anything. And one more thing…"

"What?" A little hint of annoyance tainted his voice.

"The Renzo scene…you weren't there. Remember? You weren't called in until Nino."

Frankie didn't say anything, but his mind churned.

"So how did it get there?" Kate asked. "Tell me how *your* DNA got *under* the blood of Renzo Ciccarelli when you weren't on the investigation."

More silence from Frankie, then a whisper. "Kate, how about keeping this between us until—"

"Can't do it."

"Kate…"

She sighed. "For old times' sake, you've got one week while I confirm the findings. That's all. Goodbye, Detective."

"Yeah, see you." He hung up and stared blankly at the wall, his hand balling into a fist. "Lou, we need to refocus."

"What did Kate want?"

"Nothing much, just told me about some bullshit evidence from the scene." Frankie walked to the chart and pointed to the questions he had outlined.

"Evidence," Frankie said. "We need to find out where this guy is getting his evidence."

When Lou went to get more coffee, Frankie threw the pen across the room, then kicked the chair into the table. Some fuck was going out of the way to make Frankie look dirty. He intended to find out who.

CHAPTER 30

REUNION

Brooklyn—3 Years Ago

The train pulled into Penn Station and I got off. I must have looked like a hick from West Virginia by the smile on my face and the gleam in my eyes. I couldn't help it. This was my first time in New York.

After wandering around a bit, I made my way to a phone and called the number Rosa had given me for Tony years ago, not expecting it to work and surprised when it did.

"Hello?"

"Tony?"

"Who's this?"

I paused. It was damn good to hear his voice again. "Is this Tony 'The Brain' Sannullo, the dumbest fuck I know?"

A short silence followed, then exuberance. "Rat. Don't tell me this is you. They actually let you out?"

We both laughed so hard nothing else was said for half a minute. "Where are you?"

"Train station. Just got in from Wilmington."

"I'll be there in half an hour. Maybe less. Stand outside."

I walked out of the station with a large crowd, two small bags in my hand. I stared at the mass of people milling about, then up at the buildings. People were right. New York was unlike any other city. I could *feel* the excitement in the air.

I don't know how long it took Tony to get there, but before I knew it, a maroon Coupe de Ville cut across lanes and pulled to the curb. I knew it was Tony. When the passenger door opened, Paulie stepped out, dressed to the nines in a black pin-striped suit.

"Nicky the Rat." He opened his big arms, and I ran to greet him. I would have recognized him anywhere, even though he'd put on about fifty pounds. Not fat, just bigger. Paulie had always been big, towering over us by five or six inches, but he was thick and meaty, too.

"I see you finally got that suit, Suit."

"That I did, Nicky. Got a bunch of them, thanks to Tony."

A few seconds later, Tony came over and punched me on the shoulder. "I think he wears a suit in the damn shower." He hugged me, just like a brother would. "Can't believe it's really you. It's been a long time."

Tony had changed since I last saw him. He still had the rugged good looks the girls liked, and the same quick smile. It wasn't as genuine as Paulie's big laugh, but the way it lit his eyes gave him charisma. "See you managed to keep your hair. You're looking good."

He seemed embarrassed for a second. "Yeah, I'm off the drugs now. Had trouble for a while." We chatted for a few seconds, until the horns started beeping, then Tony hollered to Paulie. "Suit, get the trunk so Nicky can put his bag in there."

Paulie popped the trunk, then came back to rearrange a few things. Sister Thomas' remark about him hanging on Tony's coattails came to mind. Tony always did like being the boss. Problem was, neither me nor Bugs listened much to anybody. I wondered how he was going to react now, because, if anything, prison made me worse and I felt certain that being a cop wouldn't have softened up Bugs. Either way, it didn't matter. I threw my bags inside then got in the back seat.

"Where to?" I asked.

"First we get a few drinks," Tony said.

I rubbed my hands across the leather. "Where the hell did you get this Caddy? It's sweet."

"It's a 1990, Rat. And it's only got 20,000 miles. Runs like new." Tony hit the gas. "We'll take a spin then get some drinks."

"Let's get Bugs," Paulie said. "He'd want to be here."

"Is he in New York?"

Tony hit the brakes while cursing at another driver. "Fuckin' idiot." When he got back on track, he returned to the conversation. "Not only is he in New York, he's a goddamn cop."

"No shit." So, there it was, confirmation of what Sister Thomas told me. "You guys see him much?"

"I just told you, he's a *cop*. Hell no, we don't see him much."

"I see him a lot," Paulie said.

"Suit, seeing him at Christmas is not *a lot*. That's once a year."

"Let's call him," I said. "You got a number?"

"We'll call him from the bar."

Tony didn't want me using his cell, so I waited till we got to the bar. I went to the back, put a few coins in the phone booth and dialed the number he gave me. Three rings later, someone answered.

"Hello?"

"Mr. Donovan, please." I did my best to sound formal, as a disguise.

A pause preceded the response. "This is Frankie. Who's this?"

"I'm sorry. I'm looking for Frankie Donovan. Is this him?"

"Yeah, I just said so. Who is this, and what do you want?"

"Oh, sorry. I have a problem at my house and wondered if you could come over and kill some *bugs*." At that, I couldn't hold it in. I started laughing. Tony and Paulie cracked up behind me.

"Who the hell is this?"

I couldn't answer, so Tony picked up the phone. "Hey, Bugs. It's Tony. Me and Suit are over at Anthony's, and you won't believe who we got with us."

FRANKIE PULLED OUT OF his precious parking space, one he probably wouldn't get back that night, and headed toward the restaurant to meet his friends. Worry set in before he got two blocks.

Suppose somebody sees me? What the fuck am I doing?

He thought about turning around and going home, but the memories of the four of them hollering "friendship and honor" kept him going. How many times had they done that over the years? Too many. And how often had they held true to it—always. Nicky taking the rap for him at Johnny's Market; Nicky saving his life at Woodside; Tony getting thirty stitches helping Mick and Bugs in a fight they had started; and Paulie suffering the wrath of a dirty cop when it should have been Tony. A sick feeling brewed in Frankie's gut. He *knew* he should go home, but...*Fuck it. I'm going. Anybody sees me, I'll figure something out.*

He pulled up to Anthony's in Bensonhurst. Valet parking whisked the car away, and he walked the few steps it took to get to the entrance. There were no bouncers guarding the doors, which resembled Ghiberti's Gates of Paradise work at the cathedral in Florence—but there was a doorman wearing gloves, who held it open for him as he approached. Frankie made a mental note to check to see if the replica of Ghiberti's masterpiece was missing.

A gust of cool air laden with smoke escaped when he entered. Frankie felt certain that smoking was banned in New York, even in bars, but perhaps this place had gotten a dispensation from the pope. The smoke was thick, hanging idle in pockets of dark corners and swirling under the lights above the pool tables. A whistle caught Frankie's attention. He looked to the back. Paulie was on his way to greet him, arms outstretched like the big bear he was. Paulie was always happy, unless Tony told him not to be. Left alone to be himself, he was one of the nicest guys on the planet.

"Paulie."

Paulie nearly dragged Frankie to the table. When he got there, he couldn't believe it. Nicky looked the same—yet different. Hair was still as dark as the soil in old man Ciotti's tomato patch, and his skin still looked like he just got off a boat from Napoli. But he looked…tougher.

It's the eyes, Frankie thought. *He's got his old man's eyes.*

I GOT UP AND came around the table. "Bugs. Damn good to see you. I've missed you guys."

"Me too, Nicky. Been way too long."

"*Way* too long." I hugged him, then we took a seat at the table with Paulie and Tony. Before long it was like old-home week, us reminiscing about the good-old days.

"Who's seen Chinski?" I asked.

The whole bunch fell silent. Finally Tony opened up. "He died in a car accident."

"Goddamn. When?"

Tony looked at Paulie for confirmation. "What, maybe a year and a half, maybe two?"

"More like two," Paulie said. "Bad thing is, he was doing real good."

"First Mick. Now Chinski. Who's next?"

Tony downed his drink and signaled for another round. "Nicky, you see, the Irish finally came out in Bugs. He's a goddamn cop."

"Better than a priest," Bugs said.

"Forget about cops and priests," Paulie said. "Nicky, how do you stay in such good shape?"

I took a sip of beer. Set the mug down. "Easy, Paulie. Just spend ten years inside and you'll be fit and trim. I recommend it to anyone." They all laughed at that, even Frankie, who seemed a little tense. Maybe being here with Tony and Paulie did that.

Hell, maybe being here with me *did that.*

Tony and Bugs got up to go to the restroom while Paulie went to make a phone call. I didn't ask why he didn't use his cell; instead, I took the opportunity to watch people. It was good to see people outside of prison, and damn good to see girls. A few couples were dancing, the music loud, but nice. Every third tune seemed to be a Sinatra song, the gaps filled by Dean Martin, Al Martino, and locals like Lou Monte and Jimmy Roselli. "Summer Wind" came on, one of my favorite Sinatra tunes. I found myself wishing I had someone like Angie to dance with. But what was she going to do? Drop her life to run to ex-con Nicky, with no job and no money?

They all returned too soon, and Paulie was eager for news. "So tell us what's new. You see anybody from home before you came up?"

"Just Sister Thomas. She's the only one who visited me, except for Mamma Rosa." I lowered my head in prayer as I said this.

"What about Angie?"

Frankie kicked Paulie then shot him a glare to kill. Paulie tried changing the subject, but the harm was done.

Yeah, what about Angie?

"She's married. Got a kid from what I hear."

Tony nodded. "Yeah, she married him right away. Guy named Marty Ferris. And she didn't wait long after you went in. Of course, she didn't have much choice, with a kid in the oven."

I did everything I could to stay in my seat. How *dare* he say something like that about Angie? The muscles in my arms tensed so bad they cramped. I slipped my hand to the seat of my chair to have something to squeeze. I'm sure my face must have shown anger. I know my eyes did. I didn't know Marty Ferris, but right then I wanted to kill him and Tony both.

"Remember when you jumped out the second story window in Sister Girard's class?" Frankie asked, in an obvious effort to change the subject.

"I remember," I said, managing a laugh. "She called Sister Thomas to kick my ass. And she did, too. Beat me with that fiberglass yardstick until it broke, then made me stand there, bent over a desk while she sent that Hannagan girl to get another one."

"That was Sister Thomas all right," Tony said.

Things sure had changed, I thought, and looked at them, their lives already established—Suit, with kids; Tony married and a house. And Bugs, a cop. I didn't even have a place to stay. I never asked why they stopped coming to visit me in prison. Or why they stopped writing. Afraid to hear the answers I guess. Just like I was afraid to see Angie.

As I was brooding, someone ordered another round of beers. We told stories long into the night, digging harder to find funny ones. It didn't end until Frankie looked at his watch.

"Shit. It's one o'clock. I'm going home to get some sleep."

"We've got to do this more often," Tony said.

"Yeah. We haven't done this in a long time," Paulie said. "You're the glue, Nicky."

Bugs pushed his chair back and stood. "I can't be seen with you assholes. Nicky's okay, but not you, Paulie. And sure as shit not Tony. I already risked my ass coming here tonight." He handed me a card. "Call me sometime."

"All right. See ya', Bugs."

"Where are you staying?"

"I don't know, I—"

"With me," Tony said. "He lived with me all his life. No sense in changing things."

"Guess I'm staying with Tony," I said, and as we left the bar I wondered if that had been another dig of Tony's, or if I was being paranoid.

I DIDN'T TALK MUCH on the way home, mostly listened to Tony and Paulie. It was good to be with friends again. We dropped Paulie off then headed to Tony's house.

Tony parked out front, and we climbed the eight or nine steps to a walk that led to his front door, a massive piece of mahogany that guarded the entrance to a three-story piece of paradise.

"Holy shit. This is yours?" I had heard Paulie talking about how nice his house was, but this...

"You'll have one just like it before long," Tony said, unlocking the door.

Not in this lifetime.

Celia, his wife, was still up. She was a cute little brunette with a button for a nose. She had an air about her that indicated she came from money and wanted others to know it. At first blush, I couldn't imagine Tony marrying her, but then I remembered that this was Tony. She fit right in with his Caddy and this house and his designer suits. Even so, I had to give her credit; it was a horrendous time to be introduced, yet she managed to be pleasant. She showed me to the guest room, then disappeared with Tony down the hall.

A large mirror in the bedroom reminded me how pitiful my wardrobe was. Tony and Paulie dressed impeccably, and Bugs wore clothes that someone would kill for. Then again, Bugs always did like the clothes, sporting the latest fashions before they became fashions. I unpacked what little I had, putting a few clothes in drawers and my toiletries in the bathroom. The letter from Angela I laid on the bed. I stared at it for a long time—strongly considered reading it again, but decided against it. I should have put it away with the letter from Mamma Rosa; instead, I went to sleep with it on my chest. Then I prayed for the courage to read it and see if I could find any reason to go see her.

Any reason at all not to hate her.

FBI AGENT JOHN HARDING reviewed the tape from the night's surveillance. Tony Sannullo and Paulie Perlano had a meet with two associates. They appeared to be out on the town, having fun, but Harding knew that the dagos often mixed fun with business when not in mixed company. Organized crime was a specialty of Harding's, what he had worked his entire career for. If he busted Tito Martelli, a promotion was almost guaranteed. And the key to Tito Martelli was Tony Sannullo, the young star of Martelli's Brooklyn operations.

Danny Maddox stood beside Harding, packing up the night-shift mess. They'd watched these guys all night, and he was tired. "Who were the two new guys?" Maddox asked.

"I'll run them through the loop tomorrow and see what comes up."

Maddox yawned. "I hope you're not thinking of starting early."

"Sleep in," Harding said. "I'm not going in until ten. Let's meet over by Tony's place. We'll catch us some dagos."

Maddox laughed. "Ten's good by me. Thanks." As he started to leave, he turned back to Harding. "You know, Agent Harding, growing up, I never even heard of all those sayings, like *dagos* and *micks*, and such." He paused. "You don't like them much do you, sir?"

"Where'd you grow up?"

"Down South, close to Memphis."

Harding nodded. "You don't hate them, because you didn't have scum like them to deal with. Goddamn dagos. There's not a crime committed up here that they don't have something to do with. When I was little…" Harding gritted his teeth, almost lost himself for a minute. "Anyway, I'm guessing you had your fair share of slurs in Memphis."

Maddox lost his smile. "Yes, sir. I guess we did." He headed for the door after that. "Good night."

CHAPTER 31

QUESTIONING

Brooklyn—3 Years Ago

The next day Agent John Harding reviewed his surveillance tapes with other members of the Organized Crime Unit. At first no one recognized the two men accompanying Tony and Paulie, then, a young agent spoke up, if tentatively.

"I think I know that guy."

"Which one?"

"The one with Mr. Sannullo. He—"

"*Mr.* Sannullo?" Harding shot him a glare to kill. "He's not a damn celebrity, Agent. The man is a *gangster.*"

"Sorry, sir."

Harding calmed down. "Which one do you recognize?"

The young agent gulped and pointed. "The one between Tony and Paulie."

"Go on."

"Well…I don't want to be wrong, but…he looks like Frankie Donovan, a detective in Brooklyn."

"Are you certain?"

"No, sir. I'm not certain. That's what I was trying to say. He just…looks like him."

A quick twist of the head brought Harding face-to-face with Agent Kent. "I want an answer before I leave here. And no mistakes. I don't want to accuse one of their own kind without something solid."

"Yes, sir."

FRANKIE HAD BEEN OUT all morning, checking leads on a case. About ten o'clock he pulled into the lot, parked, then went into headquarters.

"Morning, Detective," the desk sergeant said.

"Hey, Ted. How's it going?"

"Got visitors upstairs. And the lieutenant wants to see you."

Frankie bounded up the steps and into Lieutenant Morreau's office. It wasn't a big office, enough room for three guest chairs and a small sofa, one plant in the corner and a file cabinet. A working man's office is how Carol described it, and the paperwork spread on every square inch of flat surface showed it to be true. Morreau worked his way up from patrolman to detective, then made the big jump to lieutenant.

"You wanted me, sir?" Frankie asked as he entered.

"Sit down."

Frankie looked to the side. Two of the guest chairs were occupied by grey suits—never a good sign. Frankie sat, stared at them, then back to Lieutenant Morreau. "What's going on?"

One of the suits stood up, walked over with his hand outstretched. "John Harding, Special Agent with the FBI Organized Crime Unit."

Special Agent John Harding had a face made for geometry class—all sharp angles with a curve thrown in now and then, and topped off by a jutting forehead. His eyes were too small to be called beady; they looked as if his mother had stolen them from a weasel. Frankie reached out and took his hand. "Frankie Donovan."

"I know who you are, Detective." His voice dripped with attitude.

"Guess we're even now…*Agent.*"

The other suit, Maddox, offered a handshake. He seemed genuine. "Good morning, Detective Donovan. It sure is a fine day." He enunciated every syllable in a slow cadence that marked him as having migrated north from somewhere at least as far south as Tennessee, maybe Mississippi. Maddox was a Southern gentleman, a sharp contrast to Harding, and while his voice didn't drip with a Southern drawl, that cadence was there. And the way he ended sentences made it obvious that all that was missing was the "ma'am or sir" so commonplace down South.

Harding put on a false smile. "Detective, I'll get right to it. Last night we caught you on a surveillance tape associating with known members of a criminal organization."

Fuck me. Frankie looked to Morreau, then to Harding, letting his gaze linger. "That's a mouthful for saying I ate dinner with Tony Sannullo."

Harding's eyes went wide. He turned, staring at Lieutenant Morreau, as if to say, "I told you so" then he focused on Frankie. "You don't deny it?"

"I just told you. I had dinner with Tony. I've known him since I was five years old." There was a moment of silence before Frankie spoke again, more deliberate this time. "And as far as I know, *Agent* Harding, Tony has never been convicted of anything."

"*Being convicted* and *doing nothing wrong* are two different things. I think you know that."

"I didn't say he's never done anything wrong. Just that he's not what you accused him of." Frankie shook his head. "I know how this looks, but these guys were my friends growing up. I'm not dirty, and I'm not *associating* with them. We had a few drinks." He looked behind him and took a seat in the chair across from Morreau's desk.

"Who was the other one?" Harding asked.

"He's not with them," Frankie said quickly.

"Who is he?"

"None of your business."

Harding looked to Frankie's boss. "Lieutenant Morreau?"

Morreau wore his most frustrated expression as he stared at Frankie. "Donovan, this is no goddamn game."

Frankie sat silent for a while, then stood. "Okay, listen. I'm telling you exactly how it is. Tony called me because our old friend, Nicky Fusco, just got into town. That's the first time I've seen Nicky in ten years, and maybe the second or third time I've seen Tony or Paulie in probably three."

Harding stared while his partner took notes. "All right, Detective, I'm going to check you out, but in the meantime I'd suggest you..." He stopped, as if in thought. "Actually, I'd suggest you continue associating with them. Don't do anything different. Then—"

Frankie reached for him, but the lieutenant grabbed him.

"Detective."

He shook off Morreau's grip. "If this asshole thinks I'm gonna be a rat planted in with my friends, he's as big a dick as he looks."

Harding nodded. "Come on, Maddox. We'll take this up with the commissioner."

Frankie realized he was in deep shit. If the Feds wanted to make him look dirty, they could—and would—do it. He had to make a quick decision. "What are you guys after anyway? I don't know shit about what Tony or Paulie do."

Harding smiled, a shit-eating grin that irritated the hell out of Frankie. "That's better. I knew you'd come to your senses." Harding faced the lieutenant. "I'll get back to you on how we'll handle this." As he and his partner left, he stared at Frankie. "We'll be in touch."

CHAPTER 32

A NEW JOB

Brooklyn—3 Years Ago

It was Friday morning, which meant we headed for Cataldi's for breakfast. As soon as Tony walked in, one of the waiters hustled to get espresso, and another plopped the daily crossword on the table in front of him.

"Sit across from me, Nicky."

"Still doing those crosswords, huh?"

"Can't afford not to be sharp in my business."

"Tony, I need to get a job."

Tony set his pen on the table, leaned closer. "Nicky, I know we haven't talked about it yet, but you know that money from selling the house?"

A rotten feeling gripped me, but I held back, expecting a sad tale of investments gone sour. "What about it?"

"I invested it for you, along with some of my own stuff." He leaned forward, whispered. "We're doing good. You got enough to keep you for probably a year without doing a thing. It'll take a little while to get liquid on it, so let me know when you want me to pull it out."

I made sure my expression showed nothing, but somehow I let out a huge sigh. I didn't want Tony knowing what I'd been thinking. "That's nice, but I need to *do* something. Besides, there can't be that much, and from what I've seen of prices in New York, it won't last long."

"Don't worry. You can stay at my place as long as you like. Celia loves you."

"I've been staying with you all my life. I need a place of my own. I've got a few bucks I saved from prison, but I need to make my own living."

Tony waved his hand in the air. "I'll take you to see some people."

"It can't be some half-assed job. I've got to make big money."

"Yeah, so you told me. Don't worry, we'll find something." He stopped. "Here comes Suit. We'll pick this conversation up later."

The three of us talked for more than an hour, reminiscing about the old days, then Tony must have noticed I was getting anxious. "Okay, Paulie. You know what you've got to do for the day. I'm taking Nicky to meet a few people."

"Come in with us," Paulie said. "We could use you."

"Not a chance, Paulie. I just got out and I don't intend to go back in."

Paulie left the place laughing. Tony paid the bill, then we took off in his Caddy. I played with the radio while admiring the ride. "You always said you were going to have one of these. Guess you hit the big time."

"The big time is in your head. Remember what Doggs said."

"Yeah, I remember. 'If you *think* big, you *are* big.'" I laughed. "Let me tell you, Tony, I've been thinking big…but it's not happening."

We talked to half a dozen guys that day, each one a personal introduction from Tony, but the only thing they had for me was a menial job or an under-the-table one. When we got home that night, I went to bed early, contemplating my new life. I dug deep for Mamma Rosa's words of wisdom and Sister Thomas' inspiration. With that on my mind, I woke up the next morning with a smile and a bundle of energy.

I managed to keep that attitude going for three months, but every day was the same. The three months following that were worse. The economy was horrible, and every time I found a job opening that looked decent, dozens of people were ahead of me, all with no felony records.

We got together once a month or so with Bugs, but I couldn't even pay for the drinks. One morning I made up my mind to change things. I asked Tony to get me anything, under-the-table or not. We ate breakfast then headed out for a meeting with his boss, Tito Martelli.

"Nicky, understand that Tito is not like Doggs. He's Doggs times a hundred. You piss Tito off, and you'll be dead." Tony stared at me. "You remember that movie we saw as little kids about the newborn pigs? How the toughest ones pushed the others out of their way, climbed over them, did anything to get the best teat?"

"I remember."

"The story around Brooklyn is that Tito's been that way all his life. Except he pushes people into the East River, or into a grave in Jersey."

"Point taken."

"You sure you got that? I'm not shitting here."

"I got it."

"You better get it, because it'll be my ass on the line for bringing you in."

We rode in silence for a few minutes. Not actual silence, but listening to the radio, not talking. I didn't know half the music, but that's what happens when you spend ten years in prison. "I like this song."

"Yeah, that's a good one," Tony said, then turned down a side street. He pulled up to a gate, beeped the horn, and two guys came out and opened it.

"What's this place?"

"Union hall," Tony said. "Tito's got offices here."

He pulled the car up close, got out, leaving the keys in the ignition. The room we stepped into was small, with a coat room on the side. It opened into a large area with two pool tables and several card tables.

"Hey, Tony," someone called from the kitchen at the other end.

"Yo, Manny. Where's Tito?"

He gestured toward a back room, and we headed in that direction. The place smelled of coffee—good coffee—and pastries. As we moved into the next room, Tony nudged me. "I'm going to introduce you then leave." Tony stared at me. "What you and Tito work out is between the two of you. Understand?"

"Got it."

Tony opened the door, and we walked in. A guy about my size sat at a small table, coffee in hand. A plate of sfogliatelle sat in front of him. Already I liked the guy. Anybody who ate sfogliatelle was all right in my book.

"Tito," Tony said, and they embraced as he stood.

He was older than me, shorter and thinner too, and he dressed as if he were going to dinner at a fancy restaurant. On his right pinkie, he sported a diamond ring so big it begged to be stolen.

Tony turned to me. "Tito, this is my best friend, Nicky Fusco. He's someone you'll like."

We chatted a few minutes before Tony said he had to leave. "Call me, Nicky. I'll pick you up."

Tito waited for the door to close, then grabbed me by the arm. "Let's get some coffee." We walked to the kitchen, poured two cups and headed back. "I understand you knew Tony as a boy."

"His mother raised me."

"And you're looking for a job now?"

"Everyone needs work, Mr. Martelli. Even ex-convicts."

"Convicts aren't much use to me. I could maybe get you a job as a union rep."

I sunk when he said "union rep." I guess I was expecting more. *How the hell am I going to win Angie back as a union rep?* Right then I realized what my life was about, and what I had to do. "I need a lot more than that, Mr. Martelli. I can do *anything*." I stopped and stared at him. "If you have something you need done, I can do it."

"*Anything* sounds ominous. Besides, what would I need done?" He grabbed a biscotto from the plate on the table. "And call me Tito. I hate that *Mr. Martelli* shit."

"Anything," I said, and stared at him again. "I need money. Once I get enough, though, I'm quitting. You need to know that up front."

"I like a man who knows what he wants." He walked back to the door and opened it. "Manny, I'll be talking to our new friend. Make sure we're not disturbed."

When he returned to the table, a change had come over him. The laugh was gone; from the look on his face now, I didn't know if he *could* laugh. "Sit, Nicky. Tell me about yourself. Tell me about this...*anything*...you said you would do."

Here it was—out for six months, and already faced with making decisions that could put me back in. I decided not to hold back. I doubted it would have done any good anyway. This guy seemed like he could spot a lie surrounded by four truths. I brushed over my childhood, but told him about the Woodside fight, then prison. Told him everything about prison.

"Anybody fuck you in there?" His eyes burned holes in me. I figured he wanted to know how I stood up to things.

"Three guys tried it one night. They didn't make it. Only once more did someone ever try. After that, never." I didn't brag or boast. Just told him.

He nodded. After that, his questions focused on what I liked to do. Did I have a girlfriend? What was it like growing up without a mother? That kind of stuff. Then we got more coffee and told stories about the rigors of Catholic schools and nuns.

"You know, they always talk about how tough priests are, but for every story about a priest standing up to somebody, I'd bet fifty dollars to a donut he had a nun behind him backing his play." We laughed about that and told more nun stories, and then finally he stood, saying he had other appointments, and walked me to the door.

"Manny will take you home," he said. "No sense waiting for Tony."

I nodded to Manny and shook his hand. He was bigger than Paulie and had a neck so thick it would have been impossible for him to button the top of his shirt. Not fat, barrel-chest big, with fingers like links of sausage.

His eyebrows were thick and bushy, and they moved so much they could have passed for caterpillars. I turned to Tito. "When do I hear from you?"

"I'll get hold of Tony," he said, then nodded to Manny.

I walked out of there thinking I had done okay, but I wasn't sure. Tony was right; this guy was no Doggs Caputo.

No SOONER HAD NICKY left than Tito sent for Chicky, one of the most connected men in New York. Chicky knew somebody who knew somebody no matter what. If a person needed to be checked out, Chicky was the one to call.

"What's up?" Chicky asked when he came in.

"Need someone checked out." Tito handed him a piece of paper. "Name's Nicky Fusco. Served ten years down in Delaware."

Chicky looked at the paper, then stuffed it in his shirt pocket. "This will take a few days."

"Take as long as you need."

CHAPTER 33

VERY GOOD FRIENDS

Brooklyn—3 Years Ago

On the way home, I got to know Manny a little better, as much as you can from a car ride. He seemed to be everything Tito wasn't—open and honest, friendly and charming, smiles and laughter. I knew most of it was probably a front, honed to perfection by decades of practice. If it was, it worked.

Manny dropped me off at Tony's house and told me not to worry, that I'd be hearing from Tito. I got out of the car, went up to the door and knocked. Celia answered, inviting me in with the same warmth she expressed the other night.

"How about some food, Nicky? I was just making a salad."

"No thanks, Celia. I think I've already put five pounds on since I've been here." I followed her to the kitchen. Life seemed to be good for Tony. He had a magnificent house, a beautiful wife, and he was off drugs. On the other hand there was me—no permanent job, living with my friend, and fresh out of prison. I needed to do something. *Anything.*

From the corner of my eye, I caught a glimpse of a picture of Mamma Rosa above the mantle. It had been a long time since I'd taken the time to look at a picture of her. This one was so real it was scary. I stopped, admiring it.

Celia stood beside me. "Tony loves that picture."

"She was a saint."

She patted me on the shoulder. "He thinks so, too," she said, then tugged on my arm. "Come with me. If you're not going to eat, you can at least keep me company while I make the salad."

She asked a million questions while she worked, mostly about Tony. I answered them as best as I could, but it was obvious he hadn't told her much, and I didn't want to betray any trusts. I had no idea how far to go, so I played it safe. Queries about me, I avoided. I never was much for confession of any type, innocent or not. But when the conversation switched to Mamma Rosa, I opened up. She was one person I had no problem talking about.

Celia finished making the salad and started doing dishes. I offered to help twice, but she insisted I sit still and relax. "It sounds like you really loved Tony's mother."

A glass of water sat in front of me, and I was locked in a staring trance. "I loved Mamma Rosa," I said. "She was my mother too."

Celia laughed, and her laugh hurt me. "Tony told me that everybody called her that." I was about to interrupt, when she continued. "But he said you two were very good friends growing up."

The words hit me like a brick in the head. A lump built in my throat.

Very good friends? We were brothers. I paused. Swallowed pride. "We were," I said, then, in a lower tone. "We were very good friends."

CHAPTER 34

JOHNNY MUCK

Brooklyn—3 Years Ago

It took Chicky a week to get the information. He met Tito for breakfast at the union hall. Manny brought cappuccino for Tito and an espresso for Chicky.

Tito sipped his drink and bit into a biscotto. "Talk to me, Chicky boy. What have you got?"

"What you got is a genuine bona-fide fuckin' psycho."

"Tell me about it," Tito said.

"He goes in at nineteen after shooting a guy in a gang fight. About six months in, three of the toughest whiteys decide to get some sweets, so they follow Nicky into the shower." Chicky laughed so hard he spilled his espresso. "Ten minutes later Nicky comes out and they got to send the medic in to take care of two of the others. One of them with a cracked head, which damn near killed him, and the other with a full bar of 99.44% pure ivory shoved up his ass 100% of the way." Another laugh emerged. "Must have hurt *bad*."

Tito picked up a biscotto. "No shit?"

Chicky waved his hand. "That ain't even half the shit. Then—"

"You sure this is good information?"

"Tito, you know my shit's good."

"Okay."

"Anyway, this Nicky kid then starts training like he's going to the Olympics. Couple of more guys messed with him. The inside word is he killed one and blinded the other."

Tito sat silent while Chicky ate a pastry.

"I'm telling you, this kid's no slouch. My guy said even the guards were scared of him."

Tito dipped a biscotto into his cappuccino and smiled. "Thank you, Chicky. This has been helpful."

Chicky headed toward the door, but Tito called him. "Ask Manny to come in, please."

A minute later Manny popped his head in the door. "What?"

"Get Johnny Muck."

"You got it, boss."

As Manny left, Chicky came back in. "I forgot one thing. They said this kid ain't scared of nothing. Fuckin' *nothing*."

IT WAS TWO DAYS before Tito met with Johnny Muck. Johnny was a hit man, the best the mob boss had seen. Methodical. Cold. Analytical. Perfect. He'd done numerous hits for Tito and delivered on every one. There was one problem, though—Johnny Muck was getting old. He had been a hit man for the last three bosses, and the work was taking its toll.

Tito met him at a small cafe in the Bronx. Few people knew Johnny, and Tito preferred to keep it that way. He didn't even know where Johnny lived. By nature hit men were secretive, and they kept it that way with everyone. The trouble was worth it; having a top-notch hit man was profitable, but, more importantly, it gave Tito power. He didn't have enough work to keep Johnny busy, so he rented him out to other mob bosses. They paid his exorbitant fee, and, they owed Tito a favor—that was the real clincher. It gave Tito an edge, and it kept Johnny happy.

Tito sat facing the door. He raised his head when Johnny came in. It was 7:00 AM, precisely when Tito had asked Johnny to meet him. If he had said 7:02, he felt certain that he would have been staring at his watch for exactly two more minutes.

Muck didn't have his fedora on today—a good thing. He only wore his hat when doing a job. And he wasn't wearing gloves—another good sign. Tito raised a hand to draw his attention.

The waiter brought an espresso for Johnny, then, when he saw Tito's cappuccino was empty, he took the cup, promising a replacement.

"Good to see you, Johnny."

"I always liked this place," Johnny said. "Great pastries."

Tito jumped right in. "I need some help."

"What can I do?"

"Got a kid that needs testing."

Johnny Muck sipped his espresso then nibbled on the biscotto placed on the saucer beside the cup. All the while he looked around, always aware of his surroundings. "What kind of testing?"

"Your kind."

Johnny's eyes shot to the other tables while his right hand drifted toward his lap.

"Relax, Johnny. There's nobody here but you and me."

"You think I'm getting old?"

"We're all getting old, Johnny, but that's not the problem. Let's just say I like what you and I have done together, and I want you to train your successor."

The cappuccino came for Tito. Johnny waited. "Who is he?"

"Young kid from down by Philly."

"Sicilian?"

Tito shook his head. "Father came over from Napoli."

"Prison?"

"Ten years, but—"

Johnny was already shaking his head. "You know I don't do that."

Tito leaned in close. People were passing the table. "This kid is different. Trust me."

He finished his espresso in silence, then, "What did you have in mind?"

"See what he can do. If he pisses his pants or fucks up—kill him."

Muck thought it over. "Who? When?"

Tito shrugged. "Soon. Don't know what targets yet." He pointed his finger at Johnny. "And I'm not telling him what he's in for. Let's see how he thinks on his own."

A nod came with Johnny's response. "Call me."

Tito left a twenty on the table. They walked out together. When they got outside, Johnny looked both ways, then stared straight at Tito. "If he fucks up, I'll kill him."

"If he fucks up, I don't want him."

CHAPTER 35

JOHNNY MUCK TAKES
AN APPRENTICE

Brooklyn—3 Years Ago

Tony told me Tito wanted to see me on Wednesday. I had almost given up hope. "Did he tell you anything?"

"Nothing. Just said be there Wednesday at noon. I'll drop you off."

I got to the union hall early and waited for Tito. He came out thirty minutes later, walking fast. "Nicky. Sorry I'm late. Come with me."

I followed him, climbing into a silver Lincoln parked by the front door. "What have you got for me?"

"There's a guy named Johnny Muck who works for me. He needs an apprentice."

"What's he do?"

Tito took a left turn, drove maybe half a block, then looked over at me. "None of your business."

My first reaction was to be pissed off, but that would likely get me killed. "Can I assume I won't be needing my carpenter's hammer or saw, or shit like that? Because I'm not too good with tools."

The five seconds it took him to respond seemed like five minutes, but then he roared. "That's good, Nicky. I like that." He laughed all the way down the next block. He never told me what Johnny Muck did, but that was okay. I knew these people didn't deliver flowers.

Johnny Muck was tall for an Italian, a hair over six feet—more if you counted his fedora, a slick looking black one with a silver band that he wore cocked toward the left, maybe to show the gray streak on the right side of his head. The first thing I noticed when I met him were his hands. They were huge, and covered with gloves so thin I could see the ridges in his knuckles. His real name was Gianni Mucchiatto. People said that *Muck* was a natural shortening of his last name. Lots of Southern Italians, Neopolitans, in particular, loved to shorten names. Salvatore became Toto; Giuseppe became Zeppe or Beppe. Other people said that Johnny was the guy you called when you got into a mucky situation. I looked it up in a dictionary. One of the definitions was "anything filthy or vile." I preferred to think that that's where his name came from.

He wasn't dirty or vile, as in *unclean*, not in that sense. But he was the meanest, coldest, most ruthless fuck I'd ever seen. As far as I was concerned, "filthy and vile" fit Johnny Muck like the gloves he wore.

When I first met him, he wasn't about to tell me what he did. "You'll be working for me" was all he said.

Johnny had me get his car. He climbed in, cautious. "Where to?" I asked.

"Queens."

"You're going to have to help me out. I don't know my way around."

He gave me directions a few turns at a time. Fortunately, traffic wasn't bad this time of day, so I remembered where to go. He had me stop so we could get our windshield washed. Seemed odd, but I didn't question it. And he watched me as I drove, but did it without trying to look like he was. We went over a bridge, took a few more turns, then parked in a garage on the third floor.

Johnny Muck turned the car off but made no move to get out. I sat still. After a moment of silence, Johnny looked over. "Three guys in this investment firm owe Tito money."

I thought I knew what that meant, but didn't jump to conclusions. "Why send us?"

"Tito sent his regular guy a few weeks ago. These three guys beat Tito's man half to death. One held a gun on him while the other two did the work. They dumped him in front of family."

I nodded. This happened from time to time, people who thought the old mob was gone, just a few figureheads hanging around trying to collect on past glory. When it did happen, though, it was Johnny Muck's job to prove them wrong. Johnny Muck's, and now mine. I learned that these three guys were scum. Not only did they beat the guy, they let his wife and kid see it happen. Tito might have forgiven them one time, if it was just about money, but an insult—no way.

Johnny Muck asked if I was okay doing a job with no practice. I knew this was a test. "Just tell me what you want."

"Wipe the car down. We'll wait until they get back from lunch."

"So you know their schedule?"

Johnny Muck looked over at me, his eyes hard and probing. "Murder takes time, Nicky. That's the first rule of our business."

I tensed up. Gulped. I had killed people. Nobody innocent, and all in self-defense, but this would be different. On the other hand, these weren't babes in the woods. These were guys stealing from the mob. They knew *exactly* what they were risking. I looked over at Johnny. A bond had suddenly developed between us. "So we're going to kill these guys?"

"I didn't say that."

"No, you didn't."

"I was just telling you the first rule—murder takes time. That means you need to be prepared. Need to study your targets. Know everything about them."

"How long have you been watching?"

"A few weeks." Johnny eyed me again. This time it was more like a teacher. "Don't use the same places to watch from, but if you have to, don't do it at the same time of day. Don't use the same cars or wear the same clothes.

Remember that. *Sameness* is your enemy. People remember things they see over and over, but they also remember uniqueness. Never be unique."

I listened, surprised that Johnny could say all that in one sitting. "Okay," I said, then wiped down the car, making sure that everything I touched got wiped—handles, door, roof, everything. I looked across the hood at Johnny. "It's done."

Johnny opened the trunk, pulled out two briefcases, and handed me one. "This is yours," he said and popped it open. "The gun is clean. The case is clean. Make sure it comes out with you."

He had worn gloves, so there was nothing to wipe down on his side; besides, the car itself was nothing. If we left it, it would just be a stolen car left in a garage. Johnny put shades on and shut the trunk. "Let's go."

I kept up with him, walking side by side. I was shaking. I doubted Johnny was. I glanced at my hands. They looked calm, but I felt them trembling. This was not going to be as easy as I thought.

"WALK WITH YOUR HEAD down," Johnny said. "There are cameras everywhere."

We took an elevator to the fourth floor. He turned right and walked to #410, a large double-door with "Krivske, Pollard and Smythe" etched in script on the glass. Johnny went to the receptionist and leaned toward her. I learned later that this would make her shy away. Typically, the closer you got to people, the less likely they were to look at your face—really look at it.

"May I help you?" she asked.

"I'm Mr. Temple," Johnny said. "I have an appointment."

A quick check brought up the appointment he prearranged, apparently claiming to be a wealthy investor moving to New York.

She looked up and gave the welcoming smile all receptionists master. "They will be with you shortly, Mr. Temple. Would you care for something to drink?"

"No thanks." Johnny sat in the chair next to me. "Remember to touch nothing," he whispered.

Within minutes, a long-legged assistant led us to a conference room; all good assistants seemed to have long legs. I took note of the way we came in, assuming we might need a fast exit. She opened the door to a conference room, which had a long table in the center. Windows surrounded us, looking over the city.

The three men in the room greeted us, introducing themselves with even better fake smiles than the receptionist. Johnny asked if they minded shutting the blinds, as he had sensitive eyes. Two of the men quickly met his demands, their greed inspiring graciousness.

Johnny took his seat, opened his briefcase and pointed to the gun. Then he turned to me and said, "I believe you have something to show these gentlemen?"

A deep breath calmed me. I took another to be safe, wishing I could close my eyes too. Killing a person who was trying to hurt you was different than this. But I knew this was a test, and I knew if I didn't do it, that long-legged assistant would find four bodies in this conference room instead of three. I laid my case on the table, opened it, took one more breath…then reached for the gun. It had a silencer.

Adrenaline raced through my body, charging me. In one fluid move, I lifted the gun, and shot each of them in the head. They didn't have time to scream, just gasped and fell to the table. I put an extra bullet into each of them before putting the gun away.

Johnny packed up his case, threw me a cloth to clean off the blood, then started for the door. Not running, just moving. I latched my case and followed him, closing the door behind us.

As we walked down the hall, the assistant looked strangely at us. "Meeting over so soon, gentlemen?" I didn't trust myself to talk without my voice cracking, so I was glad Johnny spoke for us.

"I'm afraid it is," Johnny said.

We made it out of the building before anyone was alerted. We took the elevator to the subway. Before long, we were on our way to safety.

After that, Johnny and I did a lot of jobs. A guy in the Bronx who whacked someone without permission. Another one in Manhattan who was caught skimming dope from his boss. And two guys in Brooklyn who were selling heroin to elementary school kids. I relished every part of *that* job—made it particularly painful for them.

Before long, Tito had me doing jobs myself. The risk was greater, but the money was better. I reminded him again that I was going to quit once I got enough.

"Yeah, me too, kid," was all he said.

OVER THE NEXT FEW months, I did more work with Johnny, mostly perfecting my craft. I was a quick learner, and Johnny made sure to teach me his rules:

1. Murder takes time—Never rush. Know what you are going to do before, during, and after the job. Know your victim. Their face. Routines. Neighborhood. Family.

2. Murder has consequences—When doing a job you can never, *ever*, let it get personal. Each assignment is just a job. If you let it get personal, it *will* have consequences.

3. Murder takes patience—If someone has a routine, trust it. Wait them out, and it *will* pay off. As for yourself, never be predictable. Don't shop at the same place. Don't eat at the same place. Don't do *anything* at the same place or at the same time or on the same days.

4. Murder is invisible—To be good at this, you need to be invisible. And since you can't really be invisible, you have to practice not being noticed. There is a difference between being *seen* and being *noticed*. If you have to break rule number three, make sure you adhere to rule number four.

5. Murder is a promise—If you enter into a deal to murder someone, that is a promise, a secret pact. Once you take the assignment, you need to finish the job, or it could come back to haunt you.

6. Murder is immaculate—Don't leave any clues, and make sure you clean up loose ends.

I took all the rules to heart, but I especially practiced number one. When we saw Tito the next time, Johnny told him I was ready.

"He'll be teaching me pretty soon," he said.

Tito turned to me. "Remember, Nicky. Nobody knows what you do. Just Johnny, Manny and me."

"That's the way I like it." As I left, I wondered what to tell Bugs and them about what I did. They'd already been asking. I worried about Bugs, too. I felt I could trust him, but…he *was* a cop—not a good person for me to be associating with. One day he'd wake up and realize he really *was* a cop.

CHAPTER 36

DONNIE AMATO

Brooklyn—Current Day

When he found Donnie Amato, his heart raced. He couldn't wait to keep *this* promise. It's not that he liked killing people, but if it had to be done—and this did—then killing Donnie Amato would not keep him up at nights. Rushing these things was never good, though, so he settled in and did it right.

He sat in a booth at the diner—a red booth with tears in the seat and white fluff poking out—and sipped coffee and mopped up egg yolks with the last bite of a garlic bagel. The sausage links and fried potatoes were long gone, the plates disappearing with the first ritual cleansing by the very obtrusive and not-so-quiet waitress. As he contemplated dessert, his eyes shifted to the building across the street, a ramshackle, two-story house converted into half a dozen office spaces.

"More coffee?" the waitress asked.

He always seemed to end up in diners, perhaps because they were as anonymous as any place can get. He knew he was breaking rule number three, but at diners rule number four kicked in automatically—no one noticed anyone in a diner. He set his cup down, nodded as he looked up at her. Not a typical diner waitress, this one was both young and pretty with a pleasant demeanor.

"Thank you," he said, and made a mental note to tip her more. Not so much she'd remember him, but enough to let her know he appreciated the service. Silently, he chided himself. He shouldn't have stared.

Like clockwork, the door across the street opened, and out stepped Donnie Amato, sporting a three-quarter-length leather coat. As he checked both ways on the street his head bounced about like a hockey puck at a Ranger's game. He went a few steps, checked the street again, then walked toward his car. He'd be going home now, but not before stopping at Grant's fruit stand. After all, this *was* Wednesday. Donnie walked down the concrete pavement, eyes shifting one way, then another.

The man in the diner signaled the waitress, who hurried over with a check. He paid the bill, then left, climbing into an older model blue Chevy. Common car. Common color. Nothing anyone would take note of. He waited until Donnie started his car, then followed him the eight blocks to the fruit stand. He took it slow, never exceeding the speed limit. When he got to Donnie's house, he drove half a block past it, parking behind a donut shop on the next street. Walking back at a quick pace, he entered through the back door and waited. He had come earlier in the day to prepare, but he made a final check to ensure things were ready. The holes were drilled in the wall. He had the rope. Bag on the counter in the kitchen. He nodded, pulled out his bat and the three-pronged fork, then the gag and the lighter fluid. After that he went to the living room to wait.

DONNIE AMATO RODE HOME from the fruit stand with a huge smile on his face. They didn't have Jersey tomatoes—they weren't out yet—but he got some great looking melons from down South. Wasn't much better than prosciutto and melons. He also got enough mangos to last till next week.

He took a right onto a narrow street then one more right turn before pulling into his driveway. He walked the few steps to the house, stepped into the living room and shut the door behind him.

The first things Donnie noticed were the holes in the wall. They looked to be about two inches round and about two feet apart, chest high.

"What the hell?" he said, just before the bat smashed his ribs. He gasped for breath, and, as his head hit the floor, he noticed two more holes, ankle-high. The next hit knocked him out.

DONNIE LAY ON THE floor, unconscious. He dragged Donnie to the wall, stood him up, and secured him with a rope he pushed through the holes in the wall. Donnie's body sagged, but he was secure, upright, with his arms tight against his body. He took two plastic bags from the counter, opened the one containing sand, and poured it into a pitcher he took from Donnie's cabinet. A final check to make sure everything was ready, then he spread the evidence and waited for Donnie to wake up. With the first moan, he went to him.

"I need a name."

"Fuck you, who do you—"

He took the gag, which was actually a baby diaper, and tied it to a long three-pronged fork, the kind used for lifting turkeys or large roasts. When it was just right—nice and fluffy at the end—he jammed it into Donnie's mouth, breaking a few teeth. Donnie's head rammed against the wall. He tried to scream, eyes agape. Tried kicking him too.

"Do that again and I'll shoot you. Understand?"

Donnie nodded vigorously.

He cut the clothes from Donnie's body. A few times the knife cut into skin, drawing a little blood. Donnie tried talking, and he banged his head to draw his attention. The man got the can of lighter fluid and a box of matches. He squirted it between Donnie's toes, letting it pool just a little. Afterwards, he removed the gag.

"What the fuck are you doing?"

"A name."

"I don't know what kind of freak you are, but I got friends."

"I only want the name of one of them."

"I told you—"

He shoved the gag into Donnie's mouth, struck the match and dropped it to the floor, just beside Donnie's left foot. Flames spread across both feet and onto the floor. Donnie screamed, though nothing came out; the gag prevented that. Donnie kicked his feet and stomped, but his feet were tied to the wall. The man let the fire burn for about ten seconds, and then doused it with the sand from the pitcher. When Donnie calmed down, he removed the gag.

Donnie appeared dazed, but not enough to prevent his protestations. "What the fuck? Are you nuts? Jesus Christ." Blood oozed from his mouth.

"Don't make me put the gag back in."

"Okay. What do you want?" It seemed difficult for Donnie to talk now, with all the blood and the missing teeth.

"I already told you, the name. Who planned it?"

"All right. All right." Donnie looked right into his eyes. "Nino Tortella."

He jammed the gag so hard the prongs of the fork struck the back of Donnie's throat. "You shouldn't have lied to me." He squirted the lighter fluid on Donnie's balls and dick. It drizzled down his legs.

Donnie pleaded with his eyes, groaned, begged. His head bobbed up and down like a puppet.

He removed the gag. "The name."

"Johnny Muck. It was Johnny Muck. That's all I know." He breathed a huge sigh of relief. "Now let me go. Please?"

He nodded, repeating, "Johnny Muck," as he soaked the rag in lighter fluid. When it was drenched, he shoved it into Donnie's mouth, then lit the match and threw it on his balls. "I'll set your soul free, Donnie. How about that?"

Donnie tried screaming. Banged his head against the wall. Stomped his feet, but the fire kept burning.

He squirted a few more shots onto his hair, letting it drip down, then stood back to watch. When the fire hit his chest hair, it raced up, swarming his face. He waited until the gag caught on fire, smothering

Donnie's face in flames and engulfing his mouth. Surely it went down his throat too.

After Donnie died, he used a blanket to smother the flames then spread the remainder of the evidence. He was careful not to step in Donnie's mess—the urine or feces. Blood was bad enough; he didn't want that other stuff on his shoes. He went back to the kitchen, changed clothes, put the plastic on his shoes, then grabbed his bag and returned to the living room. He made the sign of the cross as he repeated the Trinitarian formula, "In nomine Patris, et Filii, et Spiritus Sancti." When he was done, he took his gun and shot Donnie Amato. Once in the head. Once in the heart.

An eye for an eye, he thought, *and then some.*

As he left the house, he removed the plastic from his shoes and placed it in the bag. He made the short walk to his car without encountering anyone. A good sign. It was just now getting dark; perhaps he had time yet for dinner. He didn't ask forgiveness for this one. Maybe it was because Donnie needed killing so bad. Maybe that was a bad sign. But he had no time to worry about it. Johnny Muck was still out there. And he *surely* needed killing.

CHAPTER 37

AN UNEXPECTED CALL

Brooklyn—2 Years Ago

The Fed-Ex truck took a right on Sixth Street and pulled up to #115. It was a big, three-story house built in the early part of the century. The driver jumped out, envelope in hand, and walked up the steps to the front door. Manny Rosso stepped out of the house and onto the stoop.

"Package for Mr. Martelli," the driver said.

Manny accepted the envelope, examined it as if it might be a bomb, then inked his name on the delivery slip before disappearing into the house. "Tito." His voice echoed off the hardwood floors. The kitchen was in the back, and it had a huge eating area surrounded by bay windows.

Tito sipped cappuccino while he read the paper. It was well past the acceptable hour for cappuccino—at least, that's what his father would have said, adhering to old Italian traditions—but Tito had grown to like it at any time of day, particularly late morning.

"Coming in," Manny said.

Tito held out his hand without looking up. "What have we got, Manny?"

"Fed-Ex package."

"Who sent it?"

Manny squinted as he tried to read the handwriting. "Says Giuseppe… something. Can't make it out."

Tito turned to look at him, brow furrowed. "Don't know any Giuseppe. Open it."

Manny unzipped the package, reached inside and pulled out a small box and an envelope, which he handed to Tito. Tito looked up at Manny, a question on his face, then he opened the envelope and read the letter:

Mr. Martelli:

You probably don't remember me, but we met many times before. You used to come to my house as an honored guest of my father. You used to share his coffee and his wine. And you ate my mother's cooking. Thank the good Lord she died before she saw what happened. But enough of that. I am sure you will be happy to know that you made my father's life miserable. He cursed you with his last breath. So, yes, Carlo is dead, and you are happy. The problem is, Mr. Martelli, with a few of those breaths before he died, he told me everything. He gave me the gun you used to kill Danny Zenkowski. The gun my father never disposed of. The one with your prints on it.

I am tired of hiding. Tired of looking over my shoulder and wondering when one of your goons will show up and kill me. I want $400,000. And I want it in small, untraceable bills with non-sequential serial numbers. If I find tracers, or dyes, or anything fishy about the transaction—or if I even think I'm being watched, I'll go to the FBI. I'm sure they will find my story interesting. But if you keep your end of the deal, I will disappear, and you will never hear from me again.

Inside the box is a throwaway cell phone. In three days, at precisely ten in the morning, I will call and tell you where to take the money.

Gina

*PS. Don't even think about stalling or telling me you don't have
the cash. I know you do. Three days. 10:00 AM.*

Tito threw the box across the room, then walked about the kitchen,
kicking things. "Find this bitch, Manny. Somebody better find her."

Manny held out the Fed-Ex slip. "Says it came from Baltimore. Maybe
Fifth Street, but I can't tell. The ink's smeared."

Tito yanked it from him, staring at it. "Who can read that? I don't know
how they let it pass."

"It's a package, boss. They can't look at the address on every one of
them."

Tito reached for his drink. "We gotta find her."

Manny set the box on the counter, opened it and removed the phone,
tucking it into his pocket. "I'll see what I can do with this. Put our guy
on it."

Three days later, with no clue where the girl was, Tito waited for the
call. The phone rang at 10:00 AM, just like Gina said it would. He grabbed
it. "Hello?"

"Have you got it?"

He waited a long time, as if he didn't want to answer. She waited. "Yeah,
I got it."

"Good. Write this down. I want it Fed-Exed to this address."

"Whoa. Are you nuts? Fed-Ex this much money?"

"That's right, Tito. Fed-Ex it. Now I'm going to give you the address."
She waited for him to acknowledge, and when he did, she continued.
"Send it to me at 1817 Fifth Street in Baltimore." She gave him the zip and
a phone number, then said, "Make sure it's marked for 10:30 AM delivery,
and make sure that "signature required" is checked." She again waited for
him to confirm, then, "If there is any hint of me being watched, or followed, or if there are any tracers in the money, I'll go to the Feds."

"It'll be there."

"Good, and in case you try something…I have help on this. Don't think of sending your goons."

"Don't worry. You'll get it."

"Just remember. Nobody watching, Tito."

"Yeah, yeah. Live a good life, Gina." *I'm gonna cut your heart out.*

Tito turned to Manny. "Get our best men on this. Stake out that address. Tell them to follow her, or whoever gets the money." He punched the wall, several times, hard. Tito had not clawed his way to the top to let some broad cut his legs out from under him.

Tito turned to Manny again, voice raised even more. "If she spots them, they're dead. I'll kill them myself."

"Got it," Manny said.

CHAPTER 38

SPECIAL DELIVERY

Gina waited until it was past pick-up time for Fed-Ex. She dialed the number for the depot in Baltimore. "Customer service, please."

A pleasant voice answered in a few seconds. "Customer service. How may I help you?"

Gina put panic in her voice. "Oh, thank God. I hope you can help. I'm expecting a very important package tomorrow, but there's been an emergency with my daughter, and I won't be home. Is it possible for me to pick it up before it goes out on the delivery truck?"

"I'm afraid you can't do that. I'm sorry."

"But this is an emergency. Please? My daughter is very sick. I know it has to be signed for, and no one will be there."

There was a short silence, then the customer service agent said in a low voice, "Let me check to see what we can do." She returned about thirty seconds later. "I need your name and the delivery address? And I need the zip code it was sent from."

"Right here," Gina said, and read it to her.

"Just a minute."

Gina heard some typing, then, "I've got it marked for pickup. But you'll need your license or something to verify your ID."

"Thanks so much. I really appreciate it." Gina sighed as she got in the car. After today, it would finally be over. She didn't trust Tito one bit, so she knew she'd still have to hide, but the money would make it easier.

TITO'S MEN WERE POSITIONED early, two in an abandoned house half a block south, and the other two at a gas station a block in the opposite direction. They had borrowed a guy from Tito's connections in Baltimore to watch the back alley in case she went out that way.

"Shitty place to live," Donnie said. "Looks like a fuckin' war zone."

"No wonder she blackmailed the boss. I might even do it to get out of here."

Small talk occupied time for the next hour and a half, but when it got to be 10:30 and the truck still hadn't come, they got nervous. Donnie's cell phone rang at 10:45. "Yeah?"

"It get there?" Tito asked.

"Nothing yet."

"All right. Call me."

At 11:00, his phone rang again. "Not yet," he said as he answered the phone.

"Something's wrong." Tito screamed, and hung up.

Two minutes later, Donnie's phone rang again. It was Manny. "Pack it up. Gina fucked us good. She picked the package up."

Donnie whistled. "Bet he's going nuts."

"Yeah, no shit."

GINA DROVE UP I-83 out of Baltimore toward Harrisburg, then took the turn to Hershey, PA. It was an easy drive from Baltimore, hour and a half tops, and the scenery was nice, especially crossing the Susquehanna River. She patted the bag on the seat next to her as if it were a baby. The ride was calming enough, but with $400,000 on the passenger seat, it was also exhilarating. She could have probably gotten more from Tito, but to ask for more might have pissed him off even worse. For $400,000, he might forget about her in a few years, then she'd be free and able to really live again. It had been a long time. She thought about going somewhere besides Hershey, but she had been safe there for a long time. She just hoped her luck held out.

Soon fear chased the euphoria away. The trembling started in her stomach and worked its way up, lingering in her shoulders, tracing down her arms. She gripped the wheel with both shaking hands, fighting the desire to pull over. The only thing stopping her was the fear that cops would want to know why she was on the shoulder of an interstate. She checked the rear view mirror for what seemed like the hundredth time, and fought off images of what Tito would do if he caught her. If she were lucky, he'd put a bullet in her brain—if she were lucky.

A few tears came. She managed to stifle the flood lurking inside her, but for how long she didn't know. She thought this was going to be easy—get the money, go home, live happily ever after. But nothing with the mob was happily ever after; she should have known that from living with her father all those years. He had given her mother enough nightmares to last several lifetimes.

She both loved and hated her father. He treated her well, but he was a degenerate like the rest of his mobster friends, and it cost him in the end. He lived the last years of his life afraid, and hiding in dingy apartments on the back streets of towns he hated. The problem was, he had taken her along for the ride. She hated him for that, but she hated the mob worse. Especially Tito Martelli. If she never saw another Italian for the rest of her life, it would be too soon.

Signs for Hershey flashed on the side of the road. New fears stirred inside her. Would Tito be waiting? Had he found out what she was doing? Would she open her apartment door and find a guy with a gun? She said a quick prayer. Her life was in God's hands now.

And Tito's.

TITO GOT A GUN from his closet and headed for the door, only stopping when Manny talked sense into him. "You don't know anything. Calm down, and we'll figure this out."

"I'm gonna kill Chicky and Donnie."

Manny grabbed his arm and led him to the kitchen. "It's not their fault. Who could have figured she'd be that smart? You got to admit, she pulled a fast one." He walked to the sink and got water. "Why not let her go? If Carlo is dead, it makes no difference."

"How do I know Carlo's dead? Besides, I don't want a goddamn sword hanging over my head like that Greek."

"You mean the Sword of Damocles?"

"Yeah, that's the one."

"Give the kid a break. She lost her parents. Now she's got you on her ass."

"She wouldn't have if she hadn't called. I'd damn near forgotten about her and her father both."

"That's bullshit, Tito." Manny shook his head. "What would *you* do? If you were broke. Needed money and were afraid to go anywhere. I'd do the same thing." Manny grabbed a piece of fruit from the table. "I'm telling you, Tito, I'd let her go."

"That's why you're not running this crew." Tito stared at him. "You know how long it took me to make that much money coming up? Long fuckin' time. And I ain't giving it up to some broad for nothing."

Manny shrugged. "So what do you want us to do?"

"Find her."

CHAPTER 39

DNA DOESN'T LIE

Brooklyn—Current Day

Frankie brushed the snow from his cashmere coat and kicked a dusting off his Moreschi shoes. Fucking goddamn cold weather. He hated snow more than anything, even more than his Irish father and his Sicilian mother, both of whom scarred him for life. He should have gone to Miami or Houston, anyplace where it didn't snow.

He lit a smoke then sat on the stoop outside of Donnie Amato's house, careful not to tear his pants. Frankie dreaded the thought of sitting on cold, rough concrete, but he'd have no more contamination of crime scenes. Kate would be there soon. He'd let her have the first look. Soon a car came down the block, pulling up to the curb at a crawl.

Has to be Mazzetti. He drives like an old woman.

Lou Mazzetti moved up the sidewalk even slower than he'd pulled to the curb.

"Hey, Lou, you got lead in your ass today?"

Mazzetti took the last drag on a smoke before tossing it aside. "Didn't figure Donnie was in any rush from what I heard." He sat on the stoop next to Frankie. "Hit me with a smoke, Donovan."

"You just threw one out."

"Yeah, well, I'm old."

"What the hell does that have to do with anything?"

"Us old people just don't give a shit." He held his hand out, waiting.

"Goddamn nuisance is what you are," Frankie said, but he gave him a smoke.

Kate pulled up a few minutes later, popping out of the car with an exuberance difficult to imagine for a medical examiner—not an occupation Frankie associated with good moods.

"Good afternoon, gentlemen. Waiting for me?"

"Damn right," Frankie said. "I'm not about to have my DNA on another scene without witnesses. If Morreau gets hold of that before I clear it…"

Kate stopped and looked at him. "Frankie, I have to turn it in, and the report goes out tomorrow."

Frankie shrugged. "If I get fired, I'll make you feel bad."

"You're top shit," Lou said, and used Frankie's shoulder to raise himself up.

"When are you retiring?" Kate asked

"About a hundred years from now. Can't afford to before then." Lou offered a hand to Frankie.

"When I need you to help me up, just shoot me."

"Be happy to," Lou said, and walked in with Kate.

The odor hit them as soon as the door opened. "Jesus Christ," Lou said, and ducked back outside.

Frankie turned back too. "Goddamn." He held a handkerchief over his mouth and nose. "Kate, you alive in there?"

"Sissies."

"She's right," Lou said. "We're pussies."

Lou went in, holding his breath. Frankie followed, unwrapping the white silk scarf from his neck and using it to cover his mouth.

Kate was across the room, stooping to examine Donnie's genital area. "Holding your breath will only help you for about a minute at best, boys. And if your lungs are as bad as I think, probably less. Might as well get it over with and take a long, deep breath." After she said that, she inhaled deeply.

Lou looked at Frankie then back to Kate. "Screw you."

"I don't think you have the stamina, Detective. I've seen you climb stairs."

"Well fuck you, then."

"Ah, here we go, the male genital response mechanism."

"Fuck you twice now."

Kate laughed. "Now you are into *extreme* fantasizing."

Lou laughed until his sides hurt. "You're getting awfully close to Donnie's dick, aren't you?"

"Jealous?"

"I could show you better."

Kate turned to him wearing a smirk. "Even burnt and shriveled up, I think I've got a better specimen here."

"Ouch. That's cruel. I give up."

Kate looked up at Frankie. "I better not find any of your semen down here, Donovan."

"I ought to kick your ass," Frankie said.

"You ought to do *something* with my ass, but *kicking* is not what I had in mind." She paused. "Rhymed with it, though."

Lou coughed. "I didn't know this was an X-rated investigation. If you two need the bedroom…"

"I've tried keeping Donovan in bed before, but he won't have it." Kate reached down and pulled something off the floor. "Gum anyone?"

Frankie looked closer and shook his head. "Did he set Donnie's balls on fire?"

"Everything." Kate stood up, eyes rolling. "One sadistic son-of-a-bitch. Set his feet on fire. His genitals. He also stuffed a cloth soaked in some flammable in his mouth and lit that." She nodded. "Look at the face."

Frankie winced. He'd seen it, but only as a glimpse.

"Sick fuck," Lou said.

"Guy must have done something really wrong," Frankie said.

Kate looked at him as if he were nuts and gestured toward the body. "*He* did something wrong?"

Frankie nodded. "For someone to do this. Whoever did it must have been pissed."

AFTER HER CREW GOT there, Kate finished up and left the scene to Frankie and Lou. There was the usual assortment of random evidence, including rat shit. Frankie looked in every room, went out back, even searched the basement, but there was no dead rat.

Lou was in the kitchen, leaning on the counter, when Frankie came down from the attic. "Hey, Donovan, we got a shitload of reporters outside."

"Don't tell them anything."

"I know that, but more importantly, you want to tell *me* what's going on?"

"Nothing."

"Nothing, my ass. You come into Nino's place and go ape shit over rat shit, then clam up on me. Now you're running around here looking for something that ain't here." Lou walked right up to him, face to face. "I'm asking as your partner. What's going on?"

Frankie raised his voice. "I said *nothing*, Detective. Got that?"

"I'll tell you what I got, *Detective*. According to Kate, we have your DNA at crime scenes where you didn't investigate. We got DNA underneath blood, which means it was there *before* the vics were killed." Mazzetti poked Frankie's chest with his finger. "You want to explain that to me? Because if it's not you leaving this evidence, who has *your* DNA?"

Frankie was silent for a few seconds. "All right, Lou. But this is you and me."

"Convince me."

Frankie told him about Nicky, about how he used to leave rat shit as a joke to let people know they were the ones who did the crime. And he told him about how Nicky and Tony put the rat in Tommy Flannagan's fridge. "If Nicky thinks someone betrayed him, he could do this. Maybe. And he could easily have my DNA."

Lou stood there, arms crossed, staring at him. "That's it? Rat shit?" He laughed so hard, he started choking. "There's rat shit in every home in New York. I got it in my house."

Frankie stood still, lips pursed, fist clenched. "There was also a dead rat in the fridge at Nino's."

"You're basing your hunches on dead rats? You're too stupid to be a detective."

"Hey, Mazzetti, remind me not to eat at your house. I don't like rat-shit pasta."

"Try it sometime," Lou said, and headed for the door. "I'm outta here."

Frankie double-checked everything, but there were no dead rats. He leaned against the kitchen counter, pondering.

Suppose Lou is right. What if all this is just bullshit? Then Frankie thought of the crime scene and how Tony had squirted lighter fluid down Timmy Benson's pants one time to scare him. Frankie didn't want to tell Lou about that. No sense in bringing Tony Sannullo into the picture—not yet.

Frankie walked out of Donnie Amato's house and into a wall of reporters.

Tom Mason, Channel Three, shoved his mic forward. "Detective Donovan, is this a mob hit?"

"No comment," Frankie said, and kept walking.

"Does this have anything to do with Nino Tortella's murder?" That question came from Megan Simms.

"Can't say."

A flurry of shouts hit him, but Frankie held his ground. "Not now. When we're ready, we'll make a statement. Everyone will get a fair shot." He ducked into his car, locked the door and started the engine. He wanted nothing more than to get away from these leeches.

It took thirty minutes to get home, and ten more to find a parking spot. As he trudged along the sidewalk toward his apartment he saw a familiar face on the stoop—Shawna Pavic, a good Irish girl who had the misfortune of marrying an ill-tempered Russian. Frankie had a thing with her once, but he knew she was here to get a story, and that pissed him off. Even so, he might as well be civil. "Hey, Shawna. How's it going?"

"Hi, Frankie. Been waiting for you. Figured you'd be pissed when you saw me."

"No shit?"

"Yeah, no shit. Way I figured it, you would tell those other reporters to fuck off, and then you'd head home. About now I figure you'd want a bottle of wine—which I happened to bring—and maybe even some company." She stood, pulling a bottle of Chianti from a brown paper bag.

It brought a smile to Frankie's face. "Only one other thing would have gotten you an invite into my apartment."

"And I ain't doing that, Donovan. Excuse my pissy grammar."

Frankie laughed. "Come on up."

After settling in, they shared the bottle of Chianti, along with a few smokes. Frankie filled her in on the details. He kept back the parts no one knew, like how the killer spread mounds of DNA evidence at each scene. And he held back on the burning of Donnie's balls, but she still got some gory stuff. Enough to make her salivate.

"You tell anybody where you got this and I swear I'll hang you."

"My lips are sealed."

"Don't go that far. I'd like—"

She tensed. "Screw you. This is fair play."

"Don't worry. I work with you because I trust you. That's all."

She relaxed. "Thanks. You don't know how tough it is nowadays. When you're a sweet young thing just coming up, you're the star, but at my age, things start going bad." She took a long sip of wine. "That's the difference. Guys age and get promoted. Women? We disappear."

Frankie held up his glass. "To your health and long lasting beauty."

They tapped glasses. "And yours."

Shawna finished the last of her wine a few minutes later, then stood. "I've got to go. I hope you don't think..."

"Don't give it a thought. Go write your report."

She leaned in and kissed his cheek. "You're the best, Donovan."

"You got that right."

After Shawna left, Frankie refilled his glass and lit another cigarette. Another night alone. He took a long drag, then blew a few smoke rings. What was tomorrow—Thursday? He made a vow that tomorrow would be a new day for him. A day for change. If he changed something each day, he might even become the person he wanted to be. With that in mind, he called Kate Burns and asked her to dinner.

They met at a small Chinese restaurant by her house. Frankie asked for a table near the back. Throughout dinner he talked mostly of cases they had worked, but he never let it get personal. Kate refused dessert. He ordered a piece of carrot cake, and she got tea.

"It's been a long time, Frankie. This invite have anything to do with the DNA stuff we're facing?"

He held up his hand to stop her. "No way I'd do that to you." Her question hurt, but she had a right to wonder. It *had* been a long time. "Nothing to do with it; I promise. I just felt like going out, and I didn't want to ask Mazzetti." It was a weak attempt at humor and it didn't work.

Kate shifted in her seat. "Look, Frankie, I know we kid a lot, and I like you, but…"

"But you don't want to go to bed with me, is that what you're saying?"

"In a kinder, gentler way. Yes."

"Don't bother being kind, Kate."

She looked at her teacup for an inordinately long time, took a sip then stared. "The way you said that, I was waiting for the 'no one else has' line to follow."

He laughed. It was a cover-up laugh, but he did it well. "That line was there. I stopped myself before the words came out."

Kate sipped her tea, looking at him over the rim of the cup. "How's your little friend?"

Frankie's face lit. "Alex? He's great. That boy's a survivor."

"You really like him, don't you?"

"Somebody's got to love him."

"So Frankie Donovan has a heart after all." She smiled when she said it.

"Yeah, well…"

Kate reached over and took his hand. "You want to go somewhere and talk?"

"Why, you a good listener?"

"I've gotten to be. Remember, I work with dead people all day, so when I get someone who actually speaks, I pay attention."

Dessert came, and Frankie ate it in silence, then remained silent as Kate finished her tea. When he was counting money to pay the bill, he looked her in the eyes. "Kate, I think I'll pass on the offer to talk, but I do appreciate it. It's just…"

She nodded. "You're not a talker."

"Something like that, yeah."

They stood, and before leaving the table, she leaned over and kissed him on the cheek. "The offer stands. No expiration date." She looked at him with warm eyes. "Okay?"

"Sounds good," he said, and took her arm to walk her out.

Alex wasn't around when Frankie got home, so he watched a movie alone, but mostly, he thought about Donnie Amato. He was convinced that these killings had something to do with Tito Martelli, and Tito had a connection with the mysterious girl Nicky called about, and Tony worked for Tito. But what did Nicky have to do with Tito? Frankie knew from the FBI surveillance tapes that he didn't work for Tony. Nicky had been seen a few times going to the union hall, but he didn't believe for a minute that he worked there. He was going to see Tito about something. And what did Nicky have to do with the girl? The names kept rolling around in his head—Tito, Nicky, Tony, the girl. Frankie had to figure it out, and he had to do it fast. The bodies were piling up.

CHAPTER 40

MOTIVES

Brooklyn—Current Day

The day after Donnie Amato's body was discovered, Donovan was called into Morreau's office. "You wanted me, Lieu?"

Morreau picked up a piece of paper from his desk and held it before him. "I got a report from Kate Burns that your DNA is at the scene of several of these crimes."

"Lieu, I can explain—"

Lieutenant Morreau got up and shoved the door shut, his voice raised a level or two when he continued. "What is there to explain? We've got your DNA at a scene you never investigated. Give me one good explanation."

Frankie laid his gun on the desk, then set his badge beside it. "Here you go, Lieu. I'm done." He headed for the door.

"Donovan. Get your ass back here."

Frankie turned but kept his hand on the doorknob. "I've had it up to my ass with all of you. First the FBI and their goddamn wires, then all the bullshit you run. Now I'm a suspect on my own case. Fuck you."

"If you'll sit for a minute, I can explain," Morreau said.

Frankie was hesitant, but he sat.

"I'm sorry about the way I approached the DNA thing, but I had to see your reaction. You'd have done the same thing, and don't deny it."

Frankie nodded, and Morreau went on. "Kate *did* tell me about finding your DNA, but she also told me that my DNA was found too—and I know I wasn't on the scene. So unless you planted mine, or I planted yours, someone is fucking with us."

Frankie leaned forward. "And doing a damn good job of it."

Morreau held out his hand. "So, we good?"

"Yeah, Lieu, we're good. I guess."

"So tell me how this killer is getting our DNA to spread over crime scenes. And after that, tell me the real reason why you want off this case. You dumped that badge on my desk like it was hurting you."

The last bit took Frankie by surprise. He sat silent for a moment, thinking.

You're either a cop or a gangster. Make up your mind.

"I don't want off the case. I just want to get it solved. So if that's all you got, I'm heading out."

"No, that's not all," Morreau said. "I didn't want you on this to begin with, but the captain insisted on you as the lead. I've backed you even though I haven't seen shit. And you're walking around here like the god-damn Lone Ranger hoarding data on the case as if you're the only one that matters." He slammed his fist on the desk so hard the glass rattled. "That's not the way things work around here, Detective. Not in *my* fucking house they don't." Morreau looked ready to go ten rounds with someone.

Frankie had never seen him so pissed. He stood, but held the glare his lieutenant offered. "Don't worry. I'll get this solved."

"That's what I'm talking about. You hear yourself? *I'll* get it solved. Not *we'll* get it solved."

"Sorry. *We'll* get these damn cases solved."

"You'd better. Now get the fuck out of here. You spoiled my breakfast."

Frankie headed toward the door, but then stopped. *How did the killer get Morreau's DNA?*

"Lieu, you ever eat at any of the diners or donut shops close to where the victims lived or worked?"

He stared at Frankie as if he were nuts. "How the hell do I know?"

"Hang on a minute. I'll be right back."

He returned shortly with three folders. Frankie and Morreau looked up each address for work and home. When they got to Nino Tortella's work address, Morreau stopped. "There is a diner right by there," he said. "I eat breakfast there maybe once or twice a month."

Frankie left with a smile on his face. "I'm back on it, Lieu," he said, but then corrected himself. "*We*, Lieu, *we're* back on it."

CHAPTER 41

A BUSY YEAR

Brooklyn—20 Months Ago

Manny interrupted Tito's reading, risking his foul humor. Four months had passed, and there was still no sign of Gina or his money. "Boss, I got an idea a little while back. Remember that source we got that gets us cop-type information sometimes?"

Tito nodded.

"I had Gina's phone checked out. It was bought in Hershey, PA."

"She could have bought it there to throw us off."

Manny shrugged. "She *could* have, and I agree she did good with the Fed-Ex thing, so she's smart, but maybe she didn't know we could trace this. Just maybe, she thought a throwaway phone was invisible." Manny waited while Tito absorbed this. "Hershey, PA, isn't that big. Just a bunch of fuckin' chocolate and a few piles of manure. It's worth a shot."

Tito's head was already nodding. "Put Bobbie and Little T on this. And tell those assholes we sent to Baltimore to go too. I want every mall, hair salon, and—" Tito stopped when he saw Manny shaking his head. "What?"

"Churches," Manny said. "Gina won't miss Sunday mass. All you got to do is watch every Catholic church in the area, and you'll get her."

Tito thought for a minute, then jumped up and hugged him. "You're a genius."

"Yeah, no shit."

A FEW WEEKS LATER, while Tito Martelli ate his eggs, sipped on his cappuccino, and read the morning paper, Manny's heavy footsteps clomped across the dining room floor on the way to the kitchen. "We just got a call from Chicky. He says it's urgent."

"You got a different number? I don't want to talk on that one."

"He's got a clean phone." Manny tossed him a throwaway cell phone, then turned on the kitchen fan and a few other appliances. Tito had the place swept constantly, but just in case, the extra noise would provide enough "reasonable doubt" when listening to a conversation."

Tito grabbed the phone, then dialed the number Manny gave him. "Yeah?"

"Chicky?"

"We just spotted Gina going into church. Pretty as a picture she was, all dressed in her Sunday best."

"Stay with her, Chicky. If you lose her…"

"I don't lose nobody." There was a pause, then, "You want me to—"

Tito almost jumped out of his chair. "No." He paced the kitchen. "Find out where she lives and stay on her. I'll be in touch."

Tito handed the phone back to Manny then walked to the table and sat. He scraped up the last of the eggs and slid them onto his toast, then sat back to finish his cappuccino. "Manny, get me Johnny Muck."

"You got it."

CHAPTER 42

OATHS AND FRIENDS

Brooklyn—20 Months Ago

Tony pulled up to the union hall, late for his weekly meeting with Tito. Paulie sat in the seat next to him, playing with the radio. As Tony turned into the lot, Paulie pointed to a car just leaving. "Ain't that Nicky?"

Tony stared, suspicion burning through him. "Yeah, I think it is."

"It's good to have him back with us."

"Yeah," Tony said, and pulled up to the front. "Wait outside today, Paulie. Tito wants to go over some things with me."

"No problem, but hey, Tony, I been thinking, maybe you ought to tell Nicky about that money."

"The money I invested for him?"

"It's better he find out from you than someone else."

Tony stared off into the distance. "Tell you what, Paulie. Keep your mouth shut and let me decide how to do it."

Paulie shrugged. "Whatever you say."

Tony slammed the car door. This was the third time he'd seen Nicky with Tito in just a few months. What the hell was he doing here? Nicky told Tony he was a union rep, but union reps don't go see Tito. Tony took the steps into the hall two at a time, then made his way to the kitchen without a word to anyone, just a nod now and then in response to greetings. He poured some coffee, walked to the lounge and took a seat next to Manny.

Manny loved to watch the news and hated to be disturbed, so they sat in silence. Curiosity was eating at him, but Tony waited until the timing was right.

"Manny, what was Nicky doing here?"

He waved his hand without looking over. "Nothing."

"Nothing? He's here in the middle of the day, and it's nothing?"

Manny picked up a half a sandwich and took a bite, damn near finishing it. Then he took a long swig of water from a bottle on the table. "What, you worried about your job?"

"My job? What are you talking about?"

"I'm talking about Tito's got himself a new boy, that's what. Better watch your ass, Tony."

"Watch my ass? Get outta here. I taught Nicky everything he knows."

Manny laughed so hard he coughed. "Now I know you're nuts. You *really* better watch your ass if you think that." He slapped Tony on the back and stood. "I gotta go. I'll tell Tito you're here."

Tony got up and paced. Manny's taunt stayed with him. *That fuckin' Nicky is trying to steal my job.* Something had to be done about him anyway. Sooner or later, he'd find out about Angela.

MANNY WORE A FROWN as he came out of his meeting with Tito. He motioned for Tony to go in. "Hope your news is good."

Tony walked in, already tense. "Hey, Tito."

"Tony, tell me we made a lot of money last week."

"What's wrong, boss? Somebody giving you trouble?"

"Nothing."

Tony went to pour a drink, patting Tito on the back as he passed. "Don't tell me nothing's wrong. I've known you too long for that." He opened a bottle of brandy. "Want a drink?"

"If you're getting a drink, the news must be bad. Don't make me wait."

"Guess I'll have to be the one to brighten your day. We had a great week. Best one in two or three months. Paulie pulled through with a load of smokes; Jiggles did that airport deal; everybody came through."

"In that case, pour me a glass."

Tony poured him a drink and walked it over, sitting on the edge of a sofa across from Tito. "So what's going on? Who's giving my favorite boss all this trouble?"

Tito shrugged. "Some broad."

"A broad? What, you get her pregnant?"

He laughed. "God no. She's…I got to take care of her, that's all."

Tony thought for a minute, his brain churning. He was making a leap in his assumptions here, but why the hell else would Nicky be with Tito so often if he wasn't a shooter? Nicky sure as shit wasn't running any crews. If Tony was right, this would either make Nicky shine or show him up for the pussy he was. "Why not give it to Nicky?"

"He told you what he does?" Tito's brow furrowed.

"We're best friends," Tony said, and shrugged.

Tito finished the drink, set the glass on a coaster and shook his head. "I'm giving this to someone else."

"Suit yourself. All I'm saying is if you really want to test the guy, give him this one."

"I don't need to test him."

"I don't doubt that. Remember, I'm the one who brought him to you. Just—"

"Just what?"

"Forget it. I doubt he'd do it anyway."

"What the hell are you talking about?" Tito asked, leaning forward. "Nicky does whatever I tell him to."

"Hey, Tito, forget it. You're better off getting someone else."

Tito stood and walked to the kitchen. "That's what I said to begin with."

Tony said nothing. By the time Tito returned, the whole idea of Nicky was eating at him.

"Why do you think he wouldn't do this?"

Tony had the remote in his hand. He jumped from channel to channel until he found a football game. "Forget about it. He probably would."

"I don't want to forget about it." Tito pulled on Tony's shirt. "Tell me why you said that."

Tony sighed. "Not that I doubt what you say, but there's no way Nicky would take out a broad."

"Why not?"

"It's not him, that's all. Nicky Fusco wouldn't kill a girl if Jesus Christ came down and told him to." Tony finished the brandy, set the glass down then continued watching the game.

Tito stared, assessing Tony the way only Tito could. "You worried?"

"Why should I be worried? I just gave you the best report in months."

Tito stood and walked around. "You *should* be worried. I'm happy with Nicky. He makes me a lot of money and handles a lot of problems. But I can't have a guy I can't trust." Tito wore his be-careful-what-you-say smile, the vicious one. "Of course you *know* that, don't you? Which is why you brought this up." Tito nodded to himself as if working out a problem in his head. "Does Nicky know you hate him so much?"

When Tony didn't answer, Tito paced some more, then lowered his head as he raised his eyebrows and stared at Tony. "You're rolling big dice here. If I give this to Nicky, he'll either be a hero or a corpse."

Tony shrugged, then got up to get more brandy. "I'm sure he'll do fine."

CHAPTER 43

HAPPY BIRTHDAY, TONY

Brooklyn—20 Months Ago

Frankie drove through heavy traffic on his way in. Not abnormal, but when done every day, a person prayed for those miraculous days when, for some unexplainable reason, there were few people on the road. Today was not one of them. Morreau said he had a new assignment for Frankie. He was both excited and worried, especially now that Nicky was back. Officially Nicky was a union rep for the plumbers, but Frankie didn't buy that for a minute. He didn't want to know what Nicky really did, but he suspected it wasn't good, and his hunches were usually on target. The problem was that his intuition got skewed when dealing with friends.

A half an hour later, he pulled into the parking lot. Ted greeted him with raised eyebrows and a shake of the head. The kind of look that said, "I wouldn't go up there if I were you." Frankie nodded. What the hell was happening now?

He took the steps two at a time, as he always did, but his "good morning" to Carol was strained and unfriendly.

Her eyes pointed to the ceiling as she whispered, "Top brass and Feds."

Fuck me. Despite the warning, he walked into Morreau's office wearing a smile. "Morning, Lieutenant." Frankie almost puked when he saw

Harding sitting in a chair against the wall, a smug look on his face. Maddox sat next to him. Worse, though, was the sight of Captain Jamison. *What is going on?*

Morreau stood. "Detective, I believe you know Agents Harding and Maddox, and of course, Captain Jamison."

Jamison was a wasp from way back, even had a pointed nose like a stinger to prove it. Frankie nodded. "Good to see you, Captain."

Harding stood, eager to take the lead. The asshole's personality was as stiff and inflexible as his name implied. "Good to see *you* again, Detective."

Frankie knew it had irked Harding when he wouldn't do what Harding wanted last time. Considering the captain was there, this looked to be revenge. "Agent Harding," he said, as they shook hands.

Captain Jamison didn't bother to stand. "Donovan, we've set up a special task force in conjunction with the FBI. Agent Harding has asked for you to be in on it."

Harding wore a shit-eating grin. Even his eyes were laughing. "Welcome aboard, Detective Donovan."

Frankie turned to Morreau. "What's going on?"

Morreau looked upset, but he also looked defeated. "Officially, you'll be assigned to homicide, but you'll be working with Agent Harding and Agent Maddox."

The hair on the back of Frankie's neck tingled. "Doing what?"

"Organized Crime Unit, Detective. We'll be putting bad guys away."

Frankie stood a little straighter, shook his head. "Don't want it."

"Not your choice," Morreau said. "It's been decided. You have connections with key people in Tito Martelli's organization, and we need Tito Martelli."

The room was closing in on Frankie and he didn't like it. If he agreed to work with them he'd be betraying his friends; if he declined, a desk assignment waited. "No way, Lieu."

Jamison shot up from his seat. "Donovan." He pulled out a folder. "Agent Harding has pictures of you meeting with men from Tito Martelli's organization several times during the past six months. If you aren't will-ing to help, I'll be forced to wonder about your loyalty."

"I can't do what you're asking, Captain."

Jamison got real close to him. "Do what you're told, or go on suspension."

Suspension! The threat rang in his ears, but in the back of his mind all he heard were words from long ago—a bunch of kids holding their hands together and yelling *friendship and honor.* "Suspend me," Frankie said, and started for the door.

"Walk out that door, and your career is over," Jamison said. "I'll see to it."

Frankie stopped. Stared at the door. He thought for a minute, then turned back, a feeling in his gut like a knife twisting. "What do I have to do?" he asked as he turned to face them.

TWO WEEKS LATER, AFTER indoctrination into the absolutely boring world of the FBI and their bullshit procedures, Frankie sat in a room being wired up. They wanted him to go to lunch with Tony and Paulie and tape them.

"You got it, Detective?" Harding asked. "Any reason you suspect they're onto you, give the signal."

Frankie scoffed. "Your signal is ridiculous. If I'm having lunch with Tony and Paulie and spit out a sentence that contains 'yellow scarf' they'll shoot me for the hell of it."

Harding didn't seem like he'd mind. "You have a better idea?"

"How about I say, 'She's got a nice ass.'"

"You are a crude—"

Frankie left the office laughing. "See you boys later."

FRANKIE DIDN'T WANT TO get Tony or Suit in trouble, even though they were mobsters.

And friends, that damn oath reminded him. For twenty-five years it had haunted him. He thought about the rules he'd be breaking as a cop, the threat from his captain, about what could happen to him if he didn't follow orders.

I'm not going to lose my job because of them. He rode along for a few miles, reinforcing his decision. No way would he risk his job. He worked too hard to get there. The closer he got to Cataldi's, the more the decision weighed on him.

He made two stops on the way to Cataldi's and walked in carrying a shopping bag. He was five minutes late, which would bother Nicky, but no one else.

Suit stood to greet him, arms open wide. Frankie set the bag on the table.

"What's in the bag?"

"I hope you didn't forget," Frankie said.

"What?"

Frankie handed Tony the bag. "Happy birthday."

Tony looked at him as if he were crazy. "It's not my birthday, Bugs. You know that."

Bugs laughed. "I know it, sure, but you know how Billy Flannagan is—he sends one present a year, and you never know who it's going to or when." Tony looked confused, then Frankie said, "This year it's your turn, Tony. Just like in sixth grade."

Billy Flannagan had ratted them out in sixth grade—Bugs was sending a signal: someone was watching, or listening, or both.

"Open it up," Suit said. "I gotta see what I missed."

Tony unwrapped it, threw the paper into the bag, then opened the box. Inside was a silk tie covered with the map of Ireland. He held the tie up for the others to see. "Would you look at this shit? Mick bastard." He passed the tie around, then opened the card that came with it. On the outside it looked like a plain birthday card, but inside was what Tony wanted to see.

Start laughing, Tony.

I'M WIRED.

Your friend forever,

Bugs

Tony laughed until he choked, his fist pounding on the table. The waiters knew them by now; otherwise, they might have rushed to see what was wrong. Tony handed the card to Paulie. "You gotta see this one. That goddamn Billy is hilarious."

Paulie laughed then passed it along to Nicky, who passed it to Bugs.

"I'm hungry as shit," Paulie said.

"Manicotti is great here," Tony said.

"I'll tell you what I could go for—a sub from Casapulla's."

Paulie hit the table with his fist. "Goddamn, Bugs, did you have to bring that up?" He laughed. "I'd kill somebody for a Casapulla's sub."

"Or a cheesesteak." Nicky looked as if he would get in a car and drive down there right now.

"Either one," Paulie said.

They were still talking about subs and steaks when the waiter came to take orders. Tony and Frankie both got the manicotti. Paulie ordered cheese ravioli.

"What about you, Nicky?" Frankie asked.

"Tortellini."

"Can't believe you didn't get the manicotti," Tony said.

Nicky just shook his head. "Nothing compares to Mamma Rosa's. I never order things she made for us."

"She was a pain in the ass," Tony said.

"Bullshit." Nicky damn near came over the table after him.

Tony waved his hand. "Yeah, I know, to you she was a saint, but let me tell you—"

"Nothing to say, Tony."

Tony downed the rest of his drink and slammed the glass on the table. "She wasn't *your* mother, Nicky. When the hell are you going to learn that?"

Nicky stared at him for a long time, then Paulie spread his arms across the table, separating them. "Mamma Rosa is dead," Paulie said. "I know she was your mother, Tony, but we all loved her. So for once in your life— shut the fuck up."

Tony stared for too long, but then his anger disappeared. "You're right, Paulie," he said, then turned to Nicky. "I'm sorry. I know you meant well." He laughed then. "I'll tell you what—I hope God listened to all your prayers. If he did, my mother went straight to heaven."

Nicky took a deep breath and visibly relaxed. "Non-stop."

They made small talk during the meal, Nicky telling them about his union rep job, and Frankie talking about his cases, and how things were going to shit. Espresso followed the meal, then Tony ordered limoncello. He raised the glass and they all joined above the center of the table.

"Friendship and honor," Tony said.

"Friendship and honor," they all repeated, and gulped down the cellos.

"Nectar of the Gods," Paulie said as he set his glass down. The look on his face was semi-orgasmic. "One more, then I've got to go."

They sipped the next drink, savoring it. "This has been fun," Frankie said.

Nicky pushed his chair back, reaching for money as he stood.

"Put your money away," Tony said. "It's no good here. And hey, Bugs. Call me sometime. I ain't been swimming in a while."

Bugs nodded. He knew that the reference to swimming meant when they could meet without the wire. "I know," Frankie said. "Not like back home. See you guys later." As he left the restaurant, he worried over his decision. He could have just ended his career; on the other hand, there was no way he could betray his friends. Not like this. All he had to do now was make sure the Feds didn't catch him.

Fuck the Feds. They can do their own work.

CHAPTER 44

A NEW ASSIGNMENT

Brooklyn—20 Months Ago

I got the call on my special cell phone, the one I would throw away after today's meeting. Nobody knew where I lived. Nobody knew what I did except Manny, Tito, and Johnny Muck. Nobody but Tony and a few others knew I was even alive. That's the way I liked it. It pissed Tito off that I wouldn't tell him where I lived, but the last thing I wanted was Tito Martelli dropping in unexpectedly. If he came for a visit, he wouldn't be bringing wine.

I let the phone ring two more times. "Hello?"

"We need to talk."

"You know where the parking garage is on Seventh?"

"Yeah, sure."

"Go park on any floor above the fifth, then take the elevator to the third. There will be a blue Camry near the elevator. Keys in the rear wheel, driver's side. Instructions will be inside."

"You keep getting more cautious." Tito laughed after he said it. "I like that. Keeps both of us on our toes."

"Glad you see it that way."

"I need help."

"Tell me when we meet."

I WATCHED FROM INSIDE a van I rented. Got there early to make sure Tito wasn't followed. He got off the elevator and looked around until he spotted the Camry. I kept it in long-term parking for occasions like this. It was cheap enough for the security it provided.

Tito got the keys, then opened the front door. He pulled out the envelope, read it, then threw it back on the seat, obviously cursing. It had instructed him to go back to the fifth floor. I wanted to see if anyone on this floor was watching or waiting for him to signal them. He locked the door, put the keys back and headed to the elevator, never even looking around.

Good, he's alone.

As he was about to get in the elevator, I beeped the horn, pulled up to him.

"Jump in."

Frustration showed. "What the hell, Nicky? You getting paranoid?" He got in the front seat. "Park this thing so we can talk."

I pulled into an empty spot. "What do you need, Tito?"

"Special one. And she's gotta go quick."

"She?"

"She stole money from me."

"Never killed a woman before. That's against my rules."

"Fuck rules. Besides, she's not a woman; she's a thief."

"Get Johnny. I don't like it."

"If I wanted Johnny, I wouldn't be here. Get your head out of your ass. This is business." Tito lit a smoke. Took a few drags. "Listen, this isn't some goddamn mom with kids in little league. This is a hard-core, blackmailing thief who was smart enough to steal a couple hundred grand from us. She knew what she was buying into and she sure as shit knew the consequences."

I sat silent, wondering if I could take out a woman. The money would help. It would be a nice addition to the nest egg I was building; besides, if she stole from the mob...

"How much?"

"How much? Four hundred large."

"That's a lot of money, Tito, but I meant how much for me?"

Tito laughed. "So that's what this negotiating is about. I forgot what a cold-hearted fuck you were." He remained silent for a minute, then said, "Don't worry. Be plenty in it for you."

"I like plenty, but I need to know how much *plenty* is." My dealings with Tito and those like him taught me to be suspicious. "Why so much? She dangerous?"

Tito looked around nervously, as if he was being watched. "She might be under surveillance." He was very quick to add, "I'm not sure, probably not, but…possibly."

"Who?"

More silence.

"Who, Tito?"

"Feds."

I laughed. "Now we get to it. That's why this is rich." I stared. "So how much?"

"I don't know. Double…fuck, triple. How about that?" He mumbled something else, then said, "What's the big deal? Feds are probably already watching you because of Tony."

"But now we'll have two teams of Feds. Makes it tough." I thought for a minute. "Get Johnny to do this. I don't need the Feds knocking on my door."

Tito waited the requisite amount of time, then sighed. "I don't *want* Johnny to do it."

Inside, I smiled all over. Either he really didn't want Johnny, or Johnny had turned it down. He was stuck with me. "Tell you what, Tito. I'll do it, but I keep whatever she has left from the money she took. And—"

"You're nuts."

"That's not all," I said, cutting him off. "If she has less than a hundred, that's what I get."

"A hundred large. You *are* nuts."

I slipped the car into gear and backed up. "Get Muck. The only reason I'd do this is to retire."

"Hold on a minute." Tito looked at me with anger in his eyes, then laughed. "You'll never retire."

I eyed him. "You want me to do this or not?"

"You're a cock-sucker."

"Yeah, I know. You got details?"

Tito handed me an envelope. "I need this done quick."

"I don't do things quickly."

Tito glared. "Make an exception. Now take me to my car so I can get the hell out of here."

As I DROVE HOME, I mentally prepared my trip. That night I studied the material Tito gave me—looked at her picture, memorized her phone number and address—then burned everything in a pot and carried the ashes to the dumpster. I packed before going to bed. Hershey wasn't far, so I decided to drive; besides, planes left trails.

When I got there, I called Donnie and Chicky and told them I was in the area. They'd seen me around the union hall, but had no idea who I was, so I hoped to keep out of sight. I got the address of the woman—Gina, I now knew her name to be—and her place of work, as well as the name she used: Debbie Small.

"What else you need?" Chicky asked.

"Nothing. You can go home now."

I sensed the anger over the phone. "Maybe we should—"

"Tito gave me permission to kill every one of you if you interfered with my job. If you're still here in twenty minutes I'll consider that interference."

"Yeah. All right. Fuck you. How about that?"

"That would be fine. Just get out of the area."

I went to bed that night in a small motel room outside of Hershey. For the first time in a long while I dreamed of what I'd do when I retired.

THE MORNING CRASHED IN on me, sunlight bursting through open curtains, frightening me awake. First days of surveillance were critical. They set the tone of the entire assignment.

I got to the school early. It was a two-story brick building that occupied an entire block, perched on a hill across from a church. The north side had three sets of double-doors, but only one door on the other three sides. A park bordered the west and a woods on the south. I made a mental note to see if the woods offered a good escape route. Rows of old brick homes bordered the east—row-houses filled with too many kids, and parents who didn't make enough money.

A group of young boys, maybe eight or nine years old, were walking up the street to school. I rolled the car window down. "Do you know where Ms. Small's class is?"

"Second floor," one of them said. "Third room down the hall."

"Thanks." I turned left at the corner. Her room was on the side near the woods, by the south door. I followed the streets, hugging the woods until I got to where it ended. Must have been almost half a mile deep, and it was bordered on the other side by a small, winding road. Two blocks away was the back side of a grocery store and a few small shops.

Perfect.

I got breakfast, parked the car and walked through the woods, binoculars in hand. The paths were worn from continual use. I found a tree stump and sat there to scan the area, see what *I* could see, and, who might be able to see me. It took about five minutes to spot Chicky and his guys sitting in a car up the street. What the hell were they thinking—three hoodlum-looking guys parked across from a school? I should have reported them as child molesters but I preferred knowing where they were. I figured Tito sent them to check on me.

But why? He's never done this before.

All morning I watched Gina. At recess I got to see her at work. More so at lunch. She was good with the kids—playing, laughing, disciplining. When school let out, she held their hands and escorted them across the street. This wasn't what I wanted to see. The other assignments were…well, they were guys that needed killing. Guys who betrayed the mob, drug dealers, even murderers. I did them a favor by taking them out early, and mercifully. This though… this was different.

When Gina left, I put the binoculars away and walked back to the car, checking to make sure no one was watching. I drove around for a while, then had dinner at a small restaurant. I ordered a steak, which I seldom did, and afterwards, wished I hadn't. Nothing seemed right today.

After driving around some more, I went back to the motel and watched television, then tried to read. Nothing would take my mind from the horrible feeling in my gut, the one Sister Thomas told us about in second grade. She said God put that feeling there so we knew when we were doing wrong. If we got that feeling, we needed to stop and think about what we were doing and whether it was right.

Goddamn you, Sister Thomas.

As I thought about what to do, it came to me. Whenever I had problems in the past, Sister Mary Thomas had been there to help. Sometimes she didn't know she helped me, but she did. I said the hell with it. Wilmington was only an hour and a half away. Resolving to go allowed me to sleep, though I did wake up before six and was on the road by six-thirty.

By eight I was standing in front of good old St. Elizabeth's.

CHAPTER 45

ADVICE

Wilmington—20 Months Ago

All the way to Wilmington I worried. Not about the assignment, and not even about facing Sister Thomas. I worried about Angie. What if I saw her? What if she saw me? I hated Tony for telling me about her the way he did, but I hated her more, and not just for running off and getting married. I hated her for making me love her so much.

St. Elizabeth's loomed before me. My stomach churned. I found myself wondering what the hell I was afraid of. Me, Nicky the Rat, afraid to face a nun, and an old one at that. With a deep breath, I opened the doors and climbed the steps. I almost hoped she wasn't there; then I could turn around, drive back to Hershey and finish the job.

Six steps led me to a small concrete landing, then six more, followed by eight. I pushed open the double doors at the top. Her class was the first one on the right. I peeked inside. I hadn't given much thought to what I'd do once I got here. What the hell was I thinking? Class was going on. As I turned to leave, Father Tom grabbed me by the arm.

"If it isn't Nicky Fusco. How long has it been?"

A smile came naturally. "Father Tom, good to see you."

"What brings you back, Nicky?"

I hesitated. "Nothing. Just…" I knew my face was flushing. "Actually, I was in the area and thought I'd come by to see Sister Mary Thomas."

"Wait here. I'll get her."

"No need, Father. I'll come back."

Father Tom shook his head. "No you won't."

She came out a moment later, looking not much older than the last time I'd seen her, and still with the permanent smile on her face and gleam in her eye. Wrapped around her left wrist were the ever-present rosary beads, ready to draw and inflict forgiveness on unsuspecting sinners.

Sister Mary Thomas opened her arms and embraced me. "Nicky Fusco. My favorite student."

I blushed again. "Sister Thomas, you say that to everyone."

"You should never accuse a nun of lying."

"You're right. Sorry, Sister."

"So what brings you back? I thought you were in New York."

I paused. Probably for too long. "Down here for a few days on work."

She grabbed my hand, led me toward the door. "Why don't we walk, Nicky? The Lord has blessed us with a nice day. He must have known you were coming."

To object would be useless. Once Sister Mary Thomas had her mind made up, she was worse than Mamma Rosa. "How have you been, Sister? How's Sister Theresa?"

"Sister Theresa passed away last year, I'm sorry to say. We will miss her company and wit." She sighed. "As to me, I'm fine. I have another good class, filled with good students."

I smiled as we made our way down the stairs. Optimism had found a permanent home in Sister Mary Thomas, probably coming with that smile she carried around.

"And you, Nicky? How have you been?"

"Great. I've been lucky." I held the doors open for her.

She squeezed my hand, stepped off the curb and started across the street to the park. "Yes, lucky. You lost your mother at birth. Your father at fourteen, and Rosa Sannullo went to God a few years later."

I didn't say anything. What could I say?

She sat under a giant old oak on a bench that had been there forever. Concrete sides, with small wood planks for a seat and a back, it had lasted for many years and had heard many tales—lovers' quarrels, proposals, family fights, kids plotting, girls gossiping. Sister Thomas pulled me down beside her. She stared until I held her gaze.

"Your father was a good man, Nicky. He raised a good son."

I fought my emotions, but lost, tears forming in my eyes. "Sister, you don't know." I shook my head. "Sometimes I wish I could start over."

She pulled my hand to her. I slid across the bench some. "Would you do things differently?"

I turned my head. Wouldn't let her see the tears. "I would. I truly believe I would."

"Then do it," she said. "You can never go back, Niccolo, but you can always start fresh."

"Sister, you don't—"

"I don't know what you've done?" She patted the back of my hand. "I feel like I have raised a thousand children, though I am empty from having none of my own. My children have become priests, cops, carpenters, bricklayers, plumbers, nurses, teachers—even murderers." She caught the surprised look in my eyes. "Yes, even murderers, and yet, there was good in all of them." She fought tears. "Do you remember Tommy Dougherty?"

I nodded. "The one who killed those girls up in Boston?"

"Yes, that's him. I spoke with him after he was sentenced." She paused, choking back tears, almost as if she had personally failed Tommy. "He never asked for forgiveness, at least, not from me. All he talked about was what if he had made another decision that night? He looked me in the eyes and he said, 'Sister, what if I had turned *left* at the stop sign instead of right, I would have never seen those girls and offered them a ride.' And then, Nicky, he took a big sigh. I felt his pain. He said, 'Sister, I truly believe that if I had not seen those girls that night, I would have never done anything like this. But now look what

I've done to my family."" She stood. Walked around a bit. "Think on it. Make your decisions count."

"Sister, you don't know what I've—"

"Niccolo Fusco. If you want to go to confession, find Father Tom. If you want to feel sorry for yourself, go down to Schmitty's and drown your sorrows in beer or whiskey—you'll have plenty of company. But if you want to *do* something with your life, make up your mind to change and then stick to it." She grabbed hold of my shoulders and shook. "*God* knows what you've done, boy, and you're not dead yet. He must be keeping you alive for something. Go *earn* this new life you've been granted. Start tomorrow on a new path. Hell. Don't wait for tomorrow, start *today*."

I got up from the bench and paced, cracking my knuckles and biting my lip. "Sister, you would be so ashamed if—"

She held up her hand. "I told you, if you want to confess, go to confession."

"I don't go to confession, Sister. Can't trust them."

"Yet you trust me?"

"Of course."

She remained silent while I continued pacing and cracking my knuckles. Finally, she faced me. "Don't do anything until tomorrow. Promise me that."

"Why?"

"I have to think about something. I have to pray tonight for guidance."

"Sister, I—"

"Promise me, Nicky."

"All right, Sister. I'll see you tomorrow." As I walked away, I cursed myself for not asking about Angie. It seemed as if every emotion was telling me to go see her. Say hi, if nothing else. But emotions held me back. Pride had shoved a cantaloupe down my throat, and I couldn't get past that. And past jealousy. All these years, and I was still jealous of the guy she married. Most of all though, I was envious of the life she had—married, with a child and a house. The kind of life we planned so long ago. I shook my head as I walked to the car.

Screw Angie. I'll make my own life.

Sister Mary Thomas prayed that night, knelt on the hard tile floors in the convent chapel and prayed for hours. When she finished, she went to her room and slept. Tomorrow was going to be a long day. This was a truth kept hidden for too long.

CHAPTER 46

A LONG-LOST LETTER

Wilmington—20 Months Ago

I was waiting for Sister Mary Thomas when she walked across the street from the convent. She came, long black robes flowing with each stride, her face gleaming in the morning sun. I couldn't see her smile, but I pictured it, knew it was there. That gave me comfort.

"Good morning, Sister."

"Get your car, Nicky. You're coming with me."

"Where?"

"To the bank. Bring your briefcase."

We drove in silence—not quite silence—but small talk all the way to the bank. "What are we doing here?"

"Be patient."

She took me to a safe-deposit box, opening it once the assistant left us alone. Inside was twenty thousand dollars in cash and a manila envelope, sealed at the top. "What the hell is this?" I asked. "Where did this money come from?"

"There should be a letter."

I started to open it, but she stopped me. "Not here. Bring it with you."

Curiosity burned inside of me, but I grabbed the cash and the envelope and put them in the briefcase. Once inside the car, I reached for the envelope.

She stopped me again. "Wait until I leave."

"Sister, what's going on?"

"You will see in good time. Do as I ask, please?"

I nodded. What else could I do?

We made more small talk until we got back to the school, then she opened the door to leave. She turned to me, smiled, but it was a false one, the first one of those I'd ever seen from her. Then she kissed me on the cheek. "Goodbye, Nicky."

The way she said it made it feel permanent. I watched her go, feeling sorry and sad at the same time. "Goodbye, Sister," I said as she closed the door.

I thought about driving back to Hershey before I read the letter, but I couldn't, so I parked in a nearby lot. My heart raced as I slid my finger along the edge of the envelope, careful not to rip anything. Once opened, I stared inside. There were a few keys and a letter.

> *Nicky, my son.*
>
> *If you are reading this, that means I am dead, probably long dead. It also means that Sister Mary Thomas is either dead or that she felt a burning need to give you this letter.*
>
> *My heart breaks considering either of those situations. I would like to say that if she is dead, I would be seeing her soon, but she will be going to a place I can never enter. I will have to be satisfied living my eternal life without her, as I had to live my physical life without her.*

I put the letter down. Wiped away tears. What the hell was going on? Did Pops and Sister Thomas… no, it couldn't be. She treated me like shit early on, was so tough on me…and why would Pops say he'd be in hell? It didn't make sense. I shook my head, picked the letter back up.

I'm sure you're wondering about the money—where did it come from? How did I get so much? Why did I wait this long to give it to you—you could have used it.

Lots of questions, I know. I'll answer them one by one.

First about sweet Sister Mary Thomas. Her real name is Concetta Panelli—beautiful name, isn't it? She and I were best friends growing up. Concetta was never beautiful in the sense that most people think of beauty, but after getting to know her, I thought she was the most wondrous person in the world. And she was so smart—but you already know that. We did everything together. Not actually everything. She kept her honor, but we had more love than most people experience all of their lives. We made plans to marry. To have a house that would be full of wonderful children like you. And we spoke of living to ages people only dreamed of, spending every day in bliss.

So what happened?

Foolish man that I was, I felt I needed to provide her with a lot of money, and things that I now know she would have never cared about. At the time, though, I was young, and young people do stupid things. I wish I had known Rosa Sannullo then. She always said money ruins love. I believe now that she was right.

To make money, I started working for the wrong people. One night I killed someone. After that, killing became part of the job. Soon, it became the job. I was good at it. The best, they said, but it ruined my life, because it took Concetta from me. When she found out what I'd done, she would have no part of me. What made me saddest, though, was that it drove her to the convent. She should have lived a life with someone. Should have raised children. But because of me, she is locked away behind tall doors every night, and she covers her beautiful body in black robes. I am ashamed of what I have done.

Later, I met your mother, and though at first it might have seemed a compromise to the love I had for Concetta—and perhaps even an act against her for becoming a nun—I learned to love your mother with a passion that I felt I could not feel for a woman again. Soon, she became my life. When she died, I knew it was God punishing me. He had taken the two most important people in the world away from me; however, he did leave me with you.

Rosa Sannullo helped me in the early days, always there with her advice and her superstitions, but always there, too, with her love. She is a good woman. A kind woman. Shortly after you were born, Concetta came to me. It was the first time we talked in many years. She never cried that day. But she looked me in the eyes and told me. "Dante, you have a baby now. I want you to quit what you are doing and take care of that baby."

At first I was angry that she would even say such a thing, but then I realized she was trying one last time to save my soul, though that chance was long gone, believe me. Even God can only forgive so much. But for her, for the Concetta I once loved, I swore I would do it. So from that day on, I quit. I told the people that I worked for that I was retiring and would never have anything to do with them. They didn't like it, but they never said anything. They gave me a job in the union, and I went back to my old trade of laying stone and bricks. A good occupation. One that sweats the bad out of you, or so Rosa Sannullo always said.

So now you have the story. I don't know how I died. I hope you didn't suffer because of it. But mostly I hope that the reason you are reading this is because Concetta—Sister Mary Thomas—is in heaven where she belongs. I hope it's not because you are in trouble.

Inside this envelope is a list of other safe deposit boxes and the keys to them. You will find about $350,000 in all. A lot of money, I imagine, even in the day you are reading this. I hope it is. I would have put it in investments, but this money was earned illegally. You *will have to do with the cash. I tried to give some to Sister Thomas, but she would have nothing to do with it.*

Also in the envelope is my favorite picture of your mother, one of the kindest, most gentle people I ever knew. And a lock of her hair.

I hope you can fix whatever is wrong with your life—if something is wrong—and I hope never to see you again.

Oh, and assuming Sister Thomas is still alive, say hello to her for me. Give her a kiss on the cheek and tell her that Dante says, 'Ti amo con tutto il mio cuore' (I love you with all of my heart.) And tell her that Dante says thank you.

Ti voglio bene,

Pops

I stared at the letter for a long time. So long that I didn't remember when I started it. Finally, I folded the pages, put them back in the envelope and turned the key to start the car. Hershey was waiting. It was going to be a long drive.

All the way back, I thought of the letter, at first denying what it said, then finding memories that supported what I'd read. Like the time when I was six and in the cop station. Pops came to get me, and he didn't even have to say anything. Just stared at them, then took me home. Or the time at the roach races, when Mikey the Face bet two hundred then tried backing out when Pops covered it. I'd never seen Mikey scared before that day, but he was. Now I knew why. And the comment Doggs made when Moynihan died, about how that would teach him to pick on Little Nicky.

I guess I'd known it all my life. Known *something* was fishy about Pops. Maybe I just didn't want to know.

Horns blared, and I swerved to avoid a head-on. *Goddamn. I better pay attention.* Refocused now, I kept my eyes on the road, but my mind kept drifting. Sister Thomas told me I could do anything. Start my life fresh. But then I looked at the letter, and, knowing what I did now, I wondered. Maybe it was in the genes. Maybe I had no choice. As I pondered on it, I realized I'd fallen into the same trap Pops had. I was trying to make money to impress Angie, just like Pops had tried with Sister Thomas.

What an idiot I am. Angie didn't care about that. My thoughts ran wild for the next half hour, until I forced myself to concentrate on driving. Traffic was getting worse, and I couldn't afford an accident. I made up my mind to figure things out when I got back to Hershey.

CHAPTER 47

RULE NUMBER TWO: MURDER HAS CONSEQUENCES

Hershey, Pennsylvania—20 Months Ago

I decided that night to get this over with quickly. Wasn't going to wait and watch like I normally did. Tito wanted it rushed anyway. In the morning I checked to make sure the motel room was perfectly clean and wiped down. I hadn't taken a shower, though I needed one badly, but a shower could leave hairs in the drain. I bundled the bedclothes and laid them on the floor. Once they were laundered, any of that evidence would be gone. I assured myself that this was my paranoia running wild. No one would even know I'd been here.

I got my case, went to the car, and drove to the back of the grocery store on the other side of the woods. I parked among the employees' cars, waited until no one was in sight, then took the gun from the trunk and walked into the woods. The gun fit in a small briefcase. Once I assembled it, I could make a killing shot from a hundred yards. Not sniper range, but damn good.

As I walked through the woods, I took note of alternate routes. Before long, I was sitting on the tree stump, waiting for lunch break. Gina should *not* have blackmailed Tito.

Stupid woman.

The school-bell ring alerted me, and at the same time brought back fond memories. The doors opened, and a mass of screaming kids poured out, laughter and joy echoing through the neighborhood. I smiled. How could I not? No one—*absolutely* no one—could hear that many kids laughing and not smile.

"Don't run, children."

The command wasn't as powerful as one from Sister Thomas, but it was good, firm. I looked up to see Gina—Debbie Small—admonishing the kids as they raced down the steps.

"Don't you *dare* cross that street until I get there." She picked up her pace and ran. I smiled again. She had more of the nun in her with that command.

Shit. I cursed and closed my eyes. Shook my head. I had to stop thinking like this. A job was a job. After all, didn't she blackmail the mob? How stupid is that? She needed killing. Can't leave people like that around to teach our children. Even Sister Thomas would have told her that *nobody* blackmails the mob.

When I looked up, the kids were in the park, playing catch. Gina joined them, and the kids seemed to like it. I raised the gun, sighted her in, focused…then decided to wait. No sense doing it in front of kids. For almost forty-five minutes I waited, then the bell rang, and the kids headed back to class. Gina stayed in the park, directing stragglers and waiting for the late ones to reach her before ushering them back across the street.

I sighted her in again, locked the crosshairs onto her head. She was almost to the curb, kind of bouncing in a half-jog type gait that teachers seemed to do in order to hustle kids along. When she got to the curb, she stopped, staring at the three kids she had just brought across.

"Where's Timmy?"

One of the kids turned to her, "He's coming."

"All right, you go in," she said. "I'll wait here."

It was perfect—her standing still, no kids around. I fixed the crosshairs one last time, then reached for the trigger. Her eyes were deep brown, and big, the kind that invited you in. And she had a long straight nose with a slight bump on it. It was a little big for a girl, but I'd seen worse.

Just as I put pressure on the trigger, she took her right index finger and twirled her necklace. I stopped. I squeezed my eyes closed then opened them again. After adjusting to the light, I focused. Then came that feeling in my stomach, twisting my gut inside out. And there was Gina, twirling that damn necklace and sliding the charm back and forth across her chin. All the while she stood on tiptoes, neck craned, looking for her lost kid like he was the damn prodigal son.

Fuck. Why did she have to be a twirler? *Angie* was a twirler. She used to twirl her hair all the time. Take her index finger and wrap it around a few strands of hair at the back of her neck and then just twirl. When Gina did that with her necklace, all I could think of was Angie.

Slowly, I let go of the trigger. Even slower, I disassembled the gun and packed it up. The walk back to the car seemed endless. I threw my life away once before for an oath nobody seemed to care about. Now I had my life back…but if I didn't kill Gina, I was a dead man.

CHAPTER 48

TOUGH DECISIONS

Hershey, Pennsylvania—20 Months Ago

At the motel that night, I sat and pondered. For the tenth time, I reminded myself that if I didn't do this contract, my life was over. At the very best, I'd have to go into hiding. More likely, I'd be dead. But every time I thought about pulling the trigger, I saw Angela's face. Angela's smile. Heard her laugh. Smelled her. Tasted her.

I punched the bed. Then punched it more. How could anybody's life be so fucked up? I walked to the dresser and reached into the bag. The letter from Angie was in that briefcase, calling me.

Find me, Nicky. No matter where I am, find me.

I punched the bed again. *Fucking coward. Fearless Nicky the Rat, scared to go see her, and hear she left me to fuck somebody else.*

The letter helped me make up my mind, though. That, and thoughts of those kids playing. No way I was killing her in front of those kids. I waited until 2:00 AM, crept out the door, checking to make sure the lights were out, then sneaked out into the night. A phone booth was maybe a quarter mile away, so I jogged there and dialed Debbie Small's number. She didn't answer until the seventh ring.

"Hello?"

"Gina?"

"Who is this?" Panic was in her voice, though it was tainted by sleep.

"My name isn't important. Tito Martelli sent me to kill you."

I heard the gasp, then what sounded like a squeal. "How did you find me?"

"I'm not here to kill you. Not anymore. But if you want to live, you need to follow my orders." I waited until the sobbing stopped. "Do you understand?"

"Okay, what? What do you want me to do?"

"Listen closely. Get your money and anything else you need into two small bags. Also get the evidence you have on Tito." I waited through another series of gasps, then heard a creaking noise. It sounded like attic steps being pulled down.

"Gina, listen to me. There isn't time. Get the money out of the attic later, if that is what you're doing. This is no joke. I was supposed to kill you today. I didn't. But if you don't listen to everything I say, you'll be dead before noon."

"Okay. Okay. Go on."

"Tomorrow at morning recess you will hear a gunshot. When you hear it, fall down. Don't run. Don't scream. Don't do anything but fall down." I paused. "Do you understand?"

"Fall down when I hear the shot."

"That's right."

"What about the children? I don't want them scared."

"They won't even know what's going on. They'll probably think it's a firecracker or something. You'll know the shot when you hear it though, and when you do, fall down."

"Okay, then what?"

"This is going to be difficult. It will require all of your concentration."

"Okay."

"Once you're down, count to thirty. Slowly. Make each one a second if you can."

"You mean like one, one-thousand..."

"That's exactly what I mean. Count to thirty. Then get up and walk away."

"Where?"

"There will be a crowd. People will be looking around for what the noise was. No matter what happens, walk away quickly. Don't run, and don't take your car. Walk through the neighborhood. Keep going until you find a place where you can call a cab. Do *not* use your cell phone. Do *not* call anyone you know. After tomorrow, Debbie Small is dead, do you understand?"

"How will I—"

"Just listen. Go to your house. Get the money and the bags then take the cab to the bus station. You don't need ID to ride the bus. Take it to Wilmington, Delaware. Go to St. Elizabeth's and ask for Sister Mary Thomas. Tell her that Nicky sent you, and that he asked to keep you safe until he calls. *Remember*, tell her Nicky sent you."

There was a long silence before she spoke. I heard her whispering, probably writing it down. "Bus station. Wilmington. St. Elizabeth's. Sister Thomas." She sighed. "Why are you doing this?"

"I don't know."

"You know he'll kill you."

"Sometimes you have to do what you think is right."

"When will I see you? I don't even know what you look like."

"It's better that way. I'll be in touch with Sister Thomas. She'll keep you safe."

As I hung up the phone, I heard, "Thank you, Nicky." It sounded sweet.

I WATCHED THE KIDS playing. Kids were the same the world over. At that age, they had so much innocence. I laughed. Even we were innocent then. The thought brought sadness with it. I focused on the issue at hand. Gina was nervous, but she was doing good. I checked the binoculars and saw Chicky and Donnie watching. No way they could see me, though.

Get ready, Gina.

I aimed, focused on her head, then raised the sights by several feet, making sure nothing was behind her. I squeezed the trigger smoothly. The shot boomed, went well over her head and into a brick wall. Several kids screamed. Gina went down.

Good girl. I moved quickly through the woods. By the time I exited, the gun was back in the briefcase. I checked the road, saw no one, and headed for the car. There was a lot still to do.

CHICKY DROPPED HIS COFFEE when the gun went off. "Jesus Christ, Donnie, she's down. She's down."

Donnie turned, head darting in every direction. "Get out of here, Chicky. We can't hang around."

Chicky popped the car in gear and headed out, taking a quick right turn to get to the main roads.

"Never even saw him, did you?" Donnie asked, looking in the rearview mirror.

"Not even a peek," Chicky said. "Just as well. I don't want to know who it is."

FIRST THING I DID was call Dexter, a guy I made friends with in prison. He had a brother who worked at the Philly paper and had connections everywhere. Anxiety ate at me. This was something I should have planned beforehand.

"Yo."

I could tell it was him when he answered. Nobody said "yo" quite like Dexter.

"Dex, it's Nicky."

A short silence, then. "Nicky the Rat. How 'bout that shit. What can the Dex do for you?"

"I need a story planted in the Hershey, Pennsylvania, paper."

"Might have to pull in favors to do this. Might take some grease."

"Just tell me what you need, Dex. And I'll owe you one."

"Tell me how you want it to read."

I gave him the details. He said he'd get back to me. Three hours later, he did. "All taken care of. Gonna cost you five hundred."

"Give me an address. And I meant that about owing you one. Just let me know."

I put $1,000 in an envelope and addressed it to Dexter. Paying him extra would ensure the best service in the future, and it just might help buy his silence if it came to that. I made one more call before leaving—to Sister Mary Thomas. When I got hold of her, I told her to expect Gina.

"Nicky, I cannot be involved in illegal activities."

"Sister, if you trust me, please listen. Hide her for a few days. Put her with a friend or get her a motel room. Don't let her use her own name or any identification. Within a few days, she'll have instructions in a letter I'm sending you."

I waited through a few seconds of silence, then Sister Thomas' voice came through. "Tell her not to worry. And, Nicky..."

"Yes, Sister?"

"Nothing. Be safe. God go with you."

"You too, Sister. Thanks."

I got rid of the gun on the way home. Cleaned it up real good, put it in some trash bags and buried it in the New Jersey Pine Barrens. Plenty else buried in there. One more gun wouldn't hurt. A lot of guys liked to keep their guns, but I never did. Keeping guns increased the chances of getting caught. If anyone ever came to my house, I didn't want a gun tying me to a crime.

When I got home, I wrote the letter, telling Gina what to do and where to go. I finished it with, "Once you get to Indianapolis, find an inexpensive motel. After a week, call Sister Thomas every other day until she tells you she's heard from me."

I mailed it miles from my house then went home. Tomorrow was a big day. I just prayed Dexter's connections came through for me. If not, I'd be dead.

TITO SAT AT THE kitchen table, enjoying his morning cappuccino, a paper open in front of him. When Manny came in, Tito set the paper down. "You check it out?"

Manny nodded. "Chicky saw it go down, and I checked the paper in Hershey. The obituary was there this morning. 'Debbie Small, teacher at Holy Cross. No relatives.'"

Tito sipped some more cappuccino then looked up, questions on his face. "Nothing in the paper about the shooting."

"Just a statement that the Feds have it under investigation. You hear that, Tito, the *Feds*. That means they were watching, like you thought. Must have been a trap to get you."

Tito laughed. "Good old Nicky. I warned Tony he was rolling the dice. Looks like he lost."

I WENT TO TITO the next day, told him that I was quitting, like I said I would. He didn't take me seriously at first, but after a while he accepted it. I told him I'd like to stay around, maybe get a real union rep job.

He tried convincing me, but when I held firm, he said okay. Said I could stay in my union rep position, but now I'd actually have to work for it. Pay wasn't going to be great, but that was all right. I had saved a lot, and I now had what Pops left me.

As I was leaving, I turned back to Tito. "I'm going to take a week or two off first, then I'll be back to start."

He looked at me funny, then nodded. "Yeah, sure. Whatever you want, Nicky. Call me when you get back."

As I started for the door, he called. "How much she have left?"

I knew he'd ask sooner or later. I was surprised he'd held out this long. "Almost two hundred."

"Two hundred." Greed filled his eyes. "That's a lot of money for one little job. Maybe—"

"We had a deal, Tito."

"Yeah, fuck you. How about that."

He was mumbling as I walked out the door, heading for my car. Still… something didn't sit right with me. Tito had taken that too easily. I made up my mind to be more alert, at least for the next few months.

For a few days, I did nothing. I made it a point to be seen with Tony and Suit, letting Tito know I was still around. After about a week, I gathered the money I'd hidden in the house and headed out late at night. It was time to go to Indianapolis and help Gina start a new life. I owed her that. If I had just killed her, she would have no worries.

CHAPTER 49

INDIANAPOLIS

20 Months Ago

I drove the car down to Philly and left it at the airport. Then I took a cab to Center City, and another one to a rental car center, where I got an economy class for two weeks, all under a different name. From there, I headed west to Indianapolis. With a decent day of driving, I'd be there for dinner.

I thought about a lot of things on the way out. Most of all, about how my life had changed and why I'd risked everything for a woman I didn't know. After much philosophizing, I blamed it on the church and Sister Mary Thomas. They were the ones who planted the seeds of guilt in me.

By the time I got to Indy, Gina was a wreck, trembling all the time, and looking over her shoulder every few minutes. It took me a while to calm her. The next day we went to Chicago and got her two new identities—Kathy Mynnocki and Mary Simmons. She didn't like the names, but she wasn't *too* unhappy with them. The worst thing was, I told her she couldn't teach anymore; they'd be looking for all the things she'd done in her former life.

We went back to Indianapolis and rented her a small house. Then I gave her instructions on how she'd have to live her life. She cried when

I left. It hurt, but I knew I had done the right thing. Indianapolis was a good place to hide her: big city, but growing fast; airport with quick, easy connections to a lot of nearby cities; and best of all, four interstates to jump on and be damn near anywhere in short order. Within four hours she could be in Chicago, Cincinnati, Cleveland, Detroit, Louisville, or St. Louis. As I drove back to New York, I realized I not only felt sorry for her, I kind of liked her.

At times like this I envied Bugs, out with different women all the time. I couldn't do that. I was always looking for that one special someone. The problem was, none of them were Angela.

Gina wasn't Angela either, but…something was different. Maybe I just wanted her more. Maybe it was empathy—both of us loners and without family. I picked my car up at the Philly airport, then headed for home. As I drove over the Walt Whitman bridge I reached for a cigarette that wasn't there, then shook my head. I had to get this shit out of my mind. If Tito found out she was alive, then *I* was dead.

CHAPTER 50

TONY AND TITO HAVE LUNCH

Brooklyn—18 Months Ago

It had been a few months since I left Gina, and the memories were already fading. For a while there had been a strong desire, but maybe that was just me being horny. What I needed was a "good lay" as Tony always said, but that didn't strike me as appealing. I might as well beat off. It was faster, cheaper, and I could dream about somebody I actually *wanted* to be with.

As I pushed the image of Angela out of my mind, the cell phone rang. "Hello?"

"Nicky, it's Tony. We're having lunch at Cataldi's."

It was early for lunch, but what the hell. "I'll be twenty minutes."

When I got there, Paulie and Bugs were at the table with Tony, and it looked as if at least one, if not two, limoncellos had already gone down. "You guys getting an early start on something?"

"Just another wonderful day," Paulie said.

"So I guess you've all been swimming?"

Bugs grabbed a piece of bread from the basket, but before he stuffed it in his mouth, he said. "I have."

"I don't care about swimming," Paulie said. "I'm hungry."

"What's everyone having?"

"Cannelloni," Tony said, and the grunts coming from Paulie convinced me he was too.

When the waiter came to the table, three of us ordered cannelloni. Bugs ordered manicotti. All through lunch, we talked about old days, like we did every time we got together. As the years passed, real memories of the old days faded and they became more what we *wanted* them to be. We talked about gang fights but forgot how scared we were before the fight happened. All we remembered was that one moment of euphoria afterwards. Frankie and Tony talked about girls and their conquests, ignoring the heartbreaks that went along with them.

Paulie downed his drink, ordered another round, then asked me if I was ever going to see Angie. "Take a goddamn weekend off and drive down, for Christ's sake. It's only a couple of hours."

The suggestion sounded good, I had to admit, but then reality hit. "What am I going to do, Paulie, go back and say, 'Hey, Angie, look at me. I'm a union rep.'"

Tony seemed pissed. "Why the hell would you want to see her after what she did to you?"

I didn't like his tone or his attitude. "What the hell, Tony. I was in prison. Tell me you're waiting seven years for someone?"

He let out a half-snort, accompanied by a sneer, the kind Tony was so good at. "Yeah, but she didn't even wait seven months. She's a—"

I reached for him, but he was across the table. If he'd have been closer, I'd have hit him. "Don't."

I looked at each of them. "I know you didn't like Angie much, but I won't have anyone talking bad about her." I turned, staring straight into Tony's eyes. "*Nobody.*"

Bugs changed the subject then scooped the last of his dessert onto his fork. "Fuck, that's it for me, guys."

"What?" Paulie asked.

"Tito just walked in. I can't afford to be seen with him." Bugs wiped his mouth and threw two twenties on the table.

"Put your money away," Tony said.

"Can't take a lunch from you either."

"I can," I said.

"Yeah," Tony said. "See you guys next time."

I nodded to Tito as we passed.

Within five minutes, I was on my way.

TITO WALKED TO THE table that Nicky and Bugs just left, pulled up a seat across from Tony. "Hey, Paulie, why don't you watch the car. Let Tony and me talk."

Paulie got up and left, and after the waiter took Tito's order and brought some more bread, Tito started talking. "I've been proud of you, Tony. You've been making good money."

"Thanks, Tito."

"They told me you were a smart kid when I took you on. That was the tag you had coming up, but lots of kids have that. What you've done is deliver, and that's important." He took a sip of water, then another. "Nothing is more important than delivering."

"I couldn't have done shit without Paulie. He's the best."

Tito nodded. "Yeah, I hear Paulie's good. You need good people around you. You've got a lot of good friends—Paulie, Nicky, and even Bugs is good. It's a shame he's a goddamn cop."

"At least he had the balls to give us a heads-up."

"That's what I mean—he's all right." Tito drank more water, then held his glass up for the waiter to see. "Service here has gotten bad."

"They're just busy. It's usually great."

After Tito got more water, he leaned close to Tony. "That thing we talked about before? It went good. Your boy did okay."

Tony's eyes went wide. "You mean Nicky?"

Tito looked at him as if he were nuts. "Yeah, the same Nicky who just left here ten minutes ago."

Tony wiped his mouth and crumpled the napkin, laying it on his plate.

"You see the body? If not, you paid for something you never got. But who cares? If it took care of your problem, that's all that matters."

"My men saw it go down. Manny verified it with the papers." He wiped his face with the napkin—wiped it hard, as if he were scrubbing off glue—then wagged a thick finger at Tony. "And I get what I pay for. *That's* what matters."

Tony held up his hands. "Whatever you say, Tito. But he didn't kill her. Nicky Fusco would *never* kill a broad."

Tito sat silent for a while. He ordered a cappuccino when the waiter came, and once they were alone again, he spoke. "I'm gonna have this checked out. In the meantime, you put somebody on Nicky. I want to know what he does, where he goes, what he buys, what he eats. If this guy fucked me…"

"If he fucked you, it wasn't you he was after. I'm telling you, it's the broad thing."

Tito stood, threw his napkin on the table. "You find out if he killed that girl. And if he didn't—kill them both." He stared at Tony. "That's what you want, isn't it? You've been pressing real hard on this. What's the matter, he fuck your wife or something?"

Tony's face tightened. "That's out of line. I don't care who you are."

"I'm going to have this checked out. I'll let you know what I find," he said, and stormed out of the restaurant.

CHAPTER 51

SHATTERED OATH

Brooklyn—18 Months Ago

As Tony got up and started for the door, the waiter intercepted him with check in hand.

"Mr. Sannullo—"

"Put it on the tab."

He bumped a few customers, then burst through the front doors. Paulie was waiting.

"What happened? Tito came out of there like he wanted to kill someone."

"Just the normal shit."

"Hey, Tony, don't give me that. What happened?"

Tony filled Paulie in on the details about Gina and how they had to hit her. He left out the part about hitting Nicky.

"You mean Nicky was supposed to take her out? You telling me our Nicky is a fuckin' shooter?"

"You heard it right. Problem is, he didn't do the job. Now he's fucked."

"What are we gonna do? We can't let anything happen to Nicky. I don't give a shit about Tito. This is Nicky we're talking about."

Tony stared at him as if he were a two-year-old. "You don't give a shit about Tito? Who the fuck pays for your house? Who sends your kids to private school?" When Paulie didn't say anything, Tony continued. "Don't worry. I got a plan. If we get the girl, we can convince Tito to leave Nicky alone. I promise." Tony patted Paulie's arm then headed for his car. "Meet me at Bobby's later."

Paulie started to say something else, but Tony turned on him. "And listen, you ever bring up Angie again, and I'll kick your ass."

"What the hell? All I did was tell him to go see her."

"Yeah, well, leave it alone. Nicky's better off without her. Look what happens to him when he gets with girls. This one's got him in trouble. *Big* trouble."

Paulie got into the car, still shaking his head.

TONY WONDERED ALL THE way over how to go about this. He couldn't come right out and ask Nicky, because he wasn't supposed to know; besides, that would make Nicky suspicious. First thing he'd have to do is prove that Nicky *didn't* kill her. Shouldn't be too difficult. Tito said it was in the papers, but Tony knew how easy it was to get something planted. Usually, though, the paper ran a retraction a few days later to cover their asses, using the old honest-mistake argument if anyone questioned them. He'd bet anything Tito never checked for a retraction. He picked up his cell and dialed Tito's number.

"Yeah, who's this?"

"Me."

"What are you going to ruin my day with now?"

"Just a thought for you. Maybe have somebody check the papers where you read that first story. See if there were any retractions."

"That it?"

"That's it." Tito hung up.

Tony wouldn't want to be Manny, or whoever verified that information.

TITO MARTELLI STORMED INTO the house, slamming doors as he moved from room to room. When he finally settled in the kitchen, he called for Manny.

Even before Manny got to the kitchen, Tito was screaming. "That fuckin' Nicky didn't kill her, Manny. I thought you checked this out. I thought she was dead."

Manny waited, knowing from experience that Tito could not be dealt with when he got like this. He walked to the sink, got water ready for coffee, poured iced tea for himself. Then he waited while Tito rambled. When Tito settled down, Manny spoke. "You mean Gina? If you're talking about her, I *did* check. Papers ran the obit, remember? Besides, Chicky and them saw it go down."

"You double-check? *I* just did. They printed a retraction three days later."

Manny gulped, hard. "I'll get on it."

Tito sat down, calm coming after a minute. "I want Tony in charge of this. Tell him he can have four guys. Just make sure one of them is Johnny Muck. And no matter what orders Tony gives, I want Nicky and Gina dead. But they've got to wait until we find Gina."

"Yeah, no shit."

TONY GOT THE CALL from Manny and decided to call Nicky that night, after he met with Tito and had the guys lined up. Tito had given him four men plus a driver. That should be enough to tail him and not get spotted. Besides, Tito had borrowed guys from the Bronx so Nicky wouldn't recognize them. He still didn't know where Nicky lived, so it was imperative to get him to meet. Tony dialed his number at nine o'clock. All he had was a cell phone, so there was no easy trace on it with his phone company contact, and Nicky wasn't one to stay on the line for long. After three rings, he answered.

"It's Tony."

"Long time, huh?"

"No time for fun. I need to see you."

There was hesitation on Nicky's end of the line. "Why?" His voice was heavy with suspicion.

"Not on this line. Meet me at Gerry's place. Down on—"

"I know where it is. Give me twenty minutes."

"I'll be there."

TONY WAITED ALONE IN a booth in the bar. The men were stationed blocks away, but with a good view of the bar so they could follow Nicky when he left. They were instructed to follow with extreme caution and switch off regularly with others so that Nicky didn't pick up the tail. With five cars, they should pull it off.

"What's up, Tony?"

Tony jumped. "Shit, didn't even see you come in."

Nicky slid into the seat opposite him. "What the hell is going on?"

Tony looked around as if they were being watched, then he whispered. "I know I'm not even supposed to know this, but you know that broad you did a while back? Well—"

Nicky sat up straight, eyes drifting left and right. His hands moved to his lap, poised for…something. "I don't know what the hell you're talking about."

"Forget what I know or don't know. Just listen. She's been spotted by one of Tito's men. I don't know where, and I don't know anything else about it. What I *do* know is that Tito is going nuts, talking about killing you and her both."

Nicky never flinched. Never blinked. If he really was the hit man, he was one cold fuck.

"Tony, I don't know what you're talking about. Are you shitting me? Are we on camera or something?" He held up his hand, signaling for a waiter. When he showed, Nicky ordered a glass of Chianti.

"Nicky, I—"

He held his hand out, laughing. "Listen, not that I don't appreciate your concern, because you really seem worried, but trust me, there's nothing to worry about." He laughed again. "Goddamn, Tony, I'm a union rep."

After the waiter brought the wine, Nicky talked about everything—everything *but* what Tony had brought up. "How's Celia?"

"She's okay. I'm just glad you're not involved with this. You had me worried."

He reached over and patted Tony's hand. "No need, but thanks."

They talked for another ten or fifteen minutes then Nicky said he had to go. "Some of us got a job to go to," he said, and threw a few bills on the table. "My treat tonight, since you did the worrying."

"All right, Nicky. Thanks. See you later."

TONY WALKED OUT WITH me, had his car pulled up, then drove off. I got my car, drove a few blocks behind Tony, then turned left. After I turned, I stopped in the middle of the street and got out to see if anyone was following. When I was convinced no one was, I got back in and continued, constantly checking the rearview mirror and making a lot of unexpected turns to throw off any tails. Ordinarily I would go through much more elaborate procedures, but I had already wasted too much time. If Tito really was on to Gina, she might already be dead. I made a right turn, then two lefts in succession. I thought about trying calling her from a phone booth, but then said fuck it, and dialed the number, still in memory from the day I bought her the phone.

It rang about seven times. No answer. Panic set in. Did they have her already? I dialed again, heart racing. What the hell was wrong with me? I never got nervous or scared, and here I was like a kid in his first gang fight. The phone rang four times.

"C'mon, Gina." My leg jiggled as I waited. Finally she picked up.

"This is Kathleen."

I recognized the calm, soothing voice, but with a hint of gravel in it. God, how I'd missed it. "Gina, it's Nicky. Get out. Now."

"Who is this?" The voice was still calm.

"Gina. Listen to me. It's *Nicky*. They *know* where you are. You need to get out, now."

"Oh my God, Nicky. How? Where? What do I do?"

I could almost see her biting her nails. See her frightened eyes. "Listen close. Calm down and listen."

Tears almost came through the phone. "I should never have done this. I should—"

"Shut-up, Gina." When she calmed down again, I went on. "Pack a

small bag. Take any cash you have. Get your IDs and head to the airport."
There was silence. "Are you with me?"

"Yeah," she said quietly.

"Good. Take cash. Go to the airport."

She sounded as if she were going to cry again. "They'll expect me at
the airport."

"Maybe, but here's what you do—buy a ticket to Chicago, there are
probably flights leaving every half an hour. Get one that leaves in five or
six hours. Pay cash. Then go sit by some other gate. Do *not* take the flight
to Chicago even if I don't show up. Just sit there and wait for me. If I don't
show, get another flight to anywhere and when you land, turn yourself in."

"But—"

"They won't be able to get guns past security. You'll be safe until I get to you."

I heard a few sobs, then, "Hurry, Nicky. Please?"

"Stay calm. Now get going."

My heart beat a little faster. I could only imagine what she felt like. I
suspected I was being tailed, felt it, but I decided to go straight to the airport. I had no time to be careful. If I didn't get there quick, she'd be dead.

TONY ANSWERED ON THE first ring. "Hello."

"It's me, boss. He took a flight to Indianapolis."

"Okay, thanks. I'll get somebody on it. Knowing Nicky, he probably
had her go to the airport."

Tony made a few calls then rode home in silence. He had that rotten
feeling in his gut that Sister Thomas used to tell them all about, the one
that always told you when you were doing wrong.

'God put that feeling into each and every one of us, and it is infallible.'

Tony hated himself, but what choice did he have. Sooner or later Nicky
would find out what he'd done—and when he did… Tony shook his head,
wiped his eyes with his sleeve. He prayed his mother couldn't see what he
was doing from her perch in heaven.

Forgive me if you can, Mamma. Please?

CHAPTER 52

WHERE TO NOW?

18 Months Ago

I was third off the plane, and immediately went to the flight status list for departures, checking the gates for Chicago. As I headed in that direction, I called Gina's phone. She answered on the first ring, whispering.

"Nicky?"

"You shouldn't be answering that way."

"Sorry. I'm so scared."

"Walk calmly from wherever you are and go to the main ticketing area for United."

"I'll have to leave security."

"I know. I'll meet you there. Walk slow, but steady. If anyone bothers you, scream."

I hurried to the ticketing area and stood just outside the exit, close to United's counters. I watched as she exited, checking to make sure no one followed, then walked up behind her and grabbed her arm, risking a slight cry.

She gasped, but not bad. "Just me," I said. "You did good."

She threw her arms around me. "Thank God you're here. I was so scared."

I breathed her scent in heavily before I pulled back, afraid to continue holding her. I hadn't realized attraction was this strong, or maybe it was just so long since I'd held *any* girl. *God help me,* I thought as I stared at her.

"Stay scared. This is far from over. We have to get out of here."

"I feel safe now. They wouldn't—"

I grabbed her by the shoulders, shook her. "Listen. We're *not* safe. We'll *never* be safe." I lowered my voice to a whisper. "This is the *mob*, Gina. Our only hope is to stay hidden."

She composed herself. "Where are we going?"

I grabbed her arm and headed for the exit. "We're going to do what they least expect—get a rental car and drive somewhere."

"Where?"

"Cincinnati, at least for now."

"Chicago's a lot bigger."

"No. Tito's got lots of friends in Chicago. Got some in Cincinnati, too, but not as many. Besides, we can be there in less than two hours, and I need someplace to sleep."

We took a cab to long-term parking, rode back on the bus, then took another bus to the National rental car facility. After that we hopped on Interstate 74 and had a straight shot to Cincinnati. Once we got going, I pressed her about where to live. She was tense and didn't respond well to pressure.

"I don't know," she said. "I can't think about it now."

"You *need* to think. There are a lot of places we can't go. Obviously not New York. And not Philly, Boston, Baltimore or DC. Chicago is definitely out. Same for Pittsburgh, St. Louis, Kansas City, San Francisco, Florida—"

"Is there any place we can go that's *decent*?"

"That leaves plenty of choices. "Denver, Houston, Phoenix, San Diego, Dallas, Seattle, Minneapolis, Portland..."

"This is bullshit. I can't live in Minnesota."

She was pissing me off, but I tried to be nice. "Me neither. Too damn cold. And too wet in Seattle or Portland."

"And too hot in Phoenix or Houston or Dallas." She sighed. "How about Cleveland?"

I shook my head. "That's on the no-go list."

"You didn't say Cleveland."

I slapped the steering wheel and turned to her. "If you'd let me finish, I would have gotten to Cleveland…and New Orleans, and Buffalo. And I think you know why. Don't pretend you're innocent."

Her lip curled into a sneer. "You think you're a clever fuck, don't you?"

"I think you've got a filthy mouth."

"You're a prick, Nicky. I can't stand you." She sobbed a little, then drew her knees up on the seat and wrapped her hands around them. "I wish you *had* killed me back in Hershey."

She shut up then, and nothing I did could get a word out of her. For the next hour and a half, I cursed myself. She was scared to death, and I'd treated her like shit.

"Gina, I'm sorry. Really."

She leaned her head against the window. Never moved. Never spoke. I thought I saw the light from oncoming traffic reflect off a tear on her cheek. That did me in. I hated seeing a woman cry. I stepped on the gas. The sooner we got to Cincinnati, the better.

You're a dumb fuck, Nicky. A stupid, dumb fuck.

AFTER PARKING IN THE long-term lot, we rode to the airport and took a shuttle to a Marriott hotel. I got a room with two queen-sized beds and asked for a six AM wake up call. Fifteen minutes after checking in, I was deep into a shower, which felt great even though I had to wear the same clothes when I got out. I dried, slipped on my shorts, and went into the room. "Your turn."

She closed the bathroom door behind her. While she showered, I thought of all the reasons why we shouldn't go to Cleveland, but the one huge advantage was that she wanted to go, and I needed to do something for her.

It took her less than ten minutes to shower. She returned with a towel wrapped around her head, wearing only her panties and a T-shirt. She poured herself a glass of water then plopped on the other bed. I glanced over, felt myself stiffen. As Bugs would say, 'this was one sexy broad.'

I let silence fill the air until I could stand it no longer. "Gina, I'm sorry about today. I didn't mean to be snappy with you."

She opened the nightstand drawer and pulled out the notepad, started writing.

"What's on the list?" I asked.

"Things I need to get."

"Like what?"

She stopped writing and glared. "Clothes. Toothbrush. Make-up. Those kinds of things, okay."

After being without women for so long, it was easy to forget how difficult they could be. I stared at her legs, got that feeling again.

Or how nice.

"Gina, what can I do to convince you that I'm sorry? I truly am."

"Bullshit."

I sat for five more minutes in silence, her writing all the time. *What the hell is on that list?* After another few minutes, I stood and knelt beside her bed. "I know it's tough for you. Your life's been torn apart, and you're scared. But I'm with you. I'm scared too."

She put the pen down and looked me in the eyes. "Why are *you* scared? You're a—"

I shook my head. "It doesn't matter what I am. They'll be coming for me. And they won't stop until they find me. Trust me, Gina. I'm scared."

She held my gaze for a long time. "Why didn't you kill me back in Hershey?"

I almost told her a lie, but who knew how long I'd be with her. I didn't want to start out that way. "I came close, but at the last minute you did something that reminded me of a girl I once loved."

She stopped writing and stared. Then she leaned forward and kissed my forehead. "That's sweet, Nicky. You must have a lot of good in you."

I shook my head. "I've been trying to find it again, but I think it's buried too deep." I stood and headed for the bathroom.

"Bring me that lotion when you come back. Please?"

I handed her the lotion as I sat on the bed. She opened the bottle and began rubbing her feet.

"Want me to do that? I give good foot massages." I laughed. "At least twelve or thirteen years ago I did."

Gina smiled. She had a slightly crooked smile, but it went well with the bump on the bridge of her nose. She tossed the bottle of lotion to me. "Do your best, Mr. Fusco, but be warned, I'm a taskmaster when it comes to foot massages."

I sat at the bottom of the bed with her feet draped over my thigh. I dabbed lotion onto my hand then gently massaged the lotion into her skin, making sure to cover all the parts of her feet, even between her toes. I rubbed it in until her skin soaked it up, then moved to the other foot. I looked up to her and gave her a smile to match the one she wore.

She moved, rolling to the side. Her left foot brushed against me.

"Don't, Gina. It's bad enough already."

"Why don't you rub some lotion up my legs a little?" If her words weren't invitation enough; her voice was. I moved up beside her, my face close to hers. "Gina, there is nothing in the world I want more right now than to make love to you. But I've got to tell you, it's been a long time for me. If I get started, I don't think I can stop."

"I don't want you to make love to me," she said.

I tensed, dejected, but as I let her go, she pulled me back. "I want you to *fuck* me."

The smile that popped on my face must have gone from ear to ear. "I love that filthy mouth."

Her feet dug into the bed, lifting her ass up. She slid out of her panties. "I haven't been with a man in two years."

As I kissed her, thoughts of Angela popped into my head. Fortunately I was able to push them out quickly.

We didn't rip clothes off like they do in the movies, but we were passionate. Maybe *hungry* was a better word. *Very* hungry. And I ate every part of her, from top to bottom, front to back.

It didn't last as long as either one of us wanted, but it was more than fantastic. Afterwards we lay there, talking, laughing. Then laughing some more. "You can curse any time you want."

She wrapped one of her legs around mine and stretched her arm across my chest. "Now I don't want to."

We got up in a few minutes and both took a shower, then about forty minutes later had a repeat of the lovemaking. Less wild, but still great. We slowed down enough to really enjoy it. Two hours later we showered again, and again we made love. This one I really took my time with, enjoying every scent of her, every taste. Someone could have come in and stuck a gun to my head and I wouldn't have known. Worse, I wouldn't have cared. This felt *that* good. As we lay there, wrapped around each other, it was easy to forget that we were running for our lives. I thought about doing it again, but thinking was all I could do. There was nothing left.

Gina had fallen asleep, but I couldn't. I stared at the ceiling, wondering about what happened in New York. Tito obviously knew Gina was alive, which meant he knew I didn't kill her.

So why didn't he kill me? Because he wanted her too. I thought a little more on that. *If I were Tito, I'd let it leak to Tony, then follow him, knowing he'd tell me. From there it would be easy to tail me to Gina.*

I relaxed and closed my eyes, satisfied that the thought process was complete and that I got away clean. Twice I almost drifted off to sleep, but a nagging thought kept popping into my head no matter how hard I tried squashing it. Tony could have been in on this. He might have known about the plan and set me up. That made more sense.

But why would Tony do that? I rolled over several times, careful not to wake Gina. I ended up on my back, staring at the ceiling again. Finally I banished it for good.

He wouldn't. No way Tony would do that.

CHAPTER 53

A NEW LIFE

About 1 Year Ago

We ended up in Cleveland. I don't know how she talked me into going there, but it might have had something to do with sex. No matter, we were there and trying to find a semi-permanent place to live. I already had an apartment for us, an efficiency that we sublet and would use as our official residence for the identification we carried. But I planned on finding another place to live under a different name. The subterfuge worried Gina.

By midafternoon, we found a nice place to rent, a small ranch in an older section of the city. The way it was situated we could walk to the grocery store, and there was a butcher and a fruit stand nearby. To top it off, there was a family-owned bakery that still made sfogliatelle. If asked to sum up my new life six weeks into it, it would have been easy. I had Gina, fresh fruit two blocks away, and sfogliatelle only three blocks past that. What more could anyone want?

Two months later we drove to a small town in Tennessee and got married by a Justice of the Peace, though I still promised her a Catholic wedding. In the third month, Gina got a job as an accountant, and I hired on as a salesman for a tile company. Not my life dream, but it kept me busy and put a few dollars in our pockets. When I got my first paycheck, I stopped at the bakery and picked up cannoli and sfogliatelle.

I was whistling when I walked in the door. "Guess what I have?"

Gina was at the table, a small oval one tucked into a neat corner of the tiny kitchen. There were tears in her eyes. I rushed to the table, setting the boxes down, then knelt before her. "What's wrong? Are you okay?"

She sobbed. Hugged me. "I'm okay now that you're home."

"What happened?"

She held on to me for a long time. "I'm sorry, Nicky. We got a new client today at the firm. His name was *Martelli*." Gina tried holding back the tears, but they came. "God, Nicky, when I heard that name, I lost it. All I could think of was Tito. I couldn't work the rest of the day. I was watching over my shoulder the whole time, wondering if he had already gotten to you."

I stood, walked around. Instinctively went to the window and peered out. "You checked, though. No one followed?"

"You can bet I checked. It took me an hour to get here because I took so many detours." She drank some water. "No one followed me." Gina stood and put water on for tea. She was trembling.

I stood too and rubbed her shoulders. "Are you okay?"

"I don't know how you do it."

"Do what?"

"Keep going, day after day. Go around like it's nothing, when inside you've got to be falling apart. You're human aren't you? I mean, you didn't come down here from some goddamn spaceship." She balled her hands into fists, squeezing the tension out. "I can't do what you do. I'm tired of being scared." She put the kettle on the burner but just stood there with her hand on it, as if it offered her support. "Sometimes at night I think about dying, calling Tito and saying, 'Here I am. Come get me.'"

I wrapped my arms around her and kissed the side of her head. "It takes time," I whispered. "Someday we'll look back on this and…well, we might not laugh, but we'll find good memories."

She let loose a few tears. "Don't you *ever* get scared?"

"All the time, baby. All the time."

She stepped back, looking at me as if it were the first time. "Why don't you ever tell me about it?"

I shook my head. "I don't do that stuff, Gina. I'm not trying to be macho or anything. I just grew up different." I kissed her forehead, then turned her around and rubbed her neck. "But you can talk to me anytime you want. I'm a great listener."

She pulled my hands over her shoulders and held them, silent until the tea water boiled. "I feel better now. Thanks."

"Remember, Gina, every day will get better." I walked to the window and peeked out again, then let go of the curtains and moved to the table. "Brought you some cannoli."

She set her tea on the table and grabbed one. "Thanks. I need it tonight."

I walked to the other window, pulled that curtain aside, checked the street again.

"I'm sure I wasn't followed."

"I know. I like to check, though. That's how you stay alive." I smiled at her. "Not doing a good job of making you feel safe, am I?"

She laughed. "I'm all right."

I watched her for a moment in silence. She was doing a good job of regaining composure. "Maybe we should get that Catholic wedding you've been wanting."

She set the cannoli down. "Are you proposing again?"

I got on my knees. "Guess I am."

A sexy smile popped onto her face. "I can think of other positions I'd rather have you in."

It only took me a millisecond to stand up and lead her to the bedroom. "Before or after?" I asked.

"Hmm. I think both."

"No, I mean do you want me to propose before we make love or after?"

"And I meant what I said. I want you to make love *before* you propose, *and*, after you propose." She laughed. "And if you're good, maybe later, too."

"You're going to kill me."

I WOKE EARLY AND cooked her favorite breakfast—sausage and eggs, with a wheat bagel—made coffee, and put it all on a tray, along with a rose I picked from our neighbor's garden. As I opened the bedroom door and said, "Room service," I laughed. The look on her face was priceless.

Her eyes lit up, and a smile as big as any I'd seen covered her face. She sat up, propping pillows behind her. "I can't believe you did this." I thought she was going to cry. "Nobody has ever done something like this for me."

I didn't know what to do. Had not expected that reaction. "I got tired of giving foot massages to get sex so I thought I'd try this."

She reached her arms out to me, looking for a hug. I set the tray at the foot of the bed and hugged her. "Morning, babe. Hope it's done right."

She kissed me, then picked up the rose and smelled it. "Nicky, I love you. Promise you'll stay with me forever."

"You know I will. Now will you please eat. I've got another surprise."

She perked up even more. "What?"

"I thought we'd go shopping for a new house today."

"We can't afford a new house."

Gina was always the practical one. Good thing, too, because I tended to spend recklessly when it came to her. "I've got money saved. We can use that."

"You can't buy a house with cash. Not these days." She looked lost in thought. "But that does bring up a question. When are we going to Indianapolis to get my money? Remember, I have quite a lot in a safe deposit box there."

It was Tuesday, and the weather was nice, with a good forecast. "Why don't we take off Friday and drive over? Make a weekend out of it."

"Long drive," she said.

"Yeah, but if we get an early start we can be there before noon, take care of business and have the rest of the weekend to ourselves."

She thought, smiling the whole time. "Why not? Let's do it."

WE GOT UP AT five, ate breakfast, had coffee and got out of Cleveland before six-thirty. By eight o'clock, Gina was a nervous wreck, worrying about every sound, and every car that stayed with us for more than a few minutes. Finally I had enough of it.

"Gina, why don't you tell me about this whole thing with Tito. Isn't it time?"

She seemed afraid to even talk about it, but she nodded and then started talking. She told me how her father, Carlo, had worked with Tito when he was coming up, how they killed a guy one night, some accountant who wasn't cooperating. Things got testy during the getaway, and Tito gave the gun to Carlo to get rid of it. Carlo didn't; he kept it. Knowing Tito as he did, he wanted something to hold over him if things got bad.

As Tito rose through the organization, he wanted to get rid of his liabilities. Carlo was one of them. Carlo got wind of the contract on him and went to the FBI for witness protection, but he never gave them the gun. Before they got him to testify, he disappeared. Things went fine for a while, but neither Gina nor her father liked their new lifestyle. When he died, she decided to do something about it, and blackmailed Tito. She still had the gun—and the name of the guy he killed—Danny Zenkowski.

"Took balls to do that, Gina. Not saying it was smart, but it did take guts."

"I had no choice. Do you know what they pay teachers—especially in Catholic schools?" She shook her head. "A single person can't live on that."

"We'll get your money, and combined with mine, plus what the two of us make, we'll be all right." I drove in silence for a while, but then I couldn't stand it. "Gina, you've been scared ever since I met you. Why don't we put this to bed?"

"Meaning what?"

"You said you have the gun Tito gave Carlo?"

"It's in the safe deposit with the money."

"Let's turn it in."

Her head shook so hard I thought her neck would break. "No way. No goddamn way."

"I know a detective in New York who can help."

"I told Tito if he gave me the money I'd forget him."

"The only way to stop Tito is to put him away. If he's gone, nobody will be after you."

"What about you?"

I thought for a minute. Didn't want to lie to her, but... "They'd probably even forget me. The only one I offended was Tito, so I doubt anyone else is going to risk it."

For maybe half an hour we drove in silence, then she shook her head. "I can't do it, Nicky. I *won't* do it."

"No problem. I'll take care of it."

She laughed, then when it hit her what I was saying, she hit me. "Bullshit. You're not doing that. No way I'm letting you go after Tito."

"If he's gone, we're safe. It's the only thing that makes sense."

"I'll leave if you do. I'll flat out leave." She rolled the window down, then up again. "Goddamnit, Nicky, I love you, but I'll leave your ass if you try it."

I kept silent after that. We didn't bring up the subject of Tito that night, or the next day, but there was tension between us. About halfway home on Sunday, she blurted out, "All right. You win. Call your friend, and I'll turn in the gun." She only waited a second, then added, "But I'm not testifying; in fact, I don't even want to meet him."

I felt relieved for the first time in days. "Don't worry. You won't have to meet him or anyone else."

"God, I hope so. Could this really be over?"

"You bet it could. Hell, it *is* over."

After we got home, Gina was in a great mood, and I planned on keeping it that way. I called Bugs three times in the first two days but never got an answer. "I'll get him tomorrow night," I said, "no matter how many times I have to call."

The next day, I went to work with a new sense of happiness. This was as good as life got. When I came home, Gina was sitting at the kitchen table with a letter in front of her. I saw the stern look before I recognized the torn corner of the envelope. An awful feeling grew inside me. Gina was holding the letter from Angie. As I approached, she waved it at me.

"What's this?"

"Nothing."

"*Nothing?*" There was venom in her voice. She could do that when she got angry. Especially when she was jealous.

I tried to be understanding. "It's an old letter, Gina."

"How old?"

"When I was in prison, back when I was maybe nineteen."

She scoffed, turning her head. "It's *nothing*, but you kept it all this time?"

I stared, resolve growing firmer. "It's a memory—that's all."

She lowered her head and read part of the letter aloud. "'Find me, please? No matter where I am, Nicky, Find me.'" Her voice was poison.

I reached for it, but she drew back, gripping it with both hands as if she would tear it.

I grabbed her. "You touch that and…"

"And what? You'll kill me? Is that what you were going to say?" She yanked her arm away.

"No. It's just—"

"Just what?"

I stared at her, but without hatred, and probably without enough love. "It's a letter from a girl I knew a long time ago." My head lowered again. "I've been a coward. Afraid to throw it away. So it sat in my briefcase, reminding me of my cowardice." A tear came to my eyes. "It reminds me that Nicky the Rat ain't shit." With that, I went to the bedroom and flopped on the bed.

She didn't come to me that night. When I got up in the morning, the letter was back where it belonged. I wanted to burn it. Shred it. What was I doing with my life? It had been so long since I felt anything.

Then came Gina. I now had a life with a woman I loved…and I was going to let an old letter and a woman who didn't give two shits about me ruin it? *Come on, Nicky.*

I left without seeing Gina, but when I got home she was there, happy as a lark and acting as if nothing had happened. I went to her, took her beautiful face in my hands and kissed her softly. "I love you."

"Nicky, I—"

I shook my head. "No. I love *you*, Mrs. Krasner." I took out the letter and tore it up in front of her.

She tried stopping me. "You don't have to do that."

"I want to. It's long past time for it."

She kissed me again then laughed. "That's a horrible name you picked out. *Krasner*, for God's sake."

I kissed her again. "If it's your name, I'll take it."

She pushed me back. "I don't know if I feel the same, *Richie*."

I hugged her and squeezed. I thought about the letter Pops had left. About how much he had loved Sister Thomas, but how he had grown to love my mother. That struck a chord. I think Gina was like that. I *did* love her. Really did. And nothing was going to break us apart.

I headed toward the kitchen. "What's for dinner?"

"Whatever you make," she said. "And remember, you have to get hold of your friend Bugs tonight."

CHAPTER 54

LATE-NIGHT CALL

9 Months Ago

Frankie trudged up the steps, worn out from another long day dealing with frustrating people and even worse cases. He opened the door to the apartment, lighting a cigarette before he hit the kitchen. He felt sorry for Paulie, was worried about Nicky, and disgusted with Tony. Maybe he felt sorry for himself too. Tired of living the life he did.

A bottle of water accompanied him to the chair, where he sat in silence, pondering his situation. Pretty soon he fell asleep, not waking up until the phone rang. He looked at the clock—1:00 AM. *Who the fuck is calling this late?*

"Hello."

"Bugs?"

"Nicky. Is this you?"

"It's me."

"Where the hell are you? Where did you go?"

"I'm okay."

"Okay? You had me worried to death, you prick. It's been six months. Maybe more."

"Sorry, Bugs. But listen. I need help."

"Anything, name it."

"I'm with a girl, and she's in trouble."

"What can I do?"

"Good old Bugs. You don't even ask what I want, and you're ready to help."

"Friendship and honor, remember?"

"I always remember. Not many others do, though." A slight pause, then, "Tito's after her, Bugs. Tried killing her already."

"Martelli?"

"Yeah."

"Did you call the FBI? You know—"

"She doesn't want that; besides, she has evidence that could put Tito away. This could be big for you. Bust Tito, and it makes a mark for your career."

Bust Tito, and it puts a mark on my chest.

Frankie lit a smoke. "You know I don't give a shit about that, but I *am* worried about you. If Tito's after her, and if you're protecting her, that means he's after you."

"Yeah, well, there's more to it than I'm saying, but he'd like to have both of us, which is why we aren't coming in."

Frankie sucked hard on the cigarette, draining the life out of it.

"Still straining those smokes, huh?"

"Fuck you. But, yeah, I am. What do you mean, not coming in? Why did you call?"

"Like I said, she's got evidence that could put Tito away. Murder. You want it or not?"

"What's in it for you?"

"Getting him off her ass. Way I figure it, if he's gone, nobody else will bother with her."

Silence followed, then, "Where do we meet? Where are you?"

"No need for you to know that. And no need to meet. I'll mail you the evidence and a statement. Do what you can with it."

"Be better to have a live person."

"Yeah, well, guess you'll have to do without."

"When can I expect it?"

"Within the week," Nicky said. "Give me your address."

"A week? Going somewhere else to mail it?"

Laughter, then, "Always said you were smart. Not as smart as The Brain, but smart."

Bugs gave him the address, then said good night. "Take care, Nicky. I've got your back."

"Me too, Bugs. Me too."

No sooner had he hung up than Bugs thought of all the questions he hadn't asked. Was this evidence Tito-specific, or would it affect his crew? Nicky didn't say, and Bugs wondered if Tony or Paulie might get hurt. Some smart detective he was. He checked the caller ID but it had been blocked.

Now what? Why didn't I ask Nicky what the evidence was? Shit, for that matter, why didn't I ask Nicky about a lot of things?

THE NEXT MORNING FRANKIE went to work as normal, then slipped out to the coffee shop down the street. He called Tony from the pay phone by the rest rooms, then ordered a plain coffee, took a booth, and waited. It didn't take Tony long to get there.

Tony walked in, spotted Bugs and headed towards him, stopping to order coffee. He slid into the seat opposite Bugs. "What's going on? Why the sudden meet?"

"Where's Nicky?"

Tony raised his eyebrows. "How the hell do I know?"

"I know your friends in Brooklyn are looking for him."

"No surprise there."

Bugs leaned in close. "What I need is the truth. Why is Tito after Nicky and the girl?"

Tony sighed and ordered a drink. "She's got something on Tito. I don't know what, so don't ask, but then she blackmailed him. And I mean big."

Tony took a sip of his drink. "Tito went nuts when she did that." He looked around. "Here's where it gets dicey, Bugs. You're not going to like hearing this, but he hired somebody to do Nicky and her both."

"What?"

"I swear on my mother's eyes. Nicky took her on the run."

Bugs leaned back and drained his coffee. "Fuck."

"Yeah, fuck is right. Tito's gonna kill both of them if he ever finds them. And there's nothing I can do about it. That's why I've been trying to find Nicky, to get word to him."

Bugs sucked on a dry smoke, then ordered another coffee. Instinct warned him to keep quiet, but friendship told him differently. "If I were you, I'd distance myself from Tito." He took a drink of water, rattled the ice in his glass, then continued. "I'm only here because of old times. No matter what, I don't want to see you and Suit go to prison. Tito's going down."

Tony looked at him, suspicion evident in his narrowed eyes. "What's this about? You talk to Nicky?"

"Why would you ask that? Why bring up Nicky if you don't know anything?"

"Whoa, Bugs. Don't get nervous. Just a guess, that's all. Anyway, I appreciate the heads-up, but there's no need to worry. Whatever you people are after Tito for, it can't touch me."

Frankie gave Tony his investigative stare. "You sure?"

"Absolutely positive," Tony said, and smiled. "Me and Paulie are clean." He laughed. "Maybe not *clean*, but clean enough."

Tony picked up his coffee cup as if it were a drink to toast with. "Friendship and honor."

"Friendship and honor," Bugs said, and tapped his cup against Tony's.

BUGS AND TONY LEFT together then parted ways. By the time Tony hit the end of the block, he was on the phone. "Bobby, get our phone company guy. Tell him to get records of Frankie Donovan's calls in the past few days. I want names if we can get them, but mostly I want locations. Got that?"

"Got it."

Tony gave him Bugs' phone number then hung up. Nicky had to have called him, and once he found out where Nicky had called from, it wouldn't be hard to find him. All the way home, Tony worried, regretting his life and the choices he'd made. He felt sure there was some parable about a man who dug a hole too deep and couldn't get himself out, but for the life of him he couldn't think of it. And his life might depend on remembering that solution. If ever he needed Sister Thomas' help, it was now. The hole he'd dug was so deep he couldn't see the top.

CHAPTER 55

RULE NUMBER THREE: MURDER TAKES PATIENCE

8 Months Ago

Frankie Donovan sat at his table, sipping coffee and staring at the log from the phone company. It had been almost two weeks since Nicky called and still no package. Something had gone wrong, and he intended to find out what.

Should have done this sooner. He checked the phone bill and saw he only had a few calls the week Nicky called, and only one from out of town—Cleveland. *What the hell are you doing in Cleveland?*

He drained his cup and called Carol. "Get me the numbers for whoever we need to talk to in Cleveland about a missing person." Frankie shook his head and rephrased. "No, not a missing person, a material witness. They'll look harder for that."

He finished dressing and headed in to work, giving Carol a picture of Nicky to send to the detective she spoke to. "Did you tell them it's urgent?"

"I told him, Detective." She handed him a slip of paper. "Here's his name and number."

"Let me know if you hear anything."

TONY SANNULLO WAITED FOR the nod from the four guys guarding the door to Cataldi's, then looked both ways before getting out of the car. He went to his table and sat down but ignored the crossword waiting for him, focusing on the door instead; Tito would be there any minute.

Anna brought espresso when Tito arrived. He sat across from Tony. "Anything?"

"Nothing yet. We know they're in Cleveland, but we haven't found them."

Tito's eyes darted back and forth. He signaled the waiter, who took orders for breakfast. "Cleveland is a big city."

"Yeah. Lot of places to hide."

"Remember, Tony, when she was in Hershey we found her at church?"

"We're checking, but there are a lot of churches in Cleveland."

Tito cracked his knuckles while he talked. "What else do we know about her? What does she do? What does she like?"

Tony sipped the last of his espresso, staring off into nothing. Two sips later, he burst out, "Sfogliatelle."

Tito shook his head. "Don't serve it here. You know that."

"Not me. Nicky."

"What?"

"Nicky loves sfogliatelle. He can't go a week without it. He told us that's the thing he missed most in prison. There can't be more than a few places in Cleveland that sell it—half a dozen at best."

Tito stood, walked over and kissed him. "You're a genius."

After a second espresso, Tito paid the bill, and they prepared to leave. "If you need more men let me know, but find every place in Cleveland that sells sfogliatelle, and have them watched."

As Tony walked away, Tito grabbed his arm. "Make sure you tell them that if they have a chance to take her out, do it. She has to go at all costs. We can get him later."

"I don't know about that, Tito. I wouldn't piss Nicky off like that."

Tito stopped and looked at him. "I'd rather they get them both, but she's the more important one; besides, what's he gonna do?"

"All I'm saying is, we don't want to piss Nicky off. I'd wait until we can get them both."

"You're not running this show," he said, and headed for the door.

CHAPTER 56

WHO IS WATCHING?

Current Day

Frankie's head pounded as he drove home. He'd been on this case for months and had gotten nowhere. Now Morreau was telling him that the captain put him on the case. Why the hell would the captain want *him* on it? He turned the music off so he could focus. The captain didn't know him, so why?

More than a few miles went by in traffic that looked like a beach weekend, and he still didn't have answers. He approached the question from another angle. Why would *anyone* want him on the case?

To solve it. That was the easy answer, but—and this was important—there was no reason for anyone to think Frankie would make a difference in solving this case when they already had a seasoned homicide detective on it. *So why?*

It suddenly hit him. *They want me on it, not to solve it, but to keep it unsolved.* He thought through the case as his foot switched continually from gas to brake pedals.

Was Tony behind it? Did something go wrong and Tito was cleaning up loose ends, planting evidence to make Bugs think it was Nicky. *Jesus Christ, did they kill him? Is that why I never heard from Nicky after the Cleveland call? It's been nine months.*

The logic solidified as he drove home and as he climbed the steps to his apartment, dabbing his forehead with a handkerchief to soak up sweat. For June it was unseasonably hot. When he got inside, he poured some iced tea, then turned the fan on and let it blow across his face.

The killer had to watch from somewhere. Each victim had something in their hands when they came home, and that couldn't be a coincidence. He and Lou had already checked the obvious places and turned nothing up. Of course, back then he only half-wanted to solve this crime.

After thinking about it for a while, he realized that plugging Tony into the equation made more sense. These were mob killings, straight and simple. Tito and Tony were just making them look like something else.

Frankie lit a cigarette. The only question now was whether to bring Mazzetti in or not. Lou was a good cop, damn good, but Frankie didn't know what he'd find. And he wasn't sure how much he was willing to share, even with his partner. By the time he got to the end of his smoke, he made up his mind. He dialed Lou.

"How about meeting me over by Renzo's in the morning? Maybe six-thirty or seven."

"What are we going to find that we didn't before?"

Frankie paused. He knew this would cause a shit storm. "This time I'm bringing pictures." He cringed, waiting for the berating.

"You mean pictures of your friends? So you finally decided to be a cop?"

Frankie hadn't thought of it like that, but Lou was right. "Yeah, Lou. I guess I did."

FRANKIE ROSE EARLY, DRESSED in a hurry, and took Flatbush Avenue toward Prospect Park, then cut across Washington to Atlantic and out to Renzo Ciccarelli's address. Renzo had lived in a nice, older neighborhood. It bordered trash, but somehow maintained its integrity. He parked in front of Renzo's, got out and stretched. Lou was already there.

"There's a McDonald's, a small diner, and a Dunkin Donuts. It *has* to be one of them," Lou said.

Frankie lit a smoke and started across the street. "Let's do Dunkin Donuts first."

The place was busy, maybe eight or ten people sitting in booths, another half dozen at the counter, and three in line. He ordered a plain coffee and a cinnamon roll for himself and a coffee for Lou.

"That'll be seven thirty-four," the man behind the counter said.

Frankie paid with a ten, placed the change in the tip jar, then asked the question he came for. "You ever see any of these men?" He showed them a picture, taken maybe a year ago of Nicky, Tony, Paulie, and himself seated around a table at Cataldi's.

The guy looked at him with suspicious eyes. Frankie flashed a badge. "Police business."

Now his eyes seemed more suspicious, but all he said was, "No."

Frankie nodded toward the other worker, showed her the photo. "Ever see any of these guys?"

She shook her head. "Other than you, none that I remember."

A rail-thin Pakistani or Indian guy, stared at him over a pair of glasses with a bent frame. "I told you. We saw no one."

Frankie grabbed the cinnamon roll and coffee, said "Thanks" then followed Lou out the door. Next stop was the restaurant. He hoped this would pay off, because there was no way the McDonald's would. As he approached, his hopes skyrocketed. Four cop cars were parked on the side of the building. If cops frequented this place, they might have noticed something.

The four patrol cars translated into six cops. Frankie approached the closest table, where two patrolmen were just finishing breakfast. He showed them his ID, then pulled out the picture.

"I've got reason to believe that one of these guys frequented this place for at least a few weeks while he prepared for a murder. Ever seen him?"

They looked at Frankie with doubtful eyes. "Never saw him," one guy said, and both shook their heads.

Frankie pressed it. "Take a look, goddamnit. One of these guys was here. I know it."

The older cop slapped a ten on the table as he stood. "Hey, buddy. Like we said. Never saw him. Make your case somewhere else."

No wonder people hated cops. "Have a nice fuckin' day while you're at it, okay?"

He talked to the hostess and got a seat with a good view of Renzo's place. A perfect view. It was too far away for Renzo to have noticed anyone watching him, but it offered a clear shot of his house.

"So what do you think, Donovan?"

"I think he was here, Maybe right at this table."

"Yeah, me too."

"Lou, order me coffee when she comes. I'm gonna talk to the other cops."

The next guy was helpful, said he thought he recognized the picture of Nicky, but couldn't swear to it. Frankie moved on to the next three, all sharing a table. Two guys and one female. "Hate to interrupt a good breakfast, but I'm working a tough case and could use help. Ever seen any of these guys, maybe right in this diner?" Frankie laid the picture on the table and waited.

The first guy said no, but the lady, while chewing, poked at the picture with her finger as if she were nailing it to the table. "I think I know this guy."

Frankie's pulse quickened. She pointed to Tony. "From where?"

She swallowed, took a sip of water, then continued. "I don't mean I *know* him, just that I've seen him here." She turned, pointing to the table next to where Lou was. "Used to sit right over there." She paused then pointed to the next booth. "Maybe the one next to it."

The other cop looked at the picture. "I don't recognize any of them."

She shook her head again. "That's because you guys weren't here. Besides, I noticed the guy because he was hot. This was when I was on the afternoon rounds with Pete. He stopped here almost every night for dinner, and every once in a while that guy—" Again she pointed at the photo "—was sitting at that table, reading the paper."

Reading the paper, Frankie thought, *or doing crosswords. Goddammit, it's Tony.* Frankie grabbed his coffee and brought it back to the table. "Mind if I sit?"

She slid over, extended her hand. "Patti," she said, prompting the other two to introduce themselves.

"Ted," the one who spoke first said, and, "Clarence," from the other.

"Anything else you can tell me about this guy?" Frankie asked.

"This about that guy across the street getting killed?"

Frankie nodded. "Not just him. Three others, too. That we know of." He gulped the rest of his coffee. It was getting warm, and he hated coffee to be anything but piping hot. "I'm catching more shit than you can imagine."

All three heads nodded at that statement. "You might check with the afternoon waitress crew. They come on about two. Girl named Cindy usually works the rotation where he sat, and she's a talkative one. Maybe she chatted him up." Patti finished her coffee, took a sip of water, then nudged Frankie to slide over and let her out. "Tell you one thing. Your guy's got balls if he sat here with cops every day, plotting a murder. Big brass ones."

As they said goodbye, Frankie nodded. *Yep, big brass ones.* Although that described either one of them.

Frankie and Lou went to the McDonald's, not expecting anything and that's exactly what they got. They went back to the station, worked some files, and returned to the restaurant about five. Cindy vaguely remembered a guy who came in once in a while, but she struggled with the photo. When Frankie pressed her, she picked out Tony.

"And you don't remember anything else?" Frankie asked.

"You know how many people I get in here? Look around. Would you remember one customer?"

"You're certain it's the guy you pointed to?"

She stared at it again. "If you're asking me if it could possibly, maybe, be this guy—okay, yeah. But if you're asking me to go to court and swear on it, no."

Frankie thanked her, but silently cursed. *Waitress who wants to be a lawyer. Just what I need.*

He found Pete, Patti's short-lived partner, but Pete didn't recognize anyone. Frankie left the restaurant, went back to Dunkin Donuts and questioned the night crowd, but got nothing new, so he packed it in for the day and went home.

On the way home, thoughts raced through his mind. A lot of the DNA evidence collected at the scenes turned out to be from cops. Where would a killer get that? *From a restaurant where cops hung out, that's where.*

All he would have to do is sit in that booth and collect DNA. And wasn't there gum at one of the scenes? He remembered how, in fourth grade, Tony used to wait until Sister Theresa's back was turned, then he'd yell. She'd whip around, ready to whack someone, but she could never tell who it was, and no one would say. Tony used to tell us, "With forty kids in the class, how's she going to know who did it?"

Just like now, Frankie thought as he turned onto Flatbush to head home. *How are we going to know who this is? But I know, Tony, you slippery fuck. I know.*

FOR THREE DAYS, FRANKIE and Lou investigated the sites of the other crimes. They talked to people at diners, coffee houses, fast food joints and pizza shops. They found a few more people who felt sure they recognized Nicky, but also more who swore it was Tony. On day four, Frankie got home by nine, plopped in his chair and listened to music. But the more he relaxed, the more he thought about the case. A statement from one of the delivery drivers kept haunting him. Before he knew it, he was up from the chair and had the files and folders spread across the table, smoke curling up from the cigarette in the ashtray.

He searched for the statement then stopped, reading it in detail, though it was already imprinted on his mind. This guy had identified the picture as Nicky, and he sounded credible. He said he remembered it because it was unusual. He delivered to the diner by Nino's house and saw the guy sitting at the table eating dinner. Half an hour later, he went to the restaurant by Donnie Amato's work and saw him there. He remembered thinking. *Didn't this guy just eat dinner?*

Frankie put down the notes, took a long drag of his cigarette, and let the smoke drift out slowly. This meant the killer was staking out his victims long beforehand. And it meant he was probably watching somebody else right now, sitting in a diner or a coffee house and watching the next guy he was going to kill. Frankie just had to figure out who.

He wanted to believe it was Tony. That would be the easy thing, but he knew in his heart that Tony and Nicky looked a lot alike; people used to think they were brothers. And that damn picture he'd shown people was from a cell phone, not the best quality.

Frankie got up, paced the apartment, then went to the window. He pulled the curtain back just a touch and peeked out into the street.

Who are you watching, Nicky?

CHAPTER 57

THINGS IN COMMON

Current Day

Frankie got home from another miserable day of getting nothing done. He did without wine again—he'd had too much of late—but he brewed a great cup of espresso and lit a smoke to enjoy it with. Long ago he realized he had too many vices to quit all at once, so he opted for control of them one at a time.

The "Things in Common" chart had moved to a prominent place on his living room wall, the space compliments of his ex-wife. As he stood before his ever-evolving chart, he studied the progress.

> *Common Links:*
> *Shot in head and heart:*   *All victims*
> *Something in hands when came home:*   *All victims*
> *Single:*   *All victims*
>
> *(Were they gay?)*

Frankie paused. Four guys killed and all single. Was he missing something? Was this some sexual deviant? He went to the table and pulled the files.

Tommy Devin, the second one, was single. No sign of girls in the apartment. Nothing in his address book. Neighbors didn't remember seeing any girls visit. He made a note.

"Could be gay."

The next file was on Renzo Ciccarelli, the first one killed. Single. No girlfriend.

Fuck, did I screw up? Are these guys all gay?

He leafed through the folder. Copies of *Penthouse* were found in the closet. That was something, but it didn't say much. He laid down Renzo's file and reached for Nino's.

Nino Tortella. Single. Engaged.

Phew. Frankie breathed a sigh of relief. *Hope it was a girl.*

As he looked deeper, all indications were that Nino was straight. He hurried to Donnie Amato's file.

Donnie Amato. Single. Divorced. *Good.* Wife filed for reasons of infidelity. *Even better.*

Donnie seemed to be anything but gay. *Thank God for small favors.*

Last thing he wanted was a city in turmoil over a bunch of gay bashings. Back to the chart.

Torture—Three were. Tommy wasn't. (Why?)

This one baffled him. Why not Tommy? Why the others, but not him? He wasn't even the first, so it wasn't that the killer was escalating. Frankie put a big question mark alongside his name.

Rat shit—Found at all crime scenes—but not rats.

So far, only Nino's had an actual dead rat. Frankie shook his head. This was weak. He was forcing it, trying to make it fit, and he knew in his heart it just didn't feel right.

Abundance of DNA—All.

Frankie looked at the rest of the evidence. Most of it was spotty. Baseball bats used on two, but not the other two. Pictures turned down at Nino and Tommy's house, but others had no pictures in the room. *All* were killed in their homes, though. He wrote that in the "All" column. He stepped back and studied more. He felt sure there was a mob connection, but he couldn't prove anything on three of them, and only suspected on two. The other two were clean.

He was hitting a stone wall, and when he did that he knew it was time to change things up. He traded in his espresso for wine. Sometimes he loved his own logic. This was psychology at its best—convince yourself you work better after, or while, drinking wine, so that you can drink wine. But that's only after you've convinced yourself you can't live without the other vices.

Thank God for giving us psychiatrists to make sense of what we do.

Frankie paced, stopping now and then to study his chart. He went to the other chart, too, looked it over. This was the one he made when he first suspected it was Nicky. Time to see what had changed. He grabbed his red pen and started in on the columns, crossing out items he felt no longer applied, making adjustments as needed to others.

Nicky:

Friends	*—Who are friends? Me, Tony, Suit. Anyone else?*
	Yes, the mystery girl.
Honor	*—Don't ever run. If this is Nicky, he definitely isn't running.*
	But he did run from Tito. What does that tell me?
Girls	*—?*
	The girl has something on Tito. Who is she, and how did Nicky meet her?
~~*Nuns*~~	~~*—Sister Mary Thomas, does she know anything? Would Nicky tell her?*~~
~~*Prison*~~	~~*—Have no idea what he did in there.*~~

Fearless   —No shit.
Smart   —Definitely.
Rosa   —Her teachings affected him. Respect for women.
             Pictures turned down. Protection of the girl. What else?
Tito   —Tito is after Nicky. Did he kill him?
Cleveland —He called from there, but never sent package. Why?

Frankie finished his first glass of wine, lit a smoke and walked. He liked to walk about the apartment, stare out the window, then come back to the chart. That helped him focus.

Betrayal, he thought, *that definitely belongs on the list.* He added it to the bottom.

Betrayal   —Someone betrayed Nicky.

When he finished with his editing, he stepped back and lit another smoke, contemplating. Now it was time to look at Tony's chart.

Tony:
Friends   —Me, Nicky, Suit, Tito, Manny.
             Have to question me and Nicky.
Honor   —Not sure if it still means anything to him.
             Never did. Remember Woodside.
Girls   —Has wife, Celia. Others.
             Tony was never faithful. What does that tell me?
Nuns   —Never had the respect Nicky did.
Mob   —Seems to be in tight.
             Rising fast and ambitious.
Conniving—Can no longer trust Tony. DO NOT TRUST HIM.
Smart   —Smartest guy I know.

Rosa ~~—His mother, but did he listen to her?~~

Tito —*Does Tony obey him? Or just work for him?*

How far would he go for Tito?

Brooklyn —*If something mob-related happens in Brooklyn, Tito knows, which means Tony knows.*

This was becoming more than a worry. This was a wart on Frankie's ass now. The captain was reaming out Morreau, and Morreau turned it on Frankie. And Frankie was out of ideas about where to go with this. Plus, he was pissed. He knew one of them did it, but he couldn't prove it.

Even worse, I don't want to prove it.

After another cigarette, Frankie's motivation cranked up, and he vowed to find out *why* these guys were killed. He stepped back to analyze the charts one more time. The night was getting old, and he was past tired. Smoke curled up from the ashtray, stung his eye. He reviewed everything again. Played it over in his mind. A few things stuck out.

If he assumed the killer was Tony, there could be a lot of reasons behind the killings, all mob-connected. But if it was Nicky, there was only one reason for him to be so brutal—someone betrayed him or hurt someone he loved.

Frankie thought about the girl, how Nicky was protecting her. Risking his life to help her get away from Tito. How Nicky had called him and said he was sending the evidence but never did. Based on that alone, something had clearly gone wrong. He went to the chart and scribbled in, 'Someone must have hurt girl.'

As soon as he wrote it he knew it felt right. He would run with that line of reasoning—for now, at least. If someone had hurt the girl, that explained why the killings were so brutal—Nicky was getting even for killing the person he loved. Frankie thought about it and nodded. He could see Nicky doing that. He *would* hurt you if you did him wrong.

Frankie went back to pacing; no way he could go to sleep now. He was closing in on solving the puzzle.

Someone hurt the girl. That explain why the killings were brutal, but not why Nicky didn't torture Tommy Devin. Frankie went back to his chair, turned it so he faced the chart and scrutinized it some more. *Why not Tommy?*

After ten minutes, maybe more, the answer hit him. The secret was in what the killer *did* to Tommy, not in what he *didn't* do. Tommy was shot once in the head and once in the heart.

Like everybody else. Frankie jumped up, grabbed his red pen, and raced to the chart.

'Girl was killed. Shot in head and heart.'

Satisfied for now, Frankie poured more wine and settled in to watch a movie. Before he went to bed, he wrote down things he had to do the next day:

'Search databases for female shooting victim. Head and heart.'

IN THE MORNING HE went straight to the office, not stopping to chat with Ted, but opting to climb the stairs and get to Carol before anyone else gave her work to do. "Hey, good-looking," he said when he reached her desk. "I need a favor."

"That's redundant, Detective. If you call me good-looking, you always need a favor."

"Yeah, but this is a big one."

Carol smiled, cooing. "Now *that* I'll take."

Frankie blushed. "All right, cut the shit." He leaned over her desk. "I need reports on any unsolved murders where there was a female victim shot in both the head and the chest."

"Where? Brooklyn? Bronx?"

"Anywhere. Whole goddamn country. Tap into the FBI database. Those bastards have data on everything."

"How far back you want me to go?"

"I don't know, five or six months, I guess."

"Anything else?"

Frankie shook his head. "Use your imagination, but head and chest shots are what I'm looking for. And not one or the other—it has to be both."

CHAPTER 58

YOU CAN'T HIDE FOREVER

8 Months Ago

It was Friday, and I was up early again. For some reason, I never slept on Fridays. I always seemed to pop up by six, and for no good reason. I planned on going to Chicago today to mail the gun off to Bugs, but Gina had me running errands—and when a woman is planning a wedding, a man better go along with it. I did.

Ever since the fiasco with Angie's letter, we had enjoyed ourselves, falling right back into old ways of laughing and having fun. Once or twice, Gina even mentioned kids. I told her I'd love to have some, but I worried about her; mid-thirties was tough for a first-time mother. I wanted her to do what was right for *her*, but secretly I prayed she would decide to have at least one child. We even got to the point of discussing names. The wedding was two weeks away, and we had a lot left to do.

"I *have* to get to Chicago," I said. "Bugs expected that package last week."

"Why not mail it from here and be done with it?"

"No. I trust Bugs, but I want to be careful. Mailing it from Chicago means it really could have come from anywhere. We'll do it at the airport Fed-Ex so anyone is a suspect, even people with connecting flights."

"Can I come with you?"

"Of course. We'll make a day of it."

"Then what do we do with what's left of this magnificent day?" She danced across the living room as if she were waltzing.

"I'll make a deal. You pick up some shrimp and pasta, and I'll get fresh bread. If you're a good girl, and promise me favors tonight, I'll get you cannoli."

She undid a button or two on her blouse, looked at me with sultry eyes. "The favors I'll promise, but don't act like this is for me. You're only going to get the sfogliatelle. Sometimes I think you like eating that more than other things."

"Goddamn. That hurt."

"Because I might be right?"

I hesitated long enough to draw a kick from her beautiful bare foot, which I grabbed and kissed. "I guess it's you, but the sfogliatelle comes in a close second."

"I'll remember that tonight, sweet Nicky," she said, as she slipped on her shoes. "I'll be back before you. You know where to find me."

I laughed as I left the house. "Now you're going to make me run."

She threw a kiss to me. "Bye."

I walked, didn't run, the few blocks to the bakery. Once inside, I savored the aromas that took me back to childhood. There wasn't much in life as good as this. I ordered the loaf of bread, two cannoli, and two sfogliatelle. I could have eaten four, but if I kept that up, I'd end up looking like Patsy the Whale. They bagged the bread, put the others in a box, and stuffed both inside a nice bag with handles.

"See you next week, Richie."

I almost didn't respond. It was tough to remember my fake name. "Okay, see you then," I said, and headed out the door. It was a beautiful day, and I had a beautiful life. I whistled and sang songs all the way home, while thoughts of Mamma Rosa's humming kept a smile on my face.

Nino Tortella sat in the back seat of a car across the street, halfway down the block from the bakery. He stared, then did a double take, then leaned forward and tapped Tommy Devin on the shoulder. "Hey, Tommy, what's your take? Is that him?"

Tommy looked at the picture on the seat beside him, then back at the man walking down the sidewalk with a bag from the bakery. "No doubt. It's him."

Nino punched some numbers on his phone and waited for an answer. "Yeah?"

"Bingo."

"Where?"

"Bakery, just like you said. We're following him now."

"Don't let him spot you."

"Don't worry, he—"

"And don't try *anything* with this guy. If he suspects something, he could kill you ten times before you even think of what to do. And believe me, you don't want him on your ass. He once told me what he'd do to anyone who betrayed him."

"Okay. We'll just follow."

"That's right. Follow. I want to know where he lives. And I need to find that girl."

CHAPTER 59

CAUGHT

8 Months Ago

J ohnny Muck sat in the back seat of the car, checking his gun while Tommy Devin drove. Muck wore thin leather gloves lined with Cashmere, and his favorite fedora sat on his head, cocked slightly to the left. "Park around the corner. And keep the car out of sight."

They got out of the car and went in the side door of a laundromat about a block and a half from Nicky and Gina's house. Tony Sannullo had issued orders to watch them and wait until they could get them both. Johnny had other orders, though, and Tito had sent him to make sure those orders got carried out: The girl goes no matter what.

Besides Johnny, there was Tommy Devin, Renzo Ciccarelli, Nino Tortella and Donnie Amato. Johnny looked at each of them, held them fixed with his hard-eyed glare. "Tito's holding me responsible, so I'm holding each of you responsible. Got it?"

They nodded.

"Okay, now we wait till he comes out, then we follow. Two cars. Very carefully."

"Time to see the priest," Gina said as she cooked breakfast. "I can't believe it's that close. Can you?"

I put the paper down and laughed. "Never did like going to see a priest, but this time, it's okay. Confession is going to be hell, though."

Gina flipped the eggs over and splashed them with a little grease from the bacon. "You might still be saying penance on our honeymoon."

I got up, walked over and rubbed her shoulders. "It'll be worth it, no matter how much penance he gives me." I leaned down and kissed her neck.

"Don't start that now."

"When we get back then."

"Hmm. That just might do."

We ate breakfast between talk of hotels, honeymoons, and houses, and then I looked at my watch and grabbed the briefcase. "Time we got going."

Gina went to the restroom, checked her make-up, then headed out the front door. In a minute, we were on the way to the church.

I parked in front of the fire hydrant so no one could slip in behind me, checked both side mirrors, the rearview, then got out, stepping onto a light dusting of snow. For Cleveland, a dusting was good. Could have just as easily been a blizzard. My shoes left prints as I made my way to the sidewalk, eyes darting left and right, seeking anything out of place. I learned long ago to be aware of my surroundings. I reached my hand out as Gina climbed out of the car.

"Ready, sinner?"

Gina smiled. "Sinner? It's a good thing I'm going first. That way I'll be done if Father Amelio dies when you tell him your sins."

We walked into the church together, said our prayers, then met Father Amelio, who had agreed to meet us early and hear our confessions before reviewing plans for the wedding. I smiled at him, then said to Gina, "I'll wait outside."

Gina looked at me suspiciously. "You're not chickening out, are you?"

"I feel like it, but I won't. Come get me when you're done."

I walked out the door and paced the sidewalk, kicking up a few tufts of snow now and then, and wishing more than anything that I had a cigarette. I pulled my collar up to buffer the wind, then blew on my hands to keep them warm. Life sure had changed. And all for the better. I was going to confession, and soon to be married properly.

Thanks, God. You're as good as Sister Thomas said you were.

A few minutes later the doors opened and Gina came out. She went by *Mary* now, but I would always think of her as Gina. A warm smile replaced my wary look. I rushed to greet her. She looked precious, standing there twirling that damn necklace of hers, even in this cold weather. One of these days I was going to hide that thing. As I moved toward her a sudden and wonderful smile popped onto my face. I felt it. I realized that this was the first time I had thought of that necklace without thinking of Angela.

"Feel better?" I hugged her and buried my head in her hair. "Get all those sins absolved?"

She laughed along with me and Father Amelio, who had come out to join us, then she leaned in close and whispered. "Now that I'm all clean of sin, maybe we should do something nasty to taint our souls." She tapped me on the arm. "We could make a habit of this."

"In order for that to work, I still have to confess, so…here I go." I grabbed her hand and headed toward the church.

"Not so fast," Gina said, pulling her hand away. "I'm staying out here to smoke. I have a feeling you'll be a while."

I rolled my eyes. "Come on, Father. Let's get this over with."

The few steps to the big wooden doors seemed like a walk down death row. A thousand thoughts ran through my head. *What the hell would this guy think when I told him what I'd done?* The least of my worries was the penance, which would be a lot more than a few prayers. He'd probably make me hold up the world for a month like Atlas. I wondered then if Atlas had been a shooter. I shook my head to clear it. Now I was mixing up mythology and religion, not something a priest would appreciate.

Father Amelio held the door for me. We walked through the inner doors. I touched my fingers to the holy water, half expecting it to feel like acid. I hesitated, then blessed myself, wondering if God minded such a foul sinner tainting his bowl.

I followed the priest past one confessional then he entered the door of the one closest to the front. The red curtain of death awaited me. If that walk into the church felt like the walk to death row, this was putting the noose around my neck.

Help me out, God. I parted the curtain and stepped into the darkness, kneeling on the padded cushion. Father Amelio sat on the other side of the screened window, his image looming like a shadow of a dark angel. I made the sign of the cross and repeated the words I dreaded for a long time.

"Bless me, Father, for I have sinned. It has been…fourteen years since my last confession."

GINA LIT HER SECOND cigarette, drawing lightly on the filter and blowing out the smoke in a long thin stream. Her head was tilted back, enjoying the crisp cold air. She wondered how long it would take them. It made her feel bad for Nicky. She could tell how worried he was on the way over. Big, tough Nicky, afraid to tell his sins to a priest. She realized that it wasn't so much that he was afraid to tell them to a priest, as it was he was afraid to admit them to himself.

This would be the final hurdle for them, the one thing she'd been waiting for to put their relationship into that perfect state. Not that they wouldn't fight—there'd always be some of that, but make-up sex could take care of the little stuff. It was even good for it. This would let Nicky finally be himself. She saw how he suffered, and though she had doubts when they first met, she knew he was a good man. A caring man who loved her.

A car door opened, then closed, drawing her attention to the street. Two men in overcoats walked toward the church. One of them wore a white scarf. The other was a tall gentleman sporting a hat like her father used to wear. She nodded, smiling. The tall one nodded in return, his smile warm.

"Good morning," he said, and tipped his hat.

They walked past her, slow and purposeful. She wondered if they were going to rid themselves of sin as well.

Might have a long wait, she wanted to tell them, then realized that regular confession wouldn't start for hours. *What are they doing here?* She turned to look at them, but the sound of another car door closing alerted her. Something stirred in her stomach—fear. She'd lived with the feeling for so long, she'd almost forgotten how intense *real* fear could be. It came back like a sharp jab with a needle.

Two more men approached from the street: overcoats, gloves, and the same purposeful stride. Gina glanced back toward the church. The two men who passed her were now facing her, hands reaching into their pockets.

I'm going to die! She knew then that she would die, and her body would be found on the sidewalk outside a church in Cleveland, shot full of holes. She threw her purse at the man closest to her then ran to the left, hoping to distract them. The snow made her slip, but she quickly got her footing, running fast toward a row of houses with trees in the front yards.

If she could make it into the trees—

The first bullet struck her just above the right kidney. Pain tore through her body. Her head reared back. She reached a hand toward the wound, stumbling as the pain increased. She kept running, not as fast now, but she still held hope. More rounds of gunfire sounded from behind her and, as she prayed, thinking they missed, she felt searing pain in her left leg, not far from her knee. She collapsed and rolled on the ground, staring up at the gray sky.

Thank you, God, for letting me finish confession. With that thought came images of Nicky. *If he hears shots, he'll come out after them.* She hoped he got away, but if not, she prayed he finished confession before they got him.

They were standing above her now, all pointing their guns. The first bullet shattered her skull, then…

I WAS IN THE middle of telling Father Amelio about a drug dealer I'd killed when I heard the unmistakable sound of gunfire. I knew that sound too well, and it roared in my ears like cannon shot. I tore the curtain aside and ran. Father Amelio was ahead of me, racing for the front door. He must have taught track or something, because as fast as I was, he beat me to the vestibule. Fear dug a deep trench inside of me. My stomach felt as if it had ruptured. Images raced through my head, and in each one, Gina lay on the ground—dead. I had my gun in hand by the time I got to the doors. Father Amelio guarded the exit, arms spread wide as if he were Christ on the cross.

"Get out of the way, Father."

He refused to move.

I pointed the gun at him. Priest or not, I had to get to Gina. "Get out of the way, or I swear I'll kill you."

"And they will kill you if you go out there."

I shoved him aside, pushed open the door and went out, low to the ground. Gina lay on the ground, blood staining the purity of the snow. Bullets flew into the door above me, some hitting the stone entrance. I rolled to the side, got off a few rounds before taking cover in an alcove. After waiting a few seconds, I knelt, peeked out and fired again, three shots. They were already heading for their cars. Two guys jumped into the farthest one up the street and sped away. The other two got into the car nearest me. The guy in the passenger seat had a distinct red birth mark on the right side of his face—Renzo Ciccarelli.

I'll see you soon.

I emptied the gun, trying to score a lucky hit, but they were gone. I raced to Gina, praying for a miracle. When I reached her, I knew it was hopeless. Her head was covered in blood and she'd been shot either in the heart or next to it many times. I knelt next to her, took her hand in mine.

It wasn't supposed to be like this. Not for her. Not for me. Everybody I loved died.

I brushed her hair from her face. Cleaned the blood off using snow. I wanted to pick her up and take her home. Fix her. Make her new. But Gina's beautiful brown eyes had no spark in them. I knew then she was gone forever.

I leaned down and kissed her lips—they were cold. Maybe from the weather, I didn't know. All I knew was those lips were not Gina's. I wasn't bringing her back.

A hand touched my shoulder. Startled at first, I looked up to see Father Amelio, his head shaking. "The cops will be here any minute. I'll have to say something."

I kissed Gina on the lips again, whispered, "I love you," then wiped my tears away and stood. "Tell them whatever you like."

I got in the car and headed for home. With luck I could get everything cleaned out and make a break before they came looking for me. As I drove home, images of Gina kept popping into my head. With each one came an image of Renzo. Every breath I took whispered his name. I needed to get to him. If nothing else, to find out who ordered the job and who helped him.

Be seeing you soon, Renzo. Real *soon.*

CHAPTER 60

SAY GOODBYE TO CLEVELAND

8 Months Ago

I raced home taking corners at speeds I shouldn't have, cutting people off, even running traffic lights. Instinct told me I shouldn't be doing this, but I had lost control. Between fits of crying and vows of vengeance, I found the will to slow down so the cops didn't pick me up. All I could think of was Gina, on the verge of getting what she wanted, and it was taken away from her in the most brutal fashion. I prayed she was with God now. She should be.

When I wasn't feeling sorry for Gina, I managed to drown in my own pity. After finally escaping the life my father lived, the one that ruined his own life, I found happiness. But they took that away when they killed Gina. Now *they* were going to pay. I always hated the looks in the eyes of the people I killed, that horrible realization just before they died, but there were several sets of eyes I was looking forward to seeing.

I parked the car, went into the house, and packed the few clothes I had. It took me longer than I wanted to gather Gina's things, as I found myself staring at them and reminiscing. Pictures, notes she wrote. Suddenly even a scribble on a piece of torn paper behind a refrigerator magnet was a masterpiece. And it was; it was hers. As I was packing I came across a necklace I bought her. It was her favorite—St. Anthony, the patron saint of lost items and travelers. I smiled. We were a little of both. I closed my eyes, pictured her twirling that damn thing around her mouth, whisking little St. Anthony back and forth across the bottom of her chin. It was what stopped me that day I saw Gina through the gun sites. It was what saved me. How many times since then had I watched her twirling? Whenever she was nervous, excited, happy, sad—it didn't matter; there seemed to be a special twirl for each emotion.

I tried smiling, but tears came instead. I brought the necklace up to my lips and kissed it. "They will pay, Gina. Trust me, they *will* pay."

I walked about the house, reconfirming memories, then got out before my emotions took hold. By eleven on Monday morning I had been to the banks and got our cash from the safe deposits. Then I got the gun she had as evidence on Tito. I drove the car to long-term parking, took the shuttle to the airport and caught a cab to the bus station. Kansas City was on my list. I had to go see a guy named Minnow, one of the many connections I'd made in prison. He could get me whatever I wanted.

Five days later, I left KC with everything I needed: another new identity, new car, and a new gun. Several new guns. I drove the speed limit all the way. No sense risking being picked up for speeding with guns in the car. New York was a two-day drive, but that was fine. It would take me that long to figure out what I was going to do to Renzo when I found him. There was no way he was getting a quick death. And once I got Renzo, I'd find out who else was involved.

Who knew I was in Cleveland? Who could have known? I had no contact with anyone.

That's when it hit me. *Bugs. I called Bugs about the gun. He must have tracked the call to Cleveland.*

Not only had they killed Gina, but Bugs broke the oath. I pounded the steering wheel, wanting to break it. After all I did for Bugs, and he does *this!*

As I drove over the Pennsylvania line, I realized the old Nicky Fusco was dead. There was just Nicky the Rat now. And as I thought about the things I was going to do to Bugs, I realized that I had no funny feeling in my gut. Sister Thomas might have a hard time explaining that one.

CHAPTER 61

CALL FROM CLEVELAND

Current Day

Frankie woke in the middle of the night, thinking about Nicky, once again wondering what this was all about. What the hell had happened? The missing package bothered him too. Why would Nicky call, say he's sending something, then not do it?

He wouldn't.

So that meant something happened to Nicky. Cleveland never turned up anything regarding the material witness request. So where was he? Had Tito killed him?

Where are you, Nicky? Anxiety kept Frankie up for another hour or so, but he finally went to sleep, catching a few hours before the alarm went off. After an invigorating shower, he made coffee, grabbed a bagel, and headed out the door.

It took him longer than usual to get to the station, and that put him in a foul humor. He got a good parking spot and rushed into the station, taking the steps two-at-a-time to the second floor. "Hey, Carol, anything on that report yet?"

"I already called and put pressure on them. They said I'll have it this morning."

"Bring it in as soon as you get it."

Carol walked in before his coffee even got cold. "Here you go, Detective. Six possibilities."

Frankie grabbed the report from her hand. "Thanks. I owe you."

"You keep saying that, but I never see anything."

He sat back down, eying the papers instead of her. "Yeah, well…"

Carol walked out, smiling. "You're welcome, Detective."

"Oh, yeah, thanks," Frankie said, but he was already deep into the report.

Six murders fit the description. There had been thirteen shootings, but seven had already been solved. He scanned through the remaining six, but nothing jumped out at him. Muggings, jealousy, domestic violence… none of them fit. He threw the papers down on the desk and walked back out to see Carol. "I need you to go back further. Maybe a year. And I only want unsolved cases."

This time didn't take as long. She returned within half an hour with new reports. There were four.

The first one was from Utah, and it looked like a family feud of some type. Some guy from an off-shoot Mormon sect shot one of his wives for having sex with another man. "What the hell?" Frankie said aloud. Didn't seem right that this guy could have multiple wives, but she couldn't have some fun on the quiet. Oh well…

This case definitely wasn't what he was looking for.

Next one was from Portland, Oregon. Young woman, maybe early thirties, shot in the back of the head and the chest. Boyfriend was missing. He scrambled through the papers. Boyfriend was reported to be about average height and weight. Brown or black hair.

Could be Nicky, he thought, but then he couldn't picture Nicky in Portland. Still…so far things fit. He laid that aside to check up on later. Too early to call the west coast.

The third one was from Cleveland. Frankie came to full alert. He never got to case number four. He looked at the case closer. Young woman killed at a church. Victim shot in the head with multiple chest wounds. He popped his head out the door.

"Carol, get me a number for Cleveland homicide." Carol loved it when cases were breaking. She thrived on the challenge and the excitement that ran through the office when a detective was closing in on something. Damn good, Carol was. Within minutes, she came in with the number.

After three calls, Frankie got hold of the right guy in homicide, Eddy Pollard, Detective First Class.

"Pollard."

"Detective Pollard? This is Frankie Donovan, Detective with Brooklyn homicide."

"What's up in the Big Apple?"

"A lot of goddamn killing. How about you?" He didn't know if Cleveland had a nickname, but if it did, he felt certain they weren't proud of it.

"About the same. What can I do for you, Detective?"

"I've got reason to suspect one of our cases has ties to Cleveland. You have any murders in the last six to ten months that involve a female victim, early to mid-thirties?"

A long pause. "Which doll do you want, Detective? You just hit my number one pain-in-the-ass case on the head."

"What have you got?"

"It was about seven months ago, maybe eight. Right in front of a church. Female, age thirty-four. Mary Simmons-Krasner."

Krasner. They went to school with a guy named Krasner, and he was sure the guy's first name had been Richie. *Didn't he die in a car wreck? Did Nicky take his name?*

"You there?" Pollard asked.

"Yeah, sorry. I was thinking." A short pause, then, "Detective, how was she killed?"

"Shot."

"Can you be more specific?"

"Combination of .38's and 9 mm. Multiple gunshots to the head and chest."

Frankie nearly fell off the chair. *Once in the head. Once in the heart.* How many times had he said that to himself? How many times had he wondered *why* these guys were killed that way? Now he had an answer. Nicky was killing them that way because of her.

"Any witnesses?"

"None."

"That's it? You got nothing else for me?"

"Not a damn thing."

"All right. Thanks."

Frankie made a note to have Carol search everything for Richie Krasner. Car rentals, hotels, plane flights. If Nicky was using Richie's name, maybe they could track him that way. Frankie grabbed his smokes and headed for the door. It was time to see Tony. No matter what goddamn lies he spit out, Tony *knew* what was going on and Frankie intended to find out.

CHAPTER 62

PRECAUTIONS

Current Day

A s Frankie drove to Tony's house, his cell phone rang. "Hello."

"Frankie, it's Carol. Detective Pollard from Cleveland homicide has been trying to reach you."

"Give me the number." Frankie pulled over as soon as he could and dialed.

"Pollard."

"Pollard, this is Donovan from Brooklyn."

There was an inordinately long pause, then. "Donovan, you're going to be pissed, but I had to do this."

"What?"

"Earlier when we talked, I told you there were no witnesses, but there was one. A priest."

"Why did—"

"You know the drill. I don't know you from shit, and you call all of a sudden wanting to know about a murder that, to me, sure as shit, stinks of New York connections. And you being from Brooklyn." Pollard paused again. "I had to check you out first, which is why I'm calling back. We said in the papers that she was alone, but she was with a guy named Richie

Krasner. Supposed to be her husband, but getting married again in the church, at least from what the priest said. And he said there were at least four shooters. Anyway, Richie vanished. We haven't been able to find shit on him. Went to the address on their licenses, but the place was empty. I mean dead empty. Not a stick of furniture, a towel, a dish. Not even a fingerprint. I'd like to keep it that way, if you know what I mean."

"No problem, Pollard. I appreciate this. If you ever need anything, call." Frankie was about to hang up, when he thought of something else. "Pollard, how did you swing it for everybody to go along with this charade?"

There followed an even longer pause than before. "Shit, Donovan, you got to keep this quiet."

"You know it."

"FBI came in shortly after the incident. I don't even know what brought them, unless they picked something up from her prints when we ran them. Said she had ties to someone in the Witness Protection Program. Since the whole thing stunk of mob connections, I believed them. They were the ones who wanted me to keep the guy out of it."

Frankie smiled. "Pollard, you've been a big help. I owe you one for sure."

"Whoa. Not so fast. How does what you're working on tie in to my case? Let's share, Detective."

Frankie hesitated, but decided that what the hell, the guy had played square with him. "We've got some murders up here. Four of them, and we think Krasner is the one doing it." He took a deep breath. "Listen, Pollard, this can't go anywhere. You'd cost me my job."

"Keep talking. I know how to use a lead."

"The girl was being hunted by some well-known mob types from Brooklyn, and I think I know why. If she had connections to someone in Witness Protection, it had to have something to do with that. We figure the guy was innocent, just protecting her."

"And you think this guy, Krasner, is now hunting them?"

"That's my guess."

"Are you shitting me? Who is this Krasner?"

"That's just it. He's not Richie Krasner."

"Damn. All right, Detective. Send me whatever you can, or at least keep me posted."

"I'll keep you updated, I promise. And I really do appreciate what you did for me." Frankie hung up and damn near sung a song. He was right about Nicky all along. He knew Nicky wouldn't kill them without a good reason. Frankie suddenly realized something.

Jesus Christ. He thinks it's me. That's what the rat shit is about. Nicky thinks I betrayed him.

FRANKIE LOCKED HIS DOOR after he entered. It was no longer a simple precaution. If Nicky was on the loose and really after him, he needed every edge he could get, and he had to solve this fast. The problem was, he had no idea who was involved with killing Nicky's girl. The priest said there were four of them, but there could be more. Frankie walked over and wrote on the chart.

'Nicky must have known shooters. At least one of them.'

He stepped back and stared at that. If Nicky only knew one—and Frankie would make that assumption for now—it had to be Renzo. He was the first one killed.

And Nicky would have gone to Renzo to get the other names.

He went back to the chart and wrote, 'Renzo gave him other names?' He put a question mark by it, but it felt right.

Frankie smiled as if he had actually figured something out. Assuming Nicky knew Renzo, he could have gotten the other names from him. So that brought him back to the original question, where did Nicky know Renzo from?

Frankie pulled up Renzo's file. No occupation. Three arrests for gambling. No convictions. Killed in house. No one heard or saw anything. Tons of evidence at scene. Tortured before shot. A note had been added to the file about a suspected connection to Tito Martelli during his old days in Queens, but nothing proven. So the one likely connection between Nicky and Renzo was the chance they both knew Tito. One possibility. One thread. That's all it took, though.

One thread—Tony Sannullo.

Frankie dialed Tony's number.

It took five rings for him to answer. "What the hell do you want, Bugs?"

"Someone tried killing Nicky."

"Why tell me?"

"I think it was you."

"Fuck you, Bugs."

"You know he won't stop until he gets you, Tony. He'll save you for last."

"Let him try. I'm not Nino Tortella."

Frankie laughed. "Oh, you're dead, Tony. You're dead, and you don't even know it." He hung up and cursed. He didn't care about Tony anymore.

But the stupid fuck might be taking me down with him.

CHAPTER 63

WHO'S NEXT

Current Day

Frankie jumped out of bed earlier than usual, gulped down his coffee and went to the office, marching up the steps to see Morreau.

"What do you want, Donovan?"

"I think I know who the killer is."

"This the rat-shit theory that Mazzetti told me about?" He said it without even looking up.

It didn't look as if Frankie would get cooperation on this. He sat in the chair. "You'd have to listen to the details. It's not what Lou thinks."

Morreau leaned back. "I'm listening."

Frankie told him all he knew—which was very little, and all he suspected—which was a lot more.

"So what are you asking for?" Morreau asked.

"Manpower. I think he's going to hit Tito Martelli."

"Let him."

"Yeah, I know, but we still have to protect him."

Morreau fiddled with his pen, took a sip of what had to be cold coffee by now—which forced Frankie to wince—then pulled out his duty schedule. After about half a minute, he shook his head and looked up. "You got Mazzetti. I can give you Higgins and Sapperstein."

Higgins and Sapperstein. They weren't the best, but not bad either. "I appreciate it, boss. This might pay off."

"You got a week, Donovan."

"Thanks, boss," Frankie said, and got out before Morreau changed his mind.

"Hey, Donovan."

Bugs turned to see Mazzetti shuffling his way in. "Hey, Lou. We got help on the case—and some new leads."

Mazzetti didn't laugh, but he looked as if he wanted to. "Hope it's got nothing to do with rats."

"Stick it, Mazzetti."

"All right. Fill me in after I get some coffee." As he walked off, he asked, "Who'd he give us for help?"

"Higgins and Sapperstein."

He shrugged. "We could do worse."

"Yeah, I thought so too."

FRANKIE WENT HOME EARLY, hoping to catch a short nap before dinner. He parked the car, grabbed the bag of groceries he bought on the way home, then headed for the apartment. As he was going up the steps to the front door, he stopped. Frozen. Next to the stoop on the sidewalk lay a dead rat. He shifted the bag to his left hand, undid his coat and loosened the strap on his gun. He checked the street, then looked up to his apartment window. The shades were drawn.

Moving back to the sidewalk, he nudged the rat with his shoe, turning it over. It was soft—a fresh kill. No visible marks. Again, he looked around, then entered the apartment building. He took the steps slower than usual, cautious about every sound, every movement.

When he reached his door he stopped, breathed deeply. As he pulled out his gun, he set the groceries on the floor, then, with his left hand, he grabbed the key and turned the lock as quietly as he could. He crept into the apartment, safety off, entering low. After a few steps, he knew no one was there. Could sense it. He stood, closed the door, and cleared the place, but found nothing. With his gun back in the holster, he checked the window, trying to see if he was being watched. The only likely surveillance spot was a bodega on the corner.

Frankie opened the door, brought in the groceries—which he had damn near forgotten about—then went to the corner. He waited until a customer left the store then flashed a picture of Nicky at the guy behind the counter. "Ever see him?"

The guy gave it a glance. "I don't think so."

"Look again," Frankie said, jabbing the picture with his finger.

The guy looked again. "What do you want me to say, that I saw him? Okay, I saw him."

"I don't want bullshit. You did or you didn't."

The store owner leaned over the counter. "I don't think so."

"Fuck." Frankie handed him a card. "Call me if you see him."

He walked back to his apartment on full alert.

I know that fucker is watching me. Tito might be next, but he's coming here too. As he climbed his steps for the second time, he wondered if Tony was being watched. And Paulie.

Well, fuck you, Nicky, if you think—

"Hey, FD. How's it going?"

Bugs looked over to see Alex sitting beside the stoop, flipping a coin. He hadn't noticed him coming up.

"Hey, Ace. Going good here. What are you doing?"

"Trying to decide what to do. Heads, I go steal some smokes from my mom's boyfriend. Tails, I wait till he leaves and see if he left any money."

"Money?"

"Sometimes he leaves me money if I go outside and wait while he's... you know, with my mom." He flipped the coin, but when he looked at it, a frown appeared.

"What?" Bugs asked.

"Tails," he said, with a sigh.

Bugs pulled a few smokes from his pack. "I shouldn't be doing this, but here, take these. But you need to quit before you can't make it up the steps anymore."

"You can still climb the steps." His words carried the defiance of the young.

"For now." Images of Lou Mazzetti panting for breath came to mind; Frankie shuddered. "I need to quit too."

He trudged up the steps, slower than usual, perhaps not wanting to know if he did get out of breath. He opened his door and went in. He set his stuff on the table, grabbed a bottle of water, and sat on the sofa. Thoughts of Nicky and Tony rolled around in his mind. He was tired of their shit. What the hell was he—a cop, or a gangster? He couldn't afford to live in the middle anymore. Bugs reached into his pocket, pulled out a quarter and flipped it, covering it up as it hit the back side of his hand. Heads he was a cop, tails a gangster.

He kept his hand covered for a long time. First he couldn't make a decision on his own. Now he didn't even have the courage to let fate decide for him.

"Fuck them," he said, and put the coin back in his pocket without looking. "I'm a cop, and they're both going down."

CHAPTER 64

RULE NUMBER FOUR: MURDER IS INVISIBLE

Current Day

I got up early, drove to the park and let the car sit, then walked the rest of the way. All through the morning, I thought about how to kill Johnny Muck. He deserved something special. But he wouldn't be easy. Johnny Muck was in a constant state of tension, ever-ready to strike out at someone. And if he struck, it was to kill. He had been a good teacher. Competent. Thorough. But everyone had a weakness. What was his?

I thought about it. He lived his life on alert. Never did anything as routine. Didn't shop on the same days, not even in the same places. Went to different gas stations, laundries, fruit stands. He seldom took the same routes anywhere he went, even if it meant going miles out of the way. He always suspected tails, so he was nearly impossible to follow. He would slow down, wait until a light turned yellow, then run it, all the while checking to see if anyone followed.

I tried to think of what Johnny liked. He ate almost any kind of food, so he didn't frequent one restaurant. He never went to the movies, not that I knew. As I pondered the situation, it finally hit me. Johnny loved his windshield to be clean. He always complained about dirty windshields, and was one of the few people who liked the window-washers who used to assault people at the streetlights. After Giuliani cracked down on them, it was tough to get your windows cleaned. Johnny used to look for guys who still did it. That could be my ticket. I just had to think of a plan.

It took me a while to figure it out, but after having no luck trying to follow Johnny, I narrowed my scope down to a few streets where I knew that sooner or later, he would go by. One of them was Flatbush Avenue by Prospect Park. Johnny loved to drive by the park, though I don't think he knew it was a habit. Once I remembered that, I used Johnny's own rules to catch him. I disguised myself as one of the homeless window washers with old clothes from Goodwill, let my beard grow out to be scruffy, and pulled a dirty cap down far enough to cover my forehead. Dirt smudges on my face combined to round out the effect. I waited on the corner of one of the routes he'd probably take to get out of Brooklyn from Tito's place, one that took him by the park. Had to wait eight days to finally catch him coming that way, and to get him at a red light. When I saw his car coming, I got up, made sure to use my best limp, and moved toward his car.

"Window washed, mister?" I asked as I pointed toward his windshield.

"If you can hurry."

I washed as fast as I could while faking the limp, and all the while, making sure my face was above his range of view. I pretended to drop something, and as I fumbled, I slipped a magnetic GPS under the wheel rim. By then the light was changing. I grabbed a few bucks from him and beat a hasty retreat.

Three hours later, I found the car, removed the GPS, then waited until morning to see him come out of his house. It was a nice little neighborhood in Valley Stream about fifteen miles from Tito's place. Single home with a well-kept yard and a detached garage out back.

You're mine now, Johnny.

That weekend I went to the hardware store just off Interstate 87 in New Jersey. It was a Saturday morning. No one would remember a face from a busy day like this. Aisle four had some of what I needed. I picked up one pound of sixteen-penny nails, four one-inch eye hooks, and a small drill, and put them all in the basket. The tool section had a nice twenty-two ounce claw hammer. Good grip on it too. Duct tape, superglue and rope rounded out the shopping list, which I paid for in the longest line, then loaded it in the trunk and returned to New York.

I prepared things meticulously. One of my prison contacts had hooked me up with a guy who worked at Animal Control, and through a simple exchange using P.O. boxes, he got me a handgun with tranquilizer darts, ones guaranteed to put down a two-hundred pound animal within seconds. I figured it would work on humans, too.

I WATCHED FOR A week. Johnny didn't seem to have any particular routine when he got home. No traps seemed to be set, no alarms needed to be turned off. He simply parked the car, got out and walked in. When he got there, he used a key to get in. Nothing unusual. I went to the house twice during the day when he wasn't home and knocked on the door—no dogs, and no one else answered. I risked going in. It might be safer to take him somewhere else, I figured, but I wanted it done here.

I checked the neighborhood for escape routes—always good to know the area. The whole neighborhood was full of single-family houses with detached garages and open yards—perfect for getting out easy. Six blocks away was a subway station, and maybe twelve or thirteen blocks in the other direction was a mall. Either would be good for what I had in mind. With my preparation done, I decided to move ahead.

The next afternoon, I went into his house. I didn't get things ready like I usually did. I thought I'd wait for that. I tidied up a bit and turned down a picture that might have been his mother—even an ex-wife. For the next hour or so, I did a lot of thinking. Why had God been so harsh with me? I kept trying to straighten my life out, but circumstances had forced me onto paths I didn't want to take. And now, with Gina gone...

When his car pulled up, I crouched behind the door and waited. I held the tranquilizer gun in my right hand and a .38 in my left, in case the drugs didn't work. Footsteps sounded on the walk, then up the steps. Slow and steady. The storm door opened, the key turned in the lock, and in stepped Johnny Muck. I had my .38 aimed at him, just in case. As he turned to shut the door, I shot him in the neck.

He stumbled backwards and dropped his keys. He reached for his gun, but I shoved him, and he fell into a chair. He struggled a little, trying to stand, but never mustered the ability. After a minute or so, he was out. The tranquilizer had taken a bit longer than the "few seconds" the guy had claimed, but it was pretty damn good. I made sure Johnny was really out, and then I got things ready.

I set my bag on the kitchen counter, took out the evidence and spread it around. I fastened one-inch hooks to the four corners of the dining room walls. I picked up Johnny's fedora, dusted it off and set in on the counter next to his gloves. Then I dragged Johnny to the dining room, and laid him on the hardwood floor, on his back. I tied each of his wrists and ankles to the hooks, then pulled the slack from them so he couldn't move. I had a nice gag prepared, but opted for plain old duct tape to start with. Depending on how aware Johnny was, I might have to switch.

It took about half an hour for him to come to his senses. When he did, I saw that look in his eyes I'd been waiting for. The same look he had seen himself many times. He rolled his eyes, and shook his head from side to side, squirmed what little he could. I could tell from his expression he wanted to talk, so I undid the tape.

"Nicky, you know it was just business."

I wanted to punish him right then, but I held my temper. "I know, Johnny, and I understand. But I need names."

"What do I get out of it? You let me go?"

I laughed. He did too. "You know that's not happening."

He gulped. I saw the Adam's apple dance in his throat. "I heard about Donnie."

"Shame about him," I said. "But he lied to me. I need to know all the shooters and who ordered it."

Johnny didn't hesitate with the truth; he knew he was going to die. "No other shooters. You got us all. Tony ordered the hit on you and the girl."

Tony. But how did he find me? Did Bugs tell him? I had to find out.

"You did good, Johnny." I paused. What I wanted to do was find Tony and rip his fuckin' head off. Tear his heart out. But I had to finish this. Johnny deserved my time now, even if it was to kill him. "How did Tony find me?"

"I don't know." Johnny looked up. "How'd you find *me*?"

"You taught me too well. I used rule number four—murder is invisible." I saw the puzzled look on his face. "I was the window washer who did your car last week."

As he nodded miserably in recognition, I knelt next to him, took the tube of superglue, and squirted it between his lips, put the tape back over his mouth, then used more tape to secure him. He struggled, trying his best, but very quickly, more quickly than I'd imagined, the superglue sealed his mouth. I had gloves on, so no prints would be left. I'd worn the gloves since I came in. Johnny seemed worried about what to expect. He was right to be worried.

I didn't want to do this to Johnny, especially after he'd been straight with me. But he was the one in charge of the shoot. He killed Gina, and he would have killed me.

After testing the ropes, I double-checked the tape. Didn't want his screams disturbing my work. And there *would* be screams. As Johnny lay there, I got the claw hammer and nails. He went wild-eyed when he saw the nails. Year ago during one of our talks, I told him what I'd do to someone who betrayed me. His hands were stretched to the side, as if he were being crucified, which seemed appropriate. I grabbed a nail the length of my finger, placed it on his palm, drew back the hammer and struck.

The vibrations rocked through him, spasms fighting against me even though he couldn't move. I hammered again, driving the nail halfway into the floor. Three more swings, and it was fastened tight. Surprisingly, there wasn't much blood. As I moved to his other hand, I met his gaze. His eyes were open as wide as they could go, and his face was stretched from trying to scream.

"Sorry this is taking so long, but I'm not a carpenter. Imagine how Jesus must have felt, Johnny. Remember, his friends betrayed him too."

The next hand only required three swings to finish. By the time I stood, he had passed out. I checked his pulse, afraid he might have had a heart attack, but he was just unconscious. I waited a few minutes for him to recover. His eyes were so sad. Pleading. Begging.

"I know, Johnny. It won't be long now."

I stepped over his body; he had pissed himself. Probably shit his pants too. If not, he would soon. I grabbed another nail, got close to him and whispered. "This is for Gina." I positioned the nail just to the right of his nose and drove it into his face. His head jerked up and down, bouncing off the floor. I think he was trying to kill himself. I couldn't have that. I rushed to the bedroom, got a pillow and pushed it under his head. Blood ran out of his nose and over his mouth. I placed another nail at the same spot on the left side, but then stopped. Despite what he had done, I still liked Johnny, and he had suffered enough. I stood and finished the job. Shot him once in the head and once in the heart. Then I repeated the Trinitarian formula as I made the sign of the cross.

Cleaning up this mess was easier than with the last two. I spread the remaining evidence, did the rest of my chores, then changed clothes before leaving through the front door. I stopped on my way home and called the Brooklyn precinct where Bugs worked and told them there was a body in Valley Stream they might be interested in. They told me it wasn't their jurisdiction. I insisted that they pass the message to Detective Donovan. "He'll want to know," I said, then hung up.

CHAPTER 65

MARTYRS AND SAINTS

Current Day

Frankie was lost in thought as he drove into the station. It had been over a week and he had nothing, not even a hint that Nicky was watching Tito. Now he was losing Higgins and Sapperstein. When he pulled into the lot, Mazzetti was waiting. "What's up, Lou?"

"We're visiting the wonderful community of Valley Stream today. Got another one."

"Valley Stream? How did *we* get the call?"

"Special invitation from the shooter. He said you'd want to know." He lit a smoke then cracked the window a bit, enough to let the smoke drift out. "So tell me again who this Rat guy is."

Frankie refreshed him on what he knew, but all the while he hoped this wasn't Nicky. That this was some kind of bad, horrible coincidence. When they got to the scene, the street was filled with cop cars, the crime scene unit, and a handful of reporters. Lou and Frankie flashed their badges and walked in.

A small crowd had gathered in the kitchen. A tall, black deputy eyed Frankie as he approached, holding his hand out. "You Donovan?"

Frankie nodded. "Yeah. And this is Lou Mazzetti, my partner."

"Bobby Tilton," he said, then moved toward the dining room. "Let me introduce you to Gianni Mucchiatto. Don't know him, but he must have pissed somebody off real bad."

The deputy cleared a path, and when Frankie stepped into the dining room, he damn near threw up. They had left Gianni as they found him, tied to the walls, hands nailed to the floor, and a nail hammered into his face. The look on his face was an expression no one should see. Frankie forced himself to take in the scene.

Did you do this, Nicky?

"Some friend you got there, Donovan." Mazzetti lit a smoke, but the crime scene guys stopped him.

Tilton tapped Frankie on the shoulder and nodded toward Mazzetti. "What's he mean? You know the shooter?"

Frankie shook his head. "I know one of the suspects."

"You plan on sharing, Detective?"

Frankie smiled. Already it had gone from *Donovan* to *detective.* "I'll send the file, Tilton. We've got five now."

"Five? How come we haven't heard shit about this?"

Frankie figured he might as well be nice to this guy. It was probably the biggest crime he'd ever had. "FBI thinks there are ties to bigger fish." Donovan looked around as if he'd said something wrong. "Probably shouldn't have even told you that."

Tilton was suddenly back on Frankie's side again. "Goddamn FBI. Those bastards are always screwing up an investigation."

"Tell me about it," Frankie said. He gestured toward the body. "So what do you have on this guy? Any connections? Priors?"

"Not even a parking ticket."

Frankie nodded. *He was a shooter, all right. And he must have been a good one to stay that clean.* He reached out his hand to Tilton. "Here's my card. I'll send you the files on what we've got. Let me know if you come up with anything. Especially if you get any witnesses."

"You got it."

As THEY DROVE BACK to Brooklyn, Mazzetti changed the radio station about a hundred times. He was never satisfied with what was playing even if he liked the song.

"Hey, Lou, leave a song for just once, will you? I'll listen to anything as long as it's a whole song."

Mazzetti ignored the question. "Why'd you leave so soon? We could have stayed a while to see what they get."

"They're not going to get anything, and you know it. It'll be the same as the others—DNA out of our ass, but nothing to connect us to the killer."

Frankie called the FBI to see what they had on Gianni Mucchiatto. He filled them in on the situation, then gave them Tilton's number. Frankie hung up and turned to Lou. "His street name was Johnny Muck. FBI's got nothing but suspicion on him."

"Pretty name," Lou said.

Frankie lit another cigarette. "I'm dropping you off at the station, Lou. I need to see if I can get anything out of Tony."

"And you don't want me coming?"

"He probably won't tell me anything. With you there, he *definitely* wouldn't."

"You sure you're not taking a cut from these guys?"

Frankie laughed. "You've been to my apartment."

"Sorry." Lou was quiet for a moment then turned to face Frankie. "If you ever crack that shell and want to talk to someone, let me know. Thirty years of marriage has made me an expert listener."

"I'm surprised you're not deaf."

"What?"

"I said…fuck you, wise ass."

Lou turned off the radio, something he never did without being threatened. "All shit aside, I'm a good listener, so if you need to talk sometime, I'll even buy the drinks."

"Thanks. I might actually take you up on that. Days like this make me want a friend."

"Like I said, you name the time and place. Just don't make it somewhere I got to climb steps."

"You got it."

Frankie let Mazzetti off at the station, then headed to Cataldi's. He couldn't get the picture of Johnny Muck out of his mind. When he got to the restaurant, he let them park the car, then went inside. "Tony here?"

"At his table."

Frankie made his way there.

Tony got up to greet Frankie, arms open wide. "What a surprise, Bugs. Good to see you."

"Not what you said last time we spoke."

"You know how that goes. I was pissed off."

Frankie said hi to Suit, then sat down. The waiter brought Frankie an espresso.

"What brings you, Bugs? You able to say?"

The last question was a reference to the wire. "I'm not wearing, Tony, but I *am* here officially. I came to see if you heard about Johnny Muck?"

Tony set his cup down, a puzzled look on his face. "Don't know Johnny Muck."

"How about you, Paulie? You know him?"

"Can't say I do, Bugs. Why?"

"Guess it doesn't matter, since you don't know him." Frankie took a bite of Paulie's cannolo, sipped some espresso, then wiped his mouth. "But I'll tell you this, if he was the last link between you and Gina, I'd leave town." Frankie threw a twenty on the table. "See you guys...I hope."

FRANKIE HADN'T GOTTEN TO the door when Tony was on the phone with Tito. He answered on the first ring. "Something happen to Johnny Muck?" Tony asked.

"I haven't heard from him, but I wasn't expecting to." There was silence, then, "Not a good line to talk on. Come see me later."

"All right. Later."

Near the end of the day, Tony went to Tito's. Manny answered the door and took him out back.

Tito looked nervous. "Something happened, all right. Johnny Muck was butchered." Tito paced across the flagstone patio. "Jesus Christ, tell him, Manny. Tell him what he did."

Tony looked to Manny, waiting.

"Tied him up and nailed him to the floor like he was Christ himself." Manny made the sign of the cross when he said it.

"Tell it all, Manny. Tony's a big boy."

Manny shook his head and stared Tony in the eyes. "He drove nails through each hand, and another one right through his cheekbone and into his mouth."

Tony grimaced. "Tito, we've got to do something."

Manny shook his head. "I warned you about this. Remember that shit in WWII about sleeping giants? I think you woke one when you killed Gina."

"He's one guy, Manny." But Tony said it without conviction.

"Tell that to Johnny Muck," Manny said.

"Don't worry. I'm gonna do something," Tito said. "I'm gonna kill that fuck." He threw his glass across the patio. "Get everybody here. We're gonna find him."

Tony analyzed the situation quickly. "I'm going home. I'll get Paulie and the other guys on it too."

Tito had a scowl on his face that looked painted on. "You do that, Tony. Let me know if you find anything."

"Will do," Tony said. "I'll let myself out."

Two blocks from Tito's house, he dialed Frankie's number. "Bugs, we need to talk."

"Find out what happened to Johnny?"

"Where, Bugs?"

"Danny's. One hour."

BUGS WAS AT THE bar when Tony walked in. He was alone, which surprised Bugs. He felt sure that Paulie would be with him. "Long time, Tony."

"Yeah, well, things change."

"What have you got for me?"

Tony got a glass of wine, then looked around. "Let's go where we can talk."

They found an empty booth away from the crowd and sat. "What do you know about Johnny Muck?" Tony asked.

"I know he's dead."

"All off the record?" Tony asked.

"All of it."

"Okay. Muck worked for all the families, but he owed his allegiance to Tito." He paused while a young couple walked by their booth. "Muck was one of the best shooters ever."

"So how did Nicky—"

"You won't like hearing this, but Nicky was a shooter. Best one they ever had, according to Tito."

"Are you fucking with me?"

"I wouldn't be here if I were. He's good, Bugs. And I need protection."

Frankie slammed his fist on the table, drawing attention from other patrons. "That's all I need, not only a crazy fuck, but a crazy fuck who's a hit man."

Bugs lit a smoke. "What else can you tell me?"

"You can't smoke in here."

"Fuck them, I'm a cop. Tell me what you know."

Tony leaned over the table. "He'll be coming for Tito for sure. Probably me, too."

"And me," Bugs said.

Tony's brow wrinkled. "Why you?"

"He thinks I gave him up. He called me from Cleveland…" Suddenly Bugs turned red and stared at Tony. "It was *you*, wasn't it? You tracked my calls when I gave you the heads-up about Tito." His hands balled into fists. "You whore. Not only betrayed Nicky, but you used me to do it." Bugs got up. "I'm glad Mamma Rosa is dead. She'd be ashamed."

Tony stared at the table—wouldn't look up. "You've got to help me. He'll kill me if you don't."

"Yeah, well, there is that," Frankie said, and walked out.

ALL THE WAY HOME, Frankie thought about how pissed he was at Tony. What the hell had happened to him? Of all the guys, he had figured Tony for the last one to give someone up or turn their back on them. But here he was, crawling on his belly, looking for salvation after what he'd done to Nicky.

Fuck him. I got enough to worry about.

When he got home, he went straight to the charts. He'd concluded on the way that his original assumption was right—Nicky would save Tony or Paulie for last, which meant that Tito was next. All efforts would be focused on Tito. He went to the chart of strategy, eyes scanning to the bottom, where he had written in large red letters—*WHO's NEXT?*

Frankie froze. Dropped his pen. Right next to it, in equally large red letters was

YOU

He drew his gun and crouched. The apartment was small, but there were a few places he could hide. "Nicky. You here?"

After a minute, and comfortable that the living room was clear, he stood, then methodically cleared the rest of the apartment. Breathing heavily now, he went for his files, noticing immediately they'd been moved. Inside the first folder, a note stuck out of the corner.

Hi, Bugs.

Saw your stupid charts. You shouldn't have done it, Bugs.

Remember, Friendship & Honor.

See you soon,

Your old friend.

Bugs ripped the note apart, then threw it across the room, pieces of paper falling to the floor. "Goddamn mother fucker." He was as pissed as he'd ever been in his life, but more than that, he was scared, and he couldn't shake the image of Johnny Muck's face.

CHAPTER 66

BEGGING FOR HELP

Current Day

Bugs woke early to get a good start and headed straight for the office. Morreau sometimes came in early to beat the rush. Bugs hoped it was one of those mornings. He got coffee and a cinnamon roll, then waited, doing paperwork until Morreau showed.

"What are you doing here so early, Donovan?"

"Need more surveillance."

"Can't do it. No chance."

"This guy is going to kill someone else if we don't stop him."

"Get me some coffee. I'll think about it."

Frankie went to get coffee, taking plenty of time to let Morreau think about it. When he brought it back, he could see the news was good by the look on Morreau's face "I'll give you four guys for one week. If you don't get him by then, I don't give a shit who he kills."

"Higgins and Sapp available?"

He nodded. "I'll give you Murphy and Russo too."

Frankie kissed Morreau on the head. "I love you for this, but I need more. I got Tito to watch, and now Tony Sannullo and Paulie Perlano, too."

Morreau wiped his head off. "No matter how much you beg, you're not getting anyone else. Now get out of here and catch somebody, will you?" As Frankie started to leave, Morreau called to him. "And tell Mazzetti to stop smoking in the building. Does he really think I don't know who it is?"

"I'll tell him, Lieu, but I think you know his answer."

FRANKIE HAD MET HARDING'S boss once—a guy named Clark, Gary Clark. The FBI had damn near dumped the surveillance, but Frankie knew they were dying to get Tito. He dialed Carol on his cell as he pulled out of the lot. "Hey, you sweet thing."

"Cut the crap, Donovan. What do you want?"

"Need a number for Special Agent Gary Clark. He's Harding's boss."

"Hang on."

He turned left, heading toward the FBI Organized Crime Unit headquarters, and before he got two blocks, Carol had what he needed. "You owe me," she said.

"I am forever in your debt." Frankie hung up and dialed Clark. He didn't speak to Clark, but got his assistant, and more importantly, an appointment in an hour with Agents Clark, Harding and Maddox. He grabbed a burger on the way and got to the meeting with almost fifteen minutes to spare.

When he entered Clark's office, Harding and Maddox were already there. Maybe Brooklyn-cop early and FBI-early were two different things. "Agent Clark, Harding, Maddox, good to see you again."

"What do you want?" Harding asked.

Clark glared at Harding, then turned to Frankie, all smiles. "Gloria said you mentioned Mr. Martelli in your message."

"Yes, sir, Agent Clark. I think we can get Tito…with some help from the FBI."

"Do you mean that the FBI can get Mr. Martelli with cooperation from Brooklyn Homicide?"

"That is *exactly* what I mean, sir."

Harding brushed it off, looking disgusted. "Sir, Detective Donovan hasn't delivered on one promise yet. We had him wired numerous times and never got anything. If you ask me, he leaked information."

"You're full of shit, Harding. These guys are always guarded in what they say. I'm a cop. Just because I hang out with old friends doesn't mean they'll talk about crimes in front of me. I told you that from the beginning, but you wasted your money on this bullshit." Frankie turned to Harding's boss. "I've got more important things to do than argue with him."

Clark was silent. Then he looked at Harding. "Agent Harding, we should listen to what the detective has to say. We've been after Martelli for a long time."

Frankie had him by the balls now. He turned to Harding, held out his hand. "I know how we can get Tito. I can get Tony Sannullo to wear a wire. Think about it, you'll be a hero."

Harding glared but said nothing, then Clark interjected. "Why do you think Sannullo will wear a wire?"

"Tony's scared. He wants protection, and I told him I wouldn't do it unless he wore a wire."

"Isn't he your friend, Detective Donovan?"

"Yes, sir, he is, but this is also my job."

"Let me make a call," Clark said, and nodded to the door. "You, too, Harding."

Harding scoffed, then stood rigid against the wall outside Clark's office.

Frankie smiled. "Bet you ten to one we're going to work with each other, Hard-on."

"Call me that one more time, and I'll kick your ass."

"We'll discuss that later; here comes your boss."

"All right, Detective. You've got a deal—*if* you can get Tony Sannullo to wear the wire."

"What do I get in exchange?" Frankie asked.

"Full support," Clark said. "The complete package—video and audio. Twenty-four-hour manned surveillance."

"How many men?"

"Four at night. Six during the day."

Frankie shook his head. "Four at night's okay, but I need eight during the day."

Clark thought for a minute, as if counting dollars, then agreed. "You'd better make this pay off. These are your tax dollars."

"Don't worry, sir. It'll pay off."

Tax dollars, my ass.

When Frankie called, Tony answered on the first ring. "Hey, it's Bugs. Meet me at Cataldi's in half an hour."

Tony didn't ask why. "See you then."

Bugs knew Tony was scared, but he had to drive the point home. Tony was the key to getting FBI help, and without surveillance, Tito's ass was gone. Not that Frankie minded much about Tito, but he didn't want this to get to the point where it came down to Nicky against Tony, or worse, against himself.

Frankie parked the car, walked in and sat at Tony's table, taking the seat across from him.

"What's up, Bugs?"

"We've had people watching Tito, watching you, Paulie, and even me. And with all of that, we got shit. Nicky's good. We can't even get a lead on him."

"I told you he's good." Tony looked about nervously. "So why'd you call?"

Frankie leaned over the table. "I need your help so I can keep you alive."

"What the hell are you talking about?"

"I need you to wear a wire."

Tony threw his napkin on the table. "Fuck you."

"I don't have the manpower to protect you. And Nicky has gotten everyone he wanted so far, even Johnny Muck."

"No wire, Bugs; besides, what good would it do? Let you hear him kill me? Is that what you want?"

"Listen to reason," Frankie said. "He's tortured everyone first, except Tommy Devin, and I figured that out. Tommy was the driver. He didn't shoot Gina. So, even if Nicky gets through surveillance, we got you covered with the wire. We can come in long before anything happens."

Tony fidgeted with his silverware. "Let me think about it. Let's eat first."

They ate in peace, talking about anything but business, but when they finished, Tony looked over to Bugs. "All right, you got a deal. But don't fuck me."

"I'll call with details," Frankie said, then he stopped and got Tony's attention. "Listen close. In the meantime, stay home. Go out the door of your house and you're taking your life with you. Think of Celia, Tony. Don't make her a widow."

CHAPTER 67

RATTUS RATTUS

Current Day

Frankie got up early to prepare for the FBI presentation. He knew this would be a tough audience—not just unreceptive, but hostile. He ate a light breakfast, just a bagel splattered with olive oil and garlic then an espresso to chase it away. The meeting was in a hotel, courtesy of Harding's boss. Frankie was the second to arrive; the first was a trainee.

What is he doing on an assignment like this?

"Good morning," Frankie said.

The trainee responded in a cheerful, FBI manner. "Good morning, Detective Donovan. I hope you are well today."

"I am, thanks." *This is going to be a long day.*

Pretty soon, the whole group showed up, coming in together like kids answering the school bell. Once they were seated, Frankie stood, closed the door and stared at the suits and ties sitting rigid at their desks.

"Good morning, gentlemen. Thank you for coming. They wanted me to have this talk to bring everyone up to speed. As you know, we have five murders: Renzo Ciccarelli, Tommy Devin, Nino Tortella, Donnie Amato, and Gianni Mucchiatto, otherwise known as Johnny Muck."

He paused for questions, but all he saw were eleven heads taking notes.

"Although we can't yet prove it, they all appear to be the work of one man—Niccolo Fusco, also known as 'Nicky the Rat.'"

"Where did he get the name? Did he rat somebody out?"

Frankie laughed. "You would be laughing with me, gentlemen, if you knew how ridiculous that question was." He paused, staring off into the distance. "I don't think there's anything in the world that could make Nicky Fusco rat someone out." *Not a fuckin' thing.*

Frankie took a few deep breaths, wishing he could have lit a cigarette. He looked out over the faces and put on a smile. "Nicky got the name 'Rat' when he was six years old. He was caught stealing cigarettes, and the cops took him to the station." He paused, remembering that it should have been him at the station. Nicky saved him that day, as he did many other days. Bugs shook his head. "For two hours, they tried to get him to tell which boys were with him, but he wouldn't say a word. Hell, they couldn't even get his name. After news of this spread, the local mobsters gave him the name of 'Rat' to honor him, not make fun of him."

Someone in the back snickered. A few mumbled. Frankie glared. At times like this, he realized he didn't belong here, in this office, with these people. He longed for his real friends. There were eleven agents in this class, and as he thought it, he smiled.

Suit wouldn't have heard of it. He'd have dragged someone in off the street to make it twelve.

Of these eleven co-workers, how many would drop whatever they were doing and rush to his aid if he called late one night? How many would share their last cigarette—shit, their last meal—with him if he were hungry? How many would have his back if they got in a bind where it looked as if they all might die? Frankie knew the answer. *None of them. Not a fuckin' one.*

Right now, he wanted nothing more than to rip his tie off, go get Tony and Paulie, and take them out for pasta. He'd tell them, 'Get your ass out of town. Hide.' Then he'd convince Nicky to call it quits. Make it all go away. Shit, it happened in movies. It happened when they were kids. Who knows, maybe it could happen again. Except that he couldn't trust Tony; he didn't know about Suit; and Nicky...

A smile played with him, flitted on his face. He turned, flipped on the overhead projector, then quickly shut it down and grabbed an eraser for the chalkboard, then wiped the slate clean. A long piece of white chalk lay on the shelf. Frankie picked it up, turned it in his hand.

If chalkboards were good enough for Sister Thomas, they're good enough for me.

'Rattus Rattus' he scratched out on the black slate. He turned to face the agents, all with puzzled looks on their faces. "This, gentlemen, is the genus rat. The most versatile, resilient, and innovative creature you might ever encounter. Rats can fall from a five-story building—and live. They can swim for miles in the ocean—and live. They can walk on wires, climb brick walls, hold their breath for three minutes, chew through cinder blocks...and they can jump four feet straight in the air from a fixed position."

Frankie scanned the audience again. Several of them looked a little intrigued. "If that isn't enough, they have a collapsible rib cage, which allows them to squeeze through a hole the size of a quarter." He paused. "And, oh yeah, their bite can be twenty times more powerful than a dog's." Frankie stopped, took out his handkerchief and wiped his brow. It was damn hot.

"So now that we know about rats, what the hell does that have to do with the case?"

"Good question, Agent. And to answer it, I'll quote an old wise man I once knew. He said that people tend to grow into their names, for good or bad. That said, no matter how you look at it, Nicky Fusco has become his namesake. He can, as you have read in the reports, get into and out of, almost anywhere. He goes about his business virtually unseen and is extremely dangerous. To say he's *fearless* would do him an injustice and elevate that word to a new level." He gestured at the board. "So, gentlemen, this is what we are facing."

Frankie made sure he gazed at each one of them before continuing. "And for those of you who snickered and mumbled— even for those who did it in their heads but kept it to themselves—let me tell you, if you slip up one bit, one iota, you'll be dead. Nicky Fusco takes no prisoners. He makes—no mistakes."

One of the agents spoke up. "We don't even know if it really is this guy. Isn't this all speculation?"

Bugs paced the room, tapping the chalk on his hand. "True, we don't know for sure. It could be these are just plain old mob killings made to look like the same nut is doing it…but I don't think so."

After a few more questions, Frankie wrapped the session up, then headed home, kicked off his shoes, went to the kitchen and opened a bottle of Chianti. The phone rang and he reached for it and answered.

"Hi, Bugs."

Frankie snapped to alert. "Nicky?"

"You knew I'd be calling, didn't you?"

A long pause. "I guess I did."

"Teach those agents anything today?"

A long pause again. "Look, I know what you think, but I didn't tell Tito where you were. Why don't we meet and talk."

"We'll talk, Bugs. Soon."

Frankie walked to the window, looked out. "Nicky, I know you're hurting. I feel bad for you. But I'm telling you, don't ever come into my house again. I'll put you down."

The line went dead.

CHAPTER 68

WATCHING THE WATCHERS

Current Day

I knew they'd be watching Tito close—too close for me to stake him out properly. Way too close for me to do him in the house. Between the FBI surveillance and Manny hanging on Tito's ass like a tumor, there was no way I'd take him out there. That brought up the question of where—and how.

I had to think this through. Sister Thomas always taught us to consider all options, eliminate the impossible, then choose from what remained. As I saw it, I had three options.

1. Take him at the house.
2. Take him on the road.
3. Take him at work.

They were the only places I could count on Tito being. Sister Thomas always had it right, though I doubt she would have been proud of what her teachings were being used for. I eliminated the union hall; it was better guarded than an army barracks. The road was out of the question; his car was bullet-proof, and the doors would be locked. Unless I wanted to use artillery, that option was out. That left me with one choice—his house—the choice I'd discounted. It was time to rethink.

After hours of deliberation, I decided to do more surveillance. Three times that week, I took a cab by his house, careful to sit high with my head turned, so that they couldn't see my face. I caught him coming out once. Manny came out first, followed by two other guys, then Tito, with two more behind him. Manny started the car, and Tito got in the back seat.

During these scouting trips, I also got to see where the FBI had their posts set up. One above the deli and another was down the block on the second floor of an older, well-kept home across from Tito's. Every window there had the curtains open except one room above the porch, the one with the good view of Tito's front door.

Shame on you, Bugs.

During the next few days, I saw Tito going to work two more times, using the same routine.

Shame on you, *Manny.* Watching their movements, I got the idea of how to do it. It took me two days to line up the rest of the plan, but on Thursday, I was ready. I should have planned longer, but I wasn't about to let Tito Martelli live one extra minute I didn't have to.

HARDING WAS NEARLY BOUNCING off the walls of the surveillance room. He got on the radio and called Maddox at the other house. "Did you get that? He was in the cab."

"We got him, sir. It's the second time he's been by in the past week."

"What did he do?"

"Nothing, sir. Just drove by."

Harding turned to Frankie. "We should have taken him. Goddamnit. We should have taken him."

"And done what? There's not one piece of evidence that ties him to these crimes."

"So what do we do, wait to film him killing Tito?"

Frankie turned his head. "You make me sick, Harding, acting like you give a shit."

"Don't worry. We *will* get your wop friend when he goes after Tito."

"He won't take Tito here; he'll want him to suffer."

"I have eight agents ready to go on my signal."

"Anybody on the street?"

"As soon as we see him coming out, we can cover him."

"Suppose he—"

"Detective, I've got a car with two agents on the corner, and we have six agents between here and the corner above him. And the back door is covered by your man and a sharp shooter."

Frankie nodded. "You didn't tell me you had a car on the corner." He paced for a minute, feeling nervous. "Going out for a smoke."

As soon as he got out back, he called Mazzetti. "I need back-up, Lou."

"Get a cop with lungs, will you?"

"Not that kind of back-up. I need two cars. These assholes only got one car to cover the street."

"It's a one-way street."

"Lou, get me a couple of cars."

"I'll see what I can do. Might be off-duty guys. You cover overtime?"

"I'll get it. Have them call my cell."

"Got it."

I WAITED FOR PAULIE's family to leave then walked up to his door and knocked. When he saw it was me, he froze.

"Nicky."

"You going to invite me in, Suit?" I had a gun in my hand, not pointed at him, but tucked against my stomach.

"Come on in." He stepped back as he said it, his eyes on the gun.

"I saw your family leave, or I wouldn't have come."

"Yeah, I appreciate that, Nicky. You want coffee?"

"I could use some." I followed him to the kitchen, checking each shadow as we went.

"There's nobody here," Suit said, watching me.

"Be a lot of blood if there is."

Paulie nodded. "I know. You want something to eat, or just coffee?"

"Just coffee." I laid the gun on the table within easy reach. "You hear what they did, Paulie?"

He didn't say anything for a few seconds. "If you mean about Gina? Yeah, I heard. I'm sorry. Really. I didn't know her, but I know she meant something to you."

"You have anything to do with it?"

"No way."

"When we're done, I want you to call Tony."

Paulie shook his head. "Can't do it, Little Nicky. You know I can't."

I reached for the gun and gripped it firmly. "So you can't betray Tony, but you could me. Is that it?"

"Like hell. I don't know what went on here, but if Tony did something, it must have been because Tito had him in a tight spot."

I grabbed the gun, jumped up and shoved it against Paulie's head. "A tight spot? That was my *wife*."

Paulie looked scared. "Shit, Nicky. I didn't know. All I know is Tito had a contract on Gina. There was nothing Tony could do."

That pissed me off. I took my finger off the trigger, not wanting to make a mistake. "Paulie, I want to keep you alive, but if you don't call Tony, I *will* kill you."

He nodded, but when he did, his eyes looked sad. "I know, Nicky, and Christ's sake, I don't want to die. I got kids. I got a boy who reminds me of Bugs when he was little, and another that sure as shit is the Mick reincarnated...but I won't hand you Tony on a platter."

Now I *really* wanted to squeeze the trigger. Even tried to, but couldn't do it. "All right. As long as I find out you didn't have anything to do with it, I won't kill you. But you keep quiet."

Paulie was shaking. I'd never seen him scared like this before. "Can't do that, either. I'd do the same for you. I hope you know it." His eyes teared. "I swear, Little Nicky, I never wanted this. Neither did Tony. He just fucked up. Got himself in a jam."

"'Got himself in a jam.'" I shoved the gun against his head again. "What do you call getting your wife killed? Tony *killed* her." I smacked him in the head with the gun, drawing blood. Paulie fell, bringing his hand up to his temple. He reached for a towel to stop the bleeding.

"Christ's sake. Don't kill me, Nicky. I don't mind for me, but my kids..." Paulie blessed himself, and tears welled in his eyes. "I'm sorry about what happened. I know how much you've lost already. Your mom, your pops...I don't know anybody who's lost more than you...but I swear on my mother's eyes, we didn't plan on hurting you. Ever."

I thought for probably ten seconds, and our entire childhood passed before my eyes. Images of us smoking, stealing cigarettes, fighting, laughing. It came together in the center of my mind, forcing me to lower the gun. "I don't know why, Paulie. Maybe it's because of what we had, but I can't do it."

He grabbed me and kissed my cheek. "I swear. Tony didn't mean this."

The mention of Tony's name fused my spine with steel. "Call him or give me the phone."

He handed me his. "Number's on there."

I punched the contact and waited while the phone rang. He picked up on the third ring. "Suit, where are you?"

I heard the voice, and though it hadn't been that long, it seemed like twenty years since the last time I'd heard it. "It's me," I said.

A very long silence, then. "That you, Rat?" His voice was weak, pleading.

"I'm here with Paulie."

"Is he okay?"

"Why would you care? Or is it just some of us you care about? Did you forget the oath? I didn't."

"Hey, fuck you and your stupid oaths. That was thirty years ago or something. Grow up."

"Wrong answer."

"Yeah, well, don't come around here, or I'll get you the right answer."

I didn't say anything for a moment. Then, "Did Paulie have anything to do with it? I need to know."

"Is he there? Is he hurt?"

I looked at Paulie. "Say something."

"I'm okay, but he's serious."

"You get all that, Tony?"

"Fuck you again, Rat. What do you want?"

"Did Suit have anything to do with it?"

"Nothing."

I sighed and hoped he didn't hear it. "I'm coming for you."

"Yeah, I know. But don't think I'm going down like Donnie or Muck."

"We'll see."

I hung up the phone, wiped it off on the towel Paulie had, then handed it back to him. "You're off the hook."

He looked at me, sweat covering his face. "Can't you let Tony off? For old times?"

"Can't, Paulie. And you ought to get out of here. They got FBI all over the place. You're all going down."

He took the towel back, dabbing his head. "I've been thinking that anyway. Thanks."

As I left, I turned to him. "Tell the kids good stories about me, will you, Suit? I wouldn't want them knowing the bad stuff."

"I will."

"And, Suit, leave the door unlocked when you leave. I might need the house for a few days."

"You got it." He walked over to me, gave me a big hug, then left.

I KNEW PAULIE WOULD call Tony to reinforce the fact that I was coming for him, so I headed for Cataldi's. It was only a matter of time before Tony showed up there on any given day. I found a good spot to watch from and relaxed, listening to music while I waited. It took about two hours, but he came, although he was back out again in less than twenty minutes. I followed at a safe distance, making sure he didn't pick up on it. Tony was an arrogant shit—didn't even check for tails.

Fifteen minutes later, he pulled into a parking garage. I didn't follow right away, but waited for another car go in then made the turn into the parking garage and headed up the ramp. On the fourth floor, just as the car in front of me pulled into a parking space, I saw Tony getting on the elevator. I parked two levels up then took care to clean everything in the car and brush it out real good. Afterward, I took the elevator to the floor where Tony parked and found a nice spot to wait—inside an unlocked car about thirty feet away.

The wait felt like days, but it was only about an hour and a half before he came out. I lowered myself into the seat, allowing him to pass, then slowly got up. I'd left the door ajar and made sure the overhead light wasn't on. Now I waited until he bent to open his door, then eased out of the car and moved up behind him, gun in hand.

"Get in. Don't try anything."

FRANKIE GOT TO THE surveillance apartment in half an hour. He was tired and eager for the day to be over with. "What have we got, Harding?"

"We have a wire in Tito's house."

"*In* the house? How?"

"Got a court order. We had the wire put in after he left this morning."

"He didn't leave any of his men there?"

"The past few days, he's taken everyone with him."

"Don't blame him; he's scared." Frankie looked out the window, then asked the guy at the scope. "Any sign of Nicky?"

"We still don't know if the perp is really him, Detective. We're taking your word for it at this juncture, but we have no positive identification on the man."

"You can take my word," he said, then, "What about Tony? Is he wired?"

"They did it this morning."

"Where is he?"

"He is probably on his way to that restaurant you people eat at all the time."

For the next half hour they took turns watching and listening, and arguing about damn near anything. As Frankie finished one of his shifts, he handed the headset to a young agent who had been in the morning's presentation. "Be back in a few. Going to catch a smoke."

Before he hit the door, Agent Cross called him. "Detective Donovan, we're live."

"What?"

"Live, sir. We've got action."

Frankie looked at Harding, who took the headset from the guy at the window and stared at Tito's house. "Nobody in the kitchen."

Cross turned. "Not him, sir. Mr. Sannullo."

"Give me that," Frankie said and grabbed the headset from Cross. As he put it on, he heard Tony's voice.

"Nicky, what are you doing here?"

Frankie yelled. "He's got Tony! Get some bodies over there…shit, where is he? Can we tell?"

Cross looked at the screen. "Looks like…forty-third and…hang on…"

"Tell Harding," Frankie said and headed for the door. "And get some people on it, now." As he ran out the door, he called back. "Harding, call me on my cell when you get anything." Frankie bounced down the steps, taking them two at a time, holding onto the rail. As much as he hated Tony right now, he didn't want him suffering the kind of death Nicky probably had planned for him.

Hang on, Tony. Hang on.

CHAPTER 69

JUDGMENT DAY

Current Day

"**N**icky, get the fuck out of my car."

"Don't say a word." I drove out of the garage with the gun pointed at Tony, but covered with my coat.

Despite what I told him, he started to talk as soon as we got on the street. "Why are you going this way? We—"

I shoved the gun into his side. "Shut-up." As soon as I had a chance, I pulled to the curb, reached over and undid his shirt. *A wire.* I ripped it off, tossed it out the window. "Any more?"

Tony looked desperate and shook his head. "That was it."

"Can't believe you stooped to wearing a wire."

"Where are we going?"

"You'll see."

When we got to Paulie's house, I took Tony to the kitchen. Paulie's blood stained the floor.

"Sit," I said. "And don't try anything. I'm not going to torture you like I did the others. Maybe it's Mamma Rosa. Maybe it's the friendship we had. You should thank God for whatever it is."

Tony stared at me; he had a way of staring at people that pissed them off.

"How do you want it?" I asked. While I waited for his answer, I struggled with my decision. Tony had been like a brother—hell, he *was* my brother, for all practical purposes. But he betrayed me. *He* was the reason Gina was dead. "Decide, Tony. I don't have a lot of time."

He spat at me. "You pitiful fuck. You've lived your whole life in my shadow. Raised by my mother. Relied on *me* to get good grades. Got a job with *my* boss. Then, when a tough decision has to be made, you get your ass in an uproar and fall for the girl. Well fuck you, Rat. This is the real world, not like when you played make-believe with Angela." He turned his head to one side, then looked back at me again. "And you know the saddest thing? You're still in love with Angie. I see it in your face every time somebody mentions her name."

Shooting was too good for Tony; I was going to beat him to death. I laid the gun on the counter and went for him, punching his face again and again. He fell, grabbed my legs, pulled them out from under me. We crashed to the floor. Tony grabbed an ashtray from the table and pummeled me with it. I managed to cover my head, but my arm took a bad beating. I tried everything to move him off me, but couldn't. Finally, I jammed my foot against the counter and, using all my weight, rolled him over. Then I jumped up and got the gun. "Don't move."

My hands were shaking. Shit, I think my whole body was shaking. Everything in me wanted to blow his kneecaps off, or his balls—anything to make him suffer. But when I thought of it, Mamma Rosa came to mind. I saw her smile, heard her laughter, and remembered how she used to hum those old Italian songs. No matter what Tony had done, I couldn't bring myself to kill him. I lowered the gun. "Tony, you're—"

As soon as I lowered my hand, he came at me. Instinct took over. I fired, hitting him in the gut.

Tony went down, clutching his stomach. "Guess I'm going out the way I want, Rat. Had to make it easier for you. I knew you'd do it anyway."

I grabbed a towel and knelt next to him, putting pressure on it. "Hold this. I'll get an ambulance." As he applied pressure, I called 9-1-1 and reported it, then got on the floor with him.

Tony pushed himself backwards, bracing his back against the wall. "Get out of here, Rat. Can't let them find you."

I got another towel, tried to stop the bleeding. As much as I hated Tony, I couldn't let him die alone. "I'm staying."

He shook his head. "Go. I'll be okay."

"Yeah, well…"

He gasped. "We had some good times together."

"Damn good times." I held him. Wished more than anything else that I could take that shot back.

"Nobody fucked with us, did they?"

I shook my head. "Why, Tony?"

"Too many things done wrong."

"What are you talking about?"

"You'd have killed me anyway." He grabbed my shirt. "Bugs didn't have anything to do with you in Cleveland. It was all me." Tears formed in his eyes. "Sorry, Rat. You know I didn't want it to go like this."

I wanted to believe him, but…

"Can't trust you after what you did. How am I to know Bugs didn't do it? He was the only one who knew."

"I swear. He was just…trying to give me a heads-up in case something affected me."

That sounded right, but still. "I'll know it when I look into Bugs' eyes and hold a gun to his head."

He squeezed my shirt, pulling me closer. "Nicky, I swear on my mother's eyes."

That stopped me cold. I got within inches of his face. "On Mamma Rosa's eyes? You swear it?"

Tony gulped and spit blood. "I swear. He didn't know."

"You want a priest?"

He laughed, coughing blood. "Even if I believed in that shit, I wouldn't do it. I don't want Mamma seeing me." He cried then, hard. "Shame on me, Nicky, for what I've become."

Tears now flowed from my eyes too. I held him tight. "Shame on both of us, Tony."

I felt sure the ambulance would be there any minute, but I couldn't leave. I stayed with Tony until he died, and I cried. A *lot*. After I closed his eyes, I blessed myself, repeated the words of the Trinitarian formula. "*Mi dispiace,* Mamma Rosa. I'm *so* sorry."

CHAPTER 70

A NEW SHOPPING LIST

Current Day

The phone rang and Frankie reached for it—it was Mazzetti. "What's up, Lou?"

"Where are you?"

"On my way back to the station. Why?" Something sounded funny in his voice. There was a long pause, so I pushed. "Lou?"

"Tony Sannullo is dead."

It hit Frankie like a hammer to the head. "Where?"

"Ambulance picked him up at Paulie Perlano's house."

"That doesn't make sense." I tried to figure that one out. Then, "Where are you, Lou?"

"On my way."

"I'll see you there."

Frankie drove in silence, thinking about all the good times. Wondering why it had to end this way. *Jesus Christ, Nicky. What have you done?*

It seemed to take forever to get to Paulie's, and the closer he got the more his gut wrenched. He didn't want to see Tony like this. That brought another thing to mind.

Where the hell is Paulie? Did Nicky kill him, too?

Sick as it sounded, Frankie wanted nothing more than to wake up and find out some other sick fuck was doing all this killing. But then, he wanted to win the lottery, too.

When Frankie arrived, Mazzetti was already waiting on the sidewalk in front of the house. "Any news on Paulie?" Frankie asked.

"No sign of him or the family," Lou said, "and I got people looking everywhere."

"Good."

"'Good'? What the hell does that mean?"

"If his family's missing, it might mean Paulie took them somewhere. Nicky's not killing his family."

"I don't know if Nicky did this," Lou said.

Bugs perked up, hope still burning in him. "Tell me about it."

"Looks like there could have been a fight, and Sannullo was shot just once. Punctured the lung, though." As they walked in together, Mazzetti continued. "No torture, and no shots to the head or heart."

"Then maybe it isn't him," Frankie said, and took the front steps two at a time.

"There's something else, Donovan."

Frankie paused and turned around. "What?"

"This was called in from the house, like the shooter made the call."

Frankie took a step back. "If the shooter called it in, and Tony was still alive, it must have been an accident."

"That's how I see it."

"Paulie," Frankie said.

"What?"

"It must have been Paulie. Something happened. Maybe they fought and the gun went off."

Mazzetti raised his eyebrows. "Maybe so. Let's go look."

I SAT IN THE corner of the room, hands cupped over my face, hiding tears. From who?

Whom?

How sick was this, to be correcting my own grammar after I just killed my best friend? I lit another smoke, punishing myself. It had been years since I quit, but I'd stopped on the way home and bought some. It felt like the thing to do. They tasted like shit, but I popped them in, one after the other.

"Goddamnit." I punched the wall beside me for probably the fifteenth time. My knuckles bled, more than when the nuns used to beat me, but not as much as they should have bled. It should be me dead, not Tony. I was the one who broke the contract; he was just trying to do his job. Isn't that how we lived our lives—give your word and stick to it?

I didn't. I took a contract and reneged on it.

Of course, I reneged. It was Gina. When I thought of her, the tears really flowed. How can a man fuck up so much? All I ever wanted was to grow old with Angela, have kids, love her forever. First Angie was taken away from me, then Tito took Gina.

Yes, it was Tito who took her. He's the one who should be lying there in a pool of blood.

I mustered the strength to stand. I threw the rest of the cigarettes in the trash, got a pen and paper and sat down to write a shopping list.

Drill, with 1/16 and 1/8th bits.

4" screws

Rope

Duct tape (it worked well last time)

55-gallon drum (x2)

Chain to support drum

What else? *Ah, yes,* I thought, and wrote it at the end of the list.

Railroad spike.

That, though, would have to be gathered.

MAZZETTI SAT ACROSS THE diner booth from Frankie, sipping his third cup of coffee. He set the cup down. "Donovan, I know you're upset—

probably pissed off, too—but we've got to get to work. Besides, if I drink any more coffee, I'll piss my pants."

"If this was Nicky, why did he call 9-1-1?"

"Christ, you're a dumb dago. I told you—they fight. He shoots Tony, then feels sorry for his old buddy when he sees him dying, so he calls the bus."

Frankie downed his cup, pulled out a ten and left it on the table. "Wouldn't want to take that theory to court."

"I got news for you. If we don't get some evidence, we ain't taking nothing to court."

They climbed in Frankie's car and headed toward the station. "You got everybody going to Tito's?"

"All of them," Mazzetti said. "Harding called too. Said he'd have eight guys all day and six tonight."

Frankie nodded. "We'll get him this time."

They drove halfway to the surveillance site without talking, and then Mazzetti started up a story. "I ever tell you about the rat in my apartment? Three years I tried getting rid of that bastard, but he outsmarted me every time."

"You trying to cheer me up?"

"You're supposed to ask what happened."

"Okay."

"Nothing happened. That rat proved to be smarter than me, so he's still there. But he doesn't eat much, and the mess he makes is small."

"Are you telling me you got a rat in your house?"

Mazzetti shook his head. "Dumb dago. You got a rat in *your* house, and we might never catch him. Get used to it."

"I'd rather ride in quiet."

It took about fifteen minutes to get to Tito's. Frankie parked on the next block. He and Mazzetti walked to the spot above the deli, manned by Maddox.

"Anything?" Frankie asked when he saw him.

"Nothing, Detective. Quiet as any other day."

"So was yesterday, and then Tony was taken."

"Yes, sir. I know."

Frankie looked around, too nervous to contribute much. "Tito gone yet?"

"Left about an hour ago. I think he shifts his departures so he doesn't have a routine."

"Good. That helps." Frankie checked the street, then headed for the door. "I'm going for a walk, Lou. Make sure we have coverage front and back, will you?"

"Bet your ass."

"You can be assured, sir," Maddox chimed in.

"Thanks, Maddox. I appreciate it."

"Sir?"

"Yeah?"

"I'm sorry about Mr. Sannullo. I know he was a friend."

Frankie patted him on the shoulder. "Thanks again. See you later."

CHAPTER 71

A LONG WAIT

Current Day

I decided to go for Tito quickly, though I still had some things to get ready. The shopping was done, had even gotten the railroad spike—a good, old rusty one I found loose by the tracks. And the house was ready too. All I needed was my accomplice. Anyone would do, even a homeless person. Someone like that would be even better; the less chance of recognition, the better I liked it.

By about ten that night, I had the details worked out. Within two hours, I found someone willing to do what I wanted for a couple of hundred bucks and return cab fare. I waited until 1:00 AM, then hailed a cab. I gave Tito's address. As we drove, I explained to my accomplice what would happen, and then I paid him in advance. I ducked as we got to Tito's street, reminding him to stop near the end of the block, *after* he passed Tito's house.

"Are there cars parked at the curb?" I asked the cabbie.

"All the way up and down," he said.

"Stop just before the end of the street," I said, then waited.

When the cab came to a stop, my decoy opened the door and stepped out. I slipped out with him and rolled under the car by the curb, keeping close to the sidewalk so they couldn't see me from the surveillance windows. Besides, they would be focused on the cab and the guy getting out. I lay still, watching as he walked down the street and turned the corner to the right. The plan was for him to walk two blocks. The cab would circle around and pick him up. I don't know what activity this spurred in the rooms where they were stationed, but I'm certain it generated a lot of conversation and concern.

I waited for at least an hour, then, inch by inch, I crept up the hill toward Tito's house. I wore black clothes and kept my face turned toward the sidewalk, away from their cameras. After much misery I made it to Tito's car and positioned myself right underneath it. If someone bent down, they could have seen me, but people seldom look under cars. Now all I had to do was wait.

As I lay there, I thought about how my life was about to change. Again. When I finished with Tito, I planned to leave the city, find a place where I could settle in and be happy. Maybe find…someone. I shook my head, trying to clear the thoughts. I had to focus or I wouldn't live to find that someone.

After a few more hours, the front door to Tito's house opened. It was early in the morning. Six-thirty, maybe seven. Footsteps came down the walk, then around to the driver's side. That would be Manny.

He unlocked the car, got in and started it, then beeped for Tito, a signal that all was okay. It was difficult to stay focused with the car running, but I concentrated on Tito and the men coming to the car with him. If he did his normal routine, he'd get in, and his men would shut the door behind him. That gave me about a ten-second window. I drew my gun, waiting. The footsteps drew closer. I saw Tito's brown Ferragamo shoes on the sidewalk.

When the door opened, I rolled out, jumped up, opened the door and got inside, pointing the gun at Tito's head. "Don't try anything," I said, then, "Manny, lock the doors."

The guys outside drew their guns, but mine was pointed at Tito;

besides, now that the doors were locked it was done with. The windows were bullet-proof. "Move, Manny. Now."

"Where to?" Manny asked. He kept his head straight ahead, but his eyes darted back and forth to the mirror.

"Just move." I drew my second gun, the one I'd used on Muck.

"You're dead!" Tito screamed, and when he did, I popped him with a tranquilizer dart.

"What the fuck?" Manny said. "You kill him, Nicky?"

"Just put him out. Take the first right. Be quick. If you try anything, you're dead. If we get caught, you're dead."

"We're not getting caught. I been doing this too long."

"I know that."

Manny pulled out with some speed, but not screeching-tires type speed. I looked at the obvious FBI car on the corner. It showed no signs of moving.

"Take a right at the second corner, then a quick left." I checked behind us a few times. I think we took them by surprise.

After half a dozen blocks, I had Manny take another right and an immediate left, running a red light in the process. I watched closely. Nothing. No tails.

"Sorry what they did to Gina."

I looked at Manny through the mirror. "You have anything to do with it?"

"Coordinating."

"Give any orders?"

"Passed them along, but I told Tito to let Gina go. I knew the kid."

"That true? About you being sorry?"

He nodded. "I liked her. She had balls."

I laughed. Thought about how she would stand up to anyone. "Yeah, she did." I was quiet for a minute. "I don't want to kill you. Do I have to?"

"They won't get a word out of me." He stared at me through the mirror.

"You talk, and I'll find you. It'll be worse than Johnny Muck."

Manny held up his right hand, as if swearing an oath. "I don't even know you."

"Okay, then. Do as I say, and you'll be safe."

I told Manny to go to Red Hook, where I had a car stashed. When I was convinced we had no tails, I had him pull over by an old warehouse by where I parked the car. "Give me your cell phone and your piece." As he handed them over, I got out. "Keys, too. Now put Tito in my car."

He handed me the keys, got Tito out, and set him in the back seat of my car. "That all, Nicky?" He said it with a pleading voice. He probably thought I was gonna pop him.

"Manny, look at me," I said, and when he did, I stared him down hard. "I wasn't fucking with you earlier. You say anything, and I'll find you. Hear me?"

"You lettin' me go?"

"I said I would." As I opened the door to get in, I told him, "I'd bail out if I were you. But if you don't, and if the other bosses get an idea to come after me, tell them I'm through with it. This was between me and Tito."

"Hey, Nicky. Thanks."

I nodded, got in the car and drove off. Valley Stream wasn't far away, but when you had a body in the back seat, it was. I kept the tranquilizer gun handy in case I needed to pop Tito again, but if traffic wasn't bad, I'd get there before he woke up. "Sleep well, Tito. I've got some nice surprises for you."

CHAPTER 72

RULE NUMBER FIVE: MURDER IS A PROMISE

Current Day

Frankie dialed Paulie's number at home, got the answering machine, then dialed the cell. "Suit, call me if you get this. It's Bugs."

Mazzetti lit another smoke and turned up the radio. "Donovan, I say we let this guy get Tito. Then maybe he goes underground, and we don't ever hear from him again."

"You probably *would* do that."

"I'd do it in a heartbeat. What did Tito Martelli ever do for this world but suck it dry?" He dragged hard on his cigarette then changed the radio station. "I wouldn't tell you if we were sitting next to this rat guy at the light."

"When are you retiring?" Frankie asked.

"Not soon enough."

"Be better for the NYPD if you did. They ought to do one of those forced retirement deals and get you off the streets."

"You're the one who said it, Donovan. Tito killed the guy's wife. As far as I'm concerned, fuck Tito. This is revenge, pure and simple."

"The Feds are in on it now, and they want Tito alive."

"Fuck them, too."

"So I guess I'm alone on this one, huh, Lou?"

"I got your back in a jam, but don't go finding trouble. Let's go about our business and see if it finds us."

"Lou, this guy might be after me. He already killed Tony—his best friend. Maybe Paulie."

Mazzetti shook his head. "Don't think so. Can't see it."

"We'll see what Manny has to say about it. They've got him at headquarters."

FRANKIE LOOKED THROUGH THE one-way glass at Manny, sitting there for more than three hours now. He turned to Morreau. "He hasn't lawyered up?"

"Never asked once. But he won't say shit."

"Let me try him."

"It's your case."

Frankie went in and took a seat across from Manny. He extended his hand to shake. "I don't think we ever met formally, but I'm—"

"Bugs Donovan. Yeah, I know." Manny shook hands then clasped them in front of him again.

"What happened, Manny? Where's Tito?"

"You really care, or is this just for the press?"

"I'm working a case. Whoever took Tito has killed six people so far. Maybe more."

"Wish I could help, but I never got a look at him."

"Never? Not when he jumped in your car? Or when you drove him all the way to Red Hook? Or when he took Tito with him into another car?"

Manny shook his head. "Kept behind me the whole time. Then he took my phone, my keys, and my licensed gun, and took off."

"In what kind of car?"

Manny laughed. "You know, Bugs, I was never good at knowing cars. If it's not a Caddie or a Lincoln, I don't know what it is."

A smile popped on Frankie's face. "Me, neither. How about colors, though? You any good with colors? Was this car blue, green, white?"

Manny thought, his brow wrinkling. "You know, I don't recall. I can't believe it, but I don't."

"Yeah, that's kinda what I thought you'd say." Frankie stood and pushed his chair in. "I don't have anything on you, so I guess you can go. I just hope this guy doesn't come after you."

Manny shook his hand, then whispered, "You better hope he doesn't come after *you*."

Yeah, no shit.

I TURNED THE CORNER to Johnny Muck's street, backed into the driveway, got out and opened the garage door. I grabbed the wheelbarrow, sitting next to a tool chest, and took it outside, next to the car. When I was certain no one was watching, I opened the rear door and dragged Tito into the wheelbarrow, then covered him with a blanket.

I took him inside, then dragged him to the cellar, where I tied and gagged him. I went back out, drove the car to the mall parking lot, then walked back by a different route. This would give me two options—subway or driving. When I returned, Tito was still out. I stripped him and went to the kitchen. I got the drill, drill bits, screws, rope, tape, hammer, and the railroad spike, then went back downstairs and finished preparations. I had already spread my first bag of evidence when I set things up. It took me almost a whole day to get it all ready.

I tied Tito to the wooden table, hands and legs stretched out toward the corners. He was face down and naked. Twenty minutes later he was staring at me, wide-eyed as a scared rabbit. The gag prevented him from talking, and his hands and feet were bound, but he tried valiantly to break free. I thought about what to do first. The nails worked so well with Johnny Muck that I decided to try screws this time. I put on a coat and a plastic cover then grabbed the drill, attached the appropriate driver, and got one of the four-inch screws. Tito tried talking, banging the side of his head on the table. I ignored him and went to his feet, positioning a screw in the bottom so it would go through and fasten to the table. I pressed hard against the sole of his foot then squeezed the trigger.

Tito thrashed about, bouncing the table so hard that it was difficult to hold the drill steady. Twice it slipped and I had to restart. Blood swirled around and pieces of flesh flew from the drill. Before I finished, Tito passed out.

While I waited for him to regain consciousness, I wondered what I had become. What kind of man could do something this vile? I had planned on doing this to both hands and feet, but I decided I would stop where I was. For fifteen more minutes I waited, admonishing myself for cruelty, but then, when he came to and looked at me with arrogant eyes, I wanted to hurt him again. Badly. I removed the tape and gag.

"I'm gonna kill you,."

"I don't think you're in a position to kill anyone, Tito."

He screamed again, cursing, threatening. I walked around while Tito continued. I spoke calmly in return. "You really shouldn't have come after us, Tito. And worst of all, you should have finished the job. That was one of Johnny's most important rules—finish the job."

"Yeah, well I finished the job on that bitch of yours. She's dead, and I hear she died on her back like the whore she was."

That hit a nerve. A bad nerve. I'd almost made up my mind to be merciful, to just shoot him and get it over with—but now, now he was going to pay. I grabbed the hammer and spike, then walked to the table. I put the gag back in, taped his mouth and looked him in the eyes.

"Tito, remember when you asked me if anyone fucked me in prison? Nobody did, but I figured you must have been curious, so I thought I'd let you see what it feels like."

I stuck the spike in his ass and shoved it in, hard. He screamed through the gag. I tapped the spike sideways. It still had some wiggle in it, so I hit it with the hammer, lightly. He bucked up and down as if he was fucking the table. "Don't think you're done, Tito. I was going to be nice, but you pissed me off. Your pain is just starting."

I dragged the table back a few feet, positioning it under a fifty-five-gallon drum I had rigged up. It was suspended from a pulley, and it was filled with water, making it weigh almost five hundred pounds in all. Holding it in place was a rope draped over the I-beam, which was fastened to another fifty-five gallon drum, also filled with water. I made sure that the spike was dead square in the center of the drum, then I took the drill and inserted a ⅛" bit. I walked over to the drum on the ground and drilled a hole in the bottom part of it. Water trickled out.

I went back to Tito. "As that water drains, the drum above you will lower. Eventually all five hundred pounds will be on that spike, driving it into your asshole. It will take a while, Tito, but it will get to where it needs to be. His eyes looked as if they would bulge out of his head. I left him, went to a folding chair and sat. Then I grabbed my cell and dialed Bugs' number.

FRANKIE SAT AT A booth in the coffee shop, sopping up egg yolks with his last piece of toast.

Where would he take him?

The waitress freshened his coffee. "Can I get you anything else?"

He shook his head. As he was thinking *What would I do if I were Nicky,* the answer came to him. He remembered a time when the cops were chasing them, and Nicky double-backed, hiding in the same place they had already looked. 'They'll look everywhere else before they come back here,' he said.

Now Bugs smacked the table. "That's it." He jumped up, left a ten on the table, then raced out. He called Mazzetti, told him to get men to the old Brooklyn crime scenes, then called Harding. He hated to, but because of jurisdiction issues, he could get to the other sites faster this way.

"Harding, I think he's got Tito at one of the original scenes. We'll take Renzo and Nino. You get Donnie and Johnny Muck."

"What about the other—"

"Don't need to worry about Tommy. That was an apartment." Before he hung up, he yelled. "Be quick, Harding, and take a lot of men."

As Frankie hung up, he noticed a voice mail. He hit the button to listen to it. "Yo, Bugs. It's Paulie. Sorry it took so long. Call me back."

The first smile of the day came to Frankie's face. It was great to hear Paulie's voice. As he started to return the call, the phone rang again, 'caller unknown.'

"Yeah?"

"Hell of a way to answer, Bugs."

"Nicky? That you?"

"It's me. I don't even know why I'm calling except maybe to say I'm sorry." A long pause followed. "Sorry about a lot of things, but mostly I'm sorry about Tony. That was an accident. He tried coming at me."

Nicky's voice sounded as if he'd been crying. "You okay, Rat?"

"Jesus Christ, Bugs, he died in my arms."

"Where are you?"

"Right in my arms and I couldn't save him."

"Where are you, Nicky?"

"I'm not coming for you, Bugs. You should have kept your mouth shut, but Tony told me you had nothing to do with it. I should have known. Sorry I thought different, just…shit, I don't know. I'm fucked up. Been doing everything wrong."

"Nicky—"

"How did it go so wrong?" Nicky's voice faded. "Everything went so wrong…"

"If you think it went wrong before, believe me, it hasn't started. I'm coming to arrest you." There was silence, and then the line went dead.

"Fuck." Frankie pounded the steering wheel as he cursed. "Where are you, Nicky? Which house?" He called Mazzetti. "Where are you?"

"Jesus Christ, Donovan, I'm not down the steps yet."

"Call me as soon as you get something."

Frankie thought through the crime scenes. Replayed images of each one in his head. Imagined he was Nicky.

Where would I go if I were Nicky? He'll want privacy. Which house offers the most privacy?

"Muck." *It's Johnny Muck's. I know it is.* Frankie looked in the rearview, did a u-turn and blasted his siren.

Frankie Donovan, the cop, was racing to catch him, hoping he got there before Nicky left. But Bugs Donovan, the gangster inside Frankie, prayed Nicky got away.

Run, Rat. You better run fast.

CHAPTER 73

TRAPPED

Current Day

Tito passed out intermittently, but for the most part he stayed awake. I watched him squeeze his ass cheeks and wiggle, trying to get rid of that spike. As he struggled, I reminded him of his mistake. "You shouldn't have done it, Tito. You should have left us alone."

He banged his head more and tried to cry out. I winced a few times, almost wishing I hadn't done it. Almost. Despite my sudden squeamishness, I waited until the job was done, then pulled out the gun—the new one—and shot him once in the head and once in the heart. Afterwards I made the sign of the cross and repeated the words to the Trinitarian formula.

I finished spreading the evidence. I put Tito's old gun in his coat—after making sure I got his prints on it—then went upstairs and washed off. The odor from Tito stuck to me. I scrubbed hard, changed clothes, then, as I was putting things back in the bag, I heard cars coming to a fast stop. I ran to the window and peeked out. Three cars had the street blocked. Guys were getting out.

Feds.

I ran to the back door, opened it, and raced across the yard, through a breezeway, then across another street. Two more cars were turning my way.

A garage door in front of me was open. I ducked in and closed it. The yards were small and all connected to similar yards that also had garages, trees and bushes. I needed to get to the subway or to my car before they closed me off.

HARDING JUMPED OUT OF the car, screaming orders into a radio as he hit the street. "Front and back. Block all side streets. Form a perimeter."

Harding had three agents with him. They burst through Johnny Muck's door without knocking. Guns drawn, they cleared each room on the first level within thirty seconds.

"Basement," Harding said. Two agents opened the door and started down.

"Something's here, sir."

"Careful," Harding said, but in less than half a minute, one of the agents called up.

"Got a body, sir. Good God, what a mess."

"Call it in," Harding said. "I'm going after him."

FROM THE SIDE DOOR, I watched out the window. A car screamed by the street north of me, then stopped.

Fuck me.

I looked around for something—anything—that would help. Three garages stood within a hundred feet or so, offering good places to duck into, and there were a lot of thick shrubs to hide behind. The Feds would secure the perimeter first, but once they got enough men they'd start checking house by house. I *had* to get out before they sealed the area.

I looked at the bag and thought about what was in it—in case I was caught.

Everything. The gun I'd shot Tito with, the tools, the clothes

The clothes. They'll have my DNA. What to do?

They had at least the four surrounding streets blocked, and they would check anyone leaving the area. Crowds were always the best way to escape, but I had no crowd.

So how do I get one?

I pushed myself to think in a new direction. What drew crowds? *Fires.* If anything got people out of their houses, it was fire trucks.

In less than a minute, I'd found a can of gasoline. I changed clothes and shoes, then took anything that could incriminate me from the bag and soaked it in gas. I spread gas about the garage. I hated doing this to some poor soul, but I had no choice. I took the gun, cleaned it again, and left it there. Then I dialed 9-1-1 and reported a fire, giving Johnny Muck's address. I waited about two minutes, struck a match and got out, dashing about forty or fifty yards to hide behind a shrub near the next street. It wasn't big enough to hide me for long, but it would do until the trucks arrived.

In a few minutes, I heard sirens. The trucks passed, and people flocked out of their houses. I waited until enough were passing by, then stepped out and joined the crowd. Everyone seemed chatty, talking about the fire, casting blame on an assortment of children in the neighborhood and talking about how something must be done about it. An older couple broke off from the crowd and headed in the opposite direction, toward the subway—just what I was waiting for. I joined them on the sidewalk.

"What was that all about?" I asked them. "Did someone start it on purpose?"

"I don't know," the woman said, "but it scared the daylights out of me."

The Feds were checking some people, but they let me pass. They were looking for single men walking alone. I wanted to run, but I forced myself into a slow, steady pace. When my patrons left me at the next block, I switched gears and went faster. Another Fed car raced by on its way to Muck's house, but I kept walking. Just as I was about to descend into the glorious New York City subway system, where a person can get lost in seconds—right when I about to breathe a sigh of relief—three Feds ran in. I gulped instead. Time to change plans.

FRANKIE RACED THROUGH BROOKLYN, siren blaring. He was on the phone the whole time. Mazzetti had already cleared Renzo and Nino's house, so that only left Donnie's and Muck's. Frankie felt certain it was Muck's. He called Harding again. He answered on the third ring.

"What?" Harding said.

"What have you got?"

"Tito's dead. He was here. We've lost him, but we're searching the entire area."

"Where's the subway?"

"Few blocks north of here."

"I'm almost there," Frankie said, "but send a couple of your men to the subway."

Two minutes later, he double-parked on the street and ran down the steps, flashing his badge to the guy at the bottom. Maddox and two more Feds arrived at almost the same time. When they hit the bottom, they started working the crowd. Frankie looked around.

Where are you, Nicky?

After twenty minutes of searching, Frankie realized he wasn't there.

What would Nicky do? Frankie recalled things from their youth and one more thing stuck out—the time they were running from the cops and Nicky had them hide out at the school dance. They'd stayed until the dance ended then walked some girls home for added protection. Convinced the subway was a dead end, Bugs talked Maddox and his men into coming with him. Once outside, he stood, staring around and thinking until it hit him. Green Acres Mall half a mile away.

"Come on, Maddox. We're going shopping."

Five minutes later they entered the mall. "You guys take the lower level," Bugs said. "I'll go up."

I WAS IN THE food court, seated at a table with two older ladies I'd helped with their trays. I was reading a book when Frankie came. He stood on his tiptoes, searching. Probably looking for a lone man. Someone trying not to be noticed. He must have figured out that I'd use a crowd, because no sooner did he start looking than he moved toward people bunched together. He started at one end and worked his way toward the middle. His right hand was in his pocket, no doubt gripping a gun. I risked a quick glance to the escalator, then decided to duck into the bathroom—try to hide out until they gave up.

BUGS MADE HIS WAY through the crowd, slowly. Methodically. Nicky was here; he knew it. A guy headed toward the men's room. From the back it looked like Nicky. Bugs followed but took his time, staying alert. He couldn't afford mistakes. When he got there, he grabbed orange cones from a janitor's closet and an 'out of order' sign and put them at the entrance. He went in, gun drawn.

Half a dozen guys were inside, none of them Nicky. But two stall doors were closed. Bugs held up his ID and pointed his gun. "Get out. Everyone." He kept his eyes on the stalls. "This is the police. Everyone out."

One of the doors popped open. A guy zipped up his pants and rushed out. The other door remained closed. Bugs kept his eyes moving from the floor to the space above the stall door. "Come on out, Nicky. It's over."

The sound of feet hitting the floor echoed lightly off the tile walls. The door opened. Nicky walked out, hands raised. "I'm unarmed."

"I ought to shoot you right here," Bugs said. He shoved Nicky against the wall, frisking him with one hand.

"You won't find anything."

"But I'll find gunshot residue. Washing your hands won't get it off your clothes."

Nicky laughed. "Maybe."

"Fuck your maybe, Rat. You're caught."

"Caught? For shooting a gun? *If* you can even prove that."

"What gun?" Bugs stepped back. "Turn around, asshole."

"The gun I lost."

Bugs dragged him to the sink and pressed his head against it. Shoved the gun into Nicky's temple. "You fuck. Killing Tony like you did."

"Don't push this, Bugs. You don't want to push it."

"I'm the one with the gun. I know you don't have one. Why would you? You're not a shooter, are you? If you had a gun, I might think you killed Tito." He eased the gun back, then stepped away, to be safe.

"I don't need a gun to kill you." Nicky brushed dirt from his clothes, straightened his shirt and hair. He focused on Bugs, held him with those hawk eyes. "Go ahead and shoot me if that's what you want. You already ruined my life."

"Ruined your life? Don't try to put that shit on me. You're the one who turned into scum. It was your choice, Nicky."

"*My* choice?" Nicky moved closer, and he had that look in his eyes, just like his father. "Nino, Renzo, Tommy, Donnie, even Johnny Muck… all those heads are on you, Bugs. I wouldn't have killed them if they didn't get to Gina. Who led them there?" Nicky glared. "*You* did, Bugs. *You're* to blame. Just like everything else."

That hit Bugs hard. No matter what else, Nicky was right about that. It was his fault that Tony found out and betrayed Nicky. He was about to speak when something else Nicky said made him rethink things. "What do you mean, 'everything else'?"

"*Everything.*" Nicky lowered his head, looked dejected. "Woodside. Prison. Me being a shooter." Nicky shook his head and stared at the floor. "I was clean, Bugs. Me and Angie, we—"

Bugs hadn't seen Nicky this way in a long time. He felt his pain. "What are you talking about with Woodside?"

Nicky raised his head and looked at him, the danger gone from his eyes. "Guess you don't know. Donna came to me that night when I was going to pick up Angie. She told me you were going after Woodside and that they had guns. She begged me to help you."

Bugs lowered the gun. His knees felt ready to buckle. His shoulders slumped and he leaned against the door. "Donna? How did she know they'd have guns?" He thought about the scum Donna ended up marrying from Woodside; he'd been there that night. Bugs shook his head. "Jesus Christ, why didn't you tell me? All this time…"

"When was I gonna tell you? When you *didn't* visit me in prison? Or in answer to the letters you didn't write?"

Bugs was silent. There was no defending this.

"Besides, it was over. I was in prison."

"You should have told me, Nicky."

"So you could feel bad?" Nicky shook his head. "We weren't raised like that, Bugs."

Now all kinds of shit ran through Frankie's head. Woodside—his fault. Nicky's time in prison—his fault. Everything could be blamed on him. And Nicky's wife getting killed—his fault for sure. And here he was trying to take Nicky into custody.

Nicky slowly shook his head. "Besides, you've got nothing on me. There's more of your DNA at those crime scenes than mine. And don't forget Tony, Paulie, and good old Tito." Nicky stared. "All of them have ties to the scenes."

A million thoughts ran through Bugs' head. Nicky was right. Frankie had no real evidence on him, nothing that would hold up in court. He stared at Nicky, wishing he could take back the things he'd done. "Are you done with it?"

Nicky spread his arms and turned his palms up. "There's nobody left."

"I guess you're right," Frankie said. "I'm making a judgment call here. I don't think we have enough evidence to do anything anyway, so get the fuck out of here. If I were you, I'd give it a couple of hours after the Feds leave, then I'd head out. And if I were you, I'd disappear for good this time." Frankie opened the door and they both walked out.

"Might be hard to disappear with Feds all over the place."

"Only if the Feds see you."

"A friend might help me. I used to have friends I could count on."

"Me too, Nicky." Bugs pulled out a smoke, put it in his mouth.

"You can't smoke here."

"Yeah, well…let me worry about that."

Nicky pulled out a pack of matches. He struck the match, cupped it, and offered the light to Frankie. "This is the way it should be, you know."

Frankie sucked deep on that first drag, the best-tasting one of all. "What's that?"

"Friendship. Honor. It should last forever."

Frankie nodded, took two more quick drags, then crushed out the butt on the ground. "It does. You just have to trust it."

He did another quick take to see if Maddox was anywhere near. "You know you're leaving me in a rough spot. I've got no one to pin these murders on."

"How about Tito?"

"Don't think so."

"Suppose you had Tito's gun, with Tito's prints on it?"

"That would be nice…but I don't have it. Do you?"

He shrugged. "Not me. But I bet when they search Tito's coat they'll find it."

"Another of those damn coincidences."

"Yeah, and to top it off, I'd bet this gun was the one that killed a guy named Danny Zenkowski."

"So who killed Tito?"

"Must have been a grieving family member of one of the ones he killed. Who knows?" Nicky stared past Frankie's shoulder. "You're the detective."

"Yeah. I'm curious, though—how did you know I'd get assigned the cases?"

"I didn't, but I knew Tito and Tony would be paying attention, since it was their guys getting whacked. And I knew as soon as Tony saw the clues, he'd tell you."

"He didn't."

"Yeah, well, you know what Sister Thomas used to say—the Lord works in mysterious ways. Besides, I never counted on Tony being the one who betrayed me."

Frankie nodded. "Just a suggestion, but you should leave here, maybe go on a vacation. Or better yet, go find Angela."

Nicky winced at the mention of her name, but it must have also sounded nice to him—sweet and fresh. "She's married, or did you forget?"

"I was married once," Frankie said. "Didn't take."

"Yeah, well..."

"Maybe it didn't take with Angie. Maybe she's sitting around the house waiting for Nicky the Rat to rescue her. She sure as shit can't be in love with Marty Ferris."

They had been walking while they talked and were now back in the food court. Nicky nodded to the escalators. "They your buddies?"

Three Feds were heading toward them. Bugs winked at Nicky and smiled. "See ya, Rat."

Frankie turned and walked toward Maddox. "You guys find anything?"

Nicky looked at him as they walked away. *Guess friendship and honor do last. Sometimes.*

CHAPTER 74

OLD MEMORIES

Current Day

I didn't bother to clean out the safe deposit boxes. New York was as good a place as any to keep them. I did, however, take Bugs' advice, and packed for a trip. I needed to get away. Think. Figure out what to do with my life. The mountains seemed like a good choice, so I headed into New Jersey on my way to the Poconos. I put the car on cruise control with music blaring.

I thought about what Bugs said—that I should go visit Angela. It kept eating at me. How stupid would that be, though, to show up at her house after all these years? She probably wouldn't remember me. No, she'd remember, but she might not want to see me. I decided Bugs was crazy and continued driving toward the Poconos.

Five miles later, an oldie came on the radio, a song by the Tavares, "Heaven Must Be Missing an Angel." It reminded me of Angela. I found myself smiling as I sang along.

Maybe it's a sign.

But I tried talking myself out of it. *She's probably got half a dozen kids. Hates my guts.*

At some point, as I pondered the logical reasons why I shouldn't go, I got off the interstate and took a turn toward I-95, heading south.

Wilmington wasn't that far. I could say hi and still be out in time to reach the beach by nightfall. Yeah, I'd go to the beach instead of the mountains. To Wildwood. I'd always loved Wildwood. Best boardwalk in the world.

I thought of a million reasons why I shouldn't do what I was doing in the couple of hours it took to get to Delaware. Despite my internal objections, I kept the course, heading toward my old hometown. Once I got to Wilmington, I looked her up in an online phone book, but found no listing. I checked all the social networking sites and found nothing there. I decided to check at her father's old house. I made the drive, slowing to a crawl as I drew near. I parked, sat in the car for a minute, then walked up to the door, nervous as hell. Suppose she was here?

An older woman answered. "May I help you?"

"I'm looking for Mr. Catrino," I said. "Actually I'm looking for his daughter, Angela."

Her face seemed to go blank. "I'm sorry, young man, but Mr. Catrino moved away years ago."

"Sorry to have troubled you," I said, and started down the steps.

"Young man," she called after me. "Angela lives a few blocks from here. Let me think…1022—"

My step paused, and I turned around. "Clayton Street," I said, finishing the address for her.

My old house.

"Why, yes. That's the one. Are you from around here?"

Smiles and tears fought for control. "Yeah. Long time ago." I extended my hand to say thanks. "I appreciate your help, and sorry again to have bothered you."

"No trouble at all. Tell Angela I said hello."

I couldn't believe it. Was this a good sign or a bad one? Why was Angie living in my old house? Only way to find out was to go there and ask. I pulled up the street by the park, as much to bring back old memories as to stay hidden while I worked up the nerve to see her.

What if her husband answers? What the hell do I do then?

I watched from the car, waiting, but the house seemed empty. After an hour, I felt like a fool. What the hell? Was I a stalker? A bunch of kids passed by. One small girl, a skinny little thing, was rough-housing with a few boys, playing tag and chasing each other. It reminded me of old times. After a while, most of the smaller kids left. Then a few older girls came by and sat on the bench. They seemed to be just talking, probably mulling over the events of the day. That bench had seen a lot over the years. Laughter, joy, tears. Soon, two of the girls left; one remained. She sat staring at the trees and twirling her hair. It reminded me of Angela and the way I used to watch her in class.

A man came up the walk, heading straight for her, yelling. She planted her hands on her hips in a wonderfully defiant posture and yelled back. I smiled. This one was bold. Then he smacked her across the face. Hard.

I sat up straight. Gulped.

The girl reeled from the blow and turned to run. He grabbed her arm and yanked her back.

That's it.

I walked briskly toward him. Reason reminded me of the dangers of interfering. *Don't do anything stupid. You have a record. Probably a brat kid who deserves everything she's getting. Hell, Sister Thomas gave me worse.*

She was crying. "No. Let me go."

My pace increased. I wanted to run, but I didn't want to draw attention. When he reared back to slap her again, I yelled. "Hey!" I ran.

He turned toward me, a scowl on his face. "This is none of your business."

The guy was about six-two, maybe more, and well-built. I pegged him at early thirties. "Anytime I see a young girl being hit," I said, "I make it my business." I stood in front of him.

"Fuck you."

I gritted my teeth. Looked around. A few kids were playing, and a few parents sat on other benches, paying no attention to us. No cops I could see. This man was vile, and he'd just broken a cardinal rule. There were rules for everything. Murder. Respect. Women. Children. And one of the worst was you didn't say that in front of kids. Certainly not in front of young girls. I knew I was antiquated in my thinking, but that was me. It was the way I was, and I wasn't about to change. "You shouldn't use that language in front of the girl."

"Fu—"

I grabbed his throat and squeezed until he gasped. He reached for my hand, trying to tear it off. I kidney-punched him. Dropped him to his knees. His gaping eyes begged for mercy as he fought to get free. His breaths came in short, quick gasps. He was struggling to stay alive. I locked onto his eyes. "Don't *ever* touch that girl again."

The guy was holding his throat, as if that would help him get his breath. I pushed him aside, then turned to the girl. "Are you all right?"

Tears were in her eyes. "Yes," she managed through sobs.

I saw a scar above her left eye and wondered if he gave it to her. "Is that your father?"

"Stepfather."

"Do you want me to take you home?"

I sensed a presence behind me; I turned quickly to see him standing there.

"She's coming with me."

I glared at him, ready to do something—anything.

"I lost my temper," he said. "It won't happen again." He held out his hand to the girl. "Come on, Rosa. I'm sorry."

Rosa! Her name is Rosa?

The guy reached for her. She pushed him away. "I'm not going with you," she said. "Not ever again."

"You'd better leave," I told him.

He walked away without another word. I turned and looked at the girl.

She spoke before I could. "Thank you. I'll be all right now." She walked away, heading down the street the way her friends had gone.

I walked back to the car, slid into the seat, leaned back and closed my eyes. Suddenly I sat up straight, opened my eyes and looked for the girl. *He called her Rosa.* I jumped out and yelled, "Rosa." but she was long gone.

What an idiot I am? Her name is Rosa. She twirls her hair. That's Angie's girl.

"Oh, that fuck." I thought of what I'd do if I saw that guy again.

I stared down the street at my old house. How many times had I raced to get home and change, then run up the street to see Angie? I pictured her with her green-and-white apron, cooking with Mamma Rosa and laughing. Always laughing. After almost another hour, I worked up the nerve to go to the door. What could she do but throw me out, curse me, and tell me she hated my guts?

My life was ruined either way. I got out and walked down the street and up the sidewalk. I tapped lightly on the door, then, realizing no human could have heard it, I knocked harder. I worried; I wasn't a kid anymore. Probably looked like shit.

When the door opened, my heart stopped. Or it seemed like it did. She wore the apron—green and white as always, stained with red sauce. I smelled meatballs cooking, and the sweet aroma of red sauce and garlic. I couldn't take my eyes off her.

"Hi, Angela."

She stared, squinted against the sun, then stepped back. Her hands flew to her mouth as she gasped. "Nicky! Nicky Fusco." She threw her arms around me, squeezed. "Oh my God, come inside. Please."

I stepped into the living room, tentative. I had lived in this house, yet it seemed like today was the first time I'd ever been here. And it didn't feel right. "Angela, I—"

She was crying, but trying not to. She shook her head back and forth. "Don't say anything." She cried more.

Finally I couldn't take it. I wrapped my arms around her. "Angie, I'm sorry. I didn't want to upset you."

She stepped back. "Sorry? Where have you been? I heard you got out. Why didn't you come?"

How could I explain? "I…"

Tears came again. "I thought you didn't care. I thought you hated me."

"How could I ever hate you?"

"Why didn't you call?"

"I didn't think it was right…you being married and all."

She stared at me, tears still in her eyes. "Nicky, I haven't been married for a long time. After we got divorced, I bought your old house."

I wanted to grab her, rip her clothes off and carry her to the bedroom. This was better than I dreamed of. But there were still issues to deal with, and I had no idea how she felt about them. I didn't know how *I* felt about them, and I'd had years to think about it.

"What about your child?"

"You know about her?"

"You were pregnant at the funeral."

She got that angry look in her eyes. "And *that's* what kept you away—the thought that I'd been with someone else?"

I wanted to turn and run, but I'd done enough of that. "Angie, I loved you so much that I couldn't take it. I figured you left me for someone else. I…"

She smacked me across the face. Hard. Then she smacked me again and broke into tears. "All of this time we could have been together…" She buried her face in her hands. "Oh, God, Nicky. How could you do this?"

"If it's any comfort to you, I—never mind. I'm stupid. A goddamn idiot. I'm sorry. I shouldn't have come. I just thought…" I headed for the door before I embarrassed myself more than I already had.

"Niccolo Fusco. Get your ass back here."

I turned, but the tears were in my own eyes now. "I'm leaving. Pretend I never showed up."

"What? Going to walk out on me?"

In all of the emotion I had forgotten about the baby. Hell, not a baby anymore. "Your daughter. Is she…is her name Rosa?"

She got a surprised look on her face. "How did you know?"

"I met her at the park today."

She nodded. "I should have known it was you. Rosa told me about a mysterious stranger who protected her from her stepfather." Angie smiled. "She called you handsome."

"Her father is an asshole."

"Yes, he is," she said. "And I already called the police. He's been warned before, so I'm sure they'll do something this time."

I didn't say anything, but I knew I could convince him to leave her alone.

"I'm sure you have a lot of questions, Nicky. No sense in delaying. First, it's her stepfather, not father. Actually he's not even her stepfather anymore. And yes, he *is* an asshole, which is why I divorced him years ago." She came closer. "And no, Nicky, there is no one else. There has *never* been anyone else. I kept praying you'd come back."

I felt as if I could fly. I sat on the sofa, and just stared. "I'm the stupidest man alive."

She wiped her tears with the corner of her apron. "I'll agree with you on that."

I jumped up, charged with new energy. "I'm going to find a place to stay and freshen up. Then I'll be back."

She grabbed hold of me, pulled me to her. "Wait. There's something I need to tell you, and you're not going to like it."

That stopped me dead. "I don't already. What?"

"You aren't her father."

My heart sank to new lows. "Go on."

"Remember that day I came to see you in prison, the last time?"

I nodded, dreading what I was hearing. "I remember."

She started crying. "Tony drove me, and when he picked me up, he was high—really high. On the way home, he…" She lost all control then and the tears flowed. "He…" Between fits of sobbing she managed to get out, "Rosa is *his* child, Nicky."

I fought for control. I wanted to hit something, to kill someone, but Tony was already dead. Now I wished he wasn't, so I could do him right.

"I didn't let him, Nicky. I fought him, but he was too strong." She cried more. "That's why I stopped coming to see you in prison. If you had seen me pregnant, it would have destroyed you."

I started walking out, thinking of all the reasons why I should leave—Rosa wasn't my kid, not my problem. But my hand stuck to the knob, unable to turn it. Something from deep in my mind screamed at me—it wasn't her fault, Angie needs me, Rosa needs me...

I blocked out the noise in my head, twisted the knob and opened the door, but I couldn't leave. If I tossed everything aside, I was left with the undeniable truth—I loved her. I loved her more than my pride, or my hurt. Even more than my hate. I pushed the door closed and went back to her.

What I wanted to tell her was *bullshit*. That every excuse she offered for not coming back was shit, but I knew she was right. If I *had* found out, I would have done anything to get to Tony. I looked at her. I hoped love was still in my eyes. I said the only thing I could think of that might comfort her, not trusting myself to be loving yet.

"Tony's dead, Angie. You can be thankful for that."

She sat up straight. "Dead? How?"

"I shot him."

Her eyes went wide. "What? Why? Did you know about it?"

I shook my head. "No, I didn't know anything about it, or I'd have made it worse. But he betrayed me, and now I know why. He was afraid I'd find out."

She gave me a hug. I recognized it immediately as an *Angie hug*, the kind she always gave when she knew I needed it. Here she was in all of her grief, and worried about me.

Good old Angie.

I made up my mind right then that we had to be together. If I had issues, I'd have to find a way around them. I pushed her back a little, just far enough to look into her eyes. "You must have lived with hell. I'm so sorry for not being here to help you."

She held me tight, wouldn't let go. "It's okay. I'll never forget it, but I'm over it. I was over it long ago. Kids do that to you."

We hugged in silence for a few seconds, then she said, "Sometimes, though, she does something that reminds me of Tony. And then when she does…" Angie tensed, clenching her fists. "Then I want to scream."

I pulled her back to me. "If it ever happens again, pretend it's Mamma Rosa instead." I kissed her forehead, then the tip of her nose. "I'll be here to help you through it."

And I knew it was true. My mind was made up. I was finally going to get the life I'd dreamed of. I thought about Gina and having to tell Angie about her. "There's obviously a lot we need to talk about. More than most people would have in a lifetime, but before that, I need to know if you want to be with me. Because if you do, if you meant what you said in that letter all those years ago, then nothing else matters."

"Before I answer, I need to tell you that Rosa thinks you are her father. That's what I've always told her."

"Why?"

"That was the only way I could make it—pretend she was yours. At first it was the only way I could love her. After that, it was easy."

I hugged her again. "Don't worry. We have a lot of time to figure out things like that."

"Do we, Nicky? What about Rosa?"

"What about her?"

"I don't expect you to love her, but—"

I put my finger to her lips, then kissed her. "She's half you and part Mamma Rosa. How could I *not* love her?" And when I said those words, I knew I meant them. I couldn't laugh right then, and probably wouldn't for a while, but I felt good. It was only a matter of time before Angie, Rosa and I began enjoying life the way it was meant to be. As Mamma Rosa used to say, all the ingredients were there for happiness. Who knew better than Mamma Rosa?

Angie wiped a stray tear and hugged me again. "Nicky Fusco, I want to be with you forever. And even if you want to leave, you're not going anywhere. I've waited all this time. You're not leaving me now. Besides, you still have a cute ass, and I like looking at it."

"And you still have no tits. But I like that."

We both laughed, and when we did, we fell into each other's arms, hugging. For the longest time, I held her. I cried a few silent tears, but mostly I thanked God for the chance to start over. I figured He must be the good God that Sister Thomas taught us about if He'd allow a man like me to be happy after what I'd done. I decided then and there that I'd go to confession that weekend. First thing. Finish what I started in Cleveland.

When we broke the embrace, I kissed her softly, savored the kiss. I closed my eyes and smelled her, tasted her. Remembered her. *Oh my God.*

She took my hand. "Let's go upstairs."

"What about your daughter?"

She half-frowned, half-smiled. "*Our* daughter, remember? She won't be home for hours."

"I intend to make up for lost time. It might take that long."

"Promise?"

"I promise."

She kissed me quick. "I know you will." As we climbed the stairs, she turned to me. "The best thing for you is that I taught her to cook just like Mamma Rosa. Now you'll have two chefs in the house."

When we got to the bedroom, we fell into a rhythm that was unexplainable. It had been thirteen years. We should have been ripping clothes off each other in some sort of lustful rage; instead, we moved slowly, passionately. Every movement stimulated a sensual response. We fell to the bed, naked, embracing each other and rolling over and over. Nothing touched but our lips and our bodies. After what seemed like forever, I kissed her everywhere, leaving no part of her untouched. Afterwards we made love. It was the best I'd ever felt.

Old memories, especially wonderful ones, die hard. We must have both remembered that, because the scene that played out was exactly like that one so long ago, when we first made love.

After we finished, she rolled over on top of me. We kissed. Laughed.

And when we were all done playing, she lay her head on my shoulder, arm draped across my neck. "I love you, Niccolo Fusco."

I kissed her forehead, then her nose. And said the same thing I said that first night. "And I love you, Angela Catrino."

As we lay there in each other's arms, I stared at the ceiling, letting my mind wander. I thanked God for giving me the chance to make things right. For giving me a chance to live again. I'd be with Angie forever now. Nothing would get in the way. Then I thought about Rosa, and how beautiful she was. How lucky I was to not only have Angie, but a daughter too. As I dreamt of her, I thought of the mark on her face where Marty had slapped her. And I thought of the scar I saw above her left eye. My blood boiled. Fists clenched.

I promise, Rosa. He will pay for this.

Angie reached over, must have felt my heart racing. "Are you okay, Nicky? You seem upset."

I breathed deep. Forced myself to relax. "Nothing to be upset about. Not anymore." I laughed. "I just can't believe I'm here and that we're together again. Everything will be fine now."

I thought of Rule Number Six—murder is immaculate. As I stroked Angie's hair, kissing it, a list formed in my mind.

> *Rope*
> *Tape*
> ~~*Four-inch*~~*, five-inch screws*
> *Acid—yes, acid*
> *A funnel*

I snapped out of it, shaking my head. No way was I going back to that life. I was through with it for good, and no asshole like him was going to drag me to the gutter again.

Angie must have sensed something. She turned on the light next to the bed, then rolled over to face me, with those eyes I couldn't resist. "Nicky Fusco, promise me that you're through with the past."

I leaned up to kiss her, but she pulled back. "Promise me."

I looked into her eyes for a long time, felt them burn through me. There had only been three people in my whole life I couldn't refuse—Mamma Rosa, Sister Mary Thomas, and Angie. "All right, but if—"

She stopped me with a kiss as sweet as any I've ever tasted. "Promise."

I hesitated for only a second or two, then hugged her. "I promise, Angie. And you know I always keep my promises."

EPILOGUE

'Detective First Class Frankie Donovan—Hero'

That's what the headlines said two days later. No one really believed all that shit, but the FBI wrapped it up nicely. Tito Martelli had killed those people, including a lady from Ohio and an accountant years ago in Queens. They found the gun in Tito's pocket—with ballistics matches—and the gun even had Tito's prints on it. They also had Tito's DNA at all of the crime scenes except for the Queens accountant and the girl in Cleveland. The papers never mentioned the other DNA.

The FBI had wiretaps that showed Tito meeting with the people he'd supposedly killed, with the exception again of the girl and the accountant, but there were a few phone calls from Tito's house to a hotel in Cleveland just before she died. The FBI confirmed that Tony Sannullo had been wearing a wire to get evidence on Tito, which was probably why Tony was also killed. The only mystery was who killed Tito. The media put the blame on Tony's friend Paulie "The Suit" Perlano, who was missing.

Frankie tried to discourage that speculation, but they ran with it. Anything for a story. The FBI wanted to know about the mysterious Nicky Fusco, who had been the main suspect right up to the end, but Frankie convinced them that it would look bad for the Bureau if people found out they had spent so much time and money chasing a suspect only to have to let him go. Frankie also let them have the glory for solving the case, taking only the residuals for himself and Lou.

As he walked down the hall from the press briefing, Mazzetti intercepted him. "Good job, Donovan. We did all right, didn't we?"

"I gave you the credit, Lou. After our Fed friends, of course."

"It will help my retirement."

"Don't tease me with those thoughts. I need a nice female partner." Frankie laughed, then asked if Lou wanted coffee.

"Not for me. I'm glad this worked out for you."

"Meaning what?"

"I mean about your friend, that Rat guy. Nice that it turned out not to be him after all."

Frankie wondered where he was going with this. "Yeah. That had me worried."

"Guess old Tito just went nuts, torturing and killing people."

"Not like he didn't kill people, Lou."

"I sure wish I could figure out who shot Tito. That would really tie this up."

"Could have been Paulie. Hell, it could have been anybody. Tito had a lot of enemies."

Lou reached down and scratched his leg as they walked. "Hey, Donovan, did I tell you I finally caught that rat at my house?"

"No, but I'm happy for you. I'd hate to have a rat in my house."

"Same here. Couldn't stand it. I didn't kill it, though."

"Didn't kill it? What the hell did you do with it?"

Lou raised his eyebrows and calmly said, "I let it go. We came to a kind of understanding. It stopped eating my cereal, and I stopped trying to trap it." Lou lit a smoke as he walked.

Frankie smiled. "I think you did the right thing, Lou. See you later."

FRANKIE NEARLY RAN FROM the office. It had been a long day of wrapping up paperwork on the cases. He hated paperwork, but at least it wasn't as bad as the shit the Feds had to go through. When he left Harding and

Maddox, they still had hours until they finished. As an afterthought, Frankie tried reaching Mazzetti to see if he wanted to catch dinner, but he didn't answer, so he called Kate. The phone rang four times, then clicked to the machine. He wasn't used to getting her message, and it was unexpectedly short.

"This is Kate, leave me a message."

Bugs hesitated. "Hey, uh, Kate, this is Frankie. I was checking to see what you were doing. Thought maybe…I don't know…thought maybe I'd see if that offer you made was still open." He hung up and felt stupid. Christ. He sounded like a goddamn tongue-tied kid.

He drove on, admonishing himself for three or four blocks, but then as he went through a nice neighborhood, thinking about how things had gone, he turned philosophical. Tony was dead. Paulie was gone. Nicky was gone too. All of his friends were out of his life, probably forever. It was time to get a new life. Though he wondered about Kate, he felt certain she wanted nothing to do with him. Frankie needed *something*. Nicky and Tony had dragged him back to their world, but he couldn't stand the thought of a return to his previous existence. Shawna, the hot reporter he once dated, came to mind. She was dangerous. Sexy too. But despite the feelings she stirred in him, he chased the thought away.

He drove slower than usual on the way home, wondering what the hell he was going to do with his life. He'd been going along, thinking he was sacrificing something by being a cop, not having fun like Tony and Paulie. Now he saw that was a farce, but he'd wasted thirteen years. As he turned the corner onto his street, a horn blared. He waved to a neighbor pulling out and saving him the parking space. Maybe this would be a good new life, he thought as he parked.

Frankie walked to the corner, got a bottle of wine, some candy, and a pack of smokes. Alex and Keisha sat on the stoop, occupying their normal spots. Smiles popped onto their faces as he tossed the candy to them in an underhand, softball-style pitch.

"Thanks, FD," they both said at once.

He rubbed their heads as he went past, then made the ritual climb to his apartment. Twenty minutes later, he was showered and sitting around in boxers and a T-shirt, sipping wine and smoking. As he checked to see what movies were on, someone knocked on the door.

Who the hell...?

He thought about throwing some pants on, but only for a second. *It's probably Alex.* When he opened it, he just gaped.

"Do I get to come in?" Kate asked, her hands full with pizza and wine.

Bugs stepped aside to let her in, then closed the door quickly. "What the hell are you doing here?"

"You sounded like you needed some company, so I canceled all my dates, and here I am."

He took the pizza from her and carried it to the table. He wasn't even hungry, but right now, pizza never looked so good.

Bugs suddenly realized he was in his shorts. "Damn, excuse me, Kate. I'll be right back."

"I've seen you in less," she said. "Sit down. We've got hot pizza and slightly-chilled wine."

Frankie opened the wine, got some plates, then sat next to her. They didn't talk about cases, or cops, or anything of importance. She told him about growing up in Illinois. He told her about the old neighborhood, about his father and mother, and about Tony, Paulie, and Mick. But mostly he told her about Nicky.

"We had this crazy oath we used to swear to," he said. "We'd put our fists together and raise them in the air and holler, 'Friendship and honor.' It was kind of stupid, but it worked for a long time." He stared at the blank wall with a glazed look in his eyes.

"So what ever happened with this oath?"

Bugs snapped out of it. "The oath? It's dead, Kate. All the guys are gone."

She rested her chin on her knuckles, elbows on the table. "You know, I like you Frankie. Not for sex," she quickly added, "but I'm thinking I could be a friend. If you need one, that is."

Frankie looked at her with what he knew was the best smile he'd worn in years. "You feel like watching a movie?"

"What kind?"

"You know I like old ones. Black-and-whites are best."

"I think so too," she said, then got up, kicked her shoes off, and curled up on a corner of the couch. "*Now* you can put some pants on. I don't want that thing poking out during the movie."

Frankie's laughter followed him from the room.

Kate took a sip of wine and smiled, and then she laughed too, really hard, the way she used to when they dated.

Back in the bedroom, Frankie dressed and thought about Kate. She didn't care about his barren apartment, or about his building with no elevator. And she held no grudges from before. Most important of all, she was here for him. *Here* without even being asked.

The more he thought about it, he realized she was like a friend from the old neighborhood. Maybe friendship and honor weren't dead after all. He hummed an old tune of Mamma Rosa's while he slipped on his shirt, then, as he buttoned his pants, he heard Kate's laughter bouncing off the barren walls, filling his empty bedroom.

Frankie stopped dressing, sat on the bed—and just listened.

Acknowledgments

The tough part of writing a book is not the writing, it's all the stuff that comes after that. I'll take credit for the writing. For the tough parts I am honor bound to thank the following:

My great copyeditor, Annette Lyon from Precision Editing Group.

A fantastic graphic designer, Goce Veselinovski, for the book cover.

Chris Fisher and Morgana Gallaway for the amazing layout and formatting.

And most importantly the army of beta readers who whipped this book into shape. They caught the mistakes I let slip.

Missy, my daughter-in-law, the one who suffered through those first drafts, and second, and third...

My daughter, Aliza, for spending countless nights arguing over what to edit out of the book. My sister, Rose, for her perception of human nature. My sons, Jimmy and Tony. My brother Chris, and all the others: Sahrina, Otto, Dana, Tom Connelly, Susan Henderson, Kathy Jensen, John Hannagan, Paul Campbell, and my good friend, Danette Ondi, for the keen insight and suggestions.

Magnificent authors and dear friends: Elizabeth Hull, who brings her characters to life like no other; Carlos Cortes, whose eloquence in his second language exceeds my native tongue; and Tochi Onyebuchi, whose imagination I can only hope to grasp a part of.

And to two of my oldest friends: Lee Comegys and Steve Budney. You know why.

None of this would have been possible if not for the dedicated, loving nuns at St. Elizabeth's, who inspired, encouraged, motivated, and beat an education into me.

Special thanks to my Aunt Rose and Aunt Margaret, two of the most magnificent people on earth. And to my mother and father, two of the most magnificent people no longer on earth. Lastly, to my wife, Mikki, the love of my life, the one I was meant to love from day one. She is my "Angela."

Ti amo con tutto il mio cuore.

Pictures from Wilmington

Casapulla's: entrance

Casapulla's: Louie

Serpe's: entrance

Serpe's: sfogliatelle

Mrs. Robino's: entrance

Fusco's Water Ice

Johnny's

St. Elizabeth's

For more pictures from Wilmington, visit the website at
www.giacomogiammatteo.com

About the Author

I live in Texas now, but I grew up in Cleland Heights, a mixed ethnic neighborhood in Wilmington, Delaware, that sat on the fringes of the Italian, Irish and Polish neighborhoods. The main characters of *Murder Takes Time* grew up in Cleland Heights and many of the scenes in the book were taken from real-life experiences.

Somehow I survived the transition to adulthood, but when my kids were young I left the Northeast and settled in Texas, where my wife suggested we get a few animals. I should have known better; we now have a full-blown animal sanctuary with rescues from all over. At last count we had 41 animals—12 dogs, a horse, a three-legged cat and 26 pigs. Oh, and one crazy—and very large—wild boar, who takes walks with me every day and happens to also be my best buddy.

Since this is a bio some of you might wonder what I do. By day I am a headhunter, scouring the country for top talent to fill jobs in the biotech and medical device industry. In the evening I help my wife tend the animals, and at night—late at night—I turn into a writer.

Thanks for taking a look at the book, and if you have time, please explore the website: www.giacomogiammatteo.com

And don't forget to let me know what you think.

jim@giacomogiammatteo.com

Thanks for taking the time to read the book. I hope you enjoyed it.

Authors live and die on recommendations and reviews, so if you liked the book, please tell someone about it. And if you have a spare moment, I'd love for you to put a review wherever you can: Amazon, B&N, iBooks, Kobo, Goodreads, Linked-in, Twitter or Facebook.

If you're looking for more of Frankie Donovan and Nicky Fusco, they'll be back in *Murder Has Consequences*, the second book in the Friendship & Honor Series, scheduled for an October release. In the meantime, *A Bullet For Carlos*, the first in the Blood Flows South Series, will be released in July. I think you'll like it.

Thanks again for your time,

Giacomo

If you would like to be notified of future releases please go to the website and sign up for the mailing list: **www.giacomogiammatteo.com**

If you want to email me about this book, please use:
suggestions@murdertakestime.com
For anything else: **jim@giacomogiammatteo.com**

A BULLET FOR CARLOS

Detective Connie Gianelli has a love/hate relationship with her uncle, head of a New York crime family, but when an undercover bust goes bad she is left wondering who to trust—her family, or the cops who wear the same badge she does.

You can read the first chapter at the website.